Tender Redemption

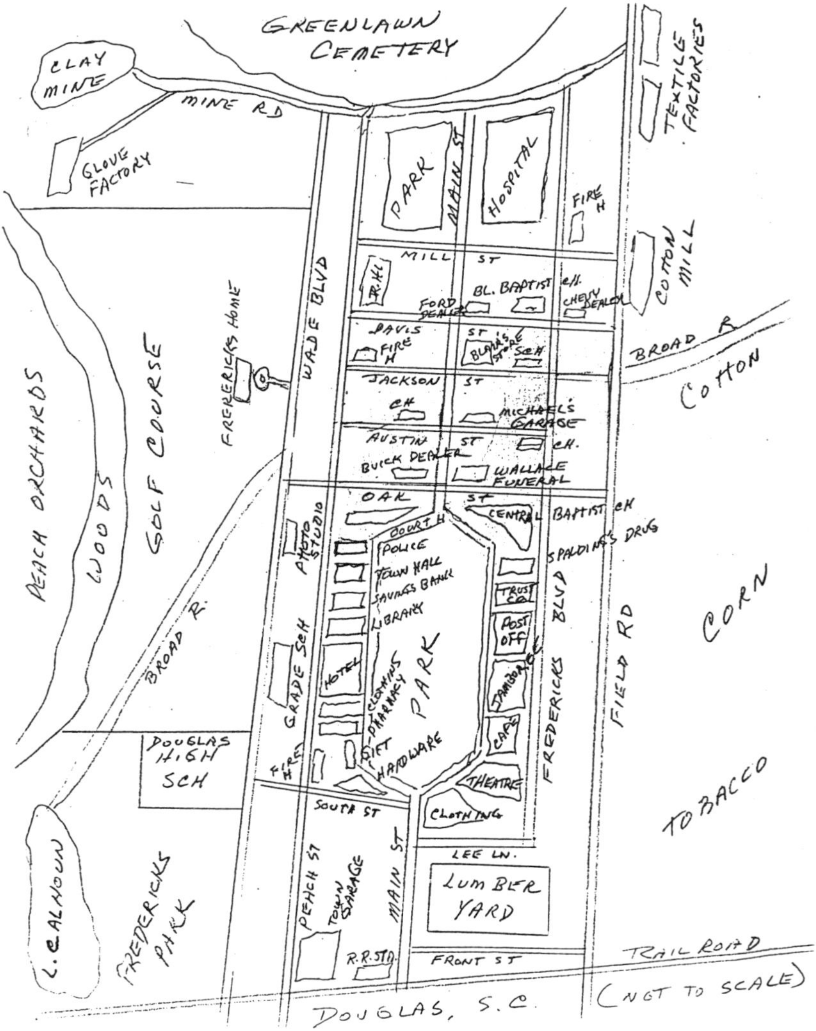
GREENLAWN CEMETERY
CLAY MINE
MINE RD
GLOVE FACTORY
TEXTILE FACTORIES
PARK
MAIN ST
HOSPITAL
FIRE H
COTTON MILL
MILL ST
BL. BAPTIST CH.
FORD DEALER
CHEVY DEALER
WADE BLVD
FREDERICKS HOME
DAVIS ST
FIRE H
BLAIR'S STORE
SCH
BROAD R
JACKSON ST
CH
MICHAEL'S GARAGE
COTTON
PEACH ORCHARDS
WOODS
GOLF COURSE
AUSTIN ST
CH.
BUICK DEALER
WALLACE FUNERAL
OAK ST
CENTRAL BAPTIST CH
PHOTO STUDIO
COURT H
POLICE
TOWN HALL
SAVINGS BANK
LIBRARY
SPALDING'S DRUG
TRUST CO.
POST OFF
BROAD R.
GRADE SCH
HOTEL
CLOTHING
PHARMACY
PARK
JAMBOREE
FREDERICKS BLVD
FIELD RD
CORN
CAFE
GIFT
HARDWARE
DOUGLAS HIGH SCH
FIRE H
THEATRE
SOUTH ST
CLOTHING
TOBACCO
L. CALHOUN
FREDERICKS PARK
PEACH ST
TOWN GARAGE
MAIN ST
LEE LN.
LUMBER YARD
R.R. STA.
FRONT ST
RAIL ROAD
(NOT TO SCALE)
DOUGLAS, S.C.

Tender Redemption

George Frederick Hambidge

VANTAGE PRESS
New York

The characters in this book are fictitious and any resemblance to actual persons is purely coincidental.

FIRST EDITION

Published by Vantage Press, Inc.
516 West 34th Street, New York, New York 10001

Manufactured in the United States of America
ISBN: 0-533-12318-6

Library of Congress Catalog Card No.: 97-90185

0 9 8 7 6 5 4 3 2 1

To Mother

Florence (Peck) Hambidge,
to whom was given the patience of Job

Contents

Preface

This is the story of a boy who spent the first fourteen years of his life with a father who was a strict disciplinarian and ruled with an iron fist. When Glen received the worst beating of his life, he knew he had no choice but to leave home. He rode out of town as a stowaway in a freight car and wound up in a medium sized town in South Carolina where he eventually became a pillar of the community. He experienced a new life; a new beginning; a life of love and respect; a tender redemption.

Acknowledgments

Mrs. John Godfrey, licensed insurance agent, retired.

Mr. Donald Hambidge, licensed surveyor, City of Danbury, CT, retired

Mr. Charles McDonald, teacher, Danbury High School, Danbury, CT.

Dr. James A. Thorburn, professor, Hammond, LA, retired.

Mrs. Frank Dooley, Simpsonville, SC.

Tender Redemption

1

Leaving Home

Nestled in the foothills of the Berkshires, in southwestern Connecticut, is the sleepy little town of Dover. The total population of the township is some twenty thousand and the town line borders on the state line of New York. We like to think of ourselves as the Gateway to New England.

In my neighborhood there was a fair complement of boys and girls. Boys played boy games and girls played girl games. Never did we mix.

It was in the early thirties when Will Daley, age fifteen, Earl Dykman, age fourteen, and I, Glen Harris, also fourteen, were sitting on the steps of a vacant house across the street from where I lived. Will was tall for his age, had black hair and dark brown eyes, and was rather handsome. Earl was a mite shorter with light brown hair and hazel eyes. I was in between in height with brown eyes and hair. Will was usually the one with the ideas and we generally followed.

"It's Halloween, let's go out tonight." Will said.

"OK with me," said Earl. "How about you, Glen?"

"Oh, you know I'm not allowed out at night."

"Suit yourself, sissy," said Will.

I resented that remark, and finally said, "Oh, all right, I'll see you later." With that, I went home.

As I walked across the street I knew that if I didn't go out I would be the laughingstock of the neighborhood. If I did go out I'd be in for a beating. I had to think about it.

Living at home was a hard life of discipline, as Father was a strict disciplinarian. He worked at a bank downtown and was a good provider even though we didn't have all that we wanted or needed. He was quick to anger and I, as the oldest boy, was the vent for his anger, it seemed.

At the supper table were my father, Glen Frederick Harris, Sr., at one end and my mother, Flora, at the opposite. I, Glen Jr., was on Father's right with Drew, age twelve, and Virginia, sixteen. On Father's left were Edward, age ten, Alan, eight, and Marjorie, or Margie, age four.

After supper Father went out, either to bowl, as he was one of the premier bowlers in town, or to a lodge meeting. Drew was downstairs working on model airplanes and I thought I'd go down and keep him company. I didn't stay long. I opened the hatch door and I was free!

I met Will and Earl down by the light at the end of the block. No one else showed up so we sauntered down Main Street. A police patrol car was coming up and we hid behind a house. We thought we might look suspicious. We found ourselves behind the houses of Main Street, Clay Place, Seaman Street and Draper Street. A patrol car stopped on Clay Place and turned on a searchlight. We hid behind a hedge until he went away.

Will saw a pail and a hose. He cut the clothesline and tied a piece to the handle of the pail. We filled the pail with water and lifted it on top of the shed roof and tied the other end of the line to the doorknob and knocked on the door. We hid behind a hedge and waited for the show. The door opened and we heard water running and a thump. The pail bounced off the man's head. We heard an oath like we had never heard before! He heard a rustle in the hedge and came running. We scattered and then we heard another oath! We were on Draper Street when Will took a wire flower border and stretched it across the road. We waited for a car to come down the hill. Soon a car came down, struck the wire, swerved and ended up facing the curb. When the driver got his bearings, he got out of the car and stepped on the wire. Another oath!

He was wrestling with the wire. It was tangled under the car. We were behind a house watching. We finally decided to leave since we didn't want to get involved. We went over to Seaman Street and took some porch furniture and placed it in the front yards of several of the houses. We let air out of a few tires. Just having fun. No damage, really. It was about midnight, I guess, when we decided to go home.

I noticed a light in the kitchen and I knew Father was home and waiting for me. I thought I could sneak in the front door and get upstairs. The door was locked—that was unusual since we never locked our doors. I went around the back and entered through the back door. The lights went out! I don't remember going through the dining room, but I do remember my father being on top of me in the living room pounding me with his fists. I was wearing a jacket with rather large buttons and he kept hitting the buttons until his knuckles were bleeding. He knocked the wind out of me for a while. When I got my wind he started in again, hitting me on my arms, sides and legs. He finally got up and turned out the lights and went to bed. I couldn't get up the stairs. I ached all over. I crawled to the sofa and tried to go to sleep. I shall never forget the hate I saw in his brown eyes.

My left side was bothering me but eventually I got to sleep. I didn't hear Father when he left for work in the morning. Later, I heard Mother in the kitchen. She came into the living room and asked if I wanted any breakfast. I thought that this was odd since I was in the habit of eating breakfast. I said I didn't feel hungry. She turned around and went back to the kitchen. Later, I gingerly stepped to the floor and stood up. My side was very sore but I made it to the door that led to the hallway and to the stairs. I got to the stairs and to the bathroom and took off my jacket and shirt. I was covered with black, blue and purple marks. My thighs were just as bad. I went to my room and slept. At noon Mother woke me.

"Care to have some lunch?"

"No, I'm not hungry."

She left the room and went down stairs. She woke me later in the afternoon.

"I think you'd better get up and come downstairs before your father comes home. He expects everyone to be at the table."

I crawled out of the bed, got dressed and freshened up a bit, and went downstairs to the living room. I was reading when Father came in. He picked up the paper and said, "I see old Hank Morgan stepped on a rake and had to go to the emergency room last night."

Mother announced that supper was ready. I didn't realize how hungry I was. I was eating like I never ate before when Father said something to me. I didn't get what he said and couldn't answer him anyway with my mouth full.

"If you would stop feeding your face you might be able to talk," he scolded. I said nothing and didn't even look at him. All I wanted to do was to get back to my room.

The next morning was Sunday and everyone was running around getting ready to go to church. Mother came into my room.

"Feel like getting up and going to church?"

"No, I think I'll just stay here."

I think she knew I was hurting. I soon heard them all leave and I got up and bathed and went downstairs. I knew that I was expected to be at the table. We had our main meal in the middle of the day on Sunday.

After dinner I went back to bed. My side was still hurting.

Monday morning I got up and had my breakfast. Mother handed me my lunch and I was off to school. I didn't go to school. I walked along the railroad until I came to some bushes and I hid, waiting for a freight train.

It must have been an hour when a slow-moving freight came along. There was a slight grade and it wasn't going very fast. Also, the trains usually stopped to take on water just up ahead. I looked for a boxcar with a door slightly open. I soon saw a likely looking car. I put my lunch in my shirt and grabbed the ladder at the front of the car and hung on. I swung my feet around and nudged the door open a little more and I was in the car. I turned around and found that I wasn't alone! At the other end of the car was a hobo just staring at me! With a smirk on his face, he asked, "What's in your shirt?"

"Nothing."

"Let's see." He took the bag and helped himself to one of my two sandwiches.

"How much money you got?"

"None."

"I thought I heard some change in your pocket." He grabbed me and took the change. "Now we're partners."

I hid a fifty-cent piece in each sock just for safekeeping so I wasn't broke. This was money I had earned from my paper route.

The train was now going at a pretty good clip. We crossed the Hudson River and not long after the train stopped. I looked out and saw many railroad tracks and many freight cars all around. The hobo said, "This is where we get off. I know where we can get a cup of coffee."

He grabbed my arm and forced me out of the car. He

was walking ahead of me. I noticed two yellow cars with green painted palm trees on the side. I figured they must be going south since I could see that they were empty. I made a dash between some cars and entered one of the yellow cars from the opposite side. I didn't think the hobo cared if I left. I sat down and ate my one and only sandwich. After an hour or so I felt a jolt. Then another jolt and soon we were moving. After a little while the car was moving and an hour or so later I looked out the left side of the car and saw the New York City skyline and knew we were going south. I didn't know where I would wind up but I had the idea that I was in for a long ride.

I did a great deal of thinking. I didn't think that I was tall enough to pass for sixteen. I decided to drop my last name of Harris and be known as Glen Fredericks. Then I thought I'd put an *H* in the middle for Henry and be known as Glen Henry Fredericks. I didn't think anyone could find me in a hurry.

I tried to doze off but didn't get much sleep. Many things were going through my head. If things got too bad I could try to get into the army. I thought I might try to get a job aboard ship. I was beginning to feel a little hungry but there was nothing I could do about it now.

It was very dark and the train was rolling along at full speed. It was away from any cities and I couldn't see any lights. *If the train stops when it gets light maybe I'll get off and get some breakfast.* I went back to sleep. I don't know how long I slept but it was still dark when I woke up. My side was hurting me; I thought this was because I was sleeping on that side. I began to think about school. If I got settled somewhere I could go to night school and get my high school diploma. The train was still moving and I dozed off again.

2

Douglas, South Carolina

I woke up; it was beginning to get light. I got up and looked out; the sun was just coming up. Not long after, the train stopped. It seemed rather warm here for early November. I saw a building with lettering on the side. It read DOUGLAS, S.C. I thought I had gone far enough. I left my roost and walked across some rail tracks and came to a street facing the tracks. It looked a bit rundown with a few apartment houses and old stores or shops of some kind. There were a few signs in the windows of some of the apartments advertising rooms for rent. I thought I'd keep that in mind just in case. I turned the corner and found myself on Main Street. A beautiful large park was in the middle. The roads on either side of the park were one way. Buildings lined the streets and it struck me as being very pretty. I saw a sign up ahead advertising a café. I thought, *At last, breakfast!* As I entered the café I saw a sign in the window: **BOY WANTED**. I took the sign out of the window and handed it to the man who looked like he was the boss.

"I'm your boy," I said.

"How old are you?" he asked.

"Sixteen," I lied.

"Follow me."

He took me downstairs and showed me how to operate the dishwasher and the dumbwaiter. He went back upstairs. He didn't ask me my name or even say if he intended to pay me. I saw a mountain of dishes, cups and silverware waiting for attention. I went to work without breakfast but anyway I had a job, I thought.

About eleven o'clock, according to the clock on the wall, the boss came down and found me mopping the floor. I finished the pile of dishes. As I put them in the dumb-waiter, I signaled the waitresses, who would lift them up. Then I would fill it up again.

"You all don't have to do that now. Wait until after lunch dishes are finished. Right now you can go up to the kitchen and Mrs. Wells will fix you something for lunch. We eat before the lunch crowd comes. I didn't have time this morning for introductions. I am Ben Wells."

"I'm Glen Fredericks."

"Hello, Glen."

I went upstairs and Mrs. Wells just looked at me.

"Hello, I'm Glen Fredericks."

"Hello, dear."

She just stood there and studied me with her steely blue eyes until I began to feel uncomfortable. Finally she said, "Please sit down at one of the booths and I'll have your lunch right soon."

There were two booths for the help. She brought a plate with a steak and two vegetables and a glass of milk. Then she brought over a piece of peach pie.

When I finished I felt as if I could move a mountain. I said, "Thank you, Mrs. Wells."

"You're welcome, dear."

I thought, *My Goodness, does she treat everyone like that?* My side was still hurting as I went downstairs and, by this time, the dishes were beginning to pile up. I sailed into them. There were two waitresses but I hadn't met them yet. I was amused when I kept hearing the waitresses say, "Y'all hurry back, ya' hea'?"

About two-forty Mr. Wells came down and found me mopping again. I thought I was going to get another bawling-out. I had finished up everything.

"My, I haven't seen this place looking so good in a long time. We're about ready to leave for the day."

"Leave?"

"Yes, we don't serve dinner. No one goes out to dinner here. We are usually out of here by three o'clock." I was so happy to think I would have the rest of the day to look for a room.

"You're doing a mighty fine job, Glen."

"Thank you, sir."

Mr. Wells and I started for the stairs when I stopped with a sharp pain in my side. Mr. Wells turned around and stared at me with his big blue eyes. His hair was beginning to turn gray.

"What's the matter, Glen?"

"Oh, I just have a sore left side. It catches me sometimes." We were at the foot of the stairs and he just stood there looking at me.

"How old did you say you were?"

"I'll be fifteen in January, sir. I'm sorry I lied but I really needed a job."

"We'll take you home. Where do you live? I don't remember seeing you-all around here before."

"Well, I just got into town this morning and I haven't had a chance to find a place."

"What, you're not from this town? Where did you come from, Glen?"

"Up north."

"Glen, you-all were hired one way or the other as soon as you walked through the door. There's more to it than just your age."

What did he mean? Why was I so readily accepted?

"Come upstairs."

We were in the dining room. The waitresses had left.

"Sit down here, Glen. I'll be right back." He went into the kitchen and was talking in a low voice to Mrs. Wells. Then I heard him on the phone. I thought, *Oh, no, he's calling the police!* He and Mrs. Wells came from the kitchen.

"We have a spare room, Glen, and Mrs. Wells and I think it would be better if you stayed with us until we decide later. Where are your bags?"

"Thank you, sir, but all I have is what you see."

I thought then that he had arranged to have the police come to the house. Anyway, I didn't think I had any choice.

We left the café and drove only about a mile, if that far, when we came to a large house sitting on a good-size lot. We sat down in the living room and the questioning began.

"Where are you-all from, Glen?" Mr. Wells asked.

"From Connecticut. I came down on a freight train. I left home because I was tired of taking any more beatings from my father. I left as soon as I got enough strength. I didn't think I had any choice. I dropped my last name, Harris, and used my middle name. I put the *H* in the middle for Henry and added *S* to Frederick. I want to be known as Glen Henry Fredericks. It isn't likely anyone will find me."

"Why did he beat you, dear?" asked Mrs. Wells.

"I went out on Halloween night. We weren't allowed out at night."

I took off my jacket and shirt and showed them the black, blue and purple marks. Mrs. Wells was crying with tears running down her face.

"Let's go upstairs, Glen," said Mr. Wells.

We went upstairs and he said, "Glen, I want to see your legs."

I lowered my pants and he saw that my thighs were the same color as my sides and arms.

"My left side hurts," I said.

"Get dressed and come downstairs, Glen. Martha, we're going downtown and we'll be back for dinner."

We drove downtown. I thought, *For sure he's going to take me to the police.* We stopped in front of an office building across from the café and on the opposite side of the park. We entered the building and went into the office of Dr. A. F. Davis. The doctor was waiting for us. He asked me to take off my jacket and shirt. He was rather large with white hair and kindly blue eyes.

"No boy should have to take that abuse."

The doctor took X rays of both sides and said that they would be ready in about an hour. I couldn't believe that Mr. Wells had called the doctor instead of the police from the café.

We left the office and continued on down Main Street. We left Douglas and kept going until we arrived in Bradford, twelve miles south. I didn't question anything Mr. Wells was going to do. I put myself in his hands.

We stopped in front of a clothing store. I came out with two pairs of slacks, two pairs of blue jeans, a sport jacket and an outer jacket for colder weather. Underwear, socks, two ties and a box of handkerchiefs. Then Mr. Wells had me try on a raincoat and I got that, also. We then stopped at a shoe store and I got a pair of sneakers and a pair of dress shoes.

Coming back, Mr. Wells said, "Glen, I can't pay you any wages since you are underage, but I can give you an allowance. I'll give you fifteen dollars per week but will withhold five dollars until the doctor and the clothes are paid for. Will that be all right with you?"

"Fine, Mr. Wells."

I was so relieved and happy I could have hugged him! I wasn't used to this.

"I didn't want to make any purchases in town. People talk," he said.

We stopped at the doctor's office.

"Hello, Ben, I have the X rays." The doctor turned on a light and there were the X rays.

"Your right side is fine, Glen, but see these three little lines on the left? They are small cracks in the ribs and that is what is bothering you. I'm going to give you a strap to wear for a month. Take it off only when bathing. Come back in thirty days. I'm sure you will be pretty well healed by then, but I want you to be careful, understand?"

"Yes, sir."

"Thanks, Doc," said Mr. Wells.

"Take good care of him, Ben."

We went home. After dinner I was tired and just wanted to go to bed. The Wellses understood and they did everything they could to make me comfortable.

The next morning I got up. Mr. Wells had already gone to the café. Mrs. Wells would take him down every morning and bring the car back and return about eight o'clock. I went back with her.

I met the waitresses, Peggy Gardiner and Shirley Fulton. Peggy was a flaming redhead with a pretty face full of freckles and Shirley was a dark-haired brunette with dark brown eyes. I felt so much better wearing the strap, especially after a good night's sleep.

That evening at the table, the Wellses agreed that I could stay there as long as I wished. Mr. Wells said that it would be better to call them Uncle Ben and Aunt Martha. I agreed and was very happy. I knew that they must have discussed me after I went to bed last night.

Before going to sleep I was trying to figure out a lot of things. *Why were they so good to me, a perfect stranger? Why did Mrs.—I mean Aunt Martha—keep calling me 'dear'? They make me feel that I am their own son. I love them but I just don't understand.*

I went to the café every morning with Aunt Martha. Every once in a while Uncle Ben would come downstairs in midmorning when it was slow and ask me to go upstairs and get a glass of milk.

Sunday mornings we went to the Central Baptist Church on Main Street, which was near the café. Uncle Ben was on the Official Board. Pastor Lloyd Masters had a wonderful delivery and his sermon was very informative and interesting. I sat with Aunt Martha. She sang the hymns with a very sweet voice and her blue eyes sparkled. Pastor Masters was rather heavyset and had a very clear voice. I could understand every word. His hair was beginning to show some gray and his blue eyes seemed very expressive.

3

Uncle Ben and Aunt Martha

For the next month I worked at the café and went to the jamboree in town on Saturday night. This was the popular entertainment in town. Al Goodwin owned the three-story building right downtown. He rented the two upper floors of offices and kept the first floor just for the jamboree. He would line up local talent each Saturday night and, once in a while, he would hire out-of-town talent at his own expense. He didn't charge admission but kept a box up front for anyone to donate something if they wished. It really was a fun evening and I had a chance to meet some young people since the younger set had their own place and adults had theirs. When anyone asked questions I just said I had come down from the North and was visiting my Uncle Ben and Aunt Martha for a spell. I was living in a dream world.

I went back to the doctor after work alone. No need to bother Uncle Ben. I told him I would walk home. He agreed. The doctor took X rays again of my left side and said to stop in the next day. I did so. He showed me three fine hairlines and said that they were healing and I didn't have to wear the strap any longer. He warned me to be careful for several more weeks.

I was putting on my shirt when he said, "Glen, sit down. I want to talk to you. I'm suppose to report you but Ben asked me not to. We are old friends. You see, Glen, Ben and Martha lost a son about two years ago. Frank was only fourteen years old and an only child. He drowned in Lake Calhoun. To them you are so much like Frank and they are hoping that you will never want to go back."

"Thank you, doctor. I don't think that I would ever want to go back. Thank you so much. This accounts for a great deal!"

I walked home slowly that afternoon. Most of the walk home my eyes would well up. This was a new life, a new beginning for me. It was like a new birth of freedom.

That night at the dinner table I mentioned the talk I had had with the doctor. I had to let them know that I knew.

"I'm sorry, really I am."

"Glen," Uncle Ben said, "he was the only child we had and we have never gotten over it. We had been thinking of adopting a boy about his age but never got around to it. Then you came along. You are so much like Frank. We felt that the Lord had something to do with your arrival."

"Glen," said Aunt Martha, "you are a wonderful God-send and we love you."

I could have hugged her, for she reminded me so much of Mother back home.

Maybe I wasn't as tough as I thought I was or perhaps I was too emotional but again I cried. Then Uncle Ben changed the subject and mentioned the great job Al Goodwin was doing with the jamboree.

"I used to play the guitar and the harmonica," I said.

"Well," said Uncle Ben, "we'll have to get you a guitar."

"Oh, I don't know. I haven't had any real lessons with the guitar."

"That's all right, Glen. I shall speak to Jack Gordon. He's the best instructor around."

I thought nothing about it until the night of my birthday. Right after dinner, Uncle Ben handed me a box. I opened it and there was a brand-new guitar and over in the corner was a harmonica! I set it to one side and gave them both a great big hug whether they liked it or not. Then I cried.

I was promoted to waiter when Shirley Fulton left. I was now working upstairs—no more heavy lifting! Uncle Ben hired a man by the name of Elmer Gage. He was a loner. He said he was forty years old; he had a room in one of the old apartment buildings by the rail tracks. He had a sense of humor and was very strong and a good worker.

I took a series of guitar lessons, just enough to learn a few chords.

I had a fairly good voice and some of the performers helped me a great deal and gave me copies of lyrics of western ballads to learn. Al Goodwin would tab me whenever he had a slow night. I had a lot of fun and looked forward to Saturday nights.

I spent my evenings during the week in night school, studying for my high school diploma. I knew I was lucky to have this opportunity and that I couldn't get very far without a high school education.

After about three and a half years of night school I received my diploma and was very proud. Uncle Ben and Aunt Martha had a surprise party for me with about a dozen friends from school, the jamboree and the church. I wasn't used to this.

I was eighteen years old and decided to go back to night school for the insurance course. A year later I was in Columbia taking my exam for my license. I passed and became a licensed insurance agent in South Carolina!

There were two front rooms in the house and Uncle Ben let me have the smaller room, which wasn't being used, for my insurance office. He hired some carpenters to put in a door so I would have my own private entrance. I was in the insurance business and writing policies in my spare time. I was still working at the café but Uncle Ben was very generous in letting me have time off when business demanded it.

On my twenty-first birthday I went to see attorney Bryan Scofield about having my name legally changed. Uncle Ben set up the appointment. The lawyer was a close friend and lodge brother of Uncle Ben. I had to have a birth certificate, so I wrote to the Dover Town Hall and sent two dollars. I received two certificates. The lawyer took care of everything even though I knew that Uncle Ben and Aunt Martha had to sign some papers. I know he asked them questions but I was now Glen Henry Fredericks, legally!

My insurance business was still in its infancy when I had to register for the draft. I wasn't very happy about it but things were looking pretty serious over in Europe. Uncle Ben and Aunt Martha talked about it and were concerned about our possible entry into another world war. They remembered the last war. We talked about what to do with my insurance business in case I was called.

A few days later Tom Shields was talking to Uncle Ben at the café. He mentioned that his granddaughter was graduating from high school and was looking for a job. She was also a straight-A student. Uncle Ben thought that she might be just the person to break into the insurance business.

I was a little perplexed. Uncle Ben was always making arrangements for me, always looking out for me and then surprising me. I couldn't get angry with him—I loved him so much. A few days later in the café, Uncle Ben called me over to the counter and said, "Glen, meet Barbra Shields. Barbra, meet my nephew, Glen."

"Pleased to meet you, Barbra."

"Thank you, sir. I'm pleased to meet you."

Uncle Ben then laid out his plan where Barbra could go

to evening classes and wait on tables during the day. Barbra thought that she might consider it but wanted to think about it. She said that she would let him know soon. We left the café and went home. On the way home Uncle Ben said, "What do you think of her, Glen?"

"Why didn't you say something to me first?"

"Oh, Glen, I'm just looking out for your own interest."

"I know, Uncle Ben. I don't know what I'd do without you but I wish you would talk things over with me. I'm not a little boy anymore, you know."

"Glen, you will always be our little boy."

After I thought about that for a moment I realized that Uncle Ben was right. Besides, Barbra really was a very pretty blue-eyed blond.

"But really, Glen, what do you think of the idea and of her helping out?"

"I think it's a great idea and she is so pretty!"

Aunt Martha quipped, "Oh, oh!"

A few days later, Barbra called Uncle Ben and said that she would give it a try. Uncle Ben hung up the phone and said, "OK, Glen, you're fired!"

"What?"

"Barbra said that she would take the job. I don't need three waitpersons."

"All right, quit kidding. What's this all about?" Aunt Martha was just sitting there smiling.

"You can now devote all your time to the insurance business and also give Barbra some help while she is taking the insurance course at evening school."

"But, Uncle Ben, I'm not even making enough to pay you anything yet."

"Don't worry about that, Glen, you are giving us more pleasure than you will ever know." Again, I couldn't help thinking how lucky I was.

For the next year Barbra was waiting on tables and going to evening school. At weekends we would get together and talk insurance and we would all wind up at the jamboree on Saturday night.

I could see that Barbra was taking a keen interest in her insurance studies. At the end of the semester, in December, Barbra completed her course and in January went to Columbia for her exam and her license. She passed and was a licensed insurance agent of property and casualty.

She left the café and spent full time in the office. Uncle Ben hired a new waitress, Debbie Shore, a high school graduate a year older than Barbra—a pretty brunette.

I was now beginning to take an interest in Douglas. In the evenings Uncle Ben, Aunt Martha and I would have discussions about the town. They had both been born there and knew about all there was to know. I bombarded them with questions and they seemed to enjoy answering me. To them, I thought, it was like going back and recalling long-ago times.

I learned that Douglas had a population of some twenty thousand people. There were two textile mills, one cotton mill, one lumber mill, one glove factory and a clay mine. Clay was used for automobile paint and in the chalk industries. On the outskirts on the left were peach orchards and on the right, tobacco, cotton and corn fields.

From my own observations and experiences, I had found that Douglas was just the right size and the people were very warm, friendly and cooperative.

I had heard of southern hospitality and felt that 90 percent was right here in Douglas! Of course, I soon learned that it was contagious throughout the South.

Every July Fourth they had a Homecoming Day celebration. Everyone looked forward to it and it seemed to be one of our part-time mayor's responsibilities to appoint a committee to plan a program. As a rule, things started off with a parade. Various units came in from the surrounding towns with firemen, school bands and a variety of floats from all over. They marched down Main Street and crossed over to Wade Boulevard and wound up at the high school field. The mayor gave a short address and made the awards. The green in the center of town was given over to the children; all sort of games and contests for prizes took place and free ice cream and cake were served. Late afternoon was time for family cookouts. At night everyone gathered at Lake Calhoun to watch a glorious fireworks display.

The more I learned the more I realized that this was my kind of town. I loved it and I loved the people.

4

World War II

On a cool April morning, four months after Pearl Harbor, I received a letter from the President of the United States: "Greetings; your friends and neighbors have selected you to serve your country," etc, etc.

I was to report at the town hall two weeks hence. Uncle Ben and Aunt Martha were a bit upset. I wasn't too concerned.

I left early in the morning. Uncle Ben and Aunt Martha drove me down and I saw Barbra getting out of her parents' car. There were about fifty young men standing around near the bus. We were all asked to enter the town hall. Mayor Lester Reed spoke for a few minutes and then presented each one of us with a small box containing a comb, nail file and clipper. When we went outside it seemed that all of Douglas had come out to see us off.

I went over to Uncle Ben to shake his hand. I tried to tell him how much I appreciated him but I choked.

"Oh, come here." He gave me a hug. Aunt Martha had tears in her eyes. She grabbed me and I thought that she would never let me go. Finally, Uncle Ben said, "Now Martha, let him go."

"Please be careful, dear," she said.

I turned around and there was Barbra just standing there. I stepped forward and the next thing I knew we were locked in each other's arms!

"I shall miss you, Glen."

"I'm sure I'm going to miss you, Barb. Take care."

"Whatever profit the business makes is yours. Uncle Ben and I insist." We kissed for the first time. I shook hands with Barbra's parents, Clay and Agnes Shields, and entered the bus.

I was sworn into the army at the armory in Columbia and from there went to Fort Bragg where I found myself in the artillery. I was assigned to surveying and fire direction. I had no training in algebra or geometry and had to go to night school three nights each week for thirteen weeks. With the help and patience of my fellow soldiers, I passed the course and, eventually, arrived in the Panama Canal Zone.

After nine months in Panama and thirteen months in California, I went to New York and then to England. Two months later I was on the Normandy coast. The battle lines were on the German–Holland border by this time. Our first battle position, a few weeks later, was on the border. We were immediately attacked by three of our fighter planes, P-47s. They strafed our position and we didn't fire back with our ack-ack guns. They went up high and circled. One plane came down to make another pass and we fired and brought him down.

The next morning they sent out a detail to investigate and, sure enough, there was a dead American lieutenant! We soon found out that we were supposed to have a different marker out each day for identification. We were not informed and someone higher up heard about this.

Jim Thornton and I were in the survey section and also in fire direction, where we computed fire direction shells to the target.

During the Battle of the Bulge, the infantry that we were supporting were pulled out and sent to the Bulge. We were sitting there with no one in front of us but we didn't know it until it was all over.

Whenever we were settled in one place we had to work a shift in fire direction. I served as vertical control operator and Jim was one of the battery computers. I'm sure that we had more responsibilities than we realized at the time. At breakfast time there was a cook who more or less looked after me. We had eggs one morning and hotcakes the next. When we were having hotcakes Sid Tallman would find out where I was sleeping and would wake me up. I have never tasted better hotcakes since, especially with the syrup they made. They were so good! At the time I was allergic to eggs.

We were on the move when, somehow, we got lost. There were cases where someone would change the road signs just to confuse us and lead us into a trap. When we realized the danger and were fired on, we got out of there in a hurry and without any casualties. Another time we were bogged down in an old barn. Shells were exploding all around us. We sneaked out about three in the morning with no injuries. The barn was never touched.

I was very happy to receive letters from Uncle Ben and Aunt Martha. They kept me posted on the home front. I received letters from Barbra and she assured me that the business was still going strong. I would also hear from Al Goodwin once in awhile. He was looking forward to having me perform at the jamboree again.

Barbra seemed to be writing more often lately and ending her letters with "Lots of Love" instead of "Sincerely." I was always glad to hear from all of them.

I tried to answer all of the letters, especially those from Uncle Ben and Aunt Martha. When I wrote to Barbra I was stuck for a complimentary closing. I thought I'd try "Affectionately Yours." In the next letter from Barbra, she asked, "Is that the best you can do?" I thought I'd have some fun and my next letter ended with "All my Love." I thought I was in trouble; otherwise that would have scared her away. Her letters kept coming with, "Lots of Love." Now I was sure I was in trouble!

Moments like these were few and far between. We had to get back to the business at hand and earn our keep. War is a twenty-four-hour-a-day job, for us and for the enemy.

We realized that we were far more fortunate than the infantry that we were supporting. We weren't engaged in hand-to-hand combat, but we did have our moments. When we were surveying we knew that the enemy was watching us but didn't bother us. They knew something big in artillery was coming in. They didn't know, however, that any high ground just beyond our infantry units would be neutralized by larger artillery before ours came in.

I shall never forget the artillery duel we had with the Germans east of Hanover. It was mountainous country and very beautiful. We were high on one mountain and the Germans were on another mountain about eight or ten miles away. Down below there was a pretty little village of white buildings with red tiled roofs. We dueled all day and finally neutralized their area. The village was not touched! We had a few casualties but nothing serious. This was our last battle with our artillery. Until the end of the war we were engaged in unorganized resistance by diehards. We were still running surveys since we still had the infantry to support and we were harassed by small groups that would snipe at us now and then but we didn't pay too much attention to them.

Another time while we were surveying, someone in the woods started to fire at us. I heard someone say, "Duck, Glen!"

I ducked and heard several bullets whiz by. They missed. We called for some infantry action and the woods were soon neutralized. By this time there was no organized resistance but the SS troops were diehards and didn't want to quit. There were also some who would put a plane together from any parts they could find and strafe our area. "Bedcheck Charlies," we called them. We downed them, of course. One day I was coming out of the mess hall and a plane came over and strafed. I ducked under a truck and my mess kit went flying. I wasn't hurt but was very angry. I was covered with mud.

After hostilities I was doing duty with the occupation forces. I later had a supply room in a pretty little German village. There was a twelve-year-old boy who spoke perfect English. He would help me in the supply room. He had two distinct profiles as he had one blue eye and one brown eye. He really was cute and a very nice little fellow. I would reward him with candy bars and also had Sunday dinner for him. We always had chicken on Sunday and it was a feast for him. I gave him his first orange and banana.

One day Henry Long, a full-blooded Indian from Oklahoma, came into the supply room and said, "Done 'et yet, Glen?"

Poor little Hans. He went out the back door and I didn't see him until the next day.

"Hans," I said, "why did you leave in such a hurry?"

"He was the first Indian I ever saw! What did he say?"

"He only asked me if I had eaten yet. Of course he said it his way. Hans, he won't hurt you."

Upstairs some of the men were using the rooms for their sleeping quarters. Henry was up there. I took Hans upstairs and introduced him to Henry. I had to hold him tight. In no time they became good friends.

A few months later I went to LeHavre, France and was booked on a Victory ship for New York. Two days out on the ocean the sea became pretty rough. We were amused at the table because the ship would roll just enough that no one had to ask for anything. Soon it would come sliding by. The next day we were not allowed out of our compartments because of the rough seas. We were locked in and our Swedish captain said, over the loudspeaker, that if anyone went up on deck he would have only nine seconds to live.

The bow of the ship would come right up out of the water and we could hear the water drop down to the sea. It would hold for a split second and then splash down to the sea. The rivets in the ship would squeak and we wondered when it was going to come apart. We stood this for eleven days! The only food we had were ice cream cups they got to each compartment several times a day. I endured it but many of the men were much too seasick and couldn't eat and were throwing up all over the place. Imagine the stench in a closed compartment under those conditions. It never bothered me and I kept on eating ice cream. The captain had a morbid sense of humor, I thought, when he announced that we had just passed the Queen Mary going back to Europe and it came within five degrees of capsizing! We were in a little Victory ship that rocked around in the ocean like a toy boat in a bathtub! That remark by the captain didn't do anything for our nerves.

When we docked in New York, most of the men in the bow of the ship were litter cases. There were ambulances all over the area. I was in the center of the ship where I received the least of the ride up and down in the ocean. I certainly had a great deal of respect for the Victory ships. I was discharged at Fort Dix in New Jersey and was back home the next day and back to reality!

5

Back to Reality

I noticed very little change in Uncle Ben but saw a little more gray in Aunt Martha's hair. All in all, though, they seemed to be in good health.

Uncle Ben got on the phone and invited Barbra and her parents, Clay and Agnes Shields, to come for dinner. Aunt Martha went all out, as she usually did, and put on quite a feast. After dinner Barbra and I went into the office and talked insurance.

I couldn't believe what that girl had done! She had more than tripled the business. We were corresponding while I was away but she never said anything about increasing the business; just mentioned that everything was fine. She put some of the profits in a separate account for me, which she didn't have to do. She tried to pay Uncle Ben rent for the office space and he wouldn't have any of that.

Since I still had a business and some cash to invest, I thought I might go back to school and take a night course in real estate and add that to the business. First, though, I got in touch with attorney Bryan Scofield to set up a partnership agreement with Barbra. She agreed but suggested that I be the senior partner. Smart girl!

The following Saturday night we went to the jamboree. Uncle Ben said that Al had called him and wanted me to bring my guitar. He had a light program and wanted me to fill in.

It was so good to be back at the jamboree. I sang "Red River Valley," then put my guitar away and went over to my table. I was still sitting with the younger set. When I arrived at the table everyone clapped and shook my hand. Barbra was holding my chair for me and when I sat down she planted a kiss on my cheek. I blushed and everyone laughed.

"What'd you do that for?"

"Oh, you figure it out," followed by a beautiful smile.

There are times when I'm not very bright, but I think I was beginning to see the light. After the jamboree some of us decided to go to Spaulding's Drugstore for milkshakes. This was a ritual for the young set before the war but I rarely joined them. Barbra told her parents that she would be home later. We had our milkshakes and I saw Barbra home. It was only a half-mile to her home and less than that to my home. We were near her home when I said, "I'm still trying to figure it out."

"Figure what out?"

"That kiss you planted on my cheek."

"Oh, that," she teased. "You're not very sharp lately. Were you gassed or something?"

I couldn't resist the smile on her face and, approaching the house, I took her in my arms and kissed her like I had never kissed anyone before. I let go. She gasped for breath, and, before she could say anything, or think, I asked, "Barbra, will you marry me?"

Her pretty blue eyes opened wide and she said, "Why, Glen, you have never even told me that you loved me!"

"I know. I've been wanting to ever since you signed off your letters with 'Lots of Love.'"

"Oh, I may think about it," she said coyly, eyeing me and studying my expression.

"Please stop teasing. Will you marry me?"

"Yes!"

I had a funny feeling, a tingling from my toes up to my head. I thought, *What have I done?* Barbra saw that I was a little out of it.

"Well, dummy, say something!"

"I think I've said enough already."

She looked puzzled.

"Oh, Barb, I'm sorry. It's just that I've never proposed before."

"You better not propose again, either."

I was so happy that I went out and bought my first car, a three-year-old Ford in very good condition. It was built the last year that cars were made during the war except for military use.

I completed the course in real estate and went to Columbia to take the exam for my license. I came back a licensed real estate agent!

There was quite a bit of acreage circling the center of town, except for a portion on the southwest owned by a Mr. Collins. He stayed mostly by himself and lived in a shack all alone. There was a lake on the property they called Lake Calhoun and Mr. Collins would let the kids swim there. This was where Frank Wells had drowned. I approached him but he wouldn't consider selling.

I felt that there would soon be a big demand for new homes by the returning servicemen. Space would be at a premium. I checked the property records at the town hall and discovered that all the vacant property on the east side of town was owned by only two parties. I inquired and they both agreed to sell. I planned to divide the acreage into half-acre building lots with a street down the middle.

Barbra set the wedding date for the next June twelfth. I gave her a list of some of my closest friends. She and her mother often worked on their list, lining up the people who would participate. So much planning!

I checked out the west end and this looked like choice land with a few rolling humps and all open acreage. I thought, *What a wonderful site for my home*. I asked Uncle Ben about it.

"That property is owned by Henry Cole's widow. She lives down on Austin Street."

I drove down there and introduced myself.

"I remember you from the jamboree. I haven't been there since my husband died."

"Mrs. Cole, I'm interested in the land you own on the west side."

"I have been thinking of putting it in the hands of a real estate agency but I just haven't gotten around to it."

"Mrs. Cole, I am a licensed real estate agent and I am really interested in buying it for my own personal use. I wouldn't put any business on it."

"No, I don't think I would like to see a shopping center or anything like that there. I understand there are about eighteen acres there. Well, perhaps we can come to some understanding, but I want to consult my lawyer and also get an appraisal."

"That's fine, Mrs. Cole. That's what you should do. Suppose you get in touch with me at your convenience. Here's my card."

She seemed to be a kind, elderly lady with gray hair and bright blue eyes.

I went over the area to really look it over. I saw one small rise and I knew then just where my house was going to be. The rest I could use for a nine-hole golf course but I wasn't going to say anything about that to anyone.

It was about two weeks later when I received a call from Mrs. Cole.

"Mr. Fredericks, do you think you could stop by this afternoon?"

"Certainly, Mrs. Cole."

I went over there and she said that she was advised to expect no less than six thousand dollars for the eighteen acres. I was elated!

"Mrs. Cole, may I give you a check for five hundred dollars as a down payment?"

"Of course, young man. I'm glad you expect to build your house there, but what will you do with the rest of the land?"

"Mrs. Cole, I intend to use all of it for my own personal use. I can assure you that it will never be used for business."

I left a very happy man. I told Barbra about it and she was happy. I went to the bank and secured a loan of two thousand dollars. I had the rest and still had a healthy surplus in the business.

6

The Wedding and a New Home

We were so very busy a week before the wedding. Uncle Ben was my best man and he got Al Goodwin to rent the jamboree room to him for a bachelor party. Al let him have the room free of charge. Uncle Ben had the dinner catered and it was delicious. Barbra had a shower a few nights before and we all were at a dinner for the wedding party put on by Clay and Agnes Shields at the hotel. Who would ever want to go through this more than once?

The wedding took place at the Central Baptist Church with Pastor Lloyd Masters officiating. Florence Parker was maid of honor and Uncle Ben was wonderful as my best man. We sent out about fifty invitations and had the reception in the social room of the church building.

Late in the afternoon we said good-bye to everyone and drove north to Washington, DC. We took tours all over the city and even visited Mount Vernon. We were in the White House, Congress, the Congressional Library, the Lincoln Memorial, the Washington Monument, the Bureau of Printing and Engraving and the Smithsonian. We walked along the Tidal Basin and stopped at the Jefferson Memorial and visited Arlington Cemetery. After two weeks of this we were ready to go home. It was during our honeymoon that I explained how I had come to Douglas and why I had changed my name.

Uncle Ben and Aunt Martha spruced up our rooms and

put the wedding presents to one side for us. I went to work on the property on the east side of town, having it surveyed into half-acre lots with a road running down the middle. I called it Fredericks Boulevard. As soon as I sold a lot I put the money right back into the project with water pipes, sewers, sidewalks and lights. I contracted with three different construction companies that provided a variety of models and prices. Anyone buying a lot was required to use one of the companies so there would be no wood-frame houses and no slum sections. That was the only restriction.

With the war over I knew there would be a run on open spaces. The men would be getting married and looking for houses. The real estate business was very active and the lots were selling far better than I thought they would.

Now I was able to focus on my own home. I had to set an example and use one of the companies I had contracted with. Barbra and I found what we wanted and, after a few modifications, we had our dream house in mind.

Barbra and I agreed to invite Uncle Ben and Aunt Martha to come live with us. They were getting along in age and the house was getting to be too much for Aunt Martha.

One night at the dinner table Barbra, out of the blue, said, "Uncle Ben and Aunt Martha [she had been asked to call them that] how would you like to come live with us in our new home when it's finished?"

They looked at each other and then looked at me.

"Barbra and I have talked it over and we really would like to have you," I said.

"We will have plenty of room. In fact, you will have your own rooms," Barbra assured them.

"Well, I don't know. What do you think, Martha?"

"I think we should give it some thought, Ben."

"Glen, I've lived in this house all my life. I was born here and Martha and I were married right here in the living room. It isn't easy to say good-bye."

"Folks," I said, "it isn't easy to say good-bye to a home you've lived in all your life, but there comes a time when we all have to make adjustments. Why not consider selling the house and either selling or leasing the café?"

"But what will I do? I can't sit around and do nothing!"

"Uncle Ben, you know how you always keep saying that you never have time for your flowers. You will have plenty of time planning the flowers and shrubbery around our new house, and it will be your home as well as ours."

"Well, as I said, I think Martha and I should think about it."

"Take your time," I said. "We won't be moving in until early next year."

The business was looking good. I was quite active with real estate. Uncle Ben hired Florence Parker when Peggy Gardiner left.

The work on our house began to take shape. Uncle Ben couldn't understand why we needed such a large house.

The house would actually be three stories because the first floor would be partially sunken and would contain a recreation room, two-door garage, furnace, workbench and a bath. The second floor would be the living room, dining room, kitchen, library and bath. Upstairs would be two master bedrooms with a bath in between. On the other side would be four bedrooms with a bath in between each two. Also a large linen closet. There would be a foyer as one entered the house with a grand staircase. Under the stairs would be a door to enter the garage, the recreation room, a closet and another bath.

The outside of the house would be finished off with red brick and the entrance would have four white columns. The driveway would be made with white crushed stone and circle in front of the house. It began to look as though we could be in our new house before the first of the year.

While the house was being built, Barbra and I were having fun designing the patio and grill area. We also planned an in-ground pool. All the rest of the property was reserved for a nine-hole golf course even though I never mentioned this to Barbra. Of course, I told Uncle Ben and asked him not to say anything about it just yet. He just shook his head. Barbra soon found out when I inadvertently left my sketches of the course on my dresser. She left them there and said nothing until she mentioned at the dinner table.

"Glen, I could use a new wardrobe and a new car. I don't think that is asking too much especially when you are planning a golf course for yourself!"

"How did you know?"

"I saw your plans, fella!"

Uncle Ben choked on his coffee.

"Barb, I really meant to tell you about that but I didn't think this was the time to spring this with all we have going on right now. Let's get the house built and then we can see about other things."

"You'd better start thinking about a nursery and everything that goes with it."

"What?"

"We're going to have a baby!"

For a minute I just stared. Uncle Ben gulped and Aunt Martha dropped her fork!

"Well," said Barbra, "what's the matter with you all? This happens all the time."

"Barbra, what next?"

"Are you happy, Glen?"

"Oh, I'm delighted! When?"

"Late March."

I was ecstatic—a baby!

It was early November and it looked as though we could be in our new home within the month. I was sitting on top of the world! It was Barbra's birthday and I drove downtown with her.

"Where are we going, Glen?"

"Oh, just out for a ride."

"Why are we stopping here?"

"Just come and follow me, Barb."

We walked into the Buick dealership and Bill Porter met us at the door.

"We're ready for you, Glen."

"Ready for what?" Barbra asked.

"Let's go out back, shall we?" asked Bill.

"Barb, happy birthday!"

She saw a beautiful brand-new blue Buick. Her color!

"Oh Glen, I love you!"

I followed her home in my five-year-old Ford and she was driving her new car as though she owned the town!

We arrived home and Barbra and Aunt Martha went out for a ride in her new car. While they were out riding Uncle Ben and I were talking about the insurance business. He knew we were, perhaps, taking on too much and wanted to help.

"Uncle Ben, I know that we will have to go easy for a little while but the business is good and I'm not worried."

"Glen, I want to put one hundred thousand dollars in the bank in your account. No arguments. You can pay me back when you can. No hurry."

"Uncle Ben, I couldn't pay you back for all you've done for me if I spent the rest of my life."

I knew it would be futile to argue with him. I paid off the mortgage as soon as the house was finished and now I thought I could concentrate on the golf course. After all, Barbra had her new car!

Uncle Ben and Aunt Martha decided to sell their house and move in with us. Barbra and I were very happy they decided to come. Uncle Ben put the old house in my hands and told me what he thought he should get for it.

We were just getting settled into our new house when a fire broke out in a house on Jackson Street. This house was the home of a colored family by the name of Melvin. Ruth Melvin was a widow and had two daughters and a son. Julie was eighteen, Donna, twelve, and David, eight. Ruth was well educated and a registered nurse at the hospital. Her late husband, Edward, had been an engineer of sorts and worked at the radio station. He had died of a massive stroke about three years previously and Ruth had been doing a wonderful job with the children.

The house had some extensive damage to the kitchen where the fire started from the stove. Grease caught fire and got out of control. There was water damage and smoke damage throughout the house. The firemen did a good job keeping the damage to a minimum.

I had the insurance and I received word when Ruth called me from a neighbor's house. I went right over and realized that the house had to be vacated until repairs could be completed. I asked if I could use a telephone. A neighbor next door let me use her phone. I called a carpenter, an electrician and painters to get them on the job as soon as possible. Then I called Barbra to see what she thought about letting the Melvins stay with us until their house was ready. She insisted that I bring them over. I went back out and found the neighbors consoling Ruth and the children.

"Ruth, I just called some people who will be up the first thing in the morning and start work on the house."

"Thank you, Mr. Fredericks."

"I also called Barbra and we would like to have you come stay with us until your house is ready."

"Oh, Mr. Fredericks, are you sure?"

"Very sure. I think you can go in now and get the things you will need and come over to our house when you can."

About an hour later Ruth and the children drove into the driveway. Uncle Ben and I helped with the luggage. We went upstairs and showed them to their rooms. Aunt Martha knew this would entail a bit more work for her but soon realized what a neat family they were. Julie was in charge of Donna and David, and Ruth was a terrific cook.

The Melvins stayed with us for three weeks. Ruth drove to the hospital every day and the children walked to school. Both the high school and the grade school were near each other just down on Wade Boulevard. Julie was a senior in high school and very neat and smart.

Donna and David had a ball in the rec room downstairs. It seemed so nice to have eight people around the dinner table. I was used to this. Ruth would stop at her house every day after work to check on the progress of her house. When the house was ready they moved back. Donna and David didn't want to leave. We missed them.

7
A New Office

A representative from Blair's Department Stores saw my ad in a real estate paper and contacted me. I spoke to Uncle Ben to see if he would approve of a Blair's store on the property. Since we didn't have a department store of that kind in Douglas, he thought it would be nice for the town. He didn't want anything that would compete too much with any business in town. I closed the sale; now we were going to have a full-blown Blair's Department Store in Douglas!

I spoke to Al Goodwin about an unoccupied office up over the jamboree building and he let me have it for a reasonable price. It was on the second floor and was spacious. I immediately moved my office and I was back in business.

I knew how Uncle Ben felt when he saw his house being ripped apart. I really felt sorry for him.

One night at the jamboree, Al Goodwin came over to me at the table and introduced me to a golf pro from Columbia. Al knew I was thinking about building a golf course.

"Glen, I want you to meet Jim Schuller. He's a club pro up in Columbia."

"Well, how do you do, Jim?"

"Hello, Glen. Al has told me about you. I understand you're interested in building a golf course?"

"Yes, I am."

"I'm staying with Al for a few weeks. I might be able to get things started for you."

Al Goodwin told me about Jim and that he had designed several courses around Columbia. On the following Monday, Jim and I went over the sketches that I had made. We walked around the area and he suggested a few changes here and there. We discussed the approximate cost, including his fee, and it staggered me!

We were doing fine and were out of debt but I knew this was going to strap us. I spoke to Barbra and she said that we could afford it.

"Let's go for it. I may want to take up golf myself."

That was all I needed. I got in touch with Jim and the next day we had a couple of 'dozers, all kinds of equipment, and dust all over the area.

I began to think Barbra would have her hands full when the baby came. I couldn't expect her to be working at the office.

"Barb, I think we ought to consider hiring a girl for the office. I'm afraid you are going to be very busy with the baby even with Aunt Martha here."

"I was thinking of that, Glen. Isn't Julie Melvin graduating this June?"

"Of course, that's a great idea. She's a straight-A student. I'll call and ask her."

I phoned the Melvin household. "Hello, Ruth?"

"Yes."

"This is Glen Fredericks."

"Oh, how are you, Mr. Fredericks?"

"Fine, Ruth. I called to see if Julie had any plans after high school."

"Well, if nothing shows up I can always get her a job at the hospital."

"Well, as you know, Barbra is due in March. She's going to have her hands full with the baby and I will need someone in the office. Do you think Julie would be interested?"

"I should think so. I'll let you talk to her."

"Hello, Mr. Fredericks."

"Hello, Julie. I was just talking to your mother and wondered if you would like to learn the insurance business? Mrs. Fredericks is going to be very busy when the baby comes."

"Oh, how wonderful! When?"

"In March sometime."

"I'm so glad for both of you but I'm afraid I don't know anything about real estate or insurance."

"Julie, you won't have to worry about real estate or insurance. You can take an insurance course at evening school and I'll pay for it."

"Mr. Fredericks, I'd love to do that!"

"OK, Julie. If you wish you can come in each day after school and get a head start. I'll pay you, of course."

"Oh, wonderful. I'll be in tomorrow afternoon. Thank you!"

"Fine, Julie. I'll see you tomorrow."

Julie would be the ideal girl for the office. She had a cheery disposition and a very pretty smile. She always dressed well.

Every afternoon after school she was in the office. After graduation she started evening classes and eventually went to Columbia and passed her exam and became a licensed insurance agent. This was quite a relief for Barbra. She was spending more time in the office than I was and I was glad to have someone to take over.

The golf course was shaping up and I thought it might be ready by early summer. Jim would come down every once in a while and check on the progress. One day Jim came down with a golf pro friend of his and introduced him to me.

"Glen, this is Matt Shoen. Matt is a club pro at a course

near Columbia."

"Hello, Matt. Glad to meet you."

"Glen, would you mind if Matt and I rated your course for you? Of course we'll handicap the fairways, too."

"Not at all. Go right ahead."

Those two fellows could have been twins with their blond hair and blue eyes.

I left them alone and, after a little while, I looked out and saw them with a tape and some instruments. They seemed to be having fun.

I was on the patio about two hours later when they came in. They gave me the course rating of 69 and the slope rating of 122. Now I could add this to the scorecards when I got them printed. I didn't know what this would do for my game. We had a cup of coffee and talked for a few moments.

"Glen," said Matt, "I'd love to come down sometime and play your course."

"Anytime, Matt. You are welcome. In fact, I'd love to play with both of you if you will give me a stroke on every green."

"No way," said Jim. "I think he's pretty good, Matt."

By early July I was on the course trying it out. Uncle Ben was having a ball mowing the greens and the fairways. I spent a fortune just on maintenance equipment and even had a golf cart. Jim figured the course would be in top shape by the following summer but it seemed playable even now.

One Saturday morning I got a call from Al Goodwin.

"Hello, Glen. How's the golf course?"

"I'm playing on it. It's great!"

"Mind if I come over?"

"Come on over. I'm just getting ready to go out now."

Al Goodwin wasn't a large man. He had light brown

hair and gray eyes but I had a feeling that he knew his way around a golf course.

In no time at all Al came over with his bag of clubs.

"Good morning, Al. I didn't know you were interested in golf."

"Glen, when I first heard that you were thinking of building a golf course I got in touch with Jim. I want to see it finished."

We went around twice and I soon learned that I was playing with someone who had been playing for quite a while.

"Al, you're pretty good. Where have you been playing?"

"I grew up on a golf course. My father was a greens keeper over in Columbia. I was on the course almost every day. Jim and I went to school together."

"Al, I've been watching you and I think I may be able to learn something."

"Glen, I'll do what I can. Just watch and use your shoulder turn and hips and keep the club on the swing line."

Needless to say, Al and I played many rounds on my course. There was hardly a day when some of the kids from high school wouldn't be on the course in the afternoon. I didn't mind.

I kept thinking about the area south of my property owned by old Mr. Collins. For several days he wasn't seen by anyone. He had a dog of mixed breed that was barking. I was on the course and down near that area and heard the dog barking. The area was rather remote and no one would hear anything unless they were in the area. I thought I would notify the police and be sure everything was all right.

The police arrived at the man's cabin and found the dog guarding the body of Mr. Collins. They consoled the dog and checked the man. They called the coroner and the man was pronounced dead.

No one knew too much about him. He did a little shopping here and there and paid his bills. On his person they found his wallet. His name was David C. Collins, and there was also the name and address of one Joseph Collins living in Durham, North Carolina. The police got in touch with him and he came down. He was a brother and sole beneficiary since there were no other relatives. Joseph searched through the cabin and found a will. It designated Joseph as the heir. After the property was probated, Joseph wanted to sell. It consisted of fourteen acres and only one building. I talked to Joseph and asked his price. He said he would sell it for five thousand dollars.

I said that I would buy it. I raided the business and gained title to the property. I went to Mayor Reed with a proposal. He was a large, kindly man with white hair and blue eyes.

"Lester, as you know, I have just acquired the Collins property. Douglas doesn't have a ballfield or a playground for the kids and I'd like to deed the land over to the city if the city will appropriate money to build a ballfield and some tennis courts. Fix up the area around Lake Calhoun and make it a safe place for swimming. It could be a nice park where everyone could benefit."

"Glen, that's a terrific idea and very generous of you. I shall bring it up at the next Common Council meeting and see what can be done."

"Thank you, Les. I hope that my proposal will be approved."

It was two weeks later when it was approved and money appropriated. I promptly turned the deed over to the city.

A month later the park was complete. It was a very

beautiful place for the kids. I received an invitation to attend the dedication of the park. The mayor wanted me on the speakers' stand. No name was mentioned but I thought that Douglas Park would do. Barbra and I sat next to Mayor Reed. Uncle Ben and Aunt Martha were in the audience.

At the ceremony, Mayor Reed spoke a few words and then called me over. He announced that I was the man who had made this possible and that I should have the honor of unveiling the plaque at the entrance. I pulled the line and the white cloth fell to the ground revealing a plaque fastened to a large rock emblazoned, FREDERICKS PARK.

Everyone cheered and I was tongue-tied! A park named after me?

I was embarrassed but honored and was lost for words for a moment. I recovered and thanked the mayor and the Common Council members.

We drove home and I learned that it really was more blessed to give than to receive. We had our own little celebration and went to the Douglas Hotel for dinner. It was a beautiful day!

8

A Daughter and a Brother

It was late March when Evelyn Arlene came into the world. She was every bit the image of her mother. Barbra had plenty of help when she came home from the hospital. Aunt Martha was with her and the baby constantly. Mother and Dad Shields were regular visitors also.

A few weeks later Barbra was rocking Evie to sleep, and seeing them together reminded me of a Sunday school song we used to sing years ago:

> I see my mother kneeling with her family each day.
> I hear the words she whispers,
> As she bows her head to pray.
> Her pleas to our Father silence all my fears,
> And I am thankful love is spoken here.

Uncle Ben decided to lease the café and he asked me to take care of the details. He was getting tired of rising early every morning. I knew he wanted to spend more time with the flowers and the shrubbery around our place. I leased the café. This relieved him of the business, yet he still had a good income from the lease arrangements.

Christmas was coming and Uncle Ben went out just beyond the golf course and cut down a beautiful pine tree. We all had fun decorating it. It was Evie's first Christmas. She watched and wondered what it was all about.

I was in the café having lunch with a client who was interested in buying a lot to build. I had only one lot left. At the table next to us were a man and a lady. I heard her call the man "Drew." I glanced over and there was something familiar about him. I didn't want to appear too conspicuous but I took another look and behold! I saw a scar on his right cheek! This was a scar he had received in a sledding accident. He ran into a car and the chains on the rear wheel of the car cut his cheek. I had goose pimples right away. I knew then that he was my brother, Drew!

After we finished lunch I shook hands with my client and we agreed to meet the next day. He left and I went over to the next table and asked, "Are you Drew Harris?"

"Yes, I am."

"From Dover, Connecticut?"

"That's right."

"I'm Glen Fredericks."

"How do you do, Glen? This is my wife, Jean, but how did you know my name?"

"Drew, I'm your brother, Glen. I'm Fredericks now." He checked my hand and saw the odd fingernail that never grew on right after a steel hoop landed on it when I was about six years old.

"My goodness, you really are Glen."

"Well, Drew, when I heard Jean call you 'Drew,' and I saw your scar, I knew you had to be my brother." His light brown hair and blue eyes gave him away.

"Glen, again, meet your sister-in-law, Jean."

"Hello, Jean. What a wonderful surprise!"

"This is a surprise, Glen. I have heard so much about you!"

"Are you staying in town tonight?"

"Well, I don't know, Glen. We only stopped for lunch. We are on our way to Florida for a couple of weeks. What do you think, Jean?"

"I think we should stay for the night so you can get to talk with your brother."

"Fine, you're staying at my place tonight and you can stay as long as you wish."

We left the café and Drew and Jean followed me home. We passed alongside the golf course and they were impressed. When we got out of the car, Drew said, "I see you have a golf course right near the place."

"Do you play, Drew?"

"No, I'm not old enough yet."

"That happens to be my golf course."

"What, your very own course?"

"Yup."

"This is a beautiful house, Glen. What do you do?"

"Real estate and insurance."

Just then Uncle Ben came out and I introduced them to him. Uncle Ben knew I came from a large family but never expected to meet any of them. We carried the bags into the house and Aunt Martha was there. I introduced them to her. I called Barbra and she came downstairs with Evie in her arms, who was a little more than a year old.

"Drew and Jean, meet Barbra and little Evie."

Barbra just stared, wondering what I was up to now.

"Hello" was all she could say.

"Barbra, we met in the café. He is really my brother."

When Barbra was convinced she handed me the baby and gave Jean a hug. Jean took the baby in her arms and kissed her.

"Drew, I'm glad to meet you." They hugged.

We went upstairs and showed them their room and spent most of the afternoon showing them around the place. They were impressed! Then we toured the town. As we drove down Fredericks Boulevard, I showed them the development I had created and then the park bearing my name. We went back home. Aunt Martha was getting dinner ready. We went out to the patio and talked and talked about everything. Drew couldn't get over my southern drawl. I didn't realize I had it. I told them how I came here on a freight car and why I changed my name and how I met Uncle Ben and Aunt Martha. He was filling me in on the home front.

"Virginia and Lloyd have two children. Jean and I have two, Ed and Ginny have three, Alan and Lilly have one and Marge is still at home. Bobby is in the air corps."

"Bobby! Who's Bobby?"

"Oh, that's right. You left before Bobby was born. He was born the following May after you left." I had a brother whom I had never seen!

"He is twenty years old, Glen."

"I can't believe it!"

"In case you want to know, Glen, he is stationed in Biloxi. I'll give you his address and you can write if you wish."

I copied his address and asked Drew if he had any pictures with him. He didn't. I checked the map and determined that Biloxi was about four hundred miles away.

"Drew, I have an appointment tomorrow with a client but after tomorrow I think I shall take a ride down there and see if I can meet my brother."

I sold my last lot the next day and Drew and Jean left for Florida. I left it up to Drew if he wanted to mention me at home.

The next morning I was on my way to Biloxi. I arrived late in the afternoon and took a room in a motor inn on the beach about three miles from Keeler Air Base. I took a quick shower and headed for the air base. I arrived at the main gate and asked the guard if I could get in touch with a

Robert Harris and have him paged. The guard was very cooperative when I told him I was his brother. He picked up the phone and asked for Information and had him paged. It was just about time for retreat. He was informed to report to the main gate immediately after retreat. I waited.

In about a half-hour I saw an airman sauntering down the street. I thought, *He's a big fellow*. I could see his blond hair and blue eyes. He stopped at the gate and was directed toward me. I got out of the car and was walking toward him.

"Hi, Bobby. I know you don't know me but I am your brother, Glen."

I know I shocked him because he didn't say anything, just stared and studied me.

"Bobby, I met Drew and Jean in a café up in South Carolina. They told me about you. I left home before you were born."

"I know I have a brother I never saw, but we were not sure if he was still alive. How did you happen to meet Drew?"

"It was a chance meeting. I happened to be in the café and sitting next to their table when I heard Jean call him 'Drew.' I glanced over and he seemed familiar. I saw his scar on his cheek and I knew that he was my brother. I went over and asked if he was Drew Harris. That's how we met."

He still had doubt in his expression. I showed him my fingernail to convince him that I really was his brother. He must have been told about my nail.

"I'm convinced, Glen, and what a surprise!"

"Bobby, have you any plans for tonight?"

"No."

"Can you get a pass? I'd like to take you out to dinner."

"I'll be right back."

He ran up the street and in about five minutes he was running down again.

Bobby and I drove to the Motor Inn on the beach and had dinner. We had so much to talk about. I was interested in any hobbies he had and what his favorite subjects were in school. Did he have a girlfriend? He loved to make model airplanes, like Drew, and he had always wanted to be in the air corps. Yes, he had a girlfriend at home. He wanted to know all about how I left home and all the experiences I had.

"Bobby, will the air corps be your career?"

"No, I don't think so."

The more we talked the more I wanted to hug him! I had to get him back to the base before ten o'clock. We parted company at the gate but not before we hugged.

On the way home the next day I kept thinking of all the ground we had covered. Father was mentioned only once, but he said that mother often mentioned me. I realized how much I had missed. To think I had a brother I never saw grow up! I began to think what I would be doing if I had stayed home. Would I have been happier? I don't think so. Here, I had found what it was like to love and be loved.

A few months later I received a letter from Germany. It was from Bobby. He sure was getting around! He said that he met a girl—a German girl! I hoped she spoke English.

9

Politics and Relatives

I returned home and was greeted by a surprise. I was used to anything by now.

"I think you're going to be a father again."

"What, again?"

We hugged and were very happy.

"When, dear?"

"About mid-September."

It seemed there was another surprise coming my way. The police commissioner died of a heart attack and, while I was away, the Common Council followed the mayor's choice and made me police commissioner!

Paul Alan was born September 18 and was a healthy baby boy with brown hair and eyes. He was my boy! Barbra and Aunt Martha had their hands full. Evie was three years old and getting into everything.

About a year later came another surprise. The doorbell rang. It was midafternoon in early October. I opened the door and a couple, I'd say in their late twenties, stood there. The lady asked, "Are you Glen Harris—I mean Fredericks?"

"I am."

"Hi, brother!"

She gave me a great big hug and kiss. I was worried, scared and speechless!

"Who are you?"

"I'm your little sister, Margie, you dope! This is my

husband, Julian, your brother-in-law."

I could see Drew had told them about me but I wasn't sure he had said anything to Mother.

"Hello, Julian. I've been getting a great number of surprises lately."

"Marge, I'm so glad you came. Please come in. I suppose you were talking to Drew?"

"Oh, yes. He gave me your address. We just got married yesterday in Maryland and made it a point to come down here to see you."

"I'm so glad you did, Marge."

Just then Barbra came into the foyer with Paul in her arms and Evie trailing.

"Marge, meet your sister-in-law, Barbra, and your niece, Evelyn, and your nephew, Paul. Barbra, this is my sister, Marge, and her husband, Julian."

"Have you any plans for tonight?"

"No, but—"

"No buts; you're staying here. And I hope you can stay a few days. We have so much to talk about."

Uncle Ben and Aunt Martha came downstairs and I made the introductions. I had to explain who Uncle Ben and Aunt Martha were, as I had with Drew and Jean.

Uncle Ben and Julian went out to the car and brought in their luggage. We showed them to their room. They freshened up and came down.

We had a little time before dinner so I took them on a tour of the town. I didn't mention the golf course or even take them out back. I thought I could show them the house later. I told them that I was in insurance and real estate. I showed them the development, driving down Fredericks Boulevard, and the park named after me and also some of the highlights of the town. We came back on Wade Boulevard. Marge said, "Look, there's a golf course."

"I know, Marge, that's mine."

We turned into the driveway. Marge was very quiet.

"You mean you own the golf course?"

"That's right. I took up golf a few years ago." I was really having fun with her.

"Glen, before you lay any more on me, what else do you have in this town?"

"Oh, Marge, I'm much too modest to tell you."

"Glen, you talk just like a southerner."

We toured the grounds and they were impressed.

At the dinner table that night I mentioned that I was police commissioner. She filled me in with the latest news from home and, of course, she wanted to know all about me.

After two days they left for home. It was so good to see them. Marge was only four years old the last time I saw her. Now she was Mrs. Julian Gleason.

Time flies and several months later I had another surprise. My brother, Alan, and his wife, Lilly, showed up at the door and, of course, I didn't know him either.

"You used to be Glen Harris?"

"Yes, and you must be Ed or Alan."

"I'm Alan, and this is my wife, Lilly."

"Well, come in. Hello, Lilly. Drew must be spreading the word."

"We're on a short trip to the Smokies and we wanted to see you while we were down here. Mom is taking care of little Al. He's just two years old."

Al and Lilly just stayed overnight and they were on their way.

I received another letter from Bobby in Germany. He had married the German girlfriend and would be bringing her back with him. He was just finishing his tour of duty. She must have spoken some English if they had agreed to marry. I hoped someday they would visit me.

I received another surprise when Julie announced that she was getting married. I knew she had a boyfriend, Albert Michaels, whom I had known for several years. They had known each other all their lives and both were members of the colored Baptist church on Davis Street.

"Mr. Fredericks," she said, "may I ask a special favor of you?"

"Of course, Julie, what is it?"

"This may seem very unusual and, if you refuse, I will understand."

"Julie, come out with it."

"The wedding is June fifteenth, only three weeks away. Will you give me away?"

I wasn't ready for anything like this and I guess I showed it. She was studying me and waiting. I soon realized that the girl didn't have a father. Turning to me was a wonderful compliment.

"Julie, for you, of course."

"I spoke to Mother and she said that she was sure you would do it. Mr. Fredericks, I am greatly honored." She hugged me. I felt so proud to think that she would even think to ask.

Albert Michaels, the groom, was owner of the auto garage on Austin Street. I always bought my gas there and had my cars maintained by him. He was a very good mechanic and very honest. A very pleasing fellow—and I was sure they would have a very happy marriage.

The wedding was a joyous occasion, perfect. I was proud to walk down the aisle with Julie on my arm. My whole family was there including Uncle Ben and Aunt Martha. Pastor Horace Hines officiated. When the pastor asked, "Who gives this bride away?" I said, "Her mother and I."

After the wedding the reception was held downstairs

in the social room. We had a delicious chicken dinner. I gave Julie and Albert a check for five hundred dollars. I thought that this would be more appreciated than some trinket. They honeymooned somewhere in Alabama and were planning to visit some cousins.

Barbra went directly to the office after the dinner. This caused me to think about hiring a girl to work in the office as Julie's assistant. I thought it would be wise to have someone to break in just in case. I talked it over with Barbra and she agreed. Barbra had enough to take care of at home without depending too much on Aunt Martha. I would speak to Julie when she returned from her trip. I thought of Florence Parker, who was still waiting on tables at the café. She was well liked by everyone and had a wonderful personality. She was a brunette with pretty brown eyes, and had been Barbra's maid of honor at our wedding.

I was at the café having a cup of coffee. Florence Parker waited on me. She had replaced Peggy Gardiner.

"Florence, how would you like to work in insurance?"

"Do you mean it?"

"Of course. I'm going to need a girl to work with Julie. She just got married, you know."

"Mr. Fredericks, I would love to give it a try but I'm not up on insurance."

"You don't have to be. Julie will break you in and, if you are interested, you can always take a course. It's all up to you."

"It sounds great, but I'll have to give a week or so notice."

"Of course. Get in touch with me."

Florence was ready to start a new career by the time Julie returned. I spoke to Julie's mother and asked to have Julie call me as soon as she returned, since they were going to live in the same house until they found their own place.

I wanted to alert Julie before she went to the office. When Julie called I told her about Florence and she was happy and said that she could use a helper. Of course, Julie would be the office manager. Florence went to evening school and then to Columbia to take her test. She passed and became an agent. Julie helped her and they got along just fine.

10
The Children

Paul was just a year old and Evie was four. They were a dream. Evie was a regular talking machine and asking questions with the rapidity of a machine gun. I thought she was going to look like her mother and be as smart as her father! Of course, Barbra had her own ideas.

Uncle Ben and Aunt Martha adored the children. Uncle Ben would take Evie all over the golf course in the golf cart and she loved it.

It was March and Evie's fifth birthday. We had a party for her. Paul was in the high chair wondering what it was all about.

Soon Evie would be going to school. Whenever we mentioned school to her she would say, "I'm not going to school. I'm gonna stay home with Mommy."

"Honey," I would say, "when the time comes I think you will change your mind."

Paul was beginning to crawl and we had to be careful we didn't step on him.

The kids continued to grow, as they always do. Evie was now ten and in the fifth grade and Paul was six and in the second grade. We planned a trip to Washington, DC, and to New York City when school closed for the summer. I wanted the children to see the sights of the nation's capital and also New York City.

Again, Uncle Ben and Aunt Martha said they didn't

feel like travelling. They'd rather stay home and take care of things.

We visited the main attractions in Washington that we saw on our honeymoon and even went to Mount Vernon. Evie remembered seeing pictures of Washington's home in her history book. We drove up to New York and took the cruise around Manhattan and the next day we went out to the Statue of Liberty. We went to the top of the Empire State Building and Barbra got dizzy. She doesn't like heights. The children were having the time of their lives.

A few years later we took the children to Florida. We left during their winter break from school. We had reservations at a beach hotel at Ormond Beach, just north of Daytona but not as crowded. We spent a week enjoying the beach and the children.

We took the children up to St. Augustine and visited Marineland. The children saw some sea life that they had never seen before. We returned home and the children couldn't wait to tell Uncle Ben and Aunt Martha all about the trip.

I was back at the office. Julie and Florence were getting along fine and really running the business. Florence was taking lessons at night school in real estate and was helping Julie with a few details in insurance. I only dropped in once in a while to see if the place was still there. I guess I considered myself semiretired.

Evie was now in high school and was on the cheerleading squad. She was at every football game and enjoyed it very much. She was also taking piano lessons. Paul was still trying to master the violin. They had their poor mother running all over the town. Of course, I helped a little.

Barbra got a phone call from school that Paul was suffering from a stomachache. She called me at the office and asked me to go over to the school and check on him. I went to the nurse's room and found Paul doubled up in pain. I called Dr. Davis and he said to bring him to his office immediately. Dr. Davis looked at him and diagnosed his condition as appendicitis. He called the hospital to prepare for a final examination and I took him to the hospital. I called Barbra and she said that she would leave right away.

The staffpeople at the hospital were wonderful. After a few tests, Paul was wheeled into the operating room and Dr. Harlan operated. Barbra and I waited. I called home and told Aunt Martha to not hold dinner for us and that Paul was in surgery for an appendectomy. "Tell Evie gently," I added.

It seemed like an eternity before Dr. Harlan came from the operating room.

"Glen, Barbra, your boy came through like a trooper. His appendix was inflamed but he will be fine."

We were in his room when they wheeled him in from the recovery room. Paul was still a little out of it. Ruth Melvin, the nurse, came in and gently slapped him on the face.

"Come, Paul, wake up."

Paul moved a little and his eyes opened. He looked around and muttered, "Mom, Dad?"

Barbra broke down and it was all I could do to compose myself. Ruth said it would be better if we let him rest. Barbra and I went down to the coffee shop to have a snack. Later we stopped by his room and he was sleeping. We went home.

The next day, Saturday, we took Evie to the hospital with us. Paul greeted us with a great big smile. We had a nice visit but didn't stay long. He looked good and was his usual cheery self.

One week after the operation Paul was home. We were so happy to have him home again but it was a chore to keep him down. He is so active and he thinks we were being mean to him. We had to remind him that he had to give himself a chance to heal.

Two weeks later Paul was back in school. We weren't concerned about him making up his school work as he is always at the top of his class.

We were soon back to normal and running the kids all over town. Football and basketball games, music lessons, dental appointments, and, of course, shopping! We are glad that we have only two children to worry about. Actually, we enjoy them very much.

Evie is in her second year of high school and is on the cheerleading squad and also on the staff of the high school newspaper. She is all of fifteen and getting prettier all the time. Paul is now eleven and in the seventh grade. They are growing up!

School is out and the July Fourth celebrations are getting under way. Barbra's Uncle Frank and Aunt Billie Dowling invited us to their place for the holiday cookout. They live on a knoll overlooking the city on North Wade Boulevard and Mine Road. Most of Barbra's relatives were there and we had a grand time. After the cookout, we gathered all the chairs and placed them on the front lawn where we enjoyed the fireworks.

During the summer we spent a couple of weeks at Charleston. We took a boat ride to Fort Sumpter and went to the beach. I even got in a little golf while Barbra and the kids went to a few flower gardens. We had a wonderful time but were glad when we finally got back home.

11
Terry

Time flies! Evie is a senior in high school and is seventeen. Paul is thirteen and a freshman. I had been trying to interest the kids in golf but they showed no interest. Barbra would come out once in a while but she wasn't caught up in it too much.

One Sunday morning as we were coming out of church the Cummings girl came up to me and asked, "Mr. Fredericks, would you care if I played on your golf course?"

"Of course not, Terry. It's open to anyone. Have you ever played golf?"

I thought that this was a foolish question since she was so young and there was no other course in town.

"Only in the backyard when I can use my brother's clubs."

"How old are you, Terry?"

"I'm twelve, but I'll be thirteen next month."

Her brother, Peter, was a frequent visitor to the golf course. We knew their parents only to speak to. Don and Helen seemed very nice.

"Terry, I have an old set of clubs in my shed behind the house. I never lock the shed so any time you want to play you may use those clubs. I'll keep plenty of old balls in the bag and plenty of tees. You will find score cards by the first tee."

"Oh, thank you, Mr. Fredericks."

The following morning I was getting ready to leave for the office when I heard someone out on the patio. I looked out and there was Terry. This was a school holiday, a teachers' convention.

"Rather early, aren't you, Terry?"

"Yes, but it's such a nice day."

"Come here, Terry." I took her to the shed and showed her the clubs that she could use. The other clubs belonged to Barbra and me.

"Thank you so much."

I left for work. I was out that morning checking on a fender bender. About eleven-thirty I went home for lunch. I found everyone out on the patio. They had decided to have lunch out there. I went out and there was Terry. She had been asked to stay for lunch. Terry was a well-mannered little girl with auburn hair and pretty brown eyes.

I checked her score card and couldn't believe it! She went around that course twice. The first time with a forty-four and the second time with a forty!

"Terry, who was keeping score?"

"I played alone and I marked every shot!"

"Terry, I have never broken ninety myself. I'd like to play a game with you some day."

"I'd love to, Mr. Fredericks."

"How about Saturday morning? If you beat me I shall buy you a set of clubs of your very own."

"Oh great, that's a deal! Oh-oh, what if I lose?"

"If you lose you will have to clean all the clubs in the shed. It will be good training for you."

I wasn't too concerned. I couldn't imagine how she could go around that course in the low forties. I didn't want to dispute her, but . . .

We were having our lunch and I noticed that Paul was doing everything he could to make Terry comfortable. I had never known Paul to take an interest in girls before, but I guessed he was growing up.

I went back to work and came home early. I had my briefcase with me since I intended to do some work at home.

Barbra greeted me with, "Did you see your son out on the course?"

"I can't believe it! He's out there with Terry and with my good clubs!"

A little later Paul came in.

"Paul, did you clean the clubs?"

"What, I have to clean them?"

"Paul, if you're going to play you will have to clean them. If you don't take care of the equipment, who will?"

"Doesn't Uncle Ben take care of things?"

"Paul, Uncle Ben is not your handyman!"

I took Paul out to the shed. The clubs were a mess, both sets! I showed Paul how to clean the clubs and the shoes, even though they hadn't used the shoes. He had to learn.

About an hour later Paul came into the library and wanted me to check the clubs. I went out and the clubs looked brand-new!

"That's more like it, Paul, but you are grounded for a week and no allowance except for lunch money."

"Dad?"

"Sorry, Paul."

I gave him a great big hug.

"OK, Dad, I understand. Dad, I'd like to have a few tips. Will you help me?"

"Paul, I would love to. You know I've been trying to interest you and Evie ever since you were little kids. If you are really interested we'll see about getting you your own set of clubs."

"Thanks, Dad, you're super."

It was Saturday morning and I was having a leisurely breakfast and reading the morning paper when I heard a noise out on the patio. I looked out and said, "Good morning, young lady. Aren't you a little early?"

"Well, we have a date and I thought I'd warm up a little."

"Have you had your breakfast?"

"Just a glass of milk."

"Come in here and have something to eat. You're going to need all the strength you can get."

She laughed and came in and Barbra gave her a bowl of cereal and a muffin.

We went out to the first tee and I gave her the honors. She teed up her ball and sent it straight down the fairway. I sent my ball straight down but not quite as far. I was impressed. Terry took a mid-iron and was just short of the green.

"Not bad," I said. Actually, she hit it beautifully. I used my four iron and got the ball to the fringe. She pitched it within four feet of the pin and picked up her ball!

"Terry, what are you doing?"

"Oh, they call that a gimme, don't they?"

Now I was beginning to see how she scored so well!

I chipped up near the hole and took a par. In her way of playing, we tied.

The next hole was a par three and there was a small stream running across the fairway just in front of the green. Since we were tied, Terry drove off first. She had a beautiful iron drive right down the middle. The ball landed just short of the stream and then trickled in. I used my trusty four iron and put it on the green. Terry retrieved her ball and tossed it to the fringe of the green.

"Terry, you don't do that!"

"I can't hit it out of the water! What am I supposed to

do? Besides, isn't that water from the rain the other day?"

I had to be careful here or I might discourage her from the game entirely. I just bit my lip, went to the green and made my putt and a birdie. She used her putter from the fringe and got it within a few feet of the hole.

"Very good, Terry."

She picked up her ball and said, "Par."

I counted six. I now had the honors, so I would tee off on the next hole first. I could see that this was going to be quite an experience!

The next hole was a par four. I drove right down the middle. Terry had a bit of a slice and it disappeared into the woods.

"I don't think I'm going to find that one. I'll hit another."

The next one was on the left side of the fairway but was playable. She took a three wood and really got it all. I matched her with my second shot. I had to admit she was pretty good. She still used her three wood and got it up short but in the sand. I flew my ball just over the bunker and was in good position. Terry took two shots to get it out of the sand and then another shot to the green. I chipped it up and on the green. Terry two putted and said, "I guess I'll have to take a bogey."

I counted seven, but, then, as I knew, we weren't playing the same game! I two-putted and I took a bogey and I didn't get into any trouble!

We were approaching the eighth hole when it started to rain a little. We were near the house so we called it quits. I let her total the score and she beat me by two strokes!

"I won!" she screamed.

"Well, Terry, I didn't think you could do it, but you won!"

"Oh, a new set of clubs!"

"Yes, Terry, I promised, but you and I are going to have a little talk about scoring."

We went into the house for some refreshments and I explained as diplomatically as possible the rules and etiquette of golf. Of course, she got her new clubs and I had to get Paul a new set also. After that, Terry and Paul were a regular twosome on the course. Poor Paul!

After dinner I went into the library to read. I began to think that about how I used to write poetry when I was young. Juvenile as it probably was, I really enjoyed doing it. The more I thought of Terry and the potential that she really had, I thought I'd try some poetry. She really was poetry in motion with her swing on the golf course. I reached for a yellow-lined pad and began to write.

Sweetheart of the Course

We eagerly step to tee number one,
Just little Terry and me.
We tee the ball for lots of fun
And hope it's a shot to see.

A steady stance, a swing to see,
Her ball rolls near the cup.
She stands aside and waits for me
To see my ball go "Dub."

We putt it out and start up course
And head for tee number two.
By now, I know, dark eyes, of course,
Is contemplating a deuce.

She concentrates on that green ahead
On the pin she trains her eye.
A swing so smooth—a steady head
Air-mails it to the sky.

I shake my head, of course in jest
I give her a frown or two.
Her drive becomes her very best
On the green—good for a deuce.

Amazed, of course, but on we tread
To the long drive number three.
Terry, now, keeps the honors, when
She sails it over the tree.

I gather my wits—await my turn
And hope I can reach the mark.
That thirteen-year-old makes her bird
And chirps away like a lark.

I have to believe now what I see
And stride to tee number four.
If Terry clears that bunker and tree
I'm not gonna play no more.

She stands on the tee—stares up north
(As though she could reach the green)
Wouldn't be surprised whatever brought
forth
From that youthful little dream.

She swings the club—a solid hit
The whirl is heard all around
The ball goes up and stays a bit
Parks near the green on the ground.

She chips it up—grins ear to ear
I'm really in deep distress
My dozen strokes behind, I fear
Won't catch that little brunette.

She grins at me on tee number five.
She knows she's got me by far
She whips the clubhead through the sky
One hundred sixty-five yards.

Accustomed to her feats by now,
Resigned to my tale of woe,
She rolls it in and takes a bow
I'm just about ready to go home!

It must be said—it's essential
And all before this is done,
That little miss has golf potential
To score a hole-in-one.

Upon the tee of number six
I sigh, will she now blow up?
Here, her big brown eyes are fixed
And the ball bounds into the cup.

We putt the green and pick up our balls
That cutie is picking up points
We enter seventh tee—par four
And I loosen up my joints.

Away it sails!—way over the hill!
I can't believe my eyes!
That dark-eyed doll just gives a shrill
Her missile just flies and flies!

She earns a par on number seven
I beat my clubs to the ground.
On number eight she looks to heaven
And drives it right over the crown.

Again, a chip to number eight green

And a delicate little putt,
That incredible dark-eyed little queen
Just taps it into the cup.

At last we stand on tee number nine.
Again, with that pert little swing,
She drills the ball right down the line
And clears about everything!

Chips to the green—a confident swing
Her ball goes ever so high
Lands on the green—around the ring
Into the cup out of sight!

It's time now to see what we did
I won't reveal my plight
But little Terry, with a great big grin,
Comes in with a twenty-five.

Now for me it's enough, while Terry, yet
Is planning to play some more.
That darlin' dark-eyed little brunette
Is the sweetheart of the course.

There is such a thing as poetic license and I suppose I used it generously. One thing I would admit, however, is that Terry would be a talented golfer once she learned the rules and etiquette of the game. She had a wonderful swing and, being so young, wonderful perception. In a few years she would be tough to beat. I do believe that she could give her brother, Peter, a good game but, of course, he would never put up with her very own version of the game.

After Terry left, Barbra wanted to know how she actually beat me on the course. I just winked and said, "She won."

"Oh, I see," she said.

12

Vacation

One fine Saturday in June, after the schools closed for the summer, we were out on the patio having a cookout. While I was cooking the hot dogs and hamburgers, Evie was looking through an American Road Atlas.

"Daddy," she quipped, "why can't we take a trip for a week or so? I'd love to see some of our national parks." Barbra was setting the table.

"Well, Glen, what do you say to that?" Barbra asked. I just kept on cooking but I thought, *Maybe that's not a bad idea.* We had no debts and had been saving money for the past several years. Besides, we hadn't had a real vacation anyway. I had just bought a new station wagon and we were in pretty good shape. The business was prospering. Evie was eighteen and Paul, fourteen. We took a weekend trip occasionally and we had traveled throughout the Smokies, but that was about all.

"Well," I said, "we may give it some thought."

"Oh, that would be super," said Paul. "When can we start?"

Uncle Ben and Aunt Martha just sat there.

"Well, Uncle Ben and Aunt Martha, when would you like to leave?" I asked.

"Oh, I don't think we ought to think about it," Uncle Ben said.

Uncle Ben and Aunt Martha were in their midsixties

and admitted that they had never traveled very much since they always had the café to run.

I said, "Folks, I think we owe it to the kids and I think we owe it to ourselves. Let's start planning later today and make some reservations. I'm sure we can have plenty of room for all of us in the wagon."

Uncle Ben and Aunt Martha agreed to come along. The more I talked the more everyone got excited.

"It could be a leisurely trip wherever we go so we can really enjoy it," said Barbra.

"Evie," I said, "I think you've started something."

Later that day we all got out the road atlas and I listened to all suggestions, especially from the kids. We left Monday morning. Julie and Florence had everything under control at the office. They got along well with each other.

We went southwest to Big Bend National Park in Texas. After two days we left for Carlsbad Caverns.

Evie and Paul couldn't get over the size of the rooms in Carlsbad Caverns.

"Look at this," Paul exclaimed when he entered the cafeteria. The room was immense and all underground!

"Air-conditioned." Evie said. It was fifty-five degrees all year round.

We visited some of the ruins of the Indians. "I don't blame them for leaving," said Paul.

We spent three days at Disneyland and the kids had a ball. We stood in line after line until the kids were satisfied. From there we went up to San Simeon Castle, built by William Randolph Hearst.

"No one should ever be this rich," whispered Evie. It was almost indescribable!

At Kings Canyon Park we saw some of the largest trees in the world. The General Sherman tree was the background for some of our pictures. The awe-inspiring view from Glacial Point at Yosemite National Park was an unforgettable experience. I don't think I could ever forget that view looking across the valley to Yosemite Falls.

"Golly, this is great!" said Paul.

The ranger put his arm on Paul's shoulder and said, "It's three thousand feet straight down, sonny!"

At night we viewed the firefall from our hotel window. They light pinecones and send them over the cliff at dark each night. The result is a spectacular firefall. Evie and Paul talked about the firefall for several days.

We travelled up to the Grand Tetons in Wyoming and then to Yellowstone National Park.

"Look, Dad, the ground is on fire!" cried Paul. The Norris Geyser basin was alive with hot steam coming out of the ground. We stayed at the Yellowstone Inn and watched Old Faithful erupt. It seemed like every hour it erupted. We took a short walk with the ranger and about a dozen or so people. The kids really learned from these walks, as we all did.

We drove across the remote areas of Wyoming and down to Rocky Mountain National Park in Colorado. Going over some of the Continental Divide routes were a bit scary, especially when it was snowing.

"Look, it's snowing," Evie said. We couldn't believe it. It turned to rain when we reached the six-thousand-foot marker.

A few days later we were in Nashville, Tennessee, where we took in the Grand Ole Opry at the Rymer Auditorium. From there we headed for home the next day.

We all had a wonderful time, even though it put a sizable dent in our savings, but Uncle Ben more than paid his share. Uncle Ben and Aunt Martha never said very much during the trip but they assured us that they enjoyed it.

We settled down to our regular routine. The kids and Barbra were out shopping for school clothes and Uncle Ben and Aunt Martha were talking about the trip and disagreeing on things that they saw. We took a mountain of pictures and the pictures usually settled many arguments. It was fun looking over the pictures and recalling incidents that we would have forgotten.

Julie announced that she was going to have a baby. Florence was just completing her course in real estate. I knew this would mean that I would be spending more time in the office. I was getting along in age and wondered if it wouldn't be wise to consider partial retirement.

Barbra and I considered either selling the business or hiring someone to run it at a fair salary. I didn't want to be hasty about it and just said that I would think about it.

Julie said that she would like to leave the office when the baby came. This was all I needed. I put an advertisement in *Real Estate News,* which was printed once a month throughout South Carolina.

I received dozens of replies and settled on a young man from Columbia who was a licensed real estate agent and insurance writer. He was working in his uncle's business and wanted to go off on his own. He sounded like the man I wanted.

His name was Leon Johnson. He was thirty-two, and he and his wife, Louise, had two children, Leon Jr., eleven, and Marjorie, eight.

I contacted him and said that I would like to meet with him. Two days later he came down to my office. We talked about what his responsibilities would be and what compensation he could expect. We came to an agreement that he would take full charge and would keep Florence Parker on the job. I was impressed with his knowledge of insurance and real estate and with his confidence.

He wanted time to look around for a suitable place to live before he sold his house in Columbia. I told him to look through some of the listings I had and he checked on several before finding what he wanted. He found a suitable place on Peach Street. He made a deposit, went back to Columbia and sold his house.

Leon and family settled into their new home in early August, three weeks before school opened, giving them plenty of time to enroll the children.

Leon took over the office and Julie and Florence got along fine with him. He knew that Julie would be leaving soon. He was a go-getter and saw possibilities to increase the business. For starters, he established a travel agency in the business and his wife, Louise, started it up. She had worked in a travel office before she married. Eventually, he would hire a girl to run that part of the business.

This freed me from the day-to-day routine and gave me time to spend with my family. I never fully realized all that Barbra was going through with the children. Once in a while I would take them here and there but this was going on constantly with Barbra. Orchestra practice, basketball, PTA, football and the dentist. Evie kept her mother busy taking her to sessions that she seemed to think were so important.

Paul and I were fierce competitors on the golf course and Terry was a frequent visitor.

I never failed to tell my children that I loved them. I would often give them a hug. I would also hug Barbra in front of them to show that it wasn't anything to be ashamed of to love and respect others. This is something I never knew anything about when I was growing up. We never let them forget that we loved them even when we had to punish them. They were always such a joy to us but they were growing up so fast. I often wished that I could slow down the clock.

13

The Family

One beautiful Saturday morning we were all having breakfast, all six of us. Looking out the window, it seemed like a perfect day to go out on the golf course. Evie was just eighteen and Paul had just turned fourteen.

"How about a foursome this morning?" I asked. "Paul and me, and, Evie, you and mother."

"Hey, neat!" exclaimed Paul.

"Mother," said Evie, "let's damage their egos!"

"Well, hon, I shall do my best."

We fetched our clubs and went to the first tee.

"Ladies first," I said. "Let's alternate and keep the order for the whole course." Everyone agreed.

"Go to it, Mother," I said.

Barbra got off a good drive and Paul was ready to go next. His drive was straight down the middle and twenty yards beyond Mother's drive. Barbra just stared at him. Evie went straight but not very far. I really let one go and outdrove everyone.

"That's the way to go, Dad," said Paul.

We were walking down the fairway when Evie said, "I shall keep score."

"Oh, no," Paul said. "Dad, I think it would be better if you kept score. You're more experienced."

"Let's settle by keeping each other's score and I will write it down. Paul, you count Evie's strokes and she will count yours. I'll count Mother's and she will count mine, OK?"

Everyone agreed, even though the girls were not smiling.

We finished the hole. Paul and I each had pars and the girls each had a bogey. The second hole, par three, Paul and I each bogeyed and the girls bogeyed. The third hole was a par four and I birdied and Paul parred. The girls each bogeyed.

Finally, the girls came up with the idea that they would play best ball. That means they would have one score between them by scoring the better of their shots. Paul and I would play regular golf. The lowest score would win. We said OK. What a mistake!

The fourth hole, par four, the girls parred and Paul and I bogeyed. The girls won the last four holes very easily. For days they would never let us forget that they had beaten us! Of course, they kept their own scores. They certainly do have their own game!

We arrived at the patio where Uncle Ben and Aunt Martha were getting things ready for a cookout lunch. We were famished and we all sat down and enjoyed an hour with our lunch. The girls enjoyed the ribbing they were giving us.

Later that afternoon, Barbra and Evie went shopping and Paul and I went up to Columbia and went to the zoo. To me these were precious moments with my fast-growing son. We returned home, had dinner, and Uncle Ben and Aunt Martha all went to the jamboree.

After the weekend I found that I was like a fish out of water. I didn't have any business to worry about anymore and I just puttered around the yard. I had to be careful to not trim something that Uncle Ben didn't think needed trimming.

Paul came home from school and asked me to take him to Blair's Department Store. He had to pick up a pair of gym trunks. He also enjoyed just looking around. He also picked up a few pairs of tube socks. We left and went down to Spaulding's Drugstore and enjoyed a milkshake together. We went home so Paul could get started on his homework.

When we arrived home we found Barbra and Uncle Ben hovering over Aunt Martha, who was lying on the sofa in the living room.

Aunt Martha seemed to be all at sea and wasn't talking to anyone. I called Dr. Davis and he came right over. He took her blood pressure—and it was very high. He ordered her to the hospital. Uncle Ben rode with her in the ambulance and Barbra and I followed. We told Evie and Paul that we would be right back.

The staff went to work right away to bring down her blood pressure. There was nothing Barbra and I could do and we left. Uncle Ben wanted to stay with her.

We had our dinner and went back to the hospital and took up something for Uncle Ben to eat. We found Aunt Martha sitting up and Uncle Ben helping her to eat. She didn't look then like she needed any help. She smiled at us. We thought that she looked really great!

The nurse on duty said that it was a sudden attack and that she would be on a low-salt diet and would be taking blood pressure medication. The doctor wasn't too concerned and said she could go home the next day.

The next day Aunt Martha was home and the doctor came and laid down some very stringent rules. No more salt in cooking and no salt at the table and no more on the go all the time; in the kitchen and around the house. Aunt Martha loved to cook but she had to realize that she had to slow down. Barbra hired a woman to come in from Monday to Friday to clean, make up the beds and do the laundry. These were just some of the things that Aunt Martha was doing.

Paul and Evie were really upset and weren't a bit bashful about telling her how much they loved her. Uncle Ben and Aunt Martha weren't just part of the family—they were family.

Aunt Martha got her strength back in a hurry and seemed her old self again. It was so good to see her well again and quite a relief to Uncle Ben. Aunt Martha was his whole world.

At the table we all had to reach for the salt but we kept it away from you-know-who.

A week later Dr. Davis stopped by and said he wanted Aunt Martha to lose twenty-five pounds. He talked to Barbra to make sure Aunt Martha stuck to her diet. He checked her blood pressure and it was normal.

The hardest task Barbra had was to slow down Aunt Martha.

"I'm all right, Barbra, stop worrying about me."

"Aunt Martha, will you please go in and sit down!"

Poor Aunt Martha. She was getting scolded by everyone, including Uncle Ben. She had always been so active and now she got scolded for doing the things she had always done. Barbra relied heavily on Aunt Martha for advice on so many things but wanted to do them herself for a change. Actually, Aunt Martha was so full of energy but she soon learned that she had to pace herself.

14

Meeting Mother

I received a phone call from Drew that Father had died from a massive stroke. Drew said nothing to Mother about visiting me but he told my sisters and brothers. He thought it would be better to not say anything to Mother while Father was alive. He asked me what I thought and I said that I thought it only fair to Mother to let her know about me.

A week later I received a letter from Mother, a letter from the heart.

Dear Brother,

Drew told me all about you and that he visited with you. I am so glad that you are well and happy. I have missed you and wondered about you constantly. I wasn't happy that Drew did not say something to me sooner but I understand how you must have felt toward your father.

I didn't blame you for leaving when you did. I wanted so much to intervene but was afraid. Your father warned me to not show you any sympathy. What could I do? I was powerless to do anything for you.

I am so pleased that you are doing so well in your business and are happily married. Please try to find time to come up here with your family very soon. I am so happy that God was with you and that you are still with us.

Love always,
Mother

"Barb, what do you think? I really would like to see Mother."

"Of course, Glen. I know how you feel."

"But, Barb, I don't want to go up there without you and the children. She would naturally want to meet the family."

We had just returned from a three-week trip and I hesitated about asking the family to pack the wagon again. We put it up to the kids and they were both excited and anxious to meet their grandmother and their cousins in Connecticut.

I asked Uncle Ben and Aunt Martha what they thought about coming and they emphatically said that it would be better if just Barbra and the kids went with me. Besides, they had enough of traveling for a while. I called Drew and he said to come up.

Two days later we were traveling north. With one stop overnight, we were at Drew's house the following day. Drew and Jean greeted us.

"How wonderful to see you folks," Jean said.

"Folks, would you believe I got lost in town? I never expected to see such a change!"

"Yes, Glen, it certainly has grown," said Drew.

We got settled. Jean and Barbra got supper ready. I offered to take them out to dinner but they insisted on staying home. Drew and I talked about the changes around town when three young children walked in the house.

"Glen," said Drew, "these are our three children. This is Drew Jr., fourteen, Ron, nine, and Joan, four. This is your Uncle Glen we told you about." I hugged the two boys, with a great big hug and kiss for Joan. Jean and Barbra came into the room and the kids met their Aunt Barbra. Evie and Paul were in the bedrooms getting settled. They came out to meet their cousins. They all soon went outside to get acquainted with the area. Drew and I settled back and talked.

I mentioned to Drew that I thought it would be better if I went to see Mother alone tomorrow morning. Barbra and I talked it over and decided it would be better.

"I agree, Glen, it's been a long time since you have seen Mother. This should be an emotional meeting and I'm sure that you are going to see quite a change in Mother."

"Of course, Drew, I'm sure I shall."

Just then the doorbell rang and there were Bobby, Else and their two children, Bobby Jr., and Diane! This was a surprise. Jean and Drew invited them down for dinner. What a pleasant evening. No wonder they didn't want to go out for dinner!

I couldn't get over how well Else spoke English. I think she actually put most of us to shame! Paul and Evie were trying hard to get to know their cousins and to remember who belonged to whom.

The next morning I called Mother on the phone. I wanted to let her know that I was in town so she would be prepared before I arrived.

"Hello, Mother. This is Glen."

"Brother, how wonderful to hear your voice. Where are you?"

"I'm staying at Drew and Jean's house. I'll be right up."

I arrived at the house that stood on the hill where we used to fly kites. Drew had to give me directions. I couldn't get over the changes in the neighborhood. I rang the bell and Mother appeared.

"Brother!" she said, "I'm so glad to see you. Where's the family?"

"Oh, Mother! We will all be up this afternoon."

I hid my surprise. Drew had been right. I nearly choked. Her hair was snow white and she seemed a little shorter. She seemed in good health and very alert.

"Mother, I'm sorry I kept my whereabouts a secret from

you but I didn't want anything more to do with Father. I was only fourteen and I couldn't let anyone know or I would have had to go back. I never wanted to see him again. I'm sorry to have to feel this way. You didn't realize how I suffered when I left. I had three cracked ribs but didn't know it until I was X-rayed in South Carolina. The doctor strapped me up for a month until they healed.

"I never thought that I deserved such abuse. When I became twenty-one I legally had my name changed. I didn't want to carry his name. I'm sorry, Mother, but that's how I felt then and that's how I feel now."

Mother cried and I cried with her. She understood. We sat down and talked until noon. She invited me to stay and have lunch with her. Of course, I stayed.

"Mother, do you remember the last time you handed me my lunch?"

"I certainly do and I have been wondering ever since where you were. I wanted so much to comfort you after that beating." She started to cry.

"Mother, I thought you were rather cool to me. I didn't know."

I went over to her and gave her a great big hug.

That afternoon I returned with the family.

"Hi, Mother, here I am again. This is Barbra and this little lady is Evelyn, and this is Paul."

"Oh, I'm so happy to see you. Your father told me your names."

Mother and Barbra embraced and then it was Evie and Paul's turn. Mother hugged them and couldn't get over the children.

"Mother, do you feel up to going out to dinner tonight? We'd love to take you out."

"Oh, I suppose I can enjoy a meal out. Your sisters and brothers often have me over to their homes and I do appreciate it. I always said that the meals I enjoy the most are the ones I don't have to fix."

By this time the children were out exploring.

"Mother, I thought of you so much. I always found it hard to forgive Father but I realize now the pressure he was under. It wasn't easy bringing up six children during the Depression. Of course, I didn't know about Bobby. But still, he did have a violent temper and I never thought I was so bad that I deserved that kind of abuse. He just had to vent his anger."

"Glen, there were times when I wanted to say something but I was afraid."

"Mother, I'm so glad I came to see you. I love you so much."

We both cried.

The doorbell rang and Mother asked me to answer it. I opened the door.

"Brother!"

I received a great big hug. She practically fell into me. I knew, of course, that she must be Virginia.

"Brother, I'm so glad to see you. Oh, this is Lloyd."

"Howdee," said Lloyd.

"Glad to meet you, Lloyd."

"Likewise," said Lloyd.

"This is Barbra."

"Hello, Virginia and Lloyd, I'm glad to meet you all."

"Oh, Brother, this is Laura and this is Kyle."

I shook hands with Kyle and gave Laura a great big hug. Laura seemed to be about fourteen and Kyle, about eleven. They didn't stay with us very long, as Mother said that we were going out for dinner. We had a delicious seafood dinner, Mother's preference.

On the way back to Drew's, I realized that I had seen all but one of my brothers—that was Ed. Drew and I talked until rather late in the evening. Everyone had gone to bed. Drew told me about Virginia having multiple sclerosis. I could tell something was wrong but Mother never said a word about her. I'm sure this was hard for all to cope with. I got a little emotional about it.

The next morning Jean took us all out for a ride. We stopped at Bobby's house so we could see where they lived and then went to Ed and Ginny's house but they were not at home. I was disappointed.

"Don't be too upset, Glen, because you're going to see them tonight. We invited them for dinner."

That evening Ed and Ginny came in with Joy, Kay and Edward Jr. Then followed Margie, Julian and Julian Jr. We had a delicious dinner and we talked, talked, and talked. Ed never stopped!

Ed told me about some of the fellows in the old neighborhood. Will had died some years ago and Earl was living up north somewhere. Most everyone I knew was gone. Drew had filled me in before.

The next morning we were packing to get ready for our trip south.

"It's been wonderful to have you up here," said Jean.

"It's been a wonderful experience for all of us, Jean," said Barbra.

I said, "Before we leave we'll stop up and see Mother. I hope someday she will try to get down and see us. I mentioned it to her but she didn't think she was up to it."

We all said good-bye to Mother and we were on the road. We arrived home the next day. Uncle Ben and Aunt Martha were happy to see us.

15
Mayor

A few weeks later we were having an election for mayor. Mayor Lester Reed had decided to retire from politics and spend full time at his clothing store. The office of mayor was only a spare-time job anyway. The Republicans had their candidate full running while the Democrats were deadlocked. It was a close-knit town and the Democrats were in the majority, although recent elections were very close.

I was not much into politics but, once in a while, I would help out the Democrats at the voting places and also help out at dinners and other fund-raising events.

I went to the caucus to help choose a candidate. They were hopelessly deadlocked and time was running out. Al Goodwin got up and gave a speech.

"Ladies and gentlemen, there is a man in this hall tonight who has done a great deal for this town. His fair play in his business dealings are well known and no one can question his integrity. Ladies and gentlemen, I am honored to nominate Mr. Glen Fredericks!"

The hall reverberated with a thunderous roar. I looked around for the nearest exit. When the noise quieted down I heard someone second the nomination. I felt as though I was trapped, cornered, and tricked.

Someone grabbed my arm and led me to the front of the hall. Al Goodwin was standing there and he shook my hand. I wanted to wring his neck! I just looked at Al and said, "Al, I'll get you for this!"

"Glen, right now you are the only one who could break this deadlock."

A call for further nominations was called for and you could hear a pin drop. A vote was taken and I won by twelve votes! That was all and the lights went out.

I spoke to Al on the way out and said, "Al, you got me into this and you are going to help one way or the other. You are my campaign manager!"

"Well, Glen, if I can get you elected it will be worth it."

The campaign began in earnest. In a few days I saw posters all over town with my picture. Al was apparently very active.

I was receiving requests and invitations to speak to various organizations and dinners. It was a good thing I didn't have the business to think about.

I made no empty promises and was beholden to no one. I was merely being myself and spoke of continued honesty in government and my wish to continue the policies of Mayor Reed.

The Republicans nominated Ralph Drum and the campaign was on. Ralph's campaign manager, Phil Smith, wanted to know, in a radio address, why I was living under an alias. Somehow, he got wind of the fact that I had changed my name. This was brought out in our circles when I became police commissioner. It wasn't widely known. I had to go on the air and report that I had had my name changed when I became twenty-one and the reason I had changed it. That settled matters and it was never brought up again.

I was elected by a fair majority and took the helm right after the first of the year. I resigned as police commissioner. After the swearing-in ceremonies we went to the Hotel Douglas for lunch. It was a glorious occasion and I was assured that I would have plenty of support.

After the luncheon I drove home with my family. They were so proud of me and I loved them. We celebrated by all going out to the golf course and playing a round of golf. Of course, Paul and I won. We kept score!

We all spent an hour or so on the patio enjoying a Coke. Paul and I had fun ribbing Mother and Evie. We really relished our victory.

At dinner that night Aunt Martha put on a feast fit for a mayor! Uncle Ben and Aunt Martha stayed home but gave us a grand welcome.

The next day I wrote a letter to Mother about my election. I soon received letters from my sisters and my brothers congratulating me, but the most heartwarming letter of all came from Mother:

> Dear Brother,
> I am very happy to hear that you have been elected mayor of Douglas. I am so proud of you and I congratulate you.
>
> Only a mother can know the anguish of losing a son as I had for so many years. I am so grateful to God that He kept you and looked after you. In all my prayers you have always been with us. I just didn't know where until recently. I never gave up hope that I would again see you.
>
> I am so glad that you have grown up holding to the principles I have always instilled in all of my children—honesty and integrity and to always respect others as you yourself want to be respected.
>
> Now you are in politics. Whatever decisions you are called upon to make, be sure to remember that you were taught, from early childhood, the difference between right and wrong. Don't ever forget that, as the mayor, you are the servant of the people.
>
> May God bless you.
>
> Love,
> Mother

My first official act was to forward a name to the common council for a new police commissioner. My choice was Al Goodwin. He was approved by the council. I got even!

I soon learned that my political honeymoon was over. We were confronted with problems of growth in Douglas. Most of it was of my own doing because of the development I established, even though it was needed. The population nearly doubled but our grand list more than tripled. With the completion of the development and the new department store, we were in solid financial shape but the problem of growth was another matter. We needed more police and firemen and equipment and another grade school, and an addition to the high school. Also, it was brought to my attention that we needed a fire marshal. All this required us to go to bonded indebtedness. We secured the bonds and were still in pretty good shape. Our increase in taxes was minimal. We were still a hometown and we strived to keep our hometown flavor. Economically, we were in good shape.

We had a movie theater in town; the only other form of entertainment was the jamboree. We also enjoyed the high school plays and concerts. I approved an appropriation of two hundred dollars per month for the jamboree. It was only a formality since the two hundred dollars per month was my salary as part-time mayor. I donated it.

Some of the high school boys got together a golf team to play in the golf tournaments of schools in the area. We, at Douglas, had never had a golf team. The high school history teacher, Harry Birch, was their coach. They left it up to Paul to approach me about having my course as their home course. They thought that Paul would have more pull! Of course, it was the only course in town. I consented.

There were several school teams in the area and now Douglas High would have its own team and golf course. For some reason, Paul was named captain of the team!

As mayor, I was expected to chair an executive meeting at the town hall once each week. Present were the police commissioner, chief of police, fire chief, fire marshal, budget manager, tax collector, purchasing agent and my secretary to take the minutes. Also, the Common Council met once a month. Other than that it was mostly ceremonial and, from time to time, I would be asked to appear before various groups.

We had three days of hard rain and there were several roads that were washed out a little and many potholes. Nothing serious, and I noticed some equipment around fixing some spots. A few days later Ruth Melvin called me at home complaining about a couple of bad potholes on Jackson Street.

"Mr. Fredericks, I've been calling the maintenance department ever since the rain. I see trucks all over the city but no one has done anything about these potholes here."

"Ruth, I shall see what I can do right away."

"Oh, thank you Mr. Fredericks, er, I mean, Mr. Mayor."

I got on the phone and called the maintenance garage. They said that they would look into it right away. Fifteen minutes later the phone rang.

"Mr. Mayor, thank you again. The men are now working on our road!"

I didn't want to get a big head but it seemed rather nice to have some clout!

The first tournament the boys had with their golf team was with Bradford High. Uncle Ben and I watched and weren't very happy. The Bradford boys were more experienced and rolled all over our boys. We needed plenty of practice and I told them that the course was always open for practice. The next meeting was a different matter. Our boys won and this was the start of fierce competition.

16

The Loss of Virginia and Mother's Visit

Evie was getting ready to attend Clemson University and, of course, she had to have a car. Barbra and I had been letting her drive but only when we were with her. She was pretty good by the time I took her in to get her license. She passed and I bought her a second-hand Ford wagon. With all the stuff she just had to take to college she needed a truck!

Paul was just starting his second year of high school and he, too, was beginning to feel comfortable behind the wheel of a car. He couldn't wait to get his license but I wasn't encouraging it.

One evening Drew phoned me that Virginia had died. I phoned Mother and also Lloyd. All I could do was express my condolence. The funeral was the next morning and I couldn't possibly have made it.

Virginia, Drew and I grew up together. We were less than two years apart. Virginia was a beautiful blue-eyed blond and possessed a cheery personality. I still remember her saying, "When Brother and I grow up, we're going to get married."

After a few years, when she realized that we couldn't get married, she would say, "When I get married, Brother is going to be the best man."

I wasn't there when she got married and I wasn't there

when she died. My loss. Now Mrs. Lloyd Barker rests in peace.

A few months later I received a phone call from Ed, saying that he and Ginny were planning a two-week trip to visit the Smokies. I said that we would love to see them and that they should plan to spend as much time as they could with us. They knew we had plenty of room from talking to Drew.

A few days later the doorbell rang and there were Ed, Ginny—and Mother!

I was shocked to see Mother but very pleased. Ed didn't want to tell me that they were bringing Mother. Some surprise! After the introductions we got them settled and I took them out for a tour of the town. Mother couldn't get over the fact that I was mayor and with such a beautiful house. She was surprised to see that I had a street and a park named after me. We returned home and Barbra and Aunt Martha had a great feast waiting for us.

After dinner we all went out to the patio and talked for a while. Mother brought me up to date on the family. Alan and Lily had a new baby girl, Nan, and Margie and Julian had a baby boy, Gerald, which they called Jerry. Mother knew all the birthdays of not only her children, but of all the grandchildren. Not bad for someone in her mideighties!

Later we strolled around the grounds. This was Uncle Ben's turf and he was proud of his creation. Mother scolded me: "You don't need a swimming pool! You don't need a golf course!"

I got in touch with Evie at Clemson so she would be home for the weekend to see her grandmother. Mother could not get over how Evie and Paul had grown. I never expected to see Mother here. We even took in the jamboree and Mother really enjoyed it. After a few days they left. It was so wonderful to see them.

Paul was beginning to see Terry Cummings more and more lately. Terry was a pretty little girl with large brown eyes and pretty auburn hair. She was a year behind Paul in school. Wasn't it strange that only a few years ago Paul couldn't see any sense in golf?—or girls!

It was getting close to nominations of candidates for Mayor. I was encouraged to run again but was undecided. I wasn't sure that I wanted to go through another campaign. I had plenty of time on my hands but still wasn't sure.

The Republicans held their caucus first. Someone again tossed Ralph Drum's name in the ring. He was immediately nominated. Ralph and I were good friends and I had plenty of contact with him since he was a member of the Common council and a very respected gentleman.

Two weeks later the Democrats held their caucus and I was there to put up Al Goodwin's name in the ring. Someone put up my name. There were no other nominations and I was the nominee. I simply gave up. I was asked if I would accept the nomination. Everyone was looking at me including Al Goodwin. I answered in the affirmative. How could I say no to a town that had given me so much love?

I met Ralph in the café a few days later. He seemed very depressed. He felt that he was merely put up in a very hopeless election—a sacrificial lamb. I felt sorry for Ralph and really wouldn't have cared if he won the election. He was a handsome man with blond hair and brown eyes. *A nice combination*, I thought.

"Ralph," I said, "elections are sometimes a surprise. Just make a list of projects that you would like to see accomplished for your town. Be sincere and honest, as I know you will be. Remember, Ralph, people remember. Even though you may feel that the party isn't going all out to support you, the people will remember what you say and how you conduct yourself during the campaign. Two years from now you may be the most popular man in town. Don't sell the people short."

Again, Al Goodwin was my campaign manager and the campaign began. Chet Turner was Ralph's manager and on the radio, he took me to task by accusing me of robbing old David Collins of his property, and also, not taking care of my job as mayor. He said that I was going to raise taxes. Ralph got me on the phone right away and said that he had nothing to do with that radio talk. He said that they were slandering remarks that he didn't share. He promised me that he would fire Chet. He did.

Ralph went on and waged a campaign without a manager and with little support from his party.

He took my advice and made a name for himself and still had his self-respect. I won the election but it wasn't a landslide by any means.

Soon after the swearing-in ceremonies, Tom Perkins announced that he was retiring as building inspector. Ralph had a gift shop and, since the building inspector was only a spare time job, I sent his name to the Common Council and they approved. I thought that this would keep Ralph's name before the public.

17
Hurricane

Two months after the rain we had a hurricane that devastated the coastal areas and did a considerable amount of damage in Douglas. The ground was still soaked from the rain and this caused more trees to come down. Schools were closed and there were many high school students volunteering to help people, especially the elderly in their homes. It was a community problem and the entire community was involved. Everyone seemed to feel it was his problem. When I wasn't outside I was in the mayor's office coordinating projects. I was getting very little sleep. There were times when I felt so tired but I felt, as mayor, I had to be available. I thought that this was to be expected of me.

I went all over town to assess the damage. Many roads were impassable because of the trees down and debris all over the roads. I was concerned about wires down and I ordered all electricity to be turned off. Homes were damaged from fallen trees and I asked for volunteers to help the Red Cross and the Salvation Army to provide for those who had to leave their homes. The wind was still very brisk but the worst was over.

All firemen and police were put on duty and the hospital was swamped with emergency cases. I hesitated about calling for disaster relief from the governor. I knew what he must be going through with more severe damage along the coast. The governor called me because Bradford and communities all around had applied to the governor. I told him about the shape we were in. The next day I saw bulldozers and other equipment all over town clearing and sawing limbs and carting them away. Utility men were repairing the electrical damage and electricity was restored in most areas the next day. We didn't have a single fatality but many were injured. The hospital was very busy for weeks. We were very fortunate that no serious fires occurred.

There was very little damage downtown. All the wires were underground. There were a few store windows blown out and some flooding in basements. There was no structural damage to buildings. I was sure that Leon would have his hands full with insurance claims.

I surveyed the damage to the golf course; it was minimal. I lost a couple of trees. It could have been worse.

With the help we received from the state, the Red Cross, the Salvation Army and the cooperation from the police, firemen and the many volunteers, we were pretty much back to normal within the month. We were lucky compared to most communities. Basements were still flooded and the firemen were all over town pumping out basements. I was lucky that I didn't have any water in my basement. Good drainage, I guessed.

When most of the town was cleared we were faced with the problem of the roads. This was going to take another week or so before all damage was repaired.

I wrote the governor thanking him for his assistance and I wrote letters to the police and fire Departments, the Red Cross, and the Salvation Army and put a letter in the paper thanking all the many volunteers who gave their time during our hour of need. We had a wonderful town and wonderful people!

I was on the go all through the hurricane and had very little sleep. When the worst was over I began to relax but I was so very tired and I felt weak. Barbra noticed that my color wasn't good and wanted me to see the doctor. I tried to brush it off; I thought all I needed was plenty of rest.

Early one morning I started to cough. I was burning up and I knew I had a fever. Barbra was worried and, unbeknown to me, she called an ambulance. I was close to being delirious and wasn't sure what was happening. A day later, I think, I realized that I was in the hospital and in an oxygen tent. I knew no one.

A few days later I was out of the tent and was beginning to see and think more clearly.

"You had a close call with pneumonia, Glen." I recognized the voice of Dr. Davis. I was a little groggy and I didn't try to answer. I looked around and I saw a figure standing next to the doctor.

"How do you feel, Mr. Fredericks?" It was the voice of Ruth Melvin, the nurse.

I just nodded and I heard the doctor say, "I think we'd better let him rest." They left.

I began to take stock of myself. I knew I had to face reality and realize that I wasn't twenty years old anymore. I really overdid it during the storm but I was doing only what was expected of me. I had to justify it.

Later Ruth came in with a tray. I was taken off the IV feeding; they wanted me to get used to eating again.

Ruth was wonderful and stayed with me while I attempted to eat. I really enjoyed it. I was finishing when Barbra walked in. I took one look and lost it. I wept uncontrollably.

"Now, this is no way for the mayor to act." She planted a kiss on my forehead and held me tight.

"Oh, Glen, I love you so much. Please don't scare us like this again."

Just then in walked Uncle Ben and Aunt Martha. I was

so glad to see them. We talked and I was able to compose myself when Evie and Paul walked in. I think they had it planned. Evie came to me and kissed me and began to cry. That didn't do anything for me. Paul was just standing there. I took hold of his hand and I didn't want to let go. He was braver than I was but I still saw him choke a little.

Ruth came in and asked to let me rest and they all left. I was alone again with my thoughts and I felt so lucky to have so many who were so concerned and who had so much love in their hearts. I began to look around and I saw the windowsill with so many cards from so many wonderful friends.

The next day Ruth got me up and I walked around for a short time and sat down in the chair. I was sitting in the chair when Barbra came in. After a long hug she said, "I was talking to the doctor and he said that if you're a good boy he may let you go home in a day or so."

"I'll be good and I can't wait to get home."

"Glen, when you do get home don't think that you're going to go places and do things. You're going to take it easy if I have to tie you down!"

"Oh, come here." We hugged.

Two days later I was home and enjoying my family and the wonderful meals Aunt Martha fixed for me. I loved it. I was fast gaining my strength and I was even out looking over the grounds and the golf course. They wouldn't let me play golf. They hid all the clubs!

I could never forget the love I received from my family and the many friends I had in Douglas. We were always a close family, but until a crisis comes along, we tend to take everything for granted. Family love is real!

A few weeks later I was permitted to play a little golf. I was completely recovered and back to my regular routine. I visited the office and everyone was glad to see me. I paid a visit to the police and fire departments and was greeted graciously. What a town! What wonderful people! I was on top of the world!

18

The Loss of Mother and Aunt Martha

After a few weeks Drew phoned that Mother had died. I was just getting ready for bed. Barbra was reading in the living room.

"Barbra, Drew just called and said Mother just died."

"Oh Glen, I'm sorry. When is the funeral?"

"Friday morning."

"Today is only Monday. Don't you think we ought to go?" she said.

"Thanks, Hon, I was hoping we could go together."

"Of course, if you'd rather go alone—"

"No Barbra, I want you with me."

I called Drew back and said that we would be there Thursday afternoon. He invited us to stay with them. We arrived in Dover Thursday afternoon. We were cordially greeted by Drew and Jean and went to the funeral home that night. Friday morning we attended the funeral and saw the grave of Father for the first time. Mother was laid to rest and we all went to Ed and Ginny's for coffee and sandwiches. After lunch Barbra and I went back to Drew's house and stayed for the night.

About a week later I received a letter from Drew informing me that the attorney had met all concerned parties at his office and the estate was divided equally between the living children. They were all named in the will but my name was not there. Drew explained that the wills were made out about twenty years ago and no one knew of my whereabouts or if I were still alive.

I wrote back to Drew stating that I thought things should stay or stand as they were. I had no intention of contesting the will. I felt that, since I had left and changed my name, I had severed all relationship with Father. That was the end of that.

Drew later informed me that Margie and Julian bought out the rest of them and moved into Mother's house on the hill. They auctioned most of the things in the house and split the proceeds between them.

Barbra, Paul, and I had just finished our breakfast and Paul was ready to leave. Barbra and I gave him a big hug and he was off to school. I had just picked up the morning paper when Uncle Ben came running down stairs in his bathrobe.

"Glen, I can't wake Martha!"

"Are you sure?"

"Yes, please do something!"

We rushed upstairs with Uncle Ben on our heels. I raised an eyelid and knew she was gone. I couldn't get any pulse.

"Uncle Ben, it appears that she's gone. I'll call the doctor. He will have to confirm it."

Dr. Davis came right over and declared her dead. Uncle Ben was just sitting in the chair and staring into space and not saying a word. I didn't know what to say or do. Barbra was standing next to Uncle Ben and had her hand on his shoulder. What could anyone do? The doctor said it was a tired heart. She simply died in her sleep. Uncle Ben was really out of it. We thought it best to get him downstairs. We got him to lie down on the sofa in the living room. The doctor gave him a mild sedative and he seemed to relax.

I went to Wallace Funeral Home and made the necessary arrangements and then went to school to get Paul. Paul was all broken up. Aunt Martha was like a grandmother to Evie and Paul. I called Clemson and asked to have Evelyn Fredericks call home right away. Soon she called and I told her the news. She left immediately and drove home.

Aunt Martha was buried in their plot at Green Lawn Cemetery just in front of their son, Frank. It is a six-grave plot and Frank was buried in the center. Two graves in the front and two in the back, for some reason. Uncle Ben was a surprise to all of us. He seemed resigned and took it better than we expected.

After the funeral we went home and Uncle Ben went up to his rooms. Paul and Evie, though, were more upset, it seemed, than anyone else. I did my best to hold up for the sake of the family but it wasn't easy. She meant so much to all of us.

Evie had gone back to Clemson and Paul went back to school. Uncle Ben was outside somewhere tending to the grounds. He wasn't saying much to anyone and we were just letting him alone. He had to get over his loss in his own way. This was devastating to him and we knew there was nothing we could say or do that would ease the pain because we all shared his grief.

Uncle Ben never was the same man but he was able to accept reality. He would never go to the jamboree again and he stayed pretty much to himself. He often remarked that he was so lucky to have us. We were the only family he had. I let him know how indebted I was to him. He was like a daddy to me and I wanted him to know it.

19

The Teachers

It was mid-May. Evie was graduating from Clemson and Barbra and I decided to take Paul to the exercises. We were so proud to see our little girl receive her degree.

We drove back home and Evie followed in her car. It was packed and had room only for the driver! We arrived home and were greeted by Uncle Ben. He was proud of Evie and said, "If only your Aunt Martha could be here."

It was the first time he had mentioned Aunt Martha since she had died.

Evie had sent out résumés to Douglas High and Bradford High while she was in her junior year at Clemson. She was hopeful of hearing something from Douglas High.

We were all at home again every day now. School was out and it seemed so good to have the kids with us. Barbra and the children were beginning to get serious about golf. They seemed to be spending a great deal of time on the course. One morning I suggested to Paul that we take on Mother and Evie. "Of course, we'll give a stroke on the two par fives." Barbra and Evie laughed and Evie said, "Let's go!"

We went out to the course and all got off to a good start. I was impressed with the drives of both Barbra and Evie.

"You've been practicing a little," I said. I winked at Paul and said, "Paul, you and I will have to buckle down."

"Don't worry, Dad. Let them have their fun for a while."

We all parred the hole and I was very much impressed. As we were stepping to the second tee, Evie came over to me and said, "Daddy, it's only fair to tell you that I took lessons at college. I didn't play because we didn't have a girls' team. I've been giving Mother lessons, so let's forget about the handicaps. We want to beat you fair and square."

Paul and I just looked at each other and Paul said, "OK, Dad, let's play golf!"

We took the next three holes and the girls were beginning to lose their rhythm. We tied the next two holes and Paul and I won the last three holes. We had to get serious to stay ahead. We couldn't take them for granted anymore.

We were coming out of church Sunday morning when Paul said, "I wonder when Evie will be out. She's still inside talking with Owen Hodge."

"We'll wait, Paul. She'll be out soon," I said. Evie came out and we went home.

At the dinner table Evie said, "Daddy, how well do you know the Hodges?"

"Oh, they've only been with us for the last six months or so. Why do you ask?"

"Owen asked me out to dinner tomorrow night."

"I met his dad, Owen Sr., when they first came to town. He's the manager of Blair's Department store and his son is temporarily heading the hardware department while waiting for an opening somewhere. He graduated from the University of South Carolina at Aiken last year. I understand he majored in math and is interested in teaching."

"Yes, he told me he was looking for a teaching position."

Evie would date occasionally but never took anyone seriously. She seemed to beam every time Owen called. I had to admit he was rather handsome with black wavy hair and very friendly brown eyes. He had a captivating smile and seemed very well mannered and educated. Owen would take Evie to the jamboree every Saturday night. We all looked forward to the jamboree.

One Saturday night when Owen brought her home, Evie said that Owen was going for an interview in Bradford Monday morning. He was to report to the superintendent and personnel director and then to the principal of the high school. Then the board of education would make the final decision.

"Now I know what I will have to face if I ever hear."

"Don't be impatient, dear," I said. I had the feeling that Evie expected me to speak to someone for her. As mayor, perhaps it would have made some notice but I wanted her to be selected on her own merit.

Owen had graduated one year before Evie and had been working in the department store ever since. He had submitted his application a year earlier. This discouraged Evie. Would she have to wait that long? I wasn't concerned, since she had submitted her application only to Douglas High and Bradford High while she was in her junior year. I didn't want her to go off someplace miles from here. Some parents never want to let go.

As we were coming out of church Sunday, Owen Sr. came up to Barbra and me and introduced his wife, Irene. I introduced Barbra and Paul to them. They invited us to dinner at their house the next day. We gratefully accepted.

We all arrived at their home on Oak Street and were cordially received. For the first time I realized that Owen Jr. was an only child, however, he didn't seem to be spoiled. He mentioned that he thought that his interview went well.

"Now," he said, "I shall have to wait until I hear from the principal."

We had a very delicious dinner and a very enjoyable evening.

We had the Hodges over to our place the following Monday for dinner. Owen Jr. was impressed with the golf course. I told him he could come over anytime and would be welcome. He said that he used to play but hadn't had the time lately. Evie challenged him to a game but no date was mentioned.

Owen said that his interview with the principal seemed to go pretty well and he now was waiting for the next meeting of the board of education.

In mid-August Evie received a letter from the Douglas school superintendent for an appointment on Wednesday the twenty-third. The interview went well and the principal was also present. They agreed to send her application and recommendation to the board of education for final consideration. A few days later Evie received a phone call from the chairman of the board of education that her appointment was approved. She was to report to the superintendent's office on August thirtieth for orientation. She was hired! Barbra and I were very pleased.

A few days later Evie received a phone call from Owen saying he had been accepted at Bradford High, which was only twelve miles from Douglas.

It was time for school again and Paul was getting ready to enter Clemson. I bought him a used Plymouth station wagon and he was ready to leave for a new experience. We only had a two-car garage and now we had five cars when everyone was home.

It was an emotional moment when we saw Paul drive out of the driveway. It was hard to believe that he wasn't a little boy anymore. Well, we went through the same emotions when Evie left for college.

Terry would often come over and play on the golf

course. Sometimes I would go out and play a round with her. It was always an experience! She often spoke of Paul and wondered why he didn't write. I wrote to Paul and mentioned that Terry Cummings was asking for him. I let him take it from there.

20

Engaged

It was Christmas and Paul was home for the holidays. We opened our gifts on Christmas Eve since the next day would be a busy time. We invited Owen and Terry to have Christmas dinner with us. It would be an evening dinner so it wouldn't interfere with their Christmas.

After dinner we were in the living room. I was looking over Paul's gifts when I heard Owen say to Evie, "Let's go into the library."

"OK," Evie said.

They entered the library and closed the door.

"Evie, hold out your hand," Owen commanded. Evie held out her hand and Owen slipped a diamond ring on her finger.

"Evie, will you marry me?"

"Oh, Owen, I will!"

"Evie, I love you."

"Owen, I love you."

They kissed. The door opened and Evie displayed her ring for all to see. Barbra had tears in her eyes.

We all congratulated them. Barbra and I were very happy for them. I thought I'd have some fun with Paul and I said, "Well, Paul, you're next."

Paul looked at me and started to blush. Terry looked at Paul and said, "Well, what do you say to that?" Terry could kid, too!

After the holidays, Leon Johnson approached me to see if I would consider selling the business. I had a good income from the lease arrangement but it was a much larger business now with the additional travel agency and the increase in insurance. He was a good business man and had built it up quite a bit. I talked it over with Barbra. She was willing to go along with anything I decided. Leon and I came to a decision that was fair and agreeable to both of us and I sold the business, the business I had started thirty years ago and the business Barbra tripled while I was in the service. Now it had blossomed into the largest business of its kind in the area.

Evie and Owen set their wedding date for June twenty-fifth. School would be closed and they would have plenty of time for a honeymoon trip and get back in time to get settled. It was agreed that they would stay with us until they could acquire their own place.

The winter skipped by and, before we knew it, spring was upon us. There were many details to be addressed. Barbra was busy with Irene Hodge in making up the invitation list. Evie selected Ann Dooley, a high school chum, to be her maid of honor. Ann was a pretty girl with light brown hair and beautiful brown eyes. Another high school friend, Alice Fowler, a brunette, and a college friend, Eleanor Fields, a blonde, were to be attendants. Paul and Peter, Terry's brother, were to be ushers.

I was to give the bride away, although I never liked that expression. Parson Lloyd Masters would conduct the ceremony at ten o'clock in the morning at the Central Baptist Church. John Arlen, a boyhood friend of Owen and a handsome blue-eyed blond, was picked as best man. The reception would be held at the Hotel Douglas ballroom and it looked as though the guest list would reach about seventy-five. The honeymoon was kept secret. I secured the services of a photographer and it looked as though all the arrangements that could be made were made.

On the wedding day I walked down the aisle with my daughter on my arm. I was the proudest dad in the world! When we reached the altar I stepped aside and sat down with Barbra. Barbra started to sniffle. I was trying hard to be strong. I nearly lost it when I saw Evie standing there and realized that I wasn't any longer the only man in her life. When the parson asked, "Who giveth this woman away?" I choked and barely got it out with a trembling voice. "Her mother and I." My eyes began to well up and Barbra was almost uncontrollable. This was the hardest moment for both of us. Our little girl was leaving the nest.

After the picture-taking session was over, the bride and groom left for the hotel. Most of the guests were already there. There was a six-piece band and at each place setting was a little white swan figure with the date and the names of the bride and groom.

After the dinner it was my special honor to dance with the bride to the tune of "My Little Girl." We both had tears running down our faces.

The newlyweds left late in the afternoon and the festivities came to a close.

We received a card from them about a week later from Hilton Head, South Carolina.

They didn't know it yet but Owen and I had gotten together and bought a house in the development that was for sale. This would be an extra wedding present from all of us. When they returned they would be living on Fredericks Boulevard.

Now I had a decision to make. It was time for thinking about the election. Nominations were being made at the Republican caucus and the Democrats were urging me to give it another term. Of course, I didn't have any valid reason not to run since I had no other obligations. I thought of Douglas and what the town meant to me and what the town had done for me.

"Glen, please think about it," said Al Goodwin.

"I appreciate how you all feel, Al, but I don't know. There are any number of good men who would like to serve."

"Glen, you are a known quantity in town and you do have a large following in town and I'd be proud to be your campaign manager again. It's an easy job now. Everybody knows you."

"Al, if I could think of the slightest excuse not to run . . . but I can't. I would feel ungrateful for what this town has done for me. You can nominate if you wish."

I was nominated on the first ballot with no opposition. The Democrats put up Ralph Drum again. This was going to be a campaign! Ralph picked Bob Leary as his campaign manager. I knew Bob well enough since he was a deacon in my church. I was waiting for the first salvo to start. Ralph made some noise about the condition of some of the roads and was critical about the lack of parking downtown. Rather a weak start, I thought. The Republican party didn't think that they had a chance and gave Ralph very little support. I had radio spot announcements and posters all over town. We gave away bumper stickers and pins. The Republican headquarters was a very quiet place and not even open most of the time. I really felt sorry for Ralph. He was too good a man to be treated this way.

I campaigned on my record and I stunned every Republican and Democrat when I spoke of my opponent in a complimentary manner. I said at an assembly of the Women Voters League, "If Ralph Drum is elected to be your next mayor, you can be sure that you will have a continuity of honest government. Ralph deserves much more than the

Republican party is giving him. If I were not running I would vote for Ralph Drum."

Al Goodwin was in the hall and almost fell out of his chair! I received loud applause and everyone laughed.

I continued to speak well of Ralph and I meant it. When the results were tallied I won by only sixty-four votes. It was the closest mayoral election in the history of Douglas.

The Republicans met at their headquarters to wind things up. Ralph announced that he was leaving the party and would register as a Democrat.

"Ralph, I don't think it's fair to blame us for not having the following that a party should have," said Chet Turner.

"My mind is made up. I'm going to register as a Democrat."

"Traitor!" shot back Chet.

"Call me what you will but I'm going where they show more respect for their members."

Bob Leary scolded Chet for calling Ralph a traitor and a fight ensued. Ralph left the hall. Police were called to restore order.

Al Goodwin told me that he was resigning as police commissioner. He felt it was time for someone else to take it. I promptly appointed Ralph Drum as our new police commissioner. The Common Council approved.

"Ralph," I said, "I think you will make a good police commissioner. Why, you've been in business in town all your adult life and you know every police officer on the force."

I was looking forward to working with Ralph for the next couple of years.

21

A New Home and the Loss of Uncle Ben

The newlyweds arrived and were shown their new home. It was going to take a few weeks to make a few changes before they moved in but it was a surprise.

"I can't believe it," cried Evie.

"This is like a dream," said Owen.

"Owen," said Owen Sr., "you will have to add on a garage but we thought we'd leave that up to you."

"Thanks, Dad, and thanks Mr. er, I mean Dad Fredericks."

"Owen, you're welcome."

Evie and Owen were settled in their rooms in our house and we were happy to have them. Uncle Ben and Owen got along just fine. In fact, Owen was learning a great deal about flowers and plants from Uncle Ben.

Paul and Terry were getting to be a regular couple. I don't think that Terry ever looked at another boy. To tell the truth, until Terry came along, Paul never paid any attention to girls.

I received a letter from my brother Bobby saying they were planning on driving down to see me about ten days before the schools opened. I phoned him right away and said to come down as soon as possible and spend a week or so with us. He said that they would leave Thursday and would be here until the following Friday.

We were thrilled, looking forward to their visit. They arrived in midmorning. Uncle Ben helped with their luggage and we got them settled. Bobby Jr. and Diane wanted to go swimming right away.

"Oh, Bobby, let them have their fun."

"OK, kids, get into your bathing suits," Bobby allowed.

"Bobby and Else, let's tour the house and grounds."

"Glen," asked Bobby, "this is some house. How much land is there?"

"Eighteen acres. If there were more I would have had an eighteen-hole course."

Else just shook her head.

After lunch I took Bobby, Else and the kids on the usual tour of the town. I showed them the development I established and the park named after me. They couldn't get over it, although they knew about if from what they were told. I took them into the mayor's office and Else couldn't understand why I wasn't there working every day.

"Else, it's only a part-time job and I don't have to be here every day."

We went back home and Barbra had a feast for us.

We all went to church Sunday morning in two cars and then to the hotel where they always had a Sunday brunch. It was a beautiful day and I thought we might take a ride around the area. Uncle Ben, Evie, Owen, Paul and Barbra went back to the house. Bobby, Else and the kids and I went up to Columbia to see the capitol building and then we visited the zoo. We went back home and talked and talked.

Bobby, Paul and I played a little golf during the week and the kids had a ball in the pool and in the recreation room. All in all we had a wonderful time and they left Friday.

Monday morning Uncle Ben took the golf cart out to check up on some of the greens and also to smooth the bunkers. Barbra and Evie were downtown shopping and said that they would stay and have lunch out. Barbra and Evie got along like sisters. They had a great relationship.

Paul and I were on the patio cleaning all the clubs. I wanted to spend as much time with him. We always understood each other and I loved him very much. It was about noon and Paul suggested that we have a cookout on the patio, just Paul, Uncle Ben, and me.

"Fine, Paul," I said. "I shall start things and you call Uncle Ben."

I went into the house and got things ready. I heard Paul calling Uncle Ben but I thought nothing of it even though he had been out on the course all morning long. Paul came running back to the house all out of breath.

"Dad, something's wrong with Uncle Ben. He's just sitting in the cart and leaning over the wheel like he's sleeping."

I ran down to the third green. Uncle Ben was there in the cart near the sand bunker. I spoke to him but got no response. I lifted his eyelid and I didn't like it. I couldn't get any pulse.

"He's gone, Paul."

"No, he can't be!" cried Paul.

I moved Uncle Ben over and drove the cart back to the house. Paul was crying and I couldn't help but shed a few tears myself. I carried Uncle Ben into the house and placed him on the sofa in the living room. I called Dr. Davis and he came right over. His examination confirmed that Uncle Ben, like Aunt Martha, had expired with a tired heart. I think Uncle Ben died of a broken heart. Barbra and Evie were devastated when they came home.

Uncle Ben was buried next to Aunt Martha just five years later at Green Lawn Cemetery.

I was called to Attorney Scofield's office the following

day and Uncle Ben's will was read. I was the sole beneficiary to his estate. It was considerable. I knew he was rather well off but he never discussed his personal finances with me. I would never have guessed that he was worth nearly a half-million dollars!

Uncle Ben was my idol. He was everything to me that a boy could ever want. I don't doubt that God led me to Douglas and to that café so many years ago. What would have become of me if he had refused to hire me? Uncle Ben and Aunt Martha gave me love. They were the first to tell me that they loved me. They gave me a new life—a rebirth.

With all that has happened in just a few years, it began to take a toll on me. Life itself is full of trials and tribulations and we have to be strong enough to handle the good with the bad. It isn't always easy to cope with losing a loved one. Yet isn't it strange that we must have the strength to endure the valleys of our life in order to enjoy the mountains? We may mourn our loss but never forget the fond memories and the precious moments of shared joy.

About a week later Barbra and I had nothing to do so we thought we'd take a little walk. We walked north up Wade Boulevard to the Green Lawn Cemetery and visited the gravesites of Uncle Ben and Aunt Martha. Upon looking at the plot we thought we would inquire of the cemetery association to find out if we could be buried in the two available spaces in the plot. There were no living relatives and I was all but adopted by them and administrator to the estate. Without being kin we were both as close to being kin as anyone could be.

We then walked over to my development and all through Fredericks Boulevard and wound up at the entrance of Fredericks Park. We didn't go in. We had lunch at the café and then walked home. We went out to the patio and just flopped down. We were bushed but we got the walk out of our system.

The next day I wrote to the Green Lawn cemetery association and inquired about the possibility of using the two available spaces in the plot of Ben and Martha Wells, in section twelve, for my wife and me. I mentioned the fact that I was brought up by them since I was fourteen and that I was the administrator of his estate. I received a letter back about two weeks later stating that my request was granted and that it would be recorded into the cemetery records. At least this was settled and Barbra and I were relieved.

22

New England

Owen obtained the services of a local carpenter to add a garage to their new house. Paul drew up the plans. It was only a one-day job and it blended in very nicely with the house.

I would sometimes go to my mayoral office in the town hall. I just like to meet people. There are always small details to address. It was a good time to visit with the departments outside the town hall. Exposure is important.

With Uncle Ben gone, and Evie and Owen living in their home, it seemed so quiet with just Barbra and Paul there. Paul was still mourning Uncle Ben. I thought it would be good for Paul to take a trip and get his mind off of Uncle Ben. Barbra and I were seriously thinking of travelling through the New England states. We spoke to Paul about it and he was all for it. We decided to leave the day after the July Fourth festivities. We asked Evie and Owen to watch the place while we were gone. Evie had keys to the house anyway.

In mid-May, Paul approached us with a surprising suggestion. He wanted to know what we thought of asking Terry along on the trip. I looked at Barbra and Barbra looked at me and we both looked at Paul. Paul was studying our expressions.

"I don't know, Paul," I said.

"Do Terry's parents know about this?" Barbra asked.

"Well, no," admitted Paul, "but it will be more fun!"

"Paul, is this something you just thought about? Have you talked to Terry about it?"

"Oh, she suggested it!"

Barbra and I had to think about this for a while. The next morning Barbra called Helen Cummings.

"Helen, has Terry said anything to you about wanting to accompany us on a trip we are planning through the New England states?"

"This is news to me, Barbra."

"Paul sprang it on us yesterday and we were taken by surprise. Glen and I talked it over and decided we'd better check with you and Don."

"I don't know, Barbra, I think I'd better talk it over with Don when he comes home."

"Helen, we wouldn't mind taking Terry. Paul and Terry are such good friends and we would certainly treat her like a daughter."

"Barbra, I'm not worried about that. You just don't know today what kids are thinking."

"Please talk it over with Don and let me know. I know that you will talk to Terry about it."

"You can be sure, Barbra!"

The next day Helen called Barbra.

"Barbra, Don, and I have given it a great deal of thought and thought it would be a good experience for Terry. How long will you be gone and what will it cost? I might say that Terry is delighted!"

"Helen, we expect to be about three weeks and we will take care of all expenses unless you want to give Terry some spending money, but even that isn't necessary."

It was agreed that Terry would accompany us on our trip up north. Terry and Paul were jumping with joy!

I called Drew and said we were going to tour the New

England states. There would be four of us. Barbra, Paul and Paul's girlfriend, Terry. Drew said to come and spend a few days with them. He said they were planning a family cookout the second Saturday of July at Margie's house, which used to be Mother's. I promised that we would be there.

The four of us packed everything we could in my Mercury trunk and had a compartment we rented to put on the roof. We were off!

We stopped overnight in Harrisburg, Pennsylvania, and then went on to Dover.

We had an opportunity to see my sister and four brothers again and Paul discovered that there were a few more cousins around than the last time. I think we had about fifty at the cookout.

The next day we left for Mystic Seaport. We toured the *Morgan* whaling ship and the village and took in the aquarium. The kids got a kick out of the way people lived in those days.

"I'm glad I wasn't living then," Paul said.

"Paul," I said, "one hundred years from now people will be saying the same thing about us."

"Oh, Mr. Fredericks," Terry said. "I can't imagine people would ever think we might seem as primitive."

We stayed overnight at Mystic and the next day we visited some of the so-called cottages at Newport, Rhode Island.

"From Mystic to Newport," Paul said. "Some contrast!"

"Yes, Paul, this was the day of the robber barons," I said.

We went to Cape Cod and climbed the tower at Provincetown. Barbra was the last one up to the top. We spent the night on the Cape and then went on to Plymouth Rock.

"This is where they landed?" asked Paul.

"No, Paul, they first touched land over near Provincetown and then came here," I said.

We went to Boston and stayed for three nights. We visited many of the points of interest and the kids learned a great deal of history there.

We were in Lexington and Concord and I told the kids that this was where the Revolutionary War started.

"Oh yes," Terry said. "The shot heard 'round the world."

"That's right, Terry," I said.

We drove along the coast through New Hampshire and into Maine. We took a place near the beach at York. It was too cold to swim and the kids were disappointed. The next day we went to Acadia Park, the only national park in New England. We went to the top of Mount Cadillac and had a wonderful view of the rock-rimmed coast of Maine.

We went to the top of Mount Washington in New Hampshire on the cograil. Barbra and Terry were a little hesitant but finally braved it.

"This is a real thrill!" said Paul.

We drove to the Green Mountain State of Vermont and stopped at so many quaint little villages where we just had to stop and buy trinkets. The scenery was so beautiful!

We entered Massachusetts. We were riding alongside the Berkshires. The scenery all through New England was beautiful.

"It's so varied," said Barbra.

We skipped into eastern New York and then to New Jersey. We were home two days later and the kids talked about the trip for days. We had a mountain of pictures to show from our trip.

23
Leaving Office

Time for nominations was nearing and I decided that I would step down as mayor and retire from politics. Besides, it was decided by the Common Council that the office of mayor would now become a full-time position, starting with the next election. I was getting along in age and was sure that I didn't want a full-time job. The town really required it. The proposal went to referendum and passed.

At the caucus I announced that I was retiring and would refuse to run again. I heard groans all over the room. It didn't seem to matter to some and my name was put up for nomination anyway.

I immediately got up and said, "Mr. Chairman. Ladies and gentlemen. I have served as police commissioner and as your mayor and I really do appreciate all the support and cooperation I have always received. I can look around in this room and pick any number of you who would become a very good mayor. I'm getting along in age and, in fairness to me and to those who are qualified, I beg you to honor my wish and please nominate someone else.

"I love this town and I love the many friends I have made here. The day I came to Douglas was the happiest day of my life up to then."

The people clapped and many came to me and hugged me. They knew I was serious. The chairman called for nominations. I jumped up and said, "Mr. Chairman, I nominate our most able police commissioner, Ralph Drum, for the office of mayor of Douglas."

Well, I sat down and waited for the explosion. I didn't have to wait long. The hall shook with the noise of dumbstruck Democrats! Ralph Drum was in the hall and almost swallowed his pipe and the chairman dropped the mallet. All eyes were on me, they wondered if I were just joking. When they finally calmed down Al Goodwin got up and seconded the nomination. Now they were sure that we were both off our rockers.

When the chairman was able to bring order to the meeting, Al Goodwin got up again and said, "Mr. Chairman, ladies, and gentlemen. I have known Ralph for many years and so have most of you. He was a Republican and waged campaigns with very little support from his party. He has been a credit to himself and to this community as building inspector and as police commissioner. I have never heard anyone question Ralph's integrity or honesty. He became a registered Democrat and has served his community honorably whenever he was asked. If honest government is what you want then I say that Ralph Drum is your man."

There was quiet in the hall like I have never known before.

"Any more nominations?" was all the chairman could say. "If not, I'll try your minds. All in favor of the name of Ralph Drum, say 'Aye.'"

The shout could be heard all over town! Ralph Drum was nominated by acclamation!

I left the hall and was on the street when Ralph caught up with me.

"Glen, I can't believe what you've done! It's a wonder you still have your head."

"Ralph," I said, "if anyone deserves this honor, you do, and I mean it!"

"Thanks, Glen; you're one in a million!"

I went home and told Barbra that I was leaving politics. She was very happy. She said, "Glen, you have served your community well and you shouldn't have any regrets."

"I know, Hon, but I can't help wondering if I'm not letting them down. They've always done so much for me."

The doorbell rang and there was Al Goodwin.

"Hello, Al, come in."

"Glen, I thought you were going to be crucified and I seconded the nomination because I thought you were in trouble. Now I'm wondering what the Republicans are going to think of this? Whom do they have?"

"I don't know, Al, but wouldn't it be something if the Republicans also nominated Ralph, even though he bolted the party?"

"Well, Glen, at any rate, I do believe that Ralph will make a fine mayor."

Al left and Barbra and I looked forward to the days ahead with no schedules and no appointments.

The Republicans held their caucus and, after hours of bickering, they nominated Chet Turner, Ralph's former campaign manager when he was running against me as a Republican and the very man Ralph fired! I couldn't believe it!

Ralph waged a strong campaign on issues that were important and on the minds of the people. He was careful about making empty promises. He had the full support of the party and there were posters with his picture all over town.

Chet lost the election to the extent that it was an embarrassment not only to him but to his party. Ralph Drum was our new mayor! Our first full-time mayor!

There was a dinner at the hotel after the swearing-in ceremonies and I told Ralph that I would be available any time he thought I might be of assistance but I didn't want any position that would tie me down. He thanked me for all I had done for him.

A few days later the doorbell rang. A Mr. Norman Hughes, chairman of the state Democratic committee, wanted to know if I would be willing to run for governor. Gov. Edward Miller was retiring due to poor health. Mr. Hughes thought that I had enough support in this area and, with a little time, they could make me known throughout the state.

I let him know that, unequivocally, I would never consider running for governor. That was the end of that.

24

Granddaughter and Paul

Paul was in his third year at Clemson and was majoring in architecture. He was one of the star golfers on his team and was still in the orchestra with his violin. Terry was in her second year and leaning toward a business career. She was instrumental in starting a girls' golf team but there were no other teams in the area so they got together one afternoon each week and played among themselves.

Paul and Terry came home every weekend. We were so glad to see Paul and I was sure Terry's parents were just as happy. We still went to the jamboree every Saturday night. Paul would sometimes play his violin during country music.

Evie and Owen were well adjusted in their teaching positions and in their new home. During the week we were invited to their home for dinner. This was our first dinner at their home.

We were enjoying a delicious dinner (Barbra had taught Evie well) when Evie sprang a surprise.

"I thought you should be the first to know. We're going to be parents."

"Oh, Evie," cried Barbra.

I kept on eating as though I didn't hear, then, "What did you say?"

"Oh, Daddy, I'm going to have a baby!"

I looked at Owen and Barbra looked at me.

"Well, congratulations!" was all I could say. I was happy for them, of course, but a baby?

"When, dear?" Barbra asked.

"Late February, Mother."

I Just sat there thinking that just a little while ago Evie was just a little girl. I was still in shock!

We had Evie and Owen over for Thanksgiving and Paul was so proud that soon he would be an uncle.

"Just think," 'Uncle Paul.' That sounds groovy, don't you think, Dad?"

"Son, it won't be long before someone will be calling you Daddy."

I remember hearing older people saying how time flies. Now I know how they felt. I just couldn't believe that my little boy would soon be an uncle, and hey, I'd be Grandpa!

We all had a wonderful Christmas and Evie and Owen spent the day with us. Even Terry came over in the afternoon and gave Paul an ID bracelet. Imagine, a boy wearing a bracelet! How times had changed. Paul gave Terry a silver locket, something you wear around your neck, which has a place for a picture or two. I still thought of those two as little kids.

On February twenty-ninth Evie became a mother, Owen, a father, Barbra, a grandmother, I, a grandfather and Paul, an uncle. What a day! Barbra Ann arrived as a beautiful and healthy little girl. The poor kid will have a birthday only once every four years. I don't think that she will be deprived of anything. Now we will have two Barbras in the family and I will have a granddaughter to spoil. Owen was staying with us while Evie was in the hospital. I never saw a more nervous father.

"Glen," Barbra intoned, "you were a wreck when Evie came."

Evie has the rest of the school year off and won't have

to go back until September. I suppose we will have the baby once in a while but that's fine with me. I'm looking forward to getting acquainted with my very own granddaughter.

Paul and Terry were home from college for the summer and Evie and Owen were back home with the baby. Barbra was spending more time over there than here. I couldn't complain. When Barbra wasn't there Owen's parents were so Evie wasn't alone very much.

I wanted to do or go someplace with Paul. One evening Barbra, Paul and I were in the living room and I said, "Barbra, since you are spending so much time at Evie's, I thought I'd like to spend a couple of weeks or so with Paul. Just travel somewhere. How about it, Paul? Just you and me."

"What, two weeks?" cried Paul.

"Glen, I think it would be very nice. Paul, I think that you would really enjoy some time with Dad."

"This may be the last time I will spend any time with you, Paul. Will you think about it?"

"I don't know, Dad. Of course, I don't have anything planned for the summer."

"Paul, this is your last vacation from school. I want to spend some time with you. Just you and me. We won't even have an itinerary. Just travel and see some of the country together."

"Can Terry come?"

"Paul, this is just you and me!"

"Dad, I was only kidding. Boy, the expression on your face! I think it's a good idea, Dad."

Paul and I spent the next morning packing things in the Mercury trunk. Paul spent the afternoon saying good-bye to Terry. The next morning we were off. Where? Who cared?

We headed northwest and spent the night in a motor lodge near Mammoth Cave in Kentucky. The next day we visited the caves. Paul was disappointed.

"Carlsbad is bigger," he said.

We continued on to Lincoln's cabin.

"I can't believe that anyone born here could become President," Paul quipped.

We visited Battle Creek, Michigan, and went into the Kellogg Company and saw cornflakes being boxed. We crossed the Mackinac Bridge and went north to Sioux Locks. Paul had never seen locks before. We went west to Wisconsin and took a boat ride through the Wisconsin Dells. In Iowa we watched a wedding party leaving "The Little Brown Church in the Vail."

"I remember singing that in church," said Paul.

In Illinois we visited New Salem where Lincoln lived and worked in a store. We also visited the grave and home of Lincoln in Springfield.

We went to St. Louis, Missouri, and went up to the top of the Gateway Arch, six hundred and thirty feet high. We spent a few days at a resort in the Ozark hills. We leisurely explored the area and even got in a little golf. We headed south and came to a small resort town called Eureka Springs, Arkansas. It was dubbed "Little Switzerland." The Ozarks were beautiful.

Paul and I spent two nights at the resort high above the town. It was beautiful. We went southeast through Little Rock and followed Route Sixty-five, the river road. We crossed the Mississippi River and went into Natchez, Mississippi, from Louisiana. We toured some of the antebellum mansions and went north to Port Gibson. Paul noted a church building with a hand and finger pointed toward the sky.

"Look, Dad, see that steeple?"

We stopped and took pictures and a lady came over to us and asked, "Are you staying for the night?"

"Well, I think we've been driving enough for one day. I think we might."

"Fine. You can find your choice of accommodations just up the road and for dinner you can come to our roast beef dinner we're having at the church tonight. Will you come?"

"How about it, Paul, a home-cooked meal?"

"OK with me, Dad."

"Thank you very much. I'll be there and looking for you. I'm Beatrice Nelson. Everyone here calls me Bea."

"Thank you, we'll be here," I promised.

That night at the Presbyterian church we met Bea and her husband, Larry, and we learned a little Civil War history about the town. General Grant saved the town from destruction, saying, "This town is too beautiful to burn."

We had a delicious roast beef dinner and the next day we visited Jackson, the capitol. There we learned more Civil War history. We visited the Space and Rocket Center in Huntsville, Alabama. Paul really enjoyed it.

Soon we were home. I'm sure Paul enjoyed the trip very much and I'm sure he is more knowledgeable about his country and more mature. He kept a diary and was adding up the number of states we went through. He said eleven. I know that I learned a great deal but I felt privileged to have spent those precious days with my fast-growing son. I shall always cherish those moments.

We returned home early Saturday afternoon. Paul had to call Terry just to let her know we were home. He then hung up.

"Well, that was short and sweet," I said.

"Oh, she'll be right over."

She must have run all the way. I don't think it was fifteen minutes before the doorbell rang and there was Terry.

Paul had given his mother a couple of souvenirs and

he surprised me with a tie clasp and cufflinks from the Space and Rocket Center. But when Terry came in, she was inundated with trinkets from every stop we made!

"Oh, Paul, you're so wonderful that you even thought of me."

Thought of her? I don't think there was a moment when he didn't! I thought he was going through his pocket money rather quickly. I had to keep replenishing him. Paul just stood there while Terry admired her treasures. Then she looked at Paul and the next thing I knew they were locked in each other's arms. It was the first time I ever saw Paul hug and kiss a girl. I didn't think he knew how.

"Dad, Mom, may Terry stay for dinner?"

"Of course," Barbra said. "Terry, you'd better call your mother and let her know."

"Thank you, Mrs. Fredericks. I shall."

A little later Paul and Terry were out on the golf course. Terry was using Paul's clubs and Paul was using mine.

After dinner we all went to the jamboree and then we took Terry home. Paul was in space!

25
All Grown Up

Paul and Terry were back in school. Paul called home and said that he had been elected president of his class! He was still on the golf team and playing his violin in the orchestra. If I sounded like a bragging father, I couldn't help it. Barbra liked to remind me, "He's my son too, you know!"

We had always been so proud of our children. We always strived to instill in them proper values and the importance of good character and integrity; to respect others as you would have them respect you. I think we did a good job. They always had pretty much what they wanted and we taught them to value their possessions.

Paul was beginning to take things seriously. He was majoring in architecture and was planning for his future. He contacted a firm in Columbia known as Mead & Taylor, Architectural Consultants. He picked this firm from a school magazine or a school paper. He received a letter inviting him to an interview on a Saturday.

I took Paul to Columbia on the designated Saturday. Paul was armed with a recommendation from the dean of the college. Paul still had about two months before he would graduate but wanted to start making plans for his future. Smart kid.

Paul came out from the interview and seemed encouraged.

"Dad, this is quite a place!"

"How did it go?"

"I won't know for a couple of weeks but I liked the way they spent time with me."

We drove home after having lunch and then we had to wait to hear from the firm.

About three weeks later Paul received a letter offering him a position with Mead & Taylor!

"I got it!"

"Got what, Paul?" I asked.

"I got a job with Mead & Taylor!"

"Does this mean you will have to move to Columbia?" I asked.

"Dad, it's only about fifty miles."

Due to the recommendation from the dean, Paul was offered a middle management position and would be responsible for a crew of draftsmen and junior engineers. I wasn't concerned that he was taking on too much too soon. Paul was growing up and knew how to handle responsibilities.

Terry was a bit forlorn. She still had another year of college and wasn't happy that Paul would be living in Columbia alone. Poor Terry, she felt a little threatened.

Barbra and I attended the graduation exercises with Terry, of course. We were so proud when Paul delivered his address as president. What a boy!

Paul went to Columbia and found a decent apartment near the firm.

Terry and Paul had a steady correspondence going and she would come over to play golf and to keep us informed. She knew more about Paul than we did. Paul was never one to write letters very much but he certainly kept Terry informed!

Paul came home for Christmas and gave Terry a diamond. Terry showed it to us in the afternoon. This was a surprise. I suppose we thought it might happen some time, but so soon? Terry still had to finish school.

We were just getting used to our little granddaughter and now our little boy was engaged to little Terry. I can't keep up, I guess.

Terry finally graduated from Clemson with a degree in business administration. The wedding was set for June tenth. Paul made all the arrangements in Columbia. The wedding at South Baptist Church, with Parson Eugene Charls officiating, would be at ten in the morning and the reception would be held at the Holiday Inn. Peter, Terry's brother, was best man.

Peter Cummings got together with those in Douglas who grew up with Paul. He even asked Evie for names. He had tickets printed and sold them to Paul's friends from church and from high school. The bachelor party was held at the hotel. Peter made me responsible for getting Paul down there on the Saturday of the party. I called Paul and asked him to come down that Saturday in the afternoon because I had a surprise for him. I thought that would bring him down. He came down and Barbra and I presented him with a brand-new Mercury. I thought he deserved it.

Saturday night, Barbra, Paul, and I left early for the jamboree but told Paul that we would have dinner at the hotel. This was fine with Paul. We walked into the ballroom and everyone welcomed Paul! Paul was speechless and he just looked at me, puzzled. Barbra took the car back and had dinner at Evie and Owen's house. Later we met them at the jamboree.

It was a very pleasant party. Paul took a ribbing but it was all in good clean fun. He came away with nearly one thousand dollars.

The Friday night before the wedding we had a dinner at the hotel for the wedding group. It included all the members of the wedding and the parents. I spoke to Don Cummings and offered to split the cost. He agreed. I gave every member of the group a pewter tankard with their initials engraved on it. We really took care of these kids!

After dinner we went home and Paul decided to stay for the night. I was glad that he didn't intend to drive back to Columbia so late at night.

It was a beautiful day for the wedding. Evie and Owen came up with Barbra and me and Owen's parents took care of the baby.

Joan Carley, a school chum of Terry's, was maid of honor. I couldn't get over seeing little Terry in her gown. She was beautiful and so grown up! And Paul, in his tuxedo. He was a man!

At the reception Barbra and I told the newlyweds to look for a house when they returned from their honeymoon—we would buy it for them as a wedding gift.

When they returned they found a beautiful home with two acres. Terry landed a position as secretary to the trust officer of the Columbia National Bank. We hadn't known it before but Terry also received a brand-new car from her folks!

After they got settled in their new home we had a cookout at their house. Evie and Owen, with the baby, drove up to Columbia with Barbra and me. Terry's parents were there and we had a grand time.

About two weeks later we invited Owen, Evie and Paul and Terry for a cookout at our house on a Saturday. We surprised them by having their parents also, Don and Helen Cummings and Owen and Irene Hodge. We had quite a crowd. We even got a foursome together and played a round of golf. Paul and I won over Owen Sr. and Owen Jr. Don Cummings didn't play golf.

Barbra and I were always so glad to see the family, now

that we were all alone so much of the time. True, they were close by but we missed them from day to day. We also miss Aunt Martha and Uncle Ben. They were so much a part of our lives and we were proud to be a part of their lives.

Only a year after Paul started with Mead & Taylor, they suggested that Paul go back to evening classes and get his master's degree. Paul couldn't object since the firm agreed to pay for the course. It was going to be a busy schedule for Paul working every day with the responsibilities he had and going to night school at the University of South Carolina five nights each week.

Terry wasn't too happy but she realized that this was all for Paul's good. Terry's concern was being alone evenings when she was due in about two months. Her parents and parents-in-law were fifty miles away and besides, Evie and Owen were expecting again.

Paul didn't seem too concerned.

"Terry," said Paul, "if we have to we can have someone come in for a few hours each day to help."

Two months later, Paul took Terry to the hospital and in the early evening, Paul and Terry became the proud parents of a healthy baby boy they named Paul Glen Fredericks. Terry took a leave of absence from work.

One month later, Evie and Owen also became the proud parents of a healthy boy, Owen III.

Barbra was beside herself. We were both very proud of our grandchildren and Barbra wanted to help and be with the babies, but one can do just so much.

Sometimes I think that she thought that she could be in both places at once. I let her do most of the running around because I couldn't keep up with her. She would be with Evie in the morning and then with Terry in Columbia in the afternoon and come home and cook dinner. This wasn't good and I knew it couldn't go on. She was wearing herself out without realizing it. She loved those babies. Of course, Owen's mother and Terry's mother were just as busy so Evie and Terry had plenty of help.

I knew I had to come up with something to take the stress off Barbra.

"Barbra, as long as you insist on running back and forth to Columbia every afternoon, I don't think you should expect to prepare dinner. We should either hire a cook or have dinner out every night. Which is it?"

"Oh, Glen, I don't think I would be comfortable with a cook in my kitchen."

"All right, then we have dinner out until Evie and Terry can handle things themselves."

"Well, I think it might be better. It will only be for a little while, anyway."

"Fine. Let's start out by inviting Owen and Irene and Don and Helen out tomorrow night for dinner at the hotel. They've been just as busy and it will give us all a chance to enjoy a meal and relax. The dinner will be on me."

Barbra got on the phone and called Irene and Helen and they accepted the invitation. The following night we all had a leisurely dinner and we all enjoyed the relaxation.

26

Grandchildren

Paul completed his studies at the university and received his master's degree in architectural engineering. He hired a cook to come in from Monday to Friday and another woman to come in once each week to clean. Barbra and I would go up once in a while to help Terry and Terry's mother would also go up to help.

About two years later, when little Paul was beginning to walk, his dad was promoted to full partnership in the business. Now the firm was known as Mead, Taylor and Fredericks! That's my boy!

There were new responsibilities for Paul at work and also on the home front. Terry was going to have another baby soon. A girl came into the world and was named Arlene Louise. Terry had to leave her job with the bank.

The family was beginning to grow and I was beginning to slow down. I realized that I needed help around the yard and the golf course. I just couldn't keep up. I hired a lawn care company right here in town. They came in twice a month for the yard and shrubbery and twice a week for the golf course. They kept things in fine shape for me. I noticed that Paul had someone to take care of his yard.

Barbra and I were enjoying our grandchildren more and more as they grew. Poor Barbra, she was so excited she was trying to be in two places at once. We were both very proud of the children but we had to slow down. Barbra was beginning to lose weight and I had to put my foot down and make her understand that she had to take care of herself. Still, I was walking on air. Four grandchildren; two granddaughters and two grandsons! I couldn't wait to get the boys out on the course.

Evie and Owen's daughter, Barbra Ann, was seven years old and starting the third grade at school. Owen III and Paul Glen were five years old and just starting first grade. Little Arlene was just three and getting into everything as they usually do. They were all as cute as they can be.

Barbra and I look forward to having the children for a day, usually on a Saturday. This gives their parents a break and we love to have them.

One Saturday we had all four children at once. They spent most of the morning in the recreation room down stairs and most of the afternoon in the pool. Of course, one could hear them all over the place. Later in the afternoon, Evie came to pick up Barbra Ann and Owen, and Barbra and I took Paul and Arlene back to Columbia and had our dinner with Paul and Terry. We left in time to take in the jamboree.

When little Paul was eleven years old he was sitting on the sofa in the living room looking through a book of the presidents of the United States. I put my arm around him and said, "Paul, when I was your age I knew all of the presidents of the United States."

"Yeah, Grampa, when you were my age there weren't so many." He took me by surprise but I gave him a hug anyway.

Paul and Owen were twelve years old now and every time they came around they wanted me to take them out on the course. I could only give them the basics, but they were beginning to develop some degree of tempo and rhythm.

When they did improve, they would be fierce competitors. I didn't think that I had to worry about them outscoring or outdriving me for a few years yet.

Barbra Ann and Arlene were too far apart in age to be chums. Four years was too much for them to be friends while they were growing up but I did hope that they would be close after they grew up.

Paul Glen and Owen III were now entering high school, Paul in Columbia and Owen right in Douglas. Owen promptly joined the golf team as did Paul in Columbia. I didn't think it took too much effort for Owen to get on the team when he let it be known that his grandfather owned the golf course.

Owen III was spending more and more time on the course. The boy had the bug for the game of golf. Almost every afternoon several boys from the school were out on the course. I was glad to see the young people showing an interest. There were times when I went out and played with them. Some of them were very good.

I was informed by Owen III that a tournament was scheduled with Bradford on Friday, just two days away. Douglas High had only defeated Bradford High once. Douglas High had had a fairly good record this season so far and I thought that they might have a chance.

The afternoon of the tournament I had everything ready for them. I didn't allow buses in the yard but cars were everywhere and the lawn was a mess. Wade Boulevard was lined with buses and cars and could handle only one-way traffic.

I was really interested in this tournament since I was helping their coach in giving them a few pointers. Of course, the coach wasn't there.

Two hours later, after the tournament was over, I invited everyone to the patio and they were refreshed with some punch. Of course, there was always plenty of water on the course. They tallied the scores and Douglas High had won by two strokes! There was the loudest cheer I ever heard. The coach and the captain of the Bradford team congratulated the Douglas boys. One boy forgot himself and said, "Thank you, Mr. Fredericks."

Everyone looked at me and I admitted that I had helped all I could. It was perfectly all right but a surprise to Harry Birch, their coach.

I went out the next morning to check the course and, to my surprise, I couldn't find a single divot. I think I taught them well. The front yard was a different story with tire tracks all over the place. My lawn men smoothed it out and I even helped a little.

Barbra just looked at me, shook her head, and said, "It's a good thing Uncle Ben isn't around to see what they did to his yard and plants."

When the boys won it made it all worthwhile. I loved them. When I was out there with them I wished that I was their age again.

Barbra thought I was a pushover for the kids and I guess I was. I never heard any complaints from the neighbors or from the police. Of course, I used to be police commissioner and also mayor. The only damage was to my lawn and I never complained.

Barbra and I asked Paul and Terry what they thought of spending their Christmas with us. We were doing this more for us. We felt so lonely around Christmas time without the family around us when we opened presents. Christmas was on a Thursday and Paul said that his office was closing at noon on Wednesday. This would give them Thursday, Friday, Saturday, and Sunday to spend with us. They agreed and we looked forward to their visit. We spent Thanksgiving with Evie and Owen at their home.

Paul and Terry came down with the car packed with presents. We got them settled and hid the presents from the kids and we all settled down for four wonderful days of family fellowship.

Paul Glen immediately called Owen III and they soon got together. Paul and I went out to the golf course and we had a foursome, Paul and I against the two boys. The weather was cool but invigorating. For the first time the boys beat us!

On Christmas morning Paul Glen and Arlene were the first to stir. We all arose and there was a great deal of commotion and excitement with the children in anticipation of what was to come. We had our breakfast. The children were in the living room and getting very impatient.

We entered the living room. The tree was lighted and was beautiful. It should have been since we all had a hand in decorating it.

The floor was covered with presents. I thought Paul and Terry were trying to spoil their children more than we spoiled ours. At any rate, I thought that they got pretty much what they ordered from Santa. Barbra and I, among other things, each received a ten-speed bicycle. Apparently, they feel that we are not getting enough exercise. After we cleared all the papers, we had boxes of clothing, games, golf balls, tees, and golf gloves. It was a mess but it was a happy time for all. The tables had turned. Now the children were spoiling the parents.

We all sat down to a delicious turkey dinner with all the trimmings and sat and talked for the afternoon. Owen III came over and he and Paul Glen went out to play golf. Paul and I just stayed put. Arlene was busy getting acquainted with her Christmas presents.

It was so wonderful to have them with us for the rest of the weekend. We had a wonderful Christmas and Barbra and I looked forward to trying out our bikes. We would really enjoy riding our bikes in the park downtown. It wouldn't do us any harm.

I really enjoyed watching the boys come over some afternoons to practice. Bradford High was their fierce competitors and when they were having their tournament here it was pandemonium! There would be cars all over the front yard and buses and cars lined up and down Wade Boulevard. I would always have a fifty-five gallon can of punch for them and there was plenty of water on the golf course. I always got a great deal of joy out of how seriously they took their game. It was fun for all.

Owen would be over practicing some afternoons and on weekends. Once in a while I would go out with him. He was getting pretty good. Whenever he won a hole I would use my age for an excuse. He would say, "I think you're doing great, Grampa, for your age."

I guess that's what you call teen-age tactfulness. At any rate I loved the little guy. Once in a while, not often, he would come in late from practicing on the course and we'd invite him to stay for dinner. He would call home for permission. Other times Evie would invite us over for dinner when Owen was on the course and we would all go there for dinner. It gave Barbra and me a change and also a chance to see Barbra Ann, who was now a little lady all of twelve!

Barbra and I counted our blessings every day for the life we were privileged to enjoy and were very thankful for our wonderful family. *Thank you again, Uncle Ben and Aunt Martha.*

27
Hawaii

Having plenty of time on my hands gave me plenty of time to come up with some way-out ideas. I got the crazy notion of taking all four grandchildren to Hawaii. I shook it off but it kept coming back. I thought I'd have some fun with Barbra and see what her reaction would be. One night we were reading in the living room.

"Barb, what do you think of taking a trip to Hawaii with the four kids?"

Barbra kept on reading. In a few seconds she said, "Glen, you're getting a little out of it in your old age."

"I think it would be good for you and me and the kids would remember it for the rest of their lives."

"Glen, get real!"

Well, I had planted the seed in her head. *Now let's have some fun with Evie and Paul.*

"Barb, let's invite everyone here for a cookout before any cold weather sets in. The kids are growing up so fast and we really don't see very much of them."

"Fine with me, Glen," she said, as she kept on reading.

"How about this coming Saturday?"

"Fine."

I picked up the phone and called Evie and Owen answered. I invited them to a cookout that coming Saturday and he said that they would be here. I called Paul and Terry answered. I tendered the same invitation to her and she assured me that they would come.

"Well, Barb, it looks as though we will have a crowd here Saturday."

"That's fine, Glen—what? When?"

"This Saturday, hon, weren't you listening?"

"Glen, sometimes I think you have too much time to think. I'd love to see them, you know that, but Saturday is only two days away."

"Barb, plenty of time to get things ready."

"Well, now that you have set it up, I think it would be nice."

Now all I had to do is just put it to Evie and Owen, and to Paul and Terry. I didn't think they would care if we took the kids off their hands when school got out for the summer.

Barbra and I were busy Saturday morning getting things ready for the afternoon. Barbra made a couple of salads and I picked up the hot dogs, hamburgers, and buns. I also bought three deepdish apple pies.

Evie and Owen and the children came in the early afternoon and Paul and Terry came in about an hour later with the children.

It was a beautiful day and we were out on the patio. The kids were down in the recreation room. We had everything under control and were just sitting around talking. I couldn't wait to spring it on them about Hawaii.

"By the way, Mother and I are planning to go to Hawaii this summer."

"Oh, how wonderful," Evie said.

"I think it's great," said Owen.

"Dad, I think it's wonderful too," said Paul.

"Lucky you," said Terry.

Barbra just sat there not saying a word. She knew what I was leading to.

"We were wondering what you all would think if we took the four children with us?"

I watched the expressions on their faces. Evie and Owen looked at each other. Paul and Terry looked at each other. I glanced over at Barbra and she just stared at me.

"Well, what do you think?"

"Dad," said Paul, "tell me: Whose idea is this?"

"We talked about it."

"Glen, you came up with this idea all by yourself," said Barbra.

"Well, the more I think about it the more practical it seems. It will be a trip the kids will never forget."

"How long will the trip be, Dad?" asked Evie.

"Only about two weeks."

"Dad, are you serious?" Terry asked.

"I think it would be great. At any rate, give it some thought before you say anything to the kids. If you all decide that the kids can come, then I shall start making plans and reservations."

Now I was convinced that they all knew I was serious. They would have plenty of time to think it over. I didn't mention it again. I just wanted to plant the seed.

Paul and Owen came out and went out to the golf course. They wanted to work up an appetite. The two girls came out and we three men began to get things started. Paul and Owen were due to be coming in soon.

We had a wonderful time. Paul and Terry left in the early evening and Evie and Owen left shortly after.

"You sure do like to have your fun, fella," cracked Barbra.

"Well, I just gave them something to think about. I really do think it would be a wonderful trip."

I didn't know it but Barbra, Evie, and Terry were talking on the phone when I wasn't around. Barbra knew what they all thought of my crazy idea before I did.

"I think I ought to tell you, Glen, that Paul and Owen are leaving it up to Evie and Terry."

"Oh, how do you know that?"

"We've been on the phone, my dear."

"Barbra, really, what do you think?"

"I think that it's so far out that we might just have the time of our lives."

"What do the girls think about it?"

"They have both agreed to put it to the children."

"Really? Hawaii, here we come!"

By the following Saturday, everyone was excited. The kids were unanimous in their decision to go to Hawaii. I wasn't surprised at that. Kids are ready to go anywhere even if they don't know where it is.

I started making plans even though it was nearly six months away. I secured plane tickets and hotel reservations at the Reef Hotel right on Waikiki Beach. I was told that car reservations were not necessary. I wrote for brochures of all the main islands and Barbra and I read everything we could get our hands on about Hawaii. Barbra was really into it by now.

Barbra Ann phoned and asked, "Do they speak English in Hawaii?"

Arlene phoned and asked, "How long does the ferry take to go to Hawaii from California?" Apparently, she was looking at the map. The kids were wild with anticipation.

We survived the slow-moving months until school was out for the summer. Right after the July Fourth Home Day festivities we were ready to travel. Evie and Owen and Paul and Terry drove us down to Atlanta. After all our farewells we boarded our plane and we were off! The kids were experiencing their first commercial flight. We reached our altitude and Paul Glen asked, "Why do we have to fly so high?

I can't see anything."

"How fast are we going?" asked Owen.

The pilot's voice came over the loudspeaker. "Good morning, ladies and gentlemen. We have a beautiful day for flying and we are thirty-three thousand feet high and are now flying at six hundred and twenty miles air speed. The temperature outside of the window is forty-three degrees Fahrenheit—below zero." Barbra was leaning against the window. She moved away abruptly.

"I don't think I want to lean against that window."

Arlene was looking at a map of the United States taken from where every state was shown. Each state had a different color. She spoke to Barbra Ann: "Just by looking at the colors we should know where we are."

The flight was smooth and quite uneventful. We landed at Los Angeles and were told that we could leave the plane but be ready to board in one half-hour. We went out and stretched. One half-hour later we were getting ready to roll again. We were soon over the wide open Pacific ocean. The kids were really excited.

"I never saw so much water before," exclaimed Owen.

We saw the Big Island of Hawaii in the distance and soon we were flying by it. I heard Barbra Ann say, "Hey, we're not landing. I don't think the pilot saw it!"

"Hon, that's the island of Hawaii. Our island is about two hundred miles ahead of us." I assured her.

We had a good view of Waikiki Beach as we approached the airport. We were greeted by some pretty Hawaiian girls.

As we were waiting to gather our luggage, I heard over the loudspeaker, "Attention, please. Will Mr. Glen Fredericks please come to the information booth?" I wondered what that was all about.

We retrieved our bags and went to the information booth. There was a man with a black cap standing there.

"Are you Mr. Fredericks?"

"Yes, I am."

"I was sent here by the Reef Hotel to pick up you and your party."

"Well, thank you."

This was a courtesy of the hotel, a very nice gesture indeed. I was informed by the driver that all taxi cabs on the island are Cadillacs.

We checked in at the hotel and, after we got settled, we went exploring. We located the dining room and the barber shop. There were a few retail outlets. We went out to the pool and then to the beach and discovered a snack shop near the beach. We went out to Kalakaua Avenue and stopped at the International Marketplace. There were many stands selling trinkets and souvenirs. There was a restaurant and just beyond was an open-air shell where they put on shows at eight every night. We thought we'd keep that in mind. We went back to the hotel to freshen up and then went to dinner. In the evening we went out to the beach and sang songs with the beach boys. They are the boys who give instructions on surfing during the day. We went to our rooms for a good night's sleep.

The next morning we rented a car and toured the island. We took the highway to Nuuanu Pali lookout.

"What a beautiful view," cried Barbra Ann.

We got out of the car and the wind nearly blew us away.

"Hang onto your hat," I said.

The view was breathtaking but we didn't stay long. We took the boat ride to the Arizona Memorial at Pearl Harbor. Paul and Owen were a bit upset when they saw the list of names of the men who perished during the attack.

"Grandpa, do you remember this?"

"I certainly do, boys. Four months later and I was in the army."

We drove along Kalakaua Avenue and went past Diamond Head.

"Look, there's water coming out of the rocks!" exclaimed Arlene. The kids got a kick out of the blowhole. As the waves came in water rushed through a hole in the rocks and a small geyser resulted.

The next morning we flew to the island of Kauai, known as the Garden Isle. We rented a car and drove to the Waimea Canyon Lookout. We went to the rim but couldn't see anything because of the clouds and constant rain. Just east, at Waialeale, is considered to be the wettest spot on earth, with an annual rainfall of some four hundred and fifty inches.

"This is the Grand Canyon of Hawaii," I said.

Since we couldn't see much, it didn't mean too much. We saw fish ponds said to be built by small elflike men they called Menehunes, who inhabited the islands before the Polynesians came. For the first time we saw rice fields. We took a boat trip up the river to the fern grotto, a damp cave draped with lush green ferns, reached by a pleasant walk from the landing through quiet shaded woods.

"This is so different," said Arlene.

We spent the night at a lodge and the next morning we flew to the island of Maui. We spent the night at Wailuku. In the morning we drove to the top of ten-thousand-foot Mount Haleakala Crater.

On the way up Paul said, "Look, I never saw so many black rocks."

"Paul," I said, "those rocks came out of the mountain during the eruption many years ago. Four thousand feet of the mountain blew off."

"Look at the pretty plant," said Barbra Ann.

"That's the silver sword plant that grows only here and on the Big Island of Hawaii. It is never to be picked," I said. It pays to read up on this.

We reached the rim and Owen was the first to look down into the crater.

"My gosh, what a hole!"

"Yes, Owen, it's twenty-five hundred feet deep. Now you know where all those rocks came from," I said.

"Grandpa, what are those mountains way off in the distance?" Paul asked.

"Those are the two peaks on the island of Hawaii, Mauna Loa and Mauna Kea. We will be visiting that island pretty soon."

We then drove to the fairylike Ioa Needle Valley. The Needle rises twenty-two hundred feet above the valley floor.

"This area is known as the Yosemite of Hawaii," I said.

We drove around the north side of the island and saw many beautiful waterfalls and much lush foliage.

We went back to our hotel and the next day flew to the island of Hawaii. We drove along the south shore and came to the black sand beach.

"The sand is all black," said Barbra Ann.

"This is the result of the lava flows. This island is still being made and active with volcanoes," I said.

We drove to Kilauea Park and spent the night at Volcano House on the crater rim. We stood on the rim but had to back off because of the strong sulphur odor.

"That's awful," cried Arlene.

"That's sulphur; we'd better step back," I said. We drove along the west side of the island, called the Kona Coast, and then across the island where we saw cactus plants and cattle ranches.

"Just like Texas," quipped Paul.

We spent the night in Hilo and the next day we flew back to Oahu. We rented a car and drove out to a pineapple field. There was a cooler where we could buy a slice of fresh pineapple right at the field. It was delicious! We tried to eat poi, which is a starchy food something like potatoes.

"It looks like mud and tastes like mud," Owen said.

We attended an all-day event called a hukilau at Laie Beach. This was a fun day where one could help in net fishing. They haul in the net and take only enough fish for the day and free the rest. At noon they uncover the underground oven and the pig is well done from cooking overnight. They use a sauce on the meat and it melts in your mouth. There are all types of native fruits and plenty of food. Then there is an afternoon of entertainment.

The following night we went to the Hilton Hawaiian Village and enjoyed a luau. This was usually an indoor affair and was a feast for the visiting royalty. Many years ago each island had its own royal family. The hukilau was like a clambake for the common people.

At night we went to the show at the International Marketplace. It was a very nice show with beautiful Hawaiian music. Of course, the kids had to buy a few trinkets at the stands.

We spent our last day visiting the Bishop Museum and Punch Bowl Crater where many of our boys were laid to rest during the Second World War. We had fun at the Kodak show near Waikiki Beach. The hula is a very graceful event to see. It looks so easy. Every little movement of the hands and arms tells a story. They let anyone in the audience try to follow the Hawaiian girls. Barbra Ann and Arlene were doing very well, but Paul and Owen were a disaster!

It was time to pack up and get ready for the flight back home. I was tired and so was Barbra but we didn't want to show it. The kids were having the time of their lives. We spent a couple of hours in the late afternoon in the pool and in the evening we were on the beach and singing songs with the beach boys.

We had a beautiful flight back home. Evie and Owen and Paul and Terry were at the airport to greet us when we arrived at Atlanta. We had a wonderful time but we were so happy to be back home. We didn't cover everything but we did about what anyone could do in two weeks. We saw a good part of Hawaii and Barbra even admitted that it was a wonderful experience.

Barbra and I had the pleasure of bringing up our own children and now are a part of our grandchildren's lives. There is nothing more rewarding than to have a child on your lap and to tell them things they never knew before. Those innocent little eyes are glued to you with their full attention and they study you and your every expression. Such a wonderful experience!

The older we get the more we realize how short life really is. It goes by so fast. Now our children are with their children and really just starting out with their own careers. Life goes on—time marches on.

Here I lie in bed reflecting on the past. Barbra is sleeping. I often think of what would have become of me if Mr. Wells had not hired me or if I had stayed home. Would I have been happier? I doubt it. I thought of the love I received when I came to Douglas. *Thank you, Uncle Ben and Aunt Martha. Thank you for the love you gave me—the greatest gift of all. Thank you for my tender redemption. Thank you, Lord.*

I slept.

The computer had

Kade straightened and laid his hands solidly on her shoulders, turning her to face him. “Give it a rest. Let’s go back upstairs. I’ve stashed some Klinian ale for a special occasion.” He smiled crookedly. “Tonight looks like a good one to me.”

He felt her tremble at the simple physical contact. Just as before, Kade detected conflicting signals emanating from her. But she stepped back, averting her face. “You ought to be concerned, Kade. This is your ship.” Her eyes met his, sparkling with intensity. “Aren’t you worried in the least? What happened to the missing 45 kilos?”

Kade barely heard her. Something shiny in her case drew his attention. He slipped his hand around it and pulled it out. “Mariss,” he replied distractedly. “I had other things on my mind before we blasted off. If the luggage weighed right at the Nexus, I admit I probably...screwed up.” His voice fell as he held up the shiny piece of clothing. He whistled low. The skimpy item was completely see-through, a filmy nothing of creamy lingerie designed to tempt and tantalize. He could imagine how it would hug a woman’s body, Mariss’ body, outlining her curves, slipping between her thighs to fasten in back, revealing... everything.

“Put that down!”

Mariss yanked at it, but Kade kept a firm grip on it. He swung around to avoid her outstretched hands. “You been wearing things like this under your flightsuit?” he asked, cocking an eyebrow at her speculatively. She was fuming, and damned pretty while doing it, too.

“It’s none of your business, you unmannerly ingrate. But if you must know, I plan to wear that on my honeymoon.”

A tide of anger swept over Kade. “With that dolt Adrian? He probably won’t know what to do with it, or with you *in* it.”

***

“Absolutely phenomenal! This is, without a doubt, one of the best stories I’ve read and I’m anxiously awaiting Tracy Cozzens’ next one.” —*Lover’s Knot Magazine*

For my husband Steve, with love.

Other Books by
Tracy Cozzens

ARABIAN KNIGHT

ISBN: 1-893896-15-3

One Perfect Mate

***

Tracy Cozzens

ImaJinn
Books

ONE PERFECT MATE

Published by ImaJinn Books, a division of ImaJinn

ISBN: 1-893896-53-6

10 9 8 7 6 5 4 3 2 1

PUBLISHER'S NOTE:
This book is a work of fiction. Names, characters, places and incidents are products of the author's imagination or are used fictitiously. Any resemblance to actual events or locales or persons, living or dead, is entirely coincidental.

This book was previously published as an electronic book through Hardshell Word Factory.

Cover design by Patricia Lazarus

ImaJinn Books, a division of ImaJinn
P.O. Box 162, Hickory Corners, MI 49060-0162
Toll Free: 1-877-625-3592
http://www.imajinnbooks.com

ONE

Nexus Spaceport

"What do you mean, he was promoted over me?"

The furious male voice behind her startled Mariss. She forced herself not to turn around in her seat and stare. Another man responded, his tone conciliatory, but Mariss couldn't catch the words. Their conversation only partially drowned out the newscast coming from the earpiece attached to her cyber-unit.

The two men had stopped near her bank of seats in the congested spaceport, apparently oblivious to the fact one was occupied. From the corner of her eye, Mariss saw their backs were turned to her. She caught flashes of the familiar taupe uniform of Quantum Craftlines.

Mariss tried to ignore the uniformed men. She kept her eyes pinned to the screen of her cyber-unit, open on her lap. The spinning Quantum logo dissolved to a newscaster with chiseled features.

But her concentration was shot. She still wasn't comfortable with space travel, even after her week-long stay aboard the massive starcruiser from Earth. If trouble was coming, she wanted to know what form it was going to take. As unobtrusively as possible, she flicked off her earpiece so she could eavesdrop.

"I'm sorry, but they felt Lindenfeld was more qualified." It was the calmer voice.

The irate words of the first man almost cut him off. "Qualified? *Lindenfeld?* How many hours does he have on me? How many spacecraft is he checked out on?"

The other man didn't reply immediately. "Well, he has

fewer hours, but his scores are out of this world. Almost top rate."

"He has *fewer* hours? You're telling me he has fewer hours, and he moves up over me?"

"Kade, I'm sorry, but your record—the other jockeys don't have that hanging over their heads. Granted, it was years ago. And granted, the others aren't as good as you. No other pilot can touch your scores—even *they* know it. But the other guys are clean. Squeaky clean. Quantum has its reputation to consider—"

The first man let loose with a string of colorful epithets about narrow-minded, short-sighted Quantum management.

The other man grew defensive. "You haven't helped things, Kade. That incident last month on Barron Outpost, for instance, cost you months—no, years—of good will. They're watching you closely."

Mariss heard a hollow laugh. "So what else is new?"

"This time it's serious. Consider this fair warning, my friend. Tread carefully. By the book. Your career's at stake. If Quantum blacklists you, nobody will touch you."

"My career's at stake? What career?" Mariss caught a glimpse of a hand thrown wide in exasperation. "Outback runs to nowhere for five solid years—"

"At least it pays steady. Remember where you were before Quantum agreed to take a chance on you. Don't screw it up. Okay, buddy?"

His request elicited a noncommittal grunt.

"Maybe next time, Kade, it'll be your turn. Now, fly easy."

Left alone, the pilot indulged in another bout of swearing before he stormed into the crowd. Mariss looked after him, but only caught a glimpse of a broad back and dark hair.

If this bitter, frustrated man were to be piloting *her* ship, she'd prefer to wait for the next flight, even if it took weeks. But she knew it wasn't likely. Flights were leaving all the time. The chances *that* particular pilot would end up on her ship were remote, thank the Maker.

She tapped the toggle on her earpiece, and the sound returned. The announcer was giving an update on Earth economy in light of a new series of extra-terrestrial trade agreements. Footage from Earth followed.

*Earth...*Where she had lived all her life. Now so unimaginably distant as to be unreal.

Mariss lost interest in the newscast. She disconnected her cyber-unit from the armrest of her seat and closed it with a snap.

A fellow traveler settled himself in the seat on her left. Gray-haired, austere, the man opened a plasti-print magazine on his lap. He obviously had no interest in casual conversation. Mariss didn't attempt any.

Instead, she watched the passengers milling around her. The Nexus was the largest spaceport in the galaxy—centrally located, a constant hive of arriving passengers and departing ships. Over the speakers came the reassuring purr of a female announcer's voice, providing departure times, gates, delays.

As she waited, Mariss scanned the crowd, intent on any men in Quantum uniforms. She speculated about each, wondering if he were one of the men she had overheard—particularly the pilot who'd been so irate.

Growing more anxious about the upcoming flight as time passed, her attention strayed to the gate on her left, which led to the change rooms and the docking bay for her ship.

Mariss had been held up at the Nexus for several days waiting for the second leg of her journey. This morning, she had left her sleeping room for the staging area four hours early—just in case. Perhaps she could have slept in a little, taken time for breakfast. But another ship wouldn't be departing for Fredon Outpost for weeks. She reminded herself that many people—one special man in particular—found punctuality and careful planning to be a virtue.

After a while, the gray-haired traveler beside her stood and disappeared into the crowd, intent on his own schedule.

The call for her flight finally came. At the entrance to the gate, an attendant ushered her down the hall into a change room. There, a second attendant helped her and about twenty other Quantum passengers select the correct size flightsuit in one of three colors designed to calm: royal blue, sea green, or turquoise.

Mariss chose royal blue to compliment her olive complexion and dressed quickly. Her own white and grey pantsuit was tagged along with other passengers' land clothes, to be redistributed at their various destinations. Mariss touched the soft, sturdy fabric of her flightsuit. The suit gave her perfect insulation. Not only that, it was designed to be cleaned in the onboard laundry. For Quantum, it provided other benefits. In the early days of commercial spaceflight, passengers had been involved in accidents when flowing robes and loose jewelry hung up on equipment, or tight skirts made quick evacuation difficult. More than a few had blamed their injuries on Quantum.

Mariss didn't mind the limited wardrobe. She liked the practicality of the unisex suit.

She followed the attendant's directions and the glowing signs through a narrow, enclosed walkway leading to the docking bays. At a juncture in the corridor, most of the passengers turned left. Mariss saw the lighted sign for Fredon Outpost, and headed right.

At the end of the corridor, no one was waiting to help her board. Mariss found this odd. She checked her boarding pass twice, then tentatively stepped over the threshold into the heart of the ship.

Quantum prided itself on its comfort. The ship's interior was designed to hide the fact it was made of nuts and bolts and metal alloys. Bright lights illuminated walls padded in a leather-like material in unobtrusive tan and cream shades. Here and there, hints of the alloy hull showed through. The ship designers had tried hard, but there was no mistaking this was a ship—and a small, cramped one at that.

The cockpit to her left was sealed off from view by a pneumatic door. On her right was the passenger cabin—with only seven seats. This ship was a puddle-jumper compared to the massive starcruiser which had brought her to the Nexus from Earth.

Mariss selected the single window seat, hoping to see more than she had on leaving Earth in the company of three hundred other passengers. Another passenger appeared, a small, balding Oriental man with a sour expression, garbed in sea green. Mariss introduced herself. The man gave her a perfunctory nod before turning his back on her. He began stowing his gear in the bin above a seat across the aisle.

Mariss sighed. The man obviously had no interest in conversation, despite the fact they would be stuck together in this tin can for ten days. She pulled open a fold-out table between her seat and the two across from her and set her cyber-unit on it. She soon became engrossed in her latest project—cross-referencing the DNA of non-Earth plant species.

A middle-aged, ebony-skinned couple entered, whispering together as if afraid too much noise would call attention to themselves. Mariss glanced up and smiled at them. They introduced themselves as the Hudsons, traveling to meet their son at his mining station on Fredon Outpost. "This is only our second spaceflight," the man said, as if apologizing.

"Mine, too," Mariss said.

But Mr. Hudson wasn't listening. His attention was given to assuaging his wife's fears about the safety of the small ship.

"We'll be in here ten days, Donald," she said. "Ten! It's so tiny! I don't know how Robert does it. I'll be claustrophobic within an hour."

"Don't forget your pills, Betta. The doctor said—"

"I know what the doctor said. But it won't make this tiny ship any larger, will it?"

Mariss tuned out the woman's complaints and returned to her analysis. She hoped the doctor's pills worked for the lady, or this could become a tedious flight indeed.

"This seat's not taken, is it?"

Mariss glanced up to see a brassy woman with lots of make-up and flaming red hair cut in the latest fashion—shaved on one side and piled on the left side of her head in a puffed cushion. Mariss thought the style made the wearer look lopsided, but then this fashion-conscious lady probably thought Mariss' own simple, braided knot lacked flair.

"No, you're welcome to it. I'm Mariss Sakari." She raised her hand in the customary non-contact, palm-out greeting, and the woman responded in kind.

"Good to know you. Call me Lorena." She slipped her generous hips into the seat across from Mariss as if it were embracing her. "I would have been here sooner, but I was...held up." She smiled, as if to herself. "A tight connection, you know."

Mariss nodded. "That would make it hard, in this huge spaceport."

Lorena's eyes widened and she leaned forward. "You have custom eyes, don't you?"

Mariss blinked her genetically enhanced violet-blue eyes and nodded. Most people weren't so blatant in pointing out the obvious. And it *was* obvious she was a child of affluence. She wished it weren't, particularly since she was now on her own. Mariss should have been born with brown eyes, with her East Indian and Polynesian heritage. Her parents had paid generously for her unexpected eye color while she was in utero. It had been a fad then. Now it just made people assume things about her.

"*Your* type doesn't usually visit backwaters like Fredon Outpost. Why are you headed there?"

"Actually, I'm not. I'm going beyond, to a planet called Elysia. It's a fairly new colony, but they've done wonders there in a very short time."

"Beyond? Seriously?" Lorena's jaw dropped. "You're not stopping at Fredon?"

"No."

"Really." Lorena's brow creased, and she chewed her lip.

Mariss thought she looked unduly concerned by the news. Or perhaps worried. "I'll be safe. It's very civilized, just distant."

Lorena's laugh was overly bright. "Well, of course it is. I wouldn't expect a rich man's daughter to rough it like us common folk. It's just that I thought Fredon was the only stop on this flight..." She shook her head, then changed the subject. "Gawd, I'll be spending this trip with a rich bi—" She bit back her words and smiled. "*Lady.* Some people have all the luck."

Mariss sighed, irritated at the woman's assumptions. "Not necessarily."

Lorena smirked. "What? Daddy wouldn't buy you the latest-model land cruiser?"

"I never wanted one."

"Well, I doubt you wanted for much of anything," Lorena said.

Mariss sighed as Lorena's words triggered a wealth of painful memories—about wants, and unmet needs. Yes, her family had been rich. Perhaps that's why she didn't value material possessions now. Instead, she valued more profound things, things a person couldn't buy. Deeply romantic, she had always imagined spending her life with her one true mate—living together companionably, raising a family. But twice she had believed she had found him, and twice she had been terribly wrong.

Now, she was about to begin a new life with husband number three, and she was only twenty-seven. But Adrian Young would be *it.* The one. After all, the Iridion Corporation all but guaranteed their matches. As a scientist, she had great faith in their methods. She would never again trust her heart with something so important.

While they waited for departure, Mariss learned that Lorena was a clothing saleswoman who specialized in bringing the latest trends to fashion-starved places. "Outback runs can be tedious for the uninitiated. But I usually manage to find *special* compensation." She grinned.

"Outback runs!" Mariss had heard that phrase for the first time just an hour ago.

As if on cue, the same voice which had been swearing about outback runs behind her in the staging area flowed through the speakers.

"Good morning, folks. This is your captain. We'll be taking off shortly, so get your gear stowed and settle in."

"Speaking of compensation," Lorena murmured with a wicked smile.

The pilot continued, "I'll try to make this as painless as possible for all of us. You all come from connecting flights, so you know the routine. But, in case you're experiencing temporary amnesia, here goes."

The pilot had Mariss' full attention now. She would bet everything she owned—now stowed aboard this ship—that he was not following the approved Quantum script. She glanced at Lorena whose smile bore a hint of anticipation which Mariss could read quite well.

"I assume you're all wearing regulation flightsuits. Of course you are," he said patronizingly. "You each have a storage bin above your seat, numbered correspondingly. Keep your stuff in your own bin. We don't need fights over storage space while we're en route."

Mariss stood to double-check her overhead bin. It contained a bag with her toiletries and not much else. She began to close it.

"Miss? Now's the time to place that pert little fanny squarely in your seat. You can play with your things once we hit interspace."

Mariss' head shot up. She looked around for the camera, but couldn't locate it. The other passengers reacted to the chastisement by looking away from her, as if embarrassed she'd been called on the carpet. Mariss slammed the overhead bin and sat down, irritation surging through her.

The pilot continued, relentless. "Trust me, you'll be glad you're in your seat—with the seatbelt fastened—when we hit lightspeed." Mariss made a face as she buckled her belt, and Lorena laughed.

"Those little tables in front of you—" Mariss glanced at the fold-out shelf in front of her.

"Yeah, that one, miss. Put it away. They're for *after* we're spacebound. And that electronic gizmo there. Turn it off and keep it off until we're in interspace, or you'll screw up my scopes and we'll smash into the side of the spaceport. In fact, why not put it in the overhead bin?"

Mariss closed her cyber-unit and rose. Her movements were fast and furious as she reopened the bin and shoved the computer inside. This time she slammed the bin door even harder. Why the pilot had chosen to pick on her was beyond her. Once they were in stable flight, he would be on his way back here, and she would let him know personally what she thought of his manners.

"Okay, now that we've gotten *that* taken care of, listen up. See those bright blue doors? There are two fore—behind the cockpit—and two aft, past the galley and sleeping cabin." The passengers glanced around to locate the doors. "If we have to abandon ship, run for 'em. They lead to life pods. The doors open automatically. The pods hold two passengers each. There are five of you and one of me on this flight, so there's plenty of space and no reason to panic. But don't stop to collect any of your...gizmos if something happens."

He was talking about her again, Mariss thought. And his pre-flight instructions left a lot to be desired. Mrs. Hudson looked like she was going to pass out.

"Of course, if we *do* hit trouble anywhere in the vast reaches of intersystem space, well, we'll just have to hang on and hope the distress signals sent from the lifepods are picked up by a passing ship. About one chance in a billion."

"By the Maker, did he really say that?" Even Lorena was shocked. Then she shrugged. "Well, he *is* honest, at any rate. Nice quality, don't you think?"

The voice continued, "But don't lose sleep, boys and girls. I haven't lost a ship yet—at least, not since my academy days. If you want the gory details about me, it's all in the cabin databank. Well, maybe not *all*."

"Pilots," Mariss grumbled.

"I wonder if he's good-looking," Lorena said.

"Arrogant." Mariss glanced at the computer panel mounted on the cabin's front wall, glowing with lights and indicators. She had to admit she was curious, if only to satisfy herself that he was qualified. He held their lives in his hands, after all. But she wasn't about to reveal her curiosity to anyone.

"We'll be trapped in here together for ten days en route to Fredon Outpost, and one of you is going beyond that to Elysia," the pilot continued. "If you all cooperate, follow the rules, and don't give me any grief, we'll get along fine."

"That can't possibly be part of the regular spiel," Mr.

Hudson said, as if realizing for the first time that their pilot had broken from the Quantum script.

"That reminds me," the pilot said. "I had some trouble with the luggage. Passenger M. Sakari." He hesitated over the name. "Whichever one you are, you're way overweight. Seriously overweight. If this was a full flight, you would have grounded us. But, since we have no sixth or seventh passenger, I was able to accommodate your...stuff."

"You're in trouble now," Lorena said, a smile playing over her red lips.

Mariss slumped into her seat, fuming at the rebuke. The pilot may not know who she was—yet—but he was going to find out.

"That's all for now. Stay calm. We leave in just a few minutes. We're next in line—after two starcruisers, three cargo haulers and an 88-B Class passenger ship. Oh. And have a pleasant flight."

Mariss didn't miss the barely veiled sarcasm in his voice. This was definitely a man with a chip on his shoulder. "Do you think he's...safe?" she asked Lorena.

"Safe?" Lorena shrugged. "Who wants safe?" Her painted lips turned up suggestively.

"No, I mean the way he talks."

"Oh. You'd rather hear all the soft, meaningless reassurances they usually dish out, wouldn't you?"

"Not really, but the other pilots are so much more professional."

"On the big cruisers."

"Yes."

Lorena grinned. "Welcome to the outback run."

TWO

It took far too long for the ship to receive clearance to depart the Nexus. With nothing to do but wait, Mariss spent the time replaying the pilot's rude comments in her mind. She was trying to calm down, but finding it difficult.

Not long after the ship blasted through the light barrier into interspace, the cockpit door swooshed open and the captain made his appearance. Silence fell as passengers and captain eyed each other.

"I'm Captain Kadin Land. Yeah, I've heard all the jokes about a guy named Land preferring space to terra firma. And I can *land* the craft just fine." His eyes flicked past Mariss and continued around the room. "If you want to be friendly on this trip, you can call me Kade." His lips curled up in a humorless smile. With his sharp features and dark coloring, he looked almost sinister.

Around Mariss, the passengers stayed as quiet as schoolchildren called before the principal. He propped his hands on his hips. "For the next ten days, listen to me and do as I say. Sorry to sound so blunt, but this isn't a picnic. It's interstellar space travel. Mostly, that involves staying out of my way and letting me do my job. This ship isn't top-of-the-line, and it isn't the easiest thing to pilot. I have a few things to tell you about our flight. But before we go any further—"

He strode past them toward the back of the cabin. He was shorter than Mariss expected, only half a head taller than herself. His nose was prominent, aquiline. Would probably be considered large. Yet a square chin and broad cheekbones gave his features balance. He wasn't what Mariss would call handsome...dramatic, perhaps. Even compelling in a rough-hewn sort of way...

Mariss forced herself not to stare as he passed by her seat. “He’s insufferable,” she whispered to Lorena, irritated at her reaction to him.

“But would you look at that view,” Lorena said.

Mariss glanced toward the port window, but saw only blackness. That was a drawback of interspace travel. There was no view.

Lorena nudged her in the side, and Mariss followed her gaze to the captain. His back turned, he was adjusting a set of indicators along the partial wall separating the galley from the passenger cabin.

Mariss couldn’t help herself. Like Lorena, she took a good look at the man who had harassed her over the speakers. He was wearing the Quantum Craftlines official uniform—taupe slacks and short jacket, pinstriped with blue and gold. His slacks were tucked into calf-high boots of the same color. Mariss’ eyes traveled from his boots up his legs to his narrow buttocks and up his broad back. His build was compact, powerful. He made Mariss uncomfortable. His tense expression gave him a hard look, as if he’d experienced more than his share of difficulties. Worse, she found herself intrigued, which she had no business being.

Mariss wanted to be nowhere near trouble. She’d had a lifetime’s worth already. She only wanted passage to Elysia, and her uncomplicated, assured future.

A moment later, soft, calming music flowed through the speakers. At the port window, the black disappeared, replaced by a soothing mix of aqua-green, swirling with blues and hints of purples. Quantum did as much as it could to encourage its passengers to remain calm during long spaceflights. The effect made Mariss feel she was traveling underwater, instead of in the vastness of space at an incalculable speed beyond customary physics and experience. The ship and its passengers existed, yet they didn’t—not in any traditional sense.

Her eyes flicked to Lorena. Perhaps it wasn’t surprising so many passengers sought spaceflight liaisons. The travelers were so far removed from the real world, what was to prevent them? Besides, it made the time pass so much quicker.

Not that Mariss had any personal experience with spaceflight affairs, of course. There had been a man on the starcruiser flight who had made his interest plain. But Mariss was spoken for. Only fifteen more days, and she would meet her new husband. At that moment, however, she couldn't conjure up memory of Adrian's hologram. Not with Captain Kade Land standing next to her chair, staring down at her.

"What?" Mariss half expected she had done something wrong again.

A smile curled Kade's lips. "I asked your name."

Not wanting to be in a submissive position, Mariss rose—and found herself standing far too close to him. He gazed down at her, his dark eyes capturing hers. She backed into the aisle. "Mariss."

"Mariss what?"

Mariss gritted her teeth. "Sakari."

"*You're* M. Sakari? Owner of the overweight luggage?"

Mariss lifted her chin. "I am."

His eyes flicked over her severe hairstyle and minimal makeup. "Funny, I didn't take you for the clotheshorse type. What'd you pack? More gizmos?"

"The contents of my luggage is no concern of yours. As far as I am aware, Quantum has no right to pry into my possessions, as long as they don't contain any contraband. And they don't." She took a deep breath and braced herself for confrontation. "By the way, your...talk...to us over the speakers was rude and unprofessional."

"So?"

His dismissive reaction confused Mariss. "I thought—I thought you should know. I didn't appreciate it."

"I see. Well, I guess I've been enlightened, M. Sakari."

Despite his words, Mariss knew full well he hadn't been. "Good," she said, tilting her chin defiantly.

"M. Sakari..." He edged closer. Mariss held her ground as he slipped his mouth beside her ear, his voice dropping conspiratorially. "Do us all a favor and bring your petty complaints to me in private from now on. Public criticism of your captain will needlessly distress the other passengers. Got it?" Kade's voice was ice-edged, even though he maintained his pleasant smile.

"I got it, Captain," Mariss said through stiff lips.

He nodded and turned to Lorena, who was standing on his other side. Mariss tried not to watch as Lorena practically fell on him in her excitement to have his attention.

The voluptuous redhead was several inches taller than Kade. He crossed his arms and stared at her as she began talking about herself. Kade cut her short. "Nice to meet you. All of you. Now, follow me."

Kade led them through the door to the galley, past the tables into the sleeping compartment. On both sides, white sleeping capsules rested along the walls in two tiers, four on one side, three on the other. A storage bin took up the eighth space. Kade turned at the far end to face them. "Now, listen up."

The passengers muted their conversation. Five pairs of eyes turned to the man who held their lives in his hands. "I serve three meals a day, at 0800, 1300 and 1800. If you miss one, you're welcome to raid the leftovers in the galley, but stay out of the stores set aside for each day's meals."

Kade gestured toward a recessed doorway at the rear of the cabin. "That's the lavatory, complete with a shower and dryer unit. Instructions for its use are inside the door. On this flight, water will be rationed."

"Rationed! Don't you recycle it?" Mr. Hudson asked.

"The ship has recycling units, but I can't vouch for their trustworthiness," Kade said. "You'll still have plenty of water. You're each allowed one five-minute shower a day. Identify yourself to the onboard computer before the shower starts, so anything you don't use will be credited to you. So if, like passenger M. Sakari here, you have a...generous amount of hair," he gazed at Mariss, his lips tilted slightly in a teasing smile, "don't wash it every day unless you can do it quickly. Let your credit pile up some. And it might not hurt to have someone help you wash it—to make it go faster."

"Someone like you, I suppose," Mariss shot back.

Kade grinned, his gaze warming considerably. Mariss felt it in her body like a jolt of electricity. "I do have some experience along those lines, M. Sakari, if that's a request. Though it *is* outside of my regular duties as your captain. Which somehow reminds me to discuss our sleeping arrangements."

He rested his palm on the nearest capsule. "The two men—you, Mr. Hudson, and you, Mr. Lee—have been assigned to top sleeping berths, the three women to bottom berths." He glanced toward each of the women. "That way you have better access to the lavatory and don't have to climb up and down." His voice became a notch less professional as his gaze landed right on Mariss. "Of course, you can switch. If a woman prefers to be on top, I have no complaints."

Mariss narrowed her eyes, but his only response was a crooked smile.

"I'm glad to hear that," Lorena purred, drawing Kade's attention. Kade cocked an eyebrow at her, but said nothing in reply. From what Mariss knew of Lorena's willingness and Kade's character—or lack thereof—his reticence with the redhead was unexpected.

Mariss wished he hadn't singled her out for his special attention. But that was obviously the direction his mind was going. The last thing she needed was a romantic entanglement in space. Even if she had wanted to seek one out, she would have nothing to do with this jaded space jockey. She merely had to make that plain to him.

Her chance to set him straight came all too soon. The passengers were seated around the two tables awaiting dinner while Kade prepared it in the galley. The floor lights had gradually dimmed as the overhead lights increased in brightness, giving the passengers the sense that evening had fallen in the artificial confines of the spaceship.

The captain's voice came through the speakers. "Passenger M. Sakari? Would you come into the galley a moment?"

With the others' eyes on her, Mariss didn't feel she could politely refuse. She entered the white and steel kitchen, and the door slid into place behind her. Kade had taken the top off a counter unit, and his hands were deep in its guts. "What is it?"

"What do you know about coffee?"

"Making it or drinking it?"

"Making it, of course. This unit's jammed."

"Do I look like a mechanic?"

Naturally, Kade took his time deciding. He straightened slowly and cocked his hip against the counter. His gaze traveled over her body so thoroughly, Mariss felt completely undressed by the time he was through. And she was only wearing the same flightsuit everyone else was wearing. She didn't consider her body particularly special. She was slender, with gentle curves. Voluptuous women like Lorena were built for looks like Kade was giving her.

Nor was her hair anything out of the ordinary. Long, straight and black, she could do little with it except braid it and bind it and knot it out of the way.

Mariss tried to feel deeply insulted at his blatant interest, but couldn't quite manage it. She reminded herself that he was the captain, and supposed to be behaving in a professional manner. He was impudent and out-of-line, and if he continued to bother her, she would tell Quantum about it the minute they landed at Fredon Outpost.

"You look like someone who can follow simple directions. Take this handle—" He passed one end of a wrench-like gizmo to her. The other end was buried inside the unit. "Don't let go until I say." With a stubby wand, he bent over the unit. Mariss felt like a nurse assisting a doctor.

"Hold it more to the left. That's it."

Mariss sighed. "You should have asked Lorena to help. *She* likes you."

Kade snorted. "She likes notches on her belt."

"What do you mean by that?"

"She's a pilot groupie."

"A what?"

"Pilot groupie. She wants anything in a uniform." His eyes flicked up to meet hers, uncomfortably close. "Even me."

Was that a sign of humility? False modesty, more like.

She could just hear him waiting for her to reassure him how desirable he was, and then, with *that* established—

Mariss pointedly looked away, and Kade returned to his soldering. "I want you—"

Startled, Mariss dropped the tool.

"Damn! I lost it." Kade straightened. "I told you to hold on." He retrieved the tool from the floor and shoved it at her. "Try harder this time."

"If you hadn't said what you did—"

"What did I say?" Hand on his hip, he stared at her, clearly uncomprehending.

Mariss wasn't about to repeat it. She met his gaze coolly.

Kade shrugged and glanced away. "I was going to ask you to help me on this flight. Quantum's cut back on flight attendants and co-pilots, particularly for outback flights like this one. One less Quantum body means one more passenger and less pay to dish out. So I do all three jobs. Except some jobs, like this one, require two pairs of hands. So I'm electing you. Got a problem with that?"

"Why me?"

"Who else is there?"

"Mr. or Mrs. Hudson."

"Uh-uh. She's semi-hysterical, and he'll be spending all his time coddling her. Mr. Lee is sour and unpleasant. Lorena would be jumping my bones every chance she got. If I had asked *her* in here—well, everyone would have to wait quite a while for dinner." His arrogant smirk returned.

"That's disgusting. That close to our *food?*"

"Don't worry, I've been inoculated." A buzzer shrilled. Kade popped open an oven door and removed a large tray with six covered dinners. He set it on the counter. "No dinner until you help me with this unit."

"I can do without the coffee."

"Well, I can't." His brow creased in concentration as he worked over the machine. "Bastards gave me a half-assed ship," he muttered. "I told them to give it the full systems check, even on non-essential systems. Hasn't happened yet. Minimal maintenance is all they deem necessary on this run.

I can't wait to see what else is going to break."

"The ship's not safe?" Mariss accepted the handle of the tool again.

"It's safe enough. If not, I'll make it safe."

Mariss waited silently, praying nothing serious would go wrong. A moment later, Kade sighed in triumph. He replaced the cover and tapped codes on a nearby panel. The machine purred to life. "Thanks, Mariss."

His friendly tone and use of her first name caught her off-guard. She handed him the tool. "All right, Captain, I'll help you. To make our flight more bearable. But this is strictly business. I have no interest in spaceflight bed jumping, just so you know. And you have to treat me professionally. No teasing."

"Wouldn't think of it." He said this casually. But when she turned to leave, she heard him gruffly add, "Just don't tease *me*, woman."

Dinner wasn't bad, for flight food. Pasta and salad and fruit. A typical, bland spacers' meal. Once Kade cleared the dishes, the married couple retired to their berths, already exhausted from the rigors of space travel. Mr. Lee stayed at the table, reading business reports on his own cyber-unit.

Mariss retrieved her unit from her overhead bin and set it on the fold-out table. She wanted a few minutes alone to concentrate—not on her botanical data, but on her future.

She pulled up the file on Adrian Young. His face filled her screen—blond, chiseled features, square chin, electric blue eyes over a perfectly proportioned nose. Adrian Young, a botanist just as she was. His emphasis was in landscape engineering. He had worked wonders at the Colony on Elysia, turning it into a paradise, according to his file.

"Who's the hunk?"

Lorena was hanging over her shoulder. Kade was passing through on his way to the cockpit. For Mariss, the timing couldn't be more perfect. She spoke clearly, firmly. "He's my husband."

From the corner of her eye, Mariss saw Kade's steps falter. He turned around and stared at her.

Lorena spoke first. "You're married? To that man?" She sounded awestruck.

Kade also reacted. "You're *married?*" He crossed toward her and looked at the computer screen. His face turned stony.

"Not yet, but I will be. I'm on my way to be with him."

"So you're *not* married. Yet," Kade said.

"Technically, no, but—"

"What's he like?" Lorena prodded. She settled herself on the arm of Mariss' seat. Mariss expected that Lorena's excitement had more to do with the fact Mariss wasn't competition for the captain's attention than any interest in her personal life.

Mariss shrugged. "He's wonderful. He's in my field. He's healthy, good-looking, as you can see, and he's anxious to make a commitment."

"Doesn't sound real. Where'd you find him?" Lorena asked.

Mariss hesitated. "Well, *I* didn't. The CMSI did."

"The what?" Lorena looked mystified.

Kade started to chuckle. Mariss glared at him defiantly. "She means a computer picked him for her," he explained.

"That's right, the Computer Mating Service of Iridion. It helps people find their perfect mates."

This statement drew a full-fledged laugh from Kade. Mariss bristled. "It's nothing to laugh at, Captain Land. The program is rigorously controlled. They're very careful who they accept. And they have a 98 percent success rate for matings that last beyond five years."

Lorena asked, "You mean you give the computer information about yourself, and they'll find someone for you?"

"Yes. I gave them my characteristics, preferences, a psychological profile, a hologram of myself. And they gave me Adrian." Conscious that Kade was listening closely, Mariss said, "Would you like to see his hologram?"

"No," Kade said.

"Sure," Lorena said.

Mariss chose to listen to Lorena. She plugged a disk into the databank on the cabin's wall and adjusted a few readings.

In a moment, Adrian formed in the cabin, two meters of excellent male specimen. His image sparkled with the unnatural light of the hologram, revealing every particle of his towering, athletic perfection. He was clad in a blue jumpsuit which hugged his muscled frame like a second skin. His hair was honey blond, his skin tanned, golden and smooth. His flawless white teeth sparkled.

He smiled broadly and looked right at Mariss, as if he knew where she was positioned in the cabin. "Greetings, Mariss." His voice was deep, intimate. Mariss loved the sound of her name on his lips. "I have just received word you are the woman I have been waiting for. I have seen your hologram, as you have mine. Your data matches mine in every facet. We are ideally suited. I can't begin to tell you how pleased and excited I am to be making this very special connection with you. I have longed for such a perfect meshing of lives, dreams and souls as you and I will experience together.

"Since learning the identity of my mate, I have dreamed of you nightly. You have lived in my heart all of my life. Soon, you will be beside me, in the flesh, and we will begin our lives together in the Colony. I am counting the nanoseconds until we meet. I give all my love to you, Mariss Sakari." The hologram ended and Adrian vanished. But his impassioned words seemed to linger in the air.

Lorena sighed. "Gawd, I have *got* to sign myself up for this program."

Mariss found it difficult to reorient herself to the cabin around her. Her dreams were with Adrian, in the Colony. "It's not easy to be accepted into the program," she finally said. "The cost of these matches is extremely high for off-worlders, but CMSI waives the fee under certain circumstances."

"Like what?" Lorena asked.

Mariss noticed Kade was silent, for once. He stood rocklike against the bulkhead wall, his arms crossed over his chest, his face unreadable.

"You have to pass a series of screening tests, *and* be matched to a Colony resident who's seeking a mate. Adrian was waiting for his perfect mate when I signed up, so when we were matched, he paid my fee. Maybe they have a match for you, too, Lorena. But you have to be willing to move to the Colony on Elysia. That's where Adrian is."

"Ugh, you can forget that!" Lorena said. "That's way too confining for someone like me."

Kade finally spoke, his tone skeptical. "They force you to live there, huh? Now, why would that be?"

"They aren't forcing me. Besides, it won't be any hardship. Watch."

Mariss plugged in a second hologram. This one wasn't life-sized. It showed a panorama of the Colony, a serenely laid-out collection of soft white buildings amid lush greenery. Aerial walkways connected the taller buildings, but there were few of these. Most of the buildings were single-story, set amid park-like plantings and meandering pathways. In the distance, a blue globe dominated the skyline. The Colony appeared spacious, clean, and ultra modern, but was softened by a tropical setting and a clear blue sky above.

"Adrian designed much of the grounds," Mariss said with pride.

The narration began. "The Colony on Elysia was created for your comfort. Every aspect of living a full life was taken into account in its creation." The hologram showed people working out-of-doors and in well-equipped offices, playing games and sports, indulging in massages. Children were being educated in a state-of-the-art classroom as the narrator spoke in an upbeat voice about the Colony's dedication to providing a quality atmosphere for raising families.

The view shifted to a lush, exotic garden complete with waterfalls, where a beautiful couple walked hand-in-hand. The woman wore a short tunic, revealing long, shapely legs. Her unbound auburn hair cascaded over her shoulders. The man was dressed in a similar tunic, belted at the waist, with leather sandals on his feet. He was in perfect physical shape, his bare arms and legs well-muscled. "I thought these were just a couple of models for this promotional advertisement, but Adrian looks even better than him." Mariss couldn't keep the pride from her voice.

The man and woman faced each other and kissed. "Of course, I'm not exactly like her, so I was surprised Adrian was matched with me."

"Yeah, you're not in the same league as her, are you?" Kade said.

Mariss missed his sarcasm. She tried not to show her hurt. He didn't have to be so blatantly honest about how poorly she measured up.

"Well, that woman *is* pretty," Lorena acknowledged. "But she isn't around, is she, Kade?" Losing interest in the hologram, she rose and slinked over to him.

Kade looked past her, his eyes fastened on Mariss. "True. And Adrian isn't around, either. Not for a few hundred lightyears, at any rate." He shoved away from the wall and entered the cockpit. The door snapped shut behind him.

"I'm starting to wish you'd ended up on a different flight," Lorena said, clearly piqued. "You're obviously the one he's interested in. Probably thinks he can catch himself a rich girl."

Mariss closed her cyber-unit and stowed it. "He's wasting his time. I believe I just demonstrated why."

"You'd think so, wouldn't you? With that hunk waiting for you. Men can be so dense. But I'll wear him down. Just keep playing the ice princess, okay? And stay out of my way."

Ice princess? Is that what people think of me? Mariss lifted a tentative hand to her tidy, braided knot.

Lorena was staring at the closed cockpit door as if willing it to reopen. Finally, she turned to Mariss with a smile that was falsely bright. "Well, I'm going to bed. I have a feeling I'm going to need my sleep in the days ahead. See you tomorrow."

She sauntered through the galley door and disappeared. Mariss soon followed.

***

Kade rolled out of his sleeping berth in a small room behind the cockpit and sat up. The indicator told him it was the middle of the rest period which passed for night in deep space. For the past hour, he had been unable to get back to sleep. He kept replaying in his mind the conversation with

Jason Weston in the Nexus staging area. Over and over, he heard the news that Lindenfeld was taking his spot as a starcruiser pilot.

Kade rubbed his face, weary beyond belief. He'd been fooling himself. He could play by the rules for a millennium and it would get him nowhere. Quantum championed its starcruiser pilots as paragons, touted their sterling records for all to see. Unless Quantum made an effort to cover up his background, he'd never make it into that elite corps, regardless of how well he performed on the job.

So here he was, back where he'd started. He hadn't been completely honest with Weston about being an outback pilot for five years. Adding in the time before Quantum, before going commercial, he had always made outback runs. Only difference was he used to haul cargo instead of people.

Cargo would be better. He had reacted badly to the news this morning. Unprofessionally. Exactly as Quantum higher management would have predicted, based on his record. And he had turned around and taken it out on his passengers.

He was so damned sick of it. Day after day of coddling passengers who would be better put to sleep for the duration than being forced to endure a situation they were untrained for. More than one cracked under the strain of the tedium, the isolation, the feeling of going nowhere, of losing touch with reality, of nothingness pressing down on you from all sides.

What Kade really hated was that once he arrived at his destination, he had to turn right around and come back again. At most, Quantum gave him a two-day layover. Quantum's philosophy was that their ships did all the work. Why should their pilots have days off when they could just as easily relax while aboard a ship moving through space?

Fine, but even seasoned pilots grew cabin-weary. That's why he longed for a starcruiser. Besides the prestige, the pay increase, the glamour, there was the sense of flying a city in space. The finest cruisers had movie theaters, recreation rooms, lounges, casinos—all manner of attractions to keep the passengers and crew entertained.

The crew. Another problem. He had none. He was alone

in this, and growing more and more tired of carrying the burden by himself. Damn Quantum cost-cutting.

Good ol' KJC-189 had no crew but him, and none of the amenities. Little wonder civilians cracked under the strain. Kade had a good store of tranquilizer for when a break occurred, which it almost always did. He expected someone to lose it about two-thirds of the way into the trip, when they were well under way but couldn't yet see the other side.

He took a mental inventory of his passengers. He played a game with himself on these solo-crew flights. Who would crack? Not Lorena. She was used to outback runs, if what she said about herself was true. Mrs. Hudson was going to be drugged up as it was. Her husband would see to it. She already had a doctor's prescription, thank the Maker. Mr. Hudson? Possible. But he had that solid, working-man aspect about him. Sturdy. Unlikely to break. Mr. Lee was an unknown quantity. Too unemotional to crack? He hoped so.

That left Mariss Sakari. Kade had been avoiding thinking about Mariss Sakari. He wished she hadn't ended up on his flight. She was too damned distracting.

She was obviously an aristocrat of some sort with those amazing violet eyes.... An extremely pretty woman. No, pretty didn't seem the right word for it. She was different.

Perfect, olive-toned skin and delicate bone structure. Exotic and serene at first glance, a slender, delicately bred lady. The type of woman he used to dream about while living in the desolate Tass Mining Colony. The type he would have married, if things hadn't gone so wrong.

He smiled to himself. Sure, Mariss Sakari was a well-bred lady. She pretended to be cool and detached. But Kade could see right through her. When he pushed her buttons, he caught glimpses of a spontaneous, passionate woman.

He fantasized for a moment how he would comfort her if she grew afraid, hold her close, whisper reassurances to her, break past her regal demeanor to the vulnerable woman beneath...

He shook his head in exasperation. He was fooling himself. Mariss Sakari would never crack—not in this lifetime. She was too damned contrary. He couldn't believe how she'd dressed him down, then agreed to help him anyway. After he'd mercilessly baited her. During his pre-flight announcements, he hadn't been able to take his eyes off her. He had watched her every reaction as he spoke to her from the cockpit.

What had he been trying to accomplish? Perhaps he had wanted her to know he was real, not just a Quantum employee. He was a real person, a man, someone she couldn't dismiss as a second-rate pilot sentenced to fly the worst commercial route in space.

Kade slammed his fist against the bulkhead, irritated beyond measure at his irrationality. What difference could it possibly make what one passenger thought of him? Especially one engaged to Mr. Perfect, Adrian Young.

He'd had hundreds of beautiful women as passengers, he reminded himself. He kept his distance when it suited him, indulged himself when he felt like it. Once he delivered Mariss Sakari to her destination, he'd never see her again. She wasn't worth thinking about.

But he couldn't seem to help himself. Kade pressed a button on the panel by his head, and a surveillance image appeared on the screen. The passenger cabin was deserted. He tapped the button again and got a view of the galley, then the sleeping compartments. All quiet.

He rose and stretched, then slipped out the cockpit door. What he was thinking of doing was against regulations, way out of line. He would be out in no time if he were caught. But he didn't give a hang.

The passenger cabin was almost dark, the overhead lights extinguished and the floor lights dimmed for night. He stopped beside seat number five, where Mariss Sakari had been sitting, and opened the overhead bin. He took down her cyber-unit and tucked it under his arm. As silently as possible, he closed the bin. With one last look toward the sleeping compartments to make sure no one had seen, he reentered the cockpit.

THREE

Mariss rolled onto her stomach. The walls of the sleeping compartment seemed to press in on her. She pounded the pillow and tried to get comfortable. She had no trouble sleeping on the starcruiser. And the beds had been no larger. So what was the problem now?

She rolled onto her back. It was useless. She slapped the cover button, and the lid lifted gently. She rolled to her feet and padded toward the main cabin. She could not stop thinking, and that always made it hard to sleep. She needed answers. Once she had them, her mind would be at ease, and she could rest.

Mariss slipped through the silent galley and into the main cabin. She crossed to the wall databank and sat before it. As soon as she keyed in a command, she asked for silent operation, so no one would be disturbed by her nighttime data search.

The menu led her straight to Captain Kadin Land's biography. His picture came on the screen along with basic facts, such as height, weight, and so on. She knew what he looked like. But she found herself staring at his picture just the same. Why did he disturb her so? What was it about him she found compelling? He wasn't handsome. Not like Adrian. He wouldn't have been chosen to appear in the Iridion Colony's promotional advertisement. Too...sharp-looking. She studied each feature individually, then sat back and gazed at his collective face. His eyes. She couldn't stop looking at his eyes. Wide-set under thick brows, darker than the darkest night, he stared back at her. He wasn't smiling in this photo, which seemed to fit his cynical personality.

Mariss gleaned what she could from the first screen—

thirty-two years old, born on Tass Mining Colony—not a pleasant place to grow up. With Quantum for five years. Scant mention of his career before that, except he had piloted cargo ships in the Nebular Sector.

Mariss paged down into the heart of his biography. Sketchy at best. He had said the "gory details" were here, but Mariss knew they wouldn't be. This was the sanitized version that Quantum provided its passengers. His academy training was listed. But no graduation date, no degree granted. He had quit the academy—or been dismissed?

Nor was there any reference to that "incident on Barron Outpost" the other Quantum man had mentioned back at the Nexus.

Interesting...the highest flight scores of any Quantum pilot—not just those currently employed, either. The highest ever. *He obviously has what it takes*, thought Mariss. So why was he piloting this small passenger ship instead of something more prestigious?

She scrolled to the end of the file, then tapped backward through it, line by line. Perhaps she could search in more depth. She had met her second husband, a corporate computer consultant, while designing a program for her botanical data. Her love for both plants and computers had outlasted *that* disastrous relationship. Since then, she had picked up even more tricks. Some women dated in their off hours—Mariss worked on programs.

Thoughtful, she tapped her fingers on the panel thoughtfully. There might very well be a complete file on Kadin Land in the ship's database. She could find a hidden gateway, a back door...

The sound of the cockpit door sliding open startled Mariss, and she jumped to her feet. The captain was standing on the threshold. His eyes widened in surprise when he saw her. He swore under his breath. Mariss backed up against the monitor, wishing she had exited his profile. Now she prayed he wouldn't notice.

"Hello," she finally said. "I couldn't sleep." She became all too aware she was wearing only her undershirt and panties.

She jerked on the edge of the oversize undershirt, but it felt far too skimpy to cover her bare legs properly.

Kade wasn't dressed any more modestly. He wore only a tank top and shorts. His wavy, dark-brown hair was mussed, like he'd been lounging around in bed. He was pressing a black cyber-unit against his chest.

Mariss' gaze went from admiring his corded biceps to realizing what they were cradling so closely. "That's—that's my cyber-unit," she gasped.

"Damn it. You were supposed to be in bed."

"So you could pry into my things?" Outrage blossomed in her chest, and she sprang at him. "You thief!" She snatched her unit from him and pressed it to her chest, aware how warm it was from being held in his arms. "What in the name of Heaven do you think you're doing?"

"Hell if I know."

"You must have been after *something*," Mariss said, realizing how oddly flattered she felt.

He finally moved, closing the distance between them. "Okay, okay." He held up his hands. "I was completely wrong. I know it. I wanted to find out about—"

"About—" she prodded, expecting him to say, *you.*

"About—that guy you're marrying."

Mariss gaped. She took a step back. "Adrian? Adrian Young? *My* Adrian Young? Why?"

He crossed his arms and shifted his weight. "Because...because...I think I know him from somewhere."

"Oh, *do* you? From where?"

"Ah...from flight school."

"Oh, really? What class?" Mariss had Adrian's bio memorized. He had never gone anywhere near flight school. She set her unit on the table and turned on him. "You're despicable. You insult me, you harass me, you make snide comments about me, you get into my personal possessions. I tell you, I'm not surprised Quantum didn't promote you. You ought to lose your pilot's license. You—"

She jabbed her finger at his chest, and Kade grabbed it. "Hold it there one second! How in the hell do you know about the promotion?"

Mariss yanked her finger away. "I—I just do. It's obvious." He stared at her, waiting for a better explanation. Mariss shrugged. "You've made it perfectly clear you hate your job. You must have tried for a better one. It's natural you tried, and you were turned down."

"Natural? No, I don't buy it." He shook his head slowly, thoughtfully. Then understanding dawned. "Oh, I see what's going on here. You're a Quantum spy! Christ, I'm in it now." He raked his hands through his thick hair.

"Spy?"

He exhaled heavily, his voice full of resignation. "I get interested in a woman who turns out to be a damn spy for the corporation. Okay, write up your report, see if I give a hang. I've been through worse."

Mariss dropped her strident tone. He was *interested* in her? "I'm not a spy. Really. I'm just traveling to see my fiancé. I overheard your argument with another man in the staging area."

His eyes narrowed. "You *did*."

She could see he didn't believe her. "Yes, something about starcruisers and a guy named...Langerfield?"

"Lindenfeld."

"That's it. Lindenfeld. I was sitting in the seats right behind you."

"Right." Despite the awkwardness of the conversation, Kade smiled at her in relief. "I suppose that's possible."

"So what were you *really* doing with my unit?"

He cocked his head. "I was trying to find out why a gorgeous woman like you would go shopping for a man."

Despite the compliment, Mariss stiffened. "I'm not shopping. I'm choosing a life mate logically, carefully, and sensibly."

Kade snorted. "Insanity. What if you get to Elysia and find out you hate him?"

"I can't. It's guaranteed."

He smiled indulgently. "Listen, hon, that's nonsense. Whatever happened to attraction?"

Mariss bristled. "I *am* attracted to Adrian."

Kade quirked an eyebrow. "How *can* you be? You've never even met the guy!"

"In a way I have. If you've been snooping through my files, you know how complete they are."

"Sure, you know he got good grades in college—"

"The *best*."

"And his parents were some kind of bigwigs in the Earth Coalition government. And his belly button is an outie."

Mariss bit her lip to keep from smiling. Kade made Adrian's profile sound ridiculous, but he was ignoring the parts which were important to her.

His voice lowered intimately. "None of that matters, Mariss."

"Of course not," she said firmly. "It's temperament and goals which matter, and the computer matched ours. We're perfect for each other. He's my other half."

Kade laid his hands on her shoulders. She tingled as he slid them gently over her skin. "Mariss. Men and women mate because of attraction, attraction from being together, not from pictures and databanks. Animal attraction, spiritual attraction, whatever you prefer to call it. It doesn't happen with hardware and computers."

Her eyes locked on his, Mariss was intensely aware that he was drawing her closer, close enough to feel the warmth emanating from his body. Her small breasts brushed his chest and sent an alarming burst of heat through her. His voice dropped to a husky whisper. "That certain something that makes your heart jerk and your breath come fast. When you see her, you know this is something special, this is going to be *it*."

Mariss found her head tilting slightly as he brought his face closer. He was weaving a spell around her. A potent spell, taking her breath away, and with it her senses.

"No—" Mariss shoved hard against his chest and broke free of his grasp. "You're wrong, Kade. So wrong it's almost laughable. Trust me, I know."

"What do you mean you—"

Mariss' voice turned fierce. "I tried it the other way. Tried it twice! It doesn't work! I'm never going through that again. Now stay out of my way, and out of my things!" Mariss swept her cyber-unit from the table and hurried from the room.

Kade watched her go, heart hammering in his chest, blood pounding in his temples. He slammed a fist against the bulkhead. Why had he ever imagined there could be something between them? He may feel an intense attraction, but that didn't mean she did.

He turned toward the cockpit door, but realized there was more light than usual in the passenger cabin. He glanced back. Mariss had left the databank screen on. He approached it to turn it off, and found his own face looking back at him.

He wanted to believe Mariss had been as intrigued by him as he was with her. More likely, she had doubts about him as a pilot after overhearing that conversation at the Nexus. If she knew the whole truth about him, she wouldn't give him a second glance. Especially when she had a life with Adrian Young to look forward to.

The man was nearly perfect, all right. Nauseating. The top of his class, a decathlete, recipient of humanitarian honors. No doubt Mariss would fall for the guy when she met him. Hell, she was right. She didn't *need* to meet him. No, she belonged with Adrian Young far more than she ever would with a space jockey going nowhere fast.

***

"Take these out."

Mariss accepted the tray from Kade and carried it out of the galley to the passengers who were just starting to gather for breakfast. As soon as she had come from the lavatory, Kade summoned her over the speakers to the galley. She didn't want to be near him after last night, but she could hardly turn him down without making an issue of it.

Kade seemed ready to forget the night before, however. He didn't refer to it. Nor did he tease her. For once, he treated her as she wanted to be treated, in a professional manner.

She eyed him closely as he bent over the sink peeling and slicing bananas. He seemed to have lost any romantic interest he may have had for her the day before. She was glad, truly she was. In her experience romance faded quicker than a flower in deep-freeze.

“Thank you, Mariss.” Lorena took her breakfast from the tray Mariss set on the table. A moment later, Kade came out of the galley with a bowl of fresh fruit. He set it in the center, and the passengers helped themselves.

“Good morning, Kade,” Lorena purred. “Did you sleep well?”

Kade smiled back. “Exceptionally.”

Mariss looked from one to the other and back again. Had Lorena scored after all? Mariss expected to feel relief that Kade was no longer pursuing her. But to her surprise, the idea of Kade casually bedding Lorena made her uneasy. She shoved the feeling away, refusing to explore it.

“How about you, Lorena? Spend a good night?”

“Not nearly,” she sighed. “I’m hoping tonight will be more...relaxing, Captain. If you get my meaning.”

Mariss looked up, unable to hide her interest. Kade hadn’t slept with her after all.

“We at Quantum do our best to please our passengers,” Kade said, his eyes on Mariss. Feigning disinterest, she looked away. “Within reason.”

***

Mariss stared hard at the numbers in the column labeled “total.” It didn’t add up, literally. She tapped at her keyboard, again generating the table on the screen.

Around her, the cabin was quiet, with only muted conversations from the other passengers. It was the fourth day. Lunch had ended, and the lazy, boring afternoon dragged by. Mrs. Hudson napped as usual, under the influence of her calming drug. Mr. Hudson and Mr. Lee played an almost silent game of poker. Lorena prowled restlessly, waiting for opportunities to corner Kade.

Not once in the past days had Captain Land asked for her assistance. He had never really needed her help. He had been flirting. That night he’d come upon her, and held her, she had relieved him of any notion that she might be interested in him.

She was certain of it. She studied him carefully over meals, or when they gathered as a group to watch a vid-disc. He treated her no differently from the others.

Ironically, now that he was behaving professionally, Mariss found she missed their confrontations. Captain Land was spending most of his time alone in the cockpit, or assuaging the fears and concerns of the other passengers.

Except for Lorena, of course. She wasn't afraid. Mariss couldn't help watching from the corner of her eye when Lorena approached Kade, standing close to him, laying her hand on his forearm. Kade didn't seem interested in her, but the trip was far from over.

Irritated, Mariss shook her head. This voyage must be getting to her. She was spending far too much time engaging in frivolous trains of thought. She blinked and focused again on her cyber-unit's screen. These numbers were the important thing.

She snapped her unit closed and tucked it under her arm, making her way toward the closed cockpit door. Standing before it, she knocked tentatively.

She heard a grunt inside. Or was it a groan? Flushing with anxiety, she thought of Lorena, perhaps with Kade, in bed. No, she had seen Lorena moments before, behind her, sneaking food from the galley.

She knocked again. The groan sounded more like "come in" this time. The door swooshed open before her, and she entered. It closed behind her. Mariss found herself in a short hallway. Another hatch in front of her led to the cockpit. She glanced about for Kade, but didn't see him right away. On her left was a sleeping compartment, roomier than the passengers'. On the right was another room, with the lavatory, and—

Mariss started. Kade's head was inches from her feet. He was hanging almost upside down, on a steeply inclined board. His ankles were fastened into cuffs on the wall. His bare arms hung over his head, his hands scraping the floor. He wore only his shorts. Sweat coated his skin, his muscles rigid from exertion.

Mariss bit her lip, hard. An unwelcome surge of desire

swept through her. She battled back the feeling. *You can't trust this, Mariss. Remember Adrian. He's your life mate.*

"Mariss," Kade gasped, his eyes wide. With a grunt, he pulled himself up by stomach muscles as flat and hard as the shell on her cyber-unit. He unfastened the cuffs holding his ankles and rolled off the board. Grabbing a towel, he slung it over his shoulders. "Wait in the cockpit."

He disappeared into the lavatory. It also housed a shower, for Mariss could hear it running. The board he had been working out on was covered in sweat. Mariss hadn't thought about how a pilot who was forced to live in such an enclosed place as this ship for days on end managed to have such a brawny frame. This must be the answer.

Other complicated pieces of exercise equipment extruded from the wall, as well. A computer unit next to a set of pulleys showed the weight the user had been lifting last. The number read 289.

Mariss stared at the lavatory door, and tried not to think about the body of the man inside. She forced herself to turn toward the cockpit. But she paused. Curious, she stuck her head in the door of the sleeping compartment across the hall and glanced around.

His Quantum uniform lay on the bed. Quantum travel posters adorned the walls—landscapes of Yosemite Valley on Earth, of Hyonim Canyon on Garrulon, of the Crystal Wash Falls of the Moon of Janus. Popular Quantum tourist destinations—none of which were on this outback run.

On the wall above his bed was pasted a small photograph of a woman and a young boy. Probably Kade and his mother. Both wore thermal suits to protect them from frigid temperatures. The background was nothing like the posters on the walls. Iron-toned escarpments rose bleakly under a leaden sky. Tass Mining Colony, one of the dreariest places in the colonized galaxy.

Mariss felt for any child who was forced to grow up on the dead asteroid. Sure, they had schools for the workers' children, and domed living colonies with artificially provided comforts. But nothing grew on Tass. Not a tree, not a shrub, not even algae. As a botanist, Mariss could think of no more dismal place.

"I imagined you in here, but I never thought you'd be so direct."

Mariss spun around and stumbled back a step. Kade stood in the doorway of his sleeping chamber, wearing nothing but a towel wrapped around his narrow hips and a suggestive grin on his face.

Mariss couldn't get around him. His tightly muscled frame filled the doorway.

"I was just looking," she insisted. She grabbed his clothes and shoved them at him, averting her eyes from his bare chest and the play of black curls there.

"Yeah, that's what they all say," he said, his eyes sparkling. "Makes 'em feel less guilty." He tossed his clothes on a chair and slipped his arms around Mariss.

Mariss felt the heat of his body imprinting itself through the fabric of her thin flightsuit. He touched his lips to her temple, his breath warm and inviting.

In a panic, she wrapped her hand around her cyber-unit and swung it upward. It smashed into the side of his head. Kade swore. He dropped her and fell back to land on the bed. He cradled his head in his hands, shooting her a venomous look from between his fingers.

With her free hand, Mariss retrieved his uniform and hurled it at him. Holding her cyber-unit in front of her like a shield, she backed through the door. "I came on business, Captain. I advise you to become presentable. I will wait in the cockpit."

She spun on her heel and entered the cockpit. She sat carefully in one of the seats, as still as possible, waiting for her heart to cease pounding. Twice Kadin Land had managed to pull her into an embrace. She thought she had made it perfectly clear that he couldn't take such liberties with her. She *had* to make it clear.

Mariss sighed, gazing at the vast, black nothingness beyond the cockpit window. So lonely. Not a star, not a comet, no color to speak of. It was downright eerie. How could the captain spend so much time looking at it? She shuddered.

Her mind drifted. Why was this trip turning out to be so difficult? He was the captain, nothing more. And she was one of his passengers. So why did the line between their roles seem to grow so blurry at times? She knew it was partly her fault. She found it hard to look at Captain Land and not see a man under his tailored uniform.

He sensed it. He knew she was attracted to him. He had to know. She hadn't pulled back quickly enough either of the times he held her. But the captain did little to foster an image of cool, impersonal confidence. He was brash, brutally honest, far too direct for common sense. *The captain...* That was the key. She had to remember he was the captain, and nothing else.

"Get out of my seat."

Mariss glanced up to see a dour Kade standing over her, dressed properly in his uniform. He pointed sharply toward the second seat in the cockpit, as if she were a dog he was training to heel.

Primly, she stood and moved to the other seat. Kade settled into the pilot's chair. A welt had formed on his temple where she had hit him. His dark eyes were stormy as they narrowed on her. "What do you want?"

Mariss set her cyber-unit on the padded deck between them and opened it. She cleared her throat, as if preparing to make a presentation to the Earth Botanical Society. If she acted cool and professional, perhaps they could both forget what had occurred. "I couldn't stop thinking about what you said, about the weight of my luggage. I knew you had erred. It doesn't add up."

"Erred? I had erred?" he asked mockingly.

"Yes. Erred."

He cocked an eyebrow at her. "Lord knows I would hate to *err*. Please, continue."

"Before leaving Earth, I calculated the weight of all my possessions. Look here." She pointed to the table on her computer's screen. "Knowing the Quantum Craftlines weight limits—it *was* listed in the pre-flight material provided to all passengers—I allotted specific numbers of kilos to all the categories of my possessions: clothing, shoes, mementos, botanical disk texts, and so on. Then I weighed every item I planned to take with me, and listed it under its specific classification." She tapped a few keys and changed the display to a series of lists. "See?"

"Yeah, I see." He snorted. "You must have been starving for entertainment that day."

"What? No, I felt this was necessary as part of the preparation for my trip. I *scheduled* time for this. Anyway, once I determined how much my things weighed, I prioritized them, and adjusted each category according to the weight I allotted for each item. I admit I cheated a little. I increased my allowance in the clothing category and took it from the miscellaneous category so I could include a couple extra sets of—" She caught herself. She had been about to tell him of her satin lingerie, beautiful sets given to her as gifts from her co-workers at the research institute just before she left.

His eyebrows arched and his gaze dropped to her chest. "Underwear? Bras? Bust enhancers?"

Mariss glared at him. So she wasn't busty. Did he have to point it out?

He merely grinned. "You wasted hours on this, didn't you?"

"It wasn't a waste! When I checked in at Quantum, my luggage was at 99.87 kilos. *Under* the limit by .13 kilos."

"I *know* the weight limit, Mariss."

She smiled in an attempt to be friendly. "Of course you do, a fine pilot like you."

Wrong tactic. His eyes narrowed, took on a dark, flinty edge. "So, what does all this prove? You probably bought something at the Nexus, a souvenir or a book, and tossed it into your case."

"Well, yes I did."

"That explains it. What was it, a set of those ugly bowls with `Nexus' stamped across the sides?"

"No. It was very lightweight. It weighed one kilo exactly, which still wouldn't have put me over, because I used up some of my soap and other...personal-care items. The total should now be 99.95 kilos. So, you see, Captain, I am *not* overweight."

"I never said *you* were overweight. I said your luggage was. *You* are perfectly...sized."

Mariss tried hard to ignore the glint in his eyes as they played over her body. She tapped her keyboard and revealed the table again, angling it toward him. "So what are you going to do about it?"

"Do about what?"

"My luggage!"

"Your luggage is safely stowed in the cargo hold."

"You misweighed it."

"Not me. The cargo handler probably screwed up when he weighed it before loading it."

"Don't you weigh it on board, too?"

"Well, yeah, but—"

"And what did my case weigh?"

He shrugged. "It came in high. As I said."

"Then your scale needs to be calibrated." She sighed, satisfied with the logic of her argument. "You should be glad I brought this to your attention. Doesn't every kilo count on a spaceship? I mean, to calculate the right amount of fuel and all."

"Of course it counts. My scales *don't* need to be calibrated." He slammed her cyber-unit closed and leaned in close to her, his lips tight. "Your *brain* does, Mariss. Has anyone ever told you you're obsessive? That's what this proves to me. You're completely obsessive! You probably added wrong. If you just threw stuff in a case and weighed it all at once—"

Mariss sat up straighter and faced him squarely. "I did *not* add wrong! And I am *not* obsessive! *You* are careless. You're not even concerned about this. What if everyone's luggage was weighed wrong? What if your fuel was weighed wrong? What if there's far less of it than you were planning on? What if it means we run out of fuel before we reach Fredon Outpost?"

"Damn it, woman, I don't need you telling me how to fly my ship!"

"I don't care how you fly it, as long as you get me safely to Elysia, so I can get married and I don't have to worry about pilots and spaceships and luggage anymore! And I don't appreciate—"

Before the words had completely left her mouth, Mariss was violently thrown back against the seat. Control-panel lights lit up like a fireworks display. The cockpit lights flickered and went out. An alarm shrieked in deafening bursts.

Kade was already responding, his hands dancing over the controls. Outside, the unrelieved black transformed as a ribbon of light began moving toward the ship.

Mariss gripped the padded arms of the seat. "What is it? What's going on?"

"Just shut up and stay put." Kade sprang to his feet and rushed to the back of the cockpit. Mariss turned to see, but an instant later, he was back in his seat, his gaze snapping from the control panel to the view out the cockpit window. He yanked something from the console and tossed it in her lap. "Talk to them. Tell them to fasten their seatbelts."

The ship shuddered. The ribbon of light came nearer, undulating, its light shifting from pure white to pink and lavender along its edges. Her heart hammering, Mariss lifted the handset. She sucked a steadying breath into her lungs and spoke. "This is the cockpit. I mean, this is Mariss in the cockpit. I'm with the captain, and he's getting things under control. Sit down in the nearest seat and buckle your seatbelt. Okay? Thanks."

Kade moved in swift, sure motions, his hands first on one set of controls, then another. A second bank of lights blazed on. "That's bad, isn't it?" Mariss asked.

Kade didn't spare her a glance. He was already attending to a third set of controls above his head. Seconds later, the bank of lights blinked off. Outside, the river of light began to curl past the side of the ship. They no longer seemed to be heading straight for it.

"I hope everyone back there is secured now," Mariss told the other passengers. "Everyone stay calm. Captain Land has things under complete control. He's the most highly rated pilot

Quantum has, so there's nothing to worry about."

Another tense moment passed. The ship bucked one final time, then settled down into its usual calm purring. The deck lights stopped flashing, the alarm ceased its howling. Finally, the cockpit lights flickered and came back on, steady and strong.

Kade collapsed against his seat. Mariss exhaled. Now that they were out of danger, her body reacted, her hands starting to shake. She clutched the handset to still them.

"Tell them we're stabilized, and I'll be coming back shortly to explain," Kade directed.

Mariss passed the information along. She lowered the handset and studied Kade. "Can you tell me what that was all about, Captain?"

Kade leaned back and gazed out the cockpit window, unseeing. "That was a Class F vortex string. Very infrequent occurrence. It has to do with interspace travel. Some people say we're creating them by traveling beyond the speed of light—causing wrinkles where there were none. I doubt it. We don't have enough power to shift the substance of the universe."

His voice was soft, speculative. This new, philosophical side of him fascinated her. She knew he was unwinding from the adrenaline surge of a few moments ago. She also reflected on the speed with which he had manipulated the craft. He had seemed to know precisely what to do. There hadn't been even a moment's hesitation. She asked softly, "What would have happened if we had run into it?"

"Gone."

"Gone—where?"

"Nowhere. Just gone." He studied her from the corner of his eye. "We would cease to exist. Except perhaps as a collection of subatomic particles drifting in the ether of space between worlds."

Mariss shuddered. "I don't think I like space travel."

Kade chuckled. "It's not the safest way to live, Mariss. But it can be exciting to live on the edge, to rely on your gut instincts."

A tremor ran through her. *Live on the edge...* Kade made the idea sound almost appealing. Almost. She thought about Peck, her first husband. He had lived on the edge, and nearly dragged her with him into the abyss. "I prefer comfort and safety, thank you," she said coolly, as if ordering cream for her coffee.

"Sorry. All you'll get for the next several days is the illusion of safety." Kade rose. He paused right above her, looking down at her. Feeling safe, seeking comfort, that's why so many people during space travel sought the simple physical comfort of each others' arms. The thought came into her mind as she gazed up at Kade's rugged face. "You did good, Mariss. You're good under pressure. You may think you don't like it, but it likes you."

"I just spoke a few words."

"You helped me. Kept your head. I appreciate it. Now let's go. The other passengers must be terrified." He strode two steps to the hatch. Mariss retrieved her cyber-unit. She was right behind him when he turned to her once more. "By the way, what was all that about being Quantum's most highly rated pilot?"

Mariss felt her face heat. She tried to shrug it off. "Your file, in the cabin databank. It said you have the highest rating of any pilot in Quantum history."

"Ah." Kade nodded thoughtfully. "Well, don't trust everything you read. You never know when someone will be lying to you."

"You mean you're not—"

He strode from the cockpit. Mariss trailed behind, her question unanswered.

***

After dinner, filled with excited and nervous conversation about their close call, Mariss finally remembered the luggage discrepancy. She considered mentioning it to the captain, but realized how incredibly trivial it would sound. Any man who could handle a spaceship the way Kade could must know what was best for his ship. She flushed with embarrassment at her earlier insistence. She still had no doubt a mistake had been made. But to tell the captain how to run his ship—

She rose from the table and scooped up her dinner bowl. Stew tonight. Not bad. Nicely spiced. She shoved the container in the incinerator and headed for the sleeping compartments. Reading before bedtime. And sleeping in tomorrow. It was easy to grow lazy on board such a small ship.

She should use the exercise equipment in the closet next to the lavatory. But she didn't feel particularly motivated. Not like Kade, who must approach exercise like it was his religion, to maintain muscles that well-toned.

An image flashed into her mind of Kade standing before her, wearing only a towel. She wished she could have taken longer to admire him. She felt a twinge of guilt. Adrian was waiting for her, waiting to pledge his life to her. Now was not the time to be thinking of another man's pectorals.

Daydreaming, she nearly walked into Kade. "Mariss." He dropped his face near her ear and lowered his voice. "Come to the cockpit at 0100 hours, when the others are asleep. I'll answer your questions then."

Without further explanation, he left her. 0100 was the middle of the ship's artificial "night." The cockpit, alone with him? "No, I won't go," Mariss said to herself, knowing as she said it that she would, if only because the prospect of a nighttime appointment added a dash of excitement to her day.

FOUR

Kade lay in his bunk and watched the numbers change on his wall clock. This whole idea was a wild goose chase, as Earthers called it. But it was an excuse to spend time alone with Mariss while the rest of the passengers were in slumberland.

Why he was attracted to the slender, serious, and obsessive woman was a mystery he couldn't unravel. But ever since he'd laid eyes on her, he'd found it difficult to look away.

A soft tap on the cockpit door alerted him. He slapped a button on the wall, and the door slid open. At the same time, he swung his legs over his bunk and looked toward the door.

Mariss waited just inside the cockpit entryway. "Well?" she asked, as if she had another pressing appointment and he was keeping her from it. She wore her hair in a single thick braid down the back of her flightsuit. One step closer to loosening up, Kade though ruefully. Better yet, for once she had left behind that obnoxious cyber-unit.

"Let's get to it." Without further explanation, he slipped past her and moved toward the databank on the wall of the passenger cabin. He tapped a few controls, and a meter-wide panel slid back in the carpeted floor. Kade slipped through the opening, setting his feet on a narrow ladder, and began to climb down.

He thought of offering Mariss assistance, but had a hunch she would refuse it. He heard her feet on the rungs above him. The cargo hold was low-ceilinged, crammed to the centimeter with equipment, noisier than the passenger deck. Here, he had access to the guts of the ship.

Kade was less interested in glancing around the cargo hold

than in watching Mariss descend from above. His eyes fastened on her softly rounded bottom, pulling against the fabric of her blue flightsuit, her bobbing braid striking against it with every step she took.

He blinked and swallowed hard, then he reached up and lifted her off the last rung.

She immediately stepped back. "I wasn't sure what you were planning tonight. I thought it might be about my luggage," she said quickly, breathlessly. "I thought you had forgotten in all the excitement."

"Excitement?"

"The vortex phenomenon."

"Oh, right." He shrugged and gestured toward the luggage racks. "Your luggage is stored over here." He led her to a collection of racks where the cases—all of the same dimensions—were lined up side by side.

"Mine is the red case," Mariss supplied.

"Yeah, I remember it. The heavy one."

"Exactly how heavy was it? According to *your* measurements."

Kade tapped out a command on a computer panel. "One forty-five. And three hundredths."

"145.03 kilos! That's impossible." Mariss shook her head firmly, sending her braid bouncing.

"Hold on a sec." A set of remote arms extruded from the wall, planted grips on either side of her case, and held it away from the rack just long enough to take a reading. Then the arms replaced the case and retracted.

Kade studied the panel. He frowned, conscious that Mariss' impatient gaze bore into his back. "99.95 kilos." He swung around to face her. "Just like you said."

Mariss smiled softly, almost tenderly. "I like a man who can admit when he's wrong."

Kade pulled his gaze from her soft, full lips. He stiffened. "I didn't say *that.* Hold on." He turned back to the panel and read the pre-flight weights. "This could take some investigating."

Kade finally ended up reweighing all of the cases. Every

one was the same weight as before leaving the Nexus.

"Let me look in my case," Mariss suggested. "Maybe I'll see something, some evidence of...I don't know what."

"Tampering? Mariss, I can't see how—"

"Just let me look." She laid her hands on his arm, and Kade couldn't help relenting.

He ordered the remote unit to extract her case from the racks and place it on a nearby console. Mariss unlocked it swiftly. The lid swung open to reveal dividers separating shoes from clothes from books from other doodads. Everything had a place, and nothing looked out of place.

"Someone's been in here," Mariss immediately announced.

"What? That's the neatest damned case I've ever seen."

"I just know they have." Mariss was flipping through the folded garments. "I distinctly remember putting the yellow jersey on top of the royal blue robe, so it wouldn't be crushed. Look. It's jammed down in between these stacks of shirts. I didn't pack it this way."

Kade shrugged. She was doing it again, worrying over things other people wouldn't give a second thought. It irritated him that he continued to find her fascinating when her habits were quite clearly annoying as hell. "Luggage often gets a little manhandled during transport, Mariss. That's the price of space travel."

"No." Her dark eyes met his, imploring and serious. "I don't buy it, Kade."

He sighed. "You've wrapped yourself around this like a Gorgin serpent around a ju-ju tree, Mariss." Gorgins were notorious for their tenacity in sucking the life from ju-jus, surviving even fire and flood to continue their relentless pursuit of their prey. He hated to see Mariss—a woman who should be enjoying her youth and her life—waste her time on such trivial nonsense.

Kade straightened and laid his hands solidly on her shoulders, turning her to face him. "Give it a rest. Let's go back upstairs. I've stashed some Klinian ale for a special occasion." He smiled crookedly. "Tonight looks like a good one to me."

He felt her tremble at the simple physical contact. Just as before, Kade detected conflicting signals emanating from her. But she stepped back, averting her face. "You ought to be concerned, Kade. This is your ship." Her eyes met his, sparkling with intensity. "Aren't you worried in the least? What happened to the missing 45 kilos?"

Kade barely heard her. Something shiny in her case drew his attention. He slipped his hand around it and pulled it out. "Mariss," he replied distractedly. "I had other things on my mind before we blasted off. If the luggage weighed right at the Nexus, I admit I probably...screwed up." His voice fell as he held up the shiny piece of clothing. He whistled low. The skimpy item was completely see-through, a filmy nothing of creamy lingerie designed to tempt and tantalize. He could imagine how it would hug a woman's body, Mariss' body, outlining her curves, slipping between her thighs to fasten in back, revealing... everything.

"Put that down!"

Mariss yanked at it, but Kade kept a firm grip on it. He swung around to avoid her outstretched hands. "You been wearing things like this under your flightsuit?" he asked, cocking an eyebrow at her speculatively. She was fuming, and damned pretty while doing it, too.

"It's none of your business, you unmannerly ingrate. But if you must know, I plan to wear that on my honeymoon."

A tide of anger swept over Kade. "With that dolt Adrian? He probably won't know what to do with it, or with you *in* it."

"You know nothing about him," Mariss shot back, her chin tilted in that irritatingly cute, defiant way.

"Fine. Take it. I'm sure you'll both make quite a pair trying to figure it out." He flung it at her and turned away.

"Figure it out! You arrogant idiot! What makes you think I don't know how it's done?"

Kade was deeply satisfied he'd caused such a passionate outburst.

"Just because I'm not panting after you like—*Lorena*, doesn't mean I don't enjoy being with men," Mariss said through gritted teeth.

Kade rested his hands on his hips. "Gee, why would I get that idea? Let me see. You run away from me like a scared rabbit. You throw yourself at a hologram instead. Afraid of touching a *real* man's body?" He snorted. "Sounds like it to me."

"You're insufferable." Mariss stuffed her lingerie back in her case with furious, choppy movements. Kade watched her, feeling oddly victorious. She didn't seem to care that the lingerie wasn't in its assigned space. She slammed the cover of the case and threw the latches home. "Put my case away. If *you* don't care about the screwed up measurements, *I* certainly don't. Now, I'm going back to my sleeping compartment. I have better things to do than crawl around cargo bays with you in the dead of night."

She gripped the ladder and climbed up blindingly fast. As soon as she disappeared, Kade glanced at her case. He reached for the panel to order the remote unit to replace it on the rack, then paused. His hand drifted over the red plasti-steel top. His fingers slid to the latches. After a glance toward the hatch, he unfastened them. The lid lifted.

Kade dug between the neat stacks and pulled out the filmy lingerie. He tucked it inside his jacket. He knew he was being childish. But this was one particular pleasure which Adrian Young would just have to miss.

***

"It's all yours." Lorena smiled widely at Mariss. She had released her half-head of hair and washed it. She tossed back the damp tresses as she stepped away from the lavatory door. Mariss thanked her, her eyes falling to the pale skin of Lorena's bosom. The flightsuit was designed to fasten to the neck, but Lorena had gradually widened the opening so that now the crests of her breasts were visible.

"You're not done up," Mariss said wryly, her eyes flicking back to Lorena's coy gaze.

Lorena cocked her hip against the doorjamb. "Not yet, but I'm working on it," she said suggestively. "I assume you've already been done up?"

Mariss sighed. "Lorena, I was talking about your flightsuit."

"And I was talking about the captain. You may play the part of a prim lady, but we both know you'd like to rav him, too."

Mariss sighed and shook her head. "Right now, I just want to take a shower."

She moved toward the door, but Lorena blocked it. Her hazel eyes locked with Mariss'. "Just do it soon, okay? He won't let me do him until he does you, so stop playing hard to get. There are only three days left until Fredon. I have to rav him or my record will be ruined. I've been done up by every pilot in this sector, except for him." Her freshly reddened lips curled. "Besides, he's a sexual vibrant. All that locked up tension, it pours off him in waves." She cocked her head. "You know, we could *both* rav him. At the same time. I bet he'd go for that."

"I'm not interested, Lorena. *Excuse* me." Mariss shoved past her into the lavatory and locked the door behind her. Lorena had a one-track mind and assumed every other woman thought as she did. Mariss set down her bag of personal items on a small shelf and began undressing.

A vibrant. In her street vernacular, Lorena had paid Kade the highest of compliments. Mariss couldn't help agreeing with her. In fact, she still found it hard to believe Kade hadn't taken such a free gift of mindless sex and run with it as fast and hard as he could.

She shoved her flightsuit in the laundry chute and activated it. By the time she was done with her shower, the suit would be clean and dry.

She stepped into the stall and reached for the control panel. But she paused. Something wasn't right. She glanced about, saw nothing out of the ordinary. White walls, ceiling with sprayer, floor with drain, modulating panel. Nothing.

Then her conscious mind registered the oddity. It was in the air. A lingering scent, so faint as to be almost undetectable. Mariss sniffed. Cloyingly sweet, with an underlying tang. Familiar. Painfully so. Here on the ship.

The illegal serum had destroyed her first marriage. Someone had brought it aboard and used it. Lorena had just been in here. That made her the most likely candidate.

The vagon serum was made from crushed morovin plant from the Moon of Vaga. In small doses, it gave users heightened awareness of sensory input, without making them feel falsely high. Colors seemed brighter, scents richer. But cross the border into abusing the drug, and users lost their strength of will, became open to suggestions, no matter how harmful. The potential abuse of such a drug was phenomenal. It had been outlawed for decades throughout the civilized galaxy. But that didn't stop the black market from thriving.

As a botanist specializing in pharmacological botanics, Mariss was more than a little familiar with vagon. As a former wife of an addict, she'd had the misfortune to experience the harsher aspects of vagon production and addiction.

Images she had fought to suppress sprang to mind...Peck using her own laboratory tools to manufacture the serum. His denials, her own desperation. The investigation which had almost destroyed her career...

Angry with herself for still feeling the pain, Mariss quashed the memories. But that didn't remove the problem presented to her now. Her finger lingered over the emergency call button. Before she could think too much about what would happen, she pressed it.

She heard nothing. Seconds passed, a minute. Mariss left the shower and retrieved a towel from a shelf. Her flightsuit was still being processed in the laundry. She heard footsteps pounding in the corridor outside the lavatory door. She managed to cover herself with the towel just before the door slid back and Kade dove into the room.

Mariss leapt back, landing against the tiny cubicle's far wall. Kade's forward momentum brought him face-to-face with her. "Mariss? What is it? What's wrong?" He looked about wildly, but there were no visible threats in the lavatory.

Catching his breath, he stepped back and glanced her over. Mariss avoided his gaze by looking over his shoulder. Mr. Hudson and Mr. Lee were staring through the open door at her toweled body. *"Shut the door,"* Mariss hissed in Kade's ear.

Kade spun and slapped the button by the door, and it slid home. He turned his gaze on her, curiosity and concern mixing with obvious interest. "Jeez, Mariss, you know how to surprise a guy. Or is it just that you like to watch me scramble after you?" He planted a palm on the wall above her head and stared down at her, waiting for her explanation. "So what is it? See a spaceport rat aboard?"

Mariss lifted her chin, a smile playing on her lips. "Not unless I'm looking at one."

"Cute." His eyes followed her loose black hair from her scalp to her hips. "Or maybe you *do* need help washing your hair." He picked up a lock, letting it slip through his fingers like water.

Mariss edged away from him and pressed her back against the sink. She gestured to the stall across from her. "I smell vagon in the shower. Someone's been using it, and I think I know who."

"Vagon? On *my* ship?" Kade's brows creased as his face tightened. "That's the last damn thing I need. *Vagon.*" He stuck his head in the shower. "So where is it?"

"You can't *see* it, Kade. The user wouldn't leave empty ampules lying around. But you can smell it."

"No, I can't," he said flatly.

"Here. You're not trying." Mariss shoved past him and stepped into the stall. "I was just about to turn on the water when I caught a faint whiff of it. I almost missed it. But I'm very familiar with the scent, so I know what I —"

"You?" Kade's amused gaze landed on her, uncomfortably close in the confines of the stall. His powerful body filled the door. "Let me guess. You took a course on identification of illegal drugs at the university, and they let you sniff a sample."

Mariss' violet eyes shot fire. "No, that's *not* how I know about vagon. Just close your eyes and concentrate, and you'll smell it, too."

"I'd rather keep them open." His eyes drifted irreverently over her body. During their argument, she had loosened her hold on the towel, giving him a glimpse of her modest cleavage. She tightened the towel again, glaring at him. Instinctively, she stepped away. Her back immediately impacted the wall behind her. There was nowhere to go.

Kade's smile faded as his eyes drifted over her, caressing her. "Mariss, I'm not stupid. First, that thing with the luggage, interrupting my off-hours exercise and waiting for me in my sleeping chamber. Now this. I admit Lorena's more direct about it. But I can certainly pretend you don't know what you're doing, if that's what you want."

He placed a foot in the shower stall, closing the distance between them to a matter of centimeters. Vibrant, Lorena had called him. Mariss felt his presence in every nerve and fiber, and it panicked her like a cornered animal. But there was nowhere to go. She was trapped.

She struck out, slamming her bare heel onto his booted foot. It was laughably ineffective. He only grinned at her and inched closer. She eyed the alarm on the wall. The captain was supposed to protect the passengers. But who would protect her from the captain? She turned to words as her most effective defense. "That `thing with the luggage' as you call it, turned out to be true, and you know it. My luggage *was* lighter than you thought. And I *do* smell vagon, or I did a few minutes ago. It's fading now. But it was here. Someone on this ship is using it."

"Let me guess. It's Lorena, isn't it?" Mariss missed his ironic tone.

She gazed at him in surprise. "How did you know?"

Kade chuckled and shook his head. "Mariss, Mariss, Mariss. Spaceflight does odd things to people, makes their primitive side come out. It's happening to you. First eliminate the competition, then use a complicated mating ritual of feigned innocence to trap your mark—me." He grinned intimately down at her.

Her composure snapped. In a blind fury, Mariss slapped Kade's face as hard as she could. The sting in her palm felt furiously wonderful.

Kade stepped back, his hand flying to his cheek. His eyes

turned thunderous as they pinned her where she stood. Mariss felt her exposed knees shaking.

Kade's voice was low, thick with anger. "Do you know how easy it would be for me to yank that pathetic towel off your body and have you?" Their eyes clashed and held. Mariss couldn't breathe. Her heart was pounding so hard, she could hear the blood rushing in her ears.

Kade continued, his voice rigid, cold. "Well, *M. Sakari,* I don't plan to give you the satisfaction, though we both know that's what you really want. You just don't want it to be your idea. That way you can pretend you've been *faithful* to Adrian. Well, I'm not playing. From now on, stay out of my way, do you hear me? I've had enough of your antics. Save your teasing and your tantrums for that blond block of wood on Elysia. I'm sure he'll be thrilled when he finds out what he's gotten himself into."

He vanished from her sight. Mariss heard the lavatory door retract and close. She was alone again, thoroughly embarrassed and completely infuriated. She tossed the towel aside and turned the water on, hard. This time she let the water run so long, she went past her five-minute limit and well into her stored credits, forgetting to use the precious resource to shampoo her hair.

***

Mariss sat before the console in the dim light of the main cabin, working at her cyber-unit. She had hard-wired it into the cabin databank, making it a slave to her own computer. Because ships in the fleet traveled such vast distances, each one carried a storehouse of information on everything from the ship's design to personnel records. The computer didn't allow even the ship's captain to have the security code that accessed the most restricted files, except in case of an emergency. With her data-manipulation skills, Mariss found bypassing the code an entertaining exercise that helped pass the time.

In the sleeping compartment, all was quiet. Only two days remained until Fredon Outpost, thank the Maker.

A fight had broken out earlier in the day between Mr.

Hudson and Mr. Lee, then between Mr. Hudson and his wife when she interfered. Betta Hudson had broken down in tears and run to the sleeping compartment. Mariss had gone to comfort her. She heard from Lorena that the argument between the two men almost came to blows. It had started over something minor, as such arguments usually did. Mr. Lee had accused Mr. Hudson of following improper rules in the Hycladian version of poker.

Captain Land had forced the men apart, sending Mr. Hudson to check on his wife, and inviting Mr. Lee into the cockpit for a while, according to Lorena.

This hadn't been the first such instance of strained nerves. Mariss herself had gotten into more than one tiff with Lorena. Yesterday, Mariss found long red hairs in her hairbrush. Lorena hadn't even asked to borrow it. And just this morning, Lorena had been in the lavatory for two solid hours, while the rest of the passengers were waiting with crossed legs to get in. The woman was inconsiderate and shallow and rude.

Mariss turned for solace to her cyber-unit. She worked on her project, or viewed the tapes of Adrian Young and the Colony on Elysia. After Fredon Outpost, she would be almost there. Almost there. She could put this entire aggravating section of her trip behind her. She might never travel in space again, after all.

Unfortunately, for the last stretch of the trip, she would be shut up in this ship alone with Kadin Land. Completely and utterly alone. Not that it should matter. For the past few days, he had ignored her completely, so much so he seemed to go out of his way to avoid her. Which was fine with Mariss.

She couldn't fully explain why she had decided to hack into the onboard databank, except she was painfully bored. Discovering Kadin Land's secrets, whatever they might be, promised to be more entertaining than anything else she could think of. Certainly more fun than listening to Lorena moan about how irresistibly good Kadin Land was in bed.

Apparently the redhead had scored after all. Mariss had seen no evidence of it on Kade's part. She tried not to care one way or the other, but she knew it was a losing battle. She was obviously interested at some level, try as she might to deny it.

She refocused on her cyber-unit's screen and moved past the friendly interface into the underlying code. Typical setup, she thought, navigating around past configuration and encryption files. This should be fairly uncomplicated.

A sound disturbed her concentration, and she glanced up. Lorena stepped from the cockpit into the cabin. She smiled at Mariss and raised her eyebrows suggestively. "It looks like it's your turn, if you're interested. Though you'll be hard-pressed to top my performance, you little ice queen." She sauntered toward the sleeping compartments.

Mariss watched her go, a sick feeling clawing in her gut. *Slut.* She couldn't keep herself from thinking it. Nor could she hold back the wave of disgust and anger that flooded over her. Her feelings were only aggravated by the knowledge that she shouldn't care about the two of them.

Her eyes flicked to the screen. Kadin Land was buried in here somewhere, and she was going to find him.

An hour later, she hit pay dirt. Quantum Personnel Files, the heading stated. *Confidential.* Fine, she wouldn't tell anybody.

Land, Kadin Aris
Born: Tass Mining Colony, 2467.2/14
Affiliation: Earth Territories
Address: Hub 117, JK-83, Nexus Spaceport
Closest Living Relative: N/A
Hair: Dark brown
Eyes: Brown
Race: Caucasian mix; Latinate predominant
Height: 174 cm
Weight: 95.3 kg
Marital Status: Single
Rank: Pilot, second class
Quantitative score of flight abilities: 99/100.
Last test date 2497.8/08: Subscores: 98/visual acuity; 99/reaction time; 99/obstacle avoidance; 99/peripheral focus; 98/

procedure performance; 97/mental preparedness; 97/ processing of incoming data; 99/endurance; 98/tenacity; 85/ stability under pressure. Note: Quantitative score remains highest in Quantum history.

Fascinated, Mariss scanned through the data, feeling like a thief in the night. A thief of information, personal information on a man she had no business being interested in. And for what? Idle amusement is all. She'd been bored. She'd been curious. She wanted to prove she could hack into the system. But that didn't give her the right to pry. Feeling deeply ashamed, Mariss began to close the file.

A word caught her up short and she scrolled back up the screen. "Oh, no," she whispered under her breath.

FIVE

CRIMINAL RECORD. The words were in capital letters, so anyone reviewing the file would be sure not to miss them—like her.

CRIMINAL RECORD: 2487.3/12: Charged with first-degree murder of classmate Alan McChord at Spanos Pilot Academy; concurrent charge of fraud involving exams; 2487.4/26: Pled guilty to third-degree murder and first-degree fraud; 2487.4/28: Sentenced to seven years hard labor, Rebus Five. 2492.7/22: Paroled to cargo service in Harik Sector; 2494.4/28: Released from parole.

Kade had done hard time at an asteroid penal colony even more dismal than the one where he'd been raised. For murder. There had been some sort of plea bargain, but that's what lawyers were for, helping the guilty get off with less than they deserved.

The authorities had charged him with first-degree murder.... And he agreed to serve a sentence of slave labor by admitting to third-degree murder. It was a lesser charge, taking into account "mitigating circumstances." But it carried with it the full burden of guilt. And Kade must have been guilty. There was no question of that. If he hadn't murdered his classmate, why would he accept the guilty verdict rather than plead not guilty, as an innocent man would?

The details and dates blurred before her. None of them mattered except for one fact: Kade was an ex-convict.

Mariss blinked hard to remove the tears from her eyes. People could change. Perhaps. Perhaps not. She scanned down the rest of the report. The most recent entry was only a month ago.

INAPPROPRIATE CONDUCT REPORT FILED: 2498.2/11: Barron Outpost. Arrested by Outpost Police for inciting to riot. Served two days in brig. Conduct Review Board findings: Guilty of drunk and disorderly conduct unbecoming a Quantum pilot. Rank reduced. Dismissal under consideration.

Inciting to riot? Why?

Mariss read on. The final terse words echoed in her mind flatly, unemotionally. Yet they carried so much meaning.

RECOMMENDATION: Suspicion of involvement in black-market trade. Despite astounding innate abilities, may pose public-relations risk to Quantum. Maintain on deep-space, far-sector runs until skills no longer required. Review conduct closely and report.

PROMOTION POTENTIAL: None.

She probably knew more now than Kade did about his future with Quantum Craftlines. He still hoped for a promotion, she knew. She had overheard him arguing about it back at the Nexus. He still believed he had a future.

Black-market trade... A chill raced down Mariss' spine. The Vagon serum. Kade hadn't been the least concerned about one of his passengers smuggling it on board. Why, he was probably involved in it. He could even be selling it to passengers aboard this ship, or transporting it for sale elsewhere. He and Lorena, after all, were apparently close. They were probably both involved.

Mariss released the databank from her unit after downloading his entire file into her own database—just as a precaution. She had a feeling she would want to review the file again, and she had worked hours to uncover it.

She snapped her cyber-unit closed. They were almost at Fredon Outpost. There would be other pilots, other ships. She might be able to find passage to Elysia with one of them. If not, she would be alone on this ship for three days with Kadin Land. The prospect was suddenly terrifying.

***

Fredon Outpost

"Thank you, Captain."

Kade smiled as Mr. Hudson raised his hand in a friendly palm-out farewell. He'd been a fairly easy passenger, as Kade had expected. Just the one incident with Mr. Lee over their card game. Other than that, things had gone well this time out.

They were standing at the bottom of the steps leading to the ship's hatch. "Thank you," Mr. Hudson repeated enthusiastically. "We made it." He grinned and draped his arm around his wife's shoulders. "You made it a decent flight, all things considered."

"It was good to have you," Kade replied. "Enjoy your visit with your son. Who knows, I may be flying you home again."

Betta cried joyously as their tall son appeared out of the milling crowd and swept her into his arms. Donald joined the reunion, and after a final wave, the Hudson family disappeared into the crowd.

Lorena confronted Kade, but her farewell was nothing like the Hudsons'. Her garishly painted lips were tight with displeasure. "I want you to know you ruined my record, and I'm not going to forget it, Land."

Kade pasted on his regulation smile and raised his hand in salute. Lorena didn't respond in kind. "It was a pleasure having you aboard, Miss," he said mockingly.

Lorena's lips twisted up. She planted a manicured hand on her fleshy hip. "Good luck, Land. Believe me, you're going to need it." She tossed a meaningful glance toward the hatch door before sauntering toward the docking bay exit. Kade caught sight of her heading straight for the Interstellar Police clustered near the exit. She was about to receive an unpleasant surprise.

If it hadn't been for Mariss, Lorena would have gotten away with it, too. It was a ploy of smugglers to plant their goods in a fellow passenger's luggage, to divert suspicion if the contraband was discovered. He suspected Lorena had slipped the goods into Mariss' case after the Nexus Spaceport cargo master had weighed it in. Either that, or the cargo master was in on it. A woman who traveled as much as Lorena undoubtedly had built a network of contacts with spaceport employees.

Once on board his ship, Lorena had retrieved her goods to keep Mariss from finding them—and so she could enjoy them. He grimaced. And Lorena thought he'd go for her bribe. She was none too happy when she realized Kade was on to her. Unfortunately, she had admitted to incinerating the drugs while on board. Which meant without evidence, she'd probably get off scot-free.

Kade considered giving a statement to the cops. But with his record, suspicion would probably fall on him as an accomplice. Maybe he shouldn't have alerted the cops—

"Captain Land." The Oriental businessman had been patiently waiting his turn.

"Mr. Lee." Kade again raised his hand, but Mr. Lee ignored the salute.

"My name isn't Mr. Lee, Pilot Land. It's Mr. Chan. I am in fact an employee of Quantum Craftlines." He flipped open his wallet to show his ID. "I have spent this flight observing your behavior and your performance. I will be filing a report on you with Quantum management shortly."

Kade stared at him, his gut twisting. Images came to him—memories of his snide comments, his loose treatment of protocol, the irreverence of his pre-flight instructions to the passengers. He was finished. "Mr. Lee. If you'd only told me, I would have—"

"No doubt behaved differently. We seek to evaluate our pilots based on their actual performance during flight, ergo the necessity of my false identity. Good day, Land." He turned away, his cyber-unit clutched in his hand.

"Mr. Lee—I mean, Mr. Chan, wait!" Kade strode to catch

up with him. Obviously reluctant, Chan faced him. "Your report, what is it going to say? I'm about to leave on another outback run. I want to know what's going to be waiting for me when I return. You owe me that."

"Can't do. Sorry. Confidential until it's filed. For the second time, good day, Land."

This time Kade didn't make a move to stop him.

***

Mariss waited uncertainly by the hatch door, her gaze playing over the slumped shoulders of her ship's captain.

Employees of Quantum and the competing Delta-Epsilon Spacelines drove carts past to attend to their respective ships. Quantum crews were already prepping Kade's ship, fueling it, conducting systems checks, off-loading the departing passengers' luggage.

Fredon Outpost was nothing like the cool, controlled atmosphere of Nexus Spaceport. Once the docking bay was pressurized, a dozen people had appeared, baggage handlers and tourists alike. The arrival of a new ship was cause for interest here in the outback.

But despite the people, Mariss felt alone with Kade. He was oblivious to her presence, his elbows propped on his knees, his hands clasped, his dark head hanging. He looked dismal. Mariss found herself responding, despite her better sense. "Excuse me," she said softly.

Kade glanced up, his eyes barely registering Mariss' presence.

"I...I overheard. I'm sorry."

"You're sorry? What in the hell for?"

"The Quantum spy, Mr. Chan."

Kade rose to face her. He was standing a step below her, bringing their eyes to the same level. His gaze was dark and penetrating, potent. He was no longer someone to pity, but a man to be wary of. Instinctively, Mariss wanted to step back, but she held her ground out of pride, and let his attack come.

"You assume the report will be bad. Thanks for the vote of confidence."

"But you think so, too!" she shot back.

He planted his hands on his hips. “Why in the hell would I think so?”

She gestured weakly toward the steps. “The way you were sitting, all slumped over.”

His jaw muscles visibly tightened. “Maybe I’m just damned tired of skinny, dark-haired vixens eavesdropping on my personal conversations!”

Mariss narrowed her eyes. He was insufferable. And probably dangerous. She needed to get away from him, at all costs. She needed to visit the inner section of the spaceport, find another pilot to take her to Elysia. “Please step aside,” she said coolly. “I...I have to go into the spaceport for a moment.”

His hand grasped her arm. Mariss caught him casting glances toward a group of Interstellar Police clustered near the exit. “There’s no sightseeing here, Mariss. Nothing but a bar and a restaurant and shuttles to nearby gas mining stations.”

“I have to go.”

He shook his head. “Just get aboard and stay put. I want to leave right away. Besides, aren’t you anxious to meet up with Mr. Wonderful?”

Mariss yanked her arm away. “I said, I have business in the spaceport.” She shoved past him and hurried down the steps, conscious of Kade’s eyes boring into her back.

***

Her errand was a complete failure. Not only did other pilots laugh at her question, they directed her back to Kade and his Quantum flight. They certainly weren’t going to change their plans to take Mariss to an out-of-the-way planet like Elysia. She had her ticket, the ship was on time—what was her problem?

As she wandered back into the docking bay, Mariss noticed the outside of Kade’s ship for the first time. At the Nexus, she had gone straight through an accessway into the ship’s interior, and never seen it. It was lozenge-shaped, dinged and scratched in places. Nothing like one of the sleek new liners showcased in Quantum vid-ads.

The ship had been knocked around a bit, just like her pilot.

Again she felt a pinch of pity. She knew Kade would hate her for it. But she couldn't help feeling compassion for him and his situation.

She told herself Quantum was probably justified. He had done a horrible thing, killing a fellow student. She repeated the facts to herself, but she couldn't convince her heart of their truth. Deep down, she half thought he needed to be protected. From what, she couldn't begin to imagine.

But she had been wrong to seek another pilot. If she, a paying passenger, deserted him now, it would only hurt his chances with Quantum all the more.

His eyes fastened on her as she approached the ship. He stood at the foot of the steps, wearing a superior grin. "No dice, Mariss? That's too bad. Looks like you're stuck with me." He must have gotten wind of what she had been up to. His smile faded. "Now get your fanny aboard and let's get this over with. It's probably my last commercial flight, and I want to be done with it."

He stalked up the steps and through the hatch. Mariss had no choice but to follow.

***

Mariss again took up her original seat in the main cabin and buckled her seatbelt in preparation for lift-off. Kade had disappeared into the cockpit.

She glanced around at the empty seats. This trip would last too long, no matter how short it was. It hadn't even begun and the sense of isolation—alone with Kadin Land in this enclosed space—was already overwhelming.

His voice came over the speakers. "Passenger Sakari, come to the cockpit." The door to the cockpit slid back and stayed open, inviting her in.

With a sigh and—she reluctantly admitted—a sense of anticipation, Mariss unbuckled her seatbelt and entered the cockpit. "What is it?"

"Take a seat." Kade occupied the pilot's seat. He pointed at the empty co-pilot's seat. "You'll probably never go into space again, once you get to Elysia. You're going to live and die there with what's-his-name."

"Adrian Young." Tentatively, Mariss sat down.

"I thought you might like to have a real view for once."

"Yes. Yes, I would." Mariss couldn't keep the excitement from her voice. The portals in the main cabin never could offer much of a view. But here in the cockpit, the viewport stretched from one end to the other, providing a full panoramic sweep. Right now, all she saw were the docking bay and the bay doors beyond.

Kade spoke to the control room. "Flight SDC 586 prepared for lift-off. All systems go."

The control room responded. "Bay doors retracting in 0-5 minutes. Permission to depart granted." Bars of yellow light began flashing a warning to those in the docking bay to retreat to safety.

Kade wasn't watching the docking bay doors. Mariss followed his gaze. His attention was on the police below, who seemed reluctant to leave the docking bay until ushered out by spaceport officials. "Why are the police here?"

Kade shook his head. Every muscle in his face had tightened. But he maintained a casual tone. "Must be looking for somebody."

Mariss recalled how Kade had wanted to leave immediately. "You?"

He snorted. "They know who I am. Somebody else. Or something else." He sighed. His dark eyes turned to her. "Hell if I know. Fasten your seatbelt, Mariss."

She did so as Kade began the sequence to prime the engine. A few minutes later, the docking bay lights turned red, and the doors began to retract before them.

The dark of space wasn't all that greeted them. Beyond the bay doors was the rim of the largest, reddest planet Mariss had ever seen. A gas giant, the spaceport floated above it, drawing essential gases from its miles-thick atmosphere. "Fredon," Kade said simply.

After more chatter with the control room, Kade lifted the ship forward and away from Fredon Outpost. Mariss gripped the arms of the co-pilot's seat as their ship moved into the vastness of space and swung sharply downward. She gasped.

It felt as if she were standing on top of the planet, hanging in mid-space with nothing supporting her. The effect was thrilling and frightening at the same time.

Kade brought the ship around, giving Mariss a magnificent full-circle view. Her blood surged in time with the engines. *This* was flying. With the endless immensity of space just outside the window, she felt as if she were sailing among the stars.

Kade banked the ship around the outpost, which hung above Fredon, sunlight glinting off its multi-faceted alloy surface. Far below, shuttles arrived and departed from its outstretched prongs. Here and there, lights glowed along its surface, indicating living and working quarters.

"It's...unbelievable," Mariss said with reverent awe. "You can't see any of this from the passenger cabin."

"Not on this ship, anyway," Kade said wryly. He grinned at her. "Like it?"

They exchanged a smile. "I love it. Thank you. I think I understand now why you put up with the tedium of the rest of it."

Kade only laughed.

Mariss felt herself warming to him. His deep, rich laugh drew her in, made her fears seem groundless, childish even. Kade's magnetism was undeniable. Right now, Mariss felt the power of his attention, and she basked in it. The trip to Elysia wouldn't be so bad after all.

Once they had jumped to interstellar space, she changed her mind.

It started with a simple enough question. "How long will it be before we reach Elysia?" she asked.

Kade glanced at the console chronometer. "Thirty-six hours to orbit, a couple after that to get to that Colony of yours." His eyes met hers. "Anxious to meet Mr. Wonderful, no doubt."

"Adrian Young," Mariss corrected. "Of course I'm looking forward to meeting him. Though in many ways, I feel I already know him."

Kade's tone was sarcastic. "Sure you do."

"What's *that* supposed to mean?"

He shrugged. "Just that you're foolish to expect as much as you do from a stranger."

"I'm not expecting anything but companionship and commitment. For that, Adrian Young has been scientifically proven to be a perfect match for me in every way that counts. His accomplishments, his interests, his education—"

Kade snorted. "Is he applying to be your husband or your employee?"

With an effort, Mariss held her temper in check, determined not to rise to the bait. "The computer also matched our temperaments, Kade. Adrian is compassionate, loyal—"

"Sounds like a dog I had once."

"—stable—"

"Safe."

She sighed, her exasperation growing. "I don't know if I'd call him safe, but I certainly hope he is. What's wrong with safe? All that means to me is he plans on a lifetime commitment, and he's never broken the law."

"Is that so?" Kade's expression froze.

Mariss didn't notice right away. Her thoughts were back with Peck, and her first disastrous marriage—the late night visits from drug dealers, the police raid on their home, the lawyers, the explaining, the fear. "He's clean. He's straight. He's never gotten into trouble. I value that in a man."

Kade's entire demeanor had changed. He unfastened his seatbelt and headed for the hatch.

Mariss suddenly realized Kade had assumed she was talking about him. Perhaps she was, subconsciously. She fumbled to unfasten her seatbelt and called after him. "Kade, wait. I wasn't referring to your own record."

Kade froze in front of the hatch door, his back to her, his hand raised to press the button. He lowered his hand and turned to face her. His expression was unreadable, his dramatic features even more prominent in the shadowed hall. "What did you say?"

Mariss sighed. She wanted it out in the open, what she knew about him. She wanted him to explain it to her, so she could understand, so she wouldn't feel so afraid of him. "I said I wasn't talking about you. About your record."

His posture was casual, his hands resting on his hips. But Mariss sensed the tension in every muscle. "My *criminal* record?" His eyes played over her face and fastened on hers, seeking, cold.

Her reply jumbled in her throat. But Kade didn't need to hear her words to confirm it. He could read her knowledge in her eyes.

He slowly closed in on her, and she found herself pressed against the wall. He hovered over her. "How in the hell do you know about that?" He glanced away, his black brows furrowed. "Let me guess. Bruce Crosby. He told you, didn't he?" He shot an accusing look at her.

"Who?"

"On Fredon. He said something to you."

Mariss shook her head vigorously. "No, no he didn't. Don't go after him. Please."

Kade's eyes narrowed to slits. He planted a palm on the wall above her head, effectively trapping her. Mariss saw a pulse beat in his tensed jaw. "Who *should* I be 'going after,' Mariss?"

Her heart hammered against her ribcage. Kadin Land looked quite capable of murder right now. "Please. Nobody. I read about your past."

His eyes widened. "*Did* you. Where?"

"In the databank computer."

"There's nothing about it in the databank. Quantum prefers to pretend it never happened." His voice took on an even harsher edge.

"It's in your personnel file. There's a mention of it."

He stared at her as if he hadn't seen her before. "How in the hell did you get in there?"

"Carefully."

"So you're a hacker."

"Sometimes I am."

His lips curled up in a humorless smile. "Was it fun, reading my personnel file?"

Mariss realized now just how deep a hole she had dug for

herself. It was time to start climbing. "Kade, I'm sorry, but I was curious. And I—"

His eyes filled with understanding, and she faltered. Lips tightened over clenched teeth, his words were tight with fury. "That's why you went looking for another pilot. You're afraid of me." He laid his hand on her shoulder, close to her neck. He spoke low, threatening. "You know all about it now, don't you, Mariss? How I killed a man?"

Mariss swallowed hard, her heart thundering in her ears. She wished she were anywhere else but here with this man, with his half-crazed look and his dark, glittering eyes. His powerful fingers burned like molten steel as they slipped along the exposed column of her neck. "I only know what I read," she finally said, her voice little more than a croak.

"I can fill you in on the gory details, if you like. Tell me, Mariss, how does it feel to have the hand of a convicted murderer around your delicate white throat?"

Her voice shook. "Let go of me."

"Just think of it, Mariss. We're completely alone out here in the middle of nowhere. And here you are, on your way to meet your new husband, a perfect, clean male specimen, with not a mark to blacken his record. But you're stuck out here with me. *Me*, Mariss."

His thumb slipped under her chin, and he tilted her head back, his fingers tense with barely leashed power. His mesmerizing gaze trapped her. She couldn't look away.

"Terrifying prospect, isn't it? I could strangle you and no one would know."

Deep in her heart, Mariss believed he wouldn't kill her—at least not yet. She gathered her courage and spoke boldly. "Is that how you killed your classmate? By strangulation?"

His lips twisted in a wry smile. "Hell no. Takes too long. I blasted his chest open. Instant death." He released her throat and slipped his forefinger along her jaw. "This is the finger which pulled the trigger." He ran it across her lip. Mariss closed her eyes against the thrill which shot through her, followed instantly by shame at her weakness. It was all wrong, completely wrong. She mustn't feel such a deep, primitive need—not here, not now, not with this man.

She gasped and wrenched her face away. "Get away from me."

Kade dropped his hands. He stood there for a breathless moment, staring at her. Mariss felt his eyes burning into her skin. "Yes, ma'am," he said flatly. He stepped back and pressed the button to open the hatch.

Mariss almost fell through it in her haste to get away. He stopped her flight with a steely hand on her arm. With effortless strength, he swung her around to face him. "Stay on your side of the ship, Sakari, and I'll stay on mine. That's a damned order."

Mariss wrenched her arm away and he let her go. She stumbled back and the door closed in her face.

She bit back a sob, but another forced its way up her throat and she couldn't contain it. Her shoulders shaking, she buried her face in her hands, shame and fury coursing through her in equal measure. It would be an eon before they reached Elysia, and the safety of her life with Adrian Young.

***

Kade kept his word. Mariss hardly saw him, except when he passed through the passenger cabin on his way to the galley for meals. Even then, he merely grabbed what he wanted and left without a word or a glance toward her. Mariss watched his retreating back, wondering if she could stand the silence much longer.

Kadin Land was apparently used to being alone. He seemed unperturbed by it. Mariss felt every second. She regretted their confrontation, but sometimes she feared him. Mostly, she feared her attraction to him, the unspeakable daydreams that had come to plague her lonely hours. She imagined him cornering her again, demanding things from her, forcing her to confront the unmentionable torrent of passion he had tapped. She had vowed never to become victim to her feelings again, vowed it as if her life depended on it. But she had never imagined feelings could flow so intensely through her body, and her heart.

It could only be loneliness, she told herself, watching the

hologram of Adrian Young. Loneliness, pure and simple. The cure was a handful of days away, on Elysia, in the body and soul of her future life mate.

On the third day, Kade's voice came to her over the speaker, crisp and professional. "Passenger M. Sakari, secure the cabin. We're exiting interstellar space into the orbit of Elysia."

Almost there, Mariss thought. She was almost there. She slipped into the seat and fastened her belt. Kade hadn't invited her to the cockpit for the view, and she had no intention of going, anyway. She would make do with the porthole beside her seat.

The black vanished with a burst of white light. The ship shuddered, and space returned. Compared to total black, the stars seemed tremendously bright and numerous. Mariss strained to see outside the small porthole. She caught a glimpse of Elysia, its green and brown curve only partially visible. The Colony was below. Adrian would be waiting for her.

Elysia was an Earth-like planet, but still distant enough to be only sparsely colonized. A lot of work remained to be done to classify its plant species. Work Mariss hoped to be engaged in shortly.

Kade was right. She would most certainly be spending the rest of her life here. Space travel was expensive. And she had no reason to return to Earth. Her brother was occupied with his own career in the prestigious diplomatic corps. And her sister—Mariss never wanted to see her sister again. Half a galaxy away wasn't distant enough.

Mariss sighed, finally admitting to herself that the Colony's appeal wasn't only Adrian Young. It was far removed from her old life, and her old pain. That was a good part of the reason she had chosen to come here.

The ship shuddered to a stop. Mariss looked around the cabin. Something wasn't right. They were in orbit above Elysia, but she couldn't hear the engines. The cockpit door opened and Kade entered. He glanced about, barely noticing her.

A moment later, a loud bang hit the top of the ship. "What was that?" Mariss asked.

"Just stay put. We're being boarded."

"Boarded! By whom?"

"Those paragons of law and order, the star cops."

SIX

Mariss ignored his command. She unfastened her seatbelt and confronted him, her eyes wide with anxiety. "What have you done?"

"Shut up and sit down." Kade turned his back on her, his gaze pinned on the cabin ceiling and the banging above.

An access hatch was being raised by an external force. The police were docked on top of his ship, anchoring it in place with grapplers. A ladder descended, and two people wearing the blood-red uniform and helmets of the Interstellar Police appeared. Their faces were half-hidden behind smoked visors, only their mouths visible. Both held before them the largest phase-guns in the police artillery, almost a meter long and as thick as a man's arm.

"Raise your hands," commanded the heavily muscled female cop. Kade saw by her gold insignia that she outranked the man beside her.

Kade slowly lifted his hands. "I'm not armed."

Ignoring Kade's protest, the lead cop gestured with her head to her subordinate, who spun Kade around and pressed him against the bulkhead. He shoved his face into the wall and searched him roughly.

"He's clean," the cop said. He crossed to Mariss, who tentatively raised her hands. The cop patted her sides down, lingering unnecessarily. When he seemed to be through, he squeezed her butt.

"Get your damn paws off her! She's just a passenger," Kade snarled.

The female cop towered over Kade a good six inches. "Shut up, flyboy. We received a tip on you." She eyed him up and down, a smirk on her thin lips. "Cooperate, and it'll go easier. For both of you." She ordered the other cop to open the hatch leading below decks.

The male cop retracted the hatch and disappeared into the bowels of Kade's ship. "What kind of tip? A payoff, or a cut of the take?"

Without warning, the female cop smashed the butt of her gun into Kade's stomach. Pain sliced through Kade, and he doubled over with a grunt. "You're digging yourself a deeper hole, Land. We checked your file, Rebus Rat. You're in deep krod. If anything's here, you're history."

The waves of pain receded enough for Kade to straighten up. His eyes found Mariss'. Her face was chalky white. Kade figured she was scared, maybe even shocked at the tactics of the police in this sector. Kade wasn't. The only thing that surprised him was that Lorena had managed to screw him after all.

"It's here." The voice of the male cop carried through the hatch. "Want to see it in place?"

"Where'd you find it?"

"In a red luggage case. Buried in the clothing, just where she said it would be."

"That's *my* case," Mariss said. "What is it? What did you find? There's nothing special in my case."

"Mariss, don't—" But it was too late. She had started toward the hatch. The butch cop shoved her back, and she fell hard on her bottom. Kade reached down and helped her to her feet. She clung to his arm, standing half behind him.

"Looks like 35, maybe 40 kilos of prime."

"Vagon," Mariss said softly.

"Shh!" Kade hissed back.

"Shut up!" The woman cop shoved them apart. The male cop appeared through the hatch, carrying a bag of vagon serum ampules. He tossed them at Kade's feet. "Explain it, flyboy."

"Planted, of course," Kade sneered. "But you already know that."

The cop raised the butt of her rifle and swung it toward Kade's head. Kade raised his forearm to block the blow. To his shock, Mariss jumped in the way before she connected.

"No, it's not his, he knows nothing about it. The drugs are mine," Mariss said, her words tumbling out. "You found them in my luggage, didn't you? He doesn't know anything about it. He's just the pilot. I—I know the drug is illegal, but I'm a botanist, and I use it in my research. I have a card here." She reached in her front hip pocket.

The male cop stopped her. "Let me." He jammed his gloved hand in her flightsuit pocket. Kade saw him take the opportunity to feel between her legs.

The sight enraged Kade beyond all caution. He leaped at the cop and shoved him off of Mariss. With a furious cry, the cop smashed the side of his gun into Kade's head. Kade stumbled to his knees, dizzy and unable to see for several precious seconds. A wave of nausea coursed upward from his gut. With supreme effort, he fought it down. There wasn't going to be any easy, polite way out of this one. These weren't your garden-variety police. They were on the fringes of control in the wasteland of the civilized galaxy. He had to think, and he had to come up with something useful. If only his head didn't feel like it was about to shatter.

"Earth Botanical Society." The male cop read the card he'd finally fished from her suit. "Mariss Sakari. Yeah, so? You're a drug trafficker. He's a convicted felon. You're coming with us."

"Cuff 'em, Mack."

Before Mack reached him, Kade was on his feet. And before he had the cuffs out, Kade's foot struck with blinding force, knocking the massive gun out of the cop's hands. It spun out of Kade's line of sight.

Mack leapt at Kade. Kade blocked his punch and delivered one of his own, slamming the cop to his knees.

This left him exposed. The lead cop let loose with a horrific blast from her phase-gun. It seared the bulkhead inches from Kade's face. Kade dove to the floor, his quick reactions saving him, but knowing it was already too late. His destiny was sealed.

He caught sight of Mariss diving onto the deck just before

a series of blasts struck near his head, sparks shooting up from the carpet and alloy floor beneath. Suddenly, the blasting stopped, accompanied by a feminine shriek and a harsh scream.

The smoke diffused and Kade could see. "Mariss!" She was kneeling across the room from him. Incredibly, her hands were wrapped around the phase-gun he'd knocked from Mack. She looked like she thought it was going to bite her.

The lead cop lay on her back, writhing, her leg damaged by the blast from the gun. Mack was crawling over his superior's body to reach the woman's discarded phase-gun, his face set in a mask of fury.

Kade didn't want this scene to end the way it was heading. He had enough blood on his hands as it was. There was another way out, if he could make it in time. He sprang up and yanked Mariss to her feet. Half carrying, half dragging her, he leapt through the galley door just as a phase-gun blast hit the console beside them. The console burst into flames, shedding sparks everywhere.

Kade slammed the door button and it slid closed. He engaged the lock, but knew it wasn't strong enough to hold the cops for long.

"This way." He continued down the corridor, past the galley and through the sleeping cabin. At the rear, he opened one of two blue doors. To Kade, it seemed the door opened in slow motion. Kade heard phase-gun blasts striking the galley doorlock. They only had a few seconds. He glanced around, but Mariss wasn't with him. He swore, panic rising. But a heartbeat later, she reappeared, clutching her cyber-unit against her chest like a shield. As soon as the lifepod door opened wide enough, he shoved her through it and dove in after.

He landed on Mariss, but righted himself and shoved her down in a seat. He took the other one and slammed the control for the doors. He caught sight of a red uniform a split second before the door sealed shut. Kade fired the jets, and the lifepod broke away from the Quantum passenger ship.

Out in space, he could see the police craft through the small portal. It was black with red insignia, four times the size of his own passenger ship. It looked like a hawk grasping a field mouse in its talons. He set the shortest course possible toward the planet, less concerned with where they were going to land than putting as much distance between themselves and the police as he could.

They entered the upper atmosphere, and the lifepod shook with the buffeting winds. “Hold on.”

“That’s what I’ve been trying to do,” Mariss said wryly.

Kade shot her a look. Her hair was mussed, her braid nearly undone. Soot from the phase-gun blasts marred her porcelain-fine cheeks. Her eyes had a wild quality, like an animal living on the edge. She was beautiful.

“You didn’t mention you knew how to use a phase-gun.”

Mariss looked away. “That’s because I don’t.”

“Could’ve fooled me.”

“I was aiming for her chest.”

The ride grew too bumpy for conversation as they passed through the atmosphere. The aft jets powered up to slow their descent. Kade attempted to use his onboard radar to pick a relatively flat landing spot. From this height he couldn’t get more specific than a large continent on the dark side, for lack of knowing anything about the planet. As they neared, Kade could see a series of mountain ranges and a wide plain in the gray area where the dark side met the light. He angled the pod toward the plain and chose a landing spot by visual reckoning, near where the night gave way to daylight. The best he could do was trust the onboard scopes and hope he didn’t hit something substantial.

The craft impacted the ground and slid, jarring Kade so hard his teeth rattled. But his eyes were fastened on his scope, which projected the onrushing terrain 200 meters ahead. In about 100 of those meters, the ground dropped away. If they hit the drop, they would fall who knew where.

Kade rammed the reverse-propulsion lever, praying to the Maker of the Universe that it would engage in time. The pod slowed almost imperceptibly. It wouldn’t be enough. The scope showed the precipice speeding toward them, 75 meters, 60, rushing up fast. Thinking faster than he ever had, he smashed his fist on the control for the oxygen vents. He remembered they were located on the front of the lifepods—at least, he thought they were in this particular model lifepod. Quantum had rushed him through the pre-flight check-out on the ship, more anxious to assign a pilot to this abysmal run than ensure passenger safety.

45 meters.

The added reverse thrust just might give them the extra meter or two they needed to keep the craft from falling into what was rapidly resolving into a nasty drop. Of course, he was depleting their precious oxygen stores, so Elysia had better have breathable air. He thought it did. He didn't think Mariss mentioned the Colony existing under a life-dome.

40 meters, a short burst of deceleration as the gas spewed out the vents.

35 meters, the drop closing fast.

25 meters. Nothing to do but hold on.

Kade turned his gaze from the scope with its advancing red field indicating a lower altitude and certain death—to Mariss, who was oblivious to their almost certain fate. Kade didn't think of himself as a particularly thoughtful guy, but he wasn't going to tell her a thing about it. No need to scare her if they just happened to make it.

His eye flicked to the scope—25 meters. Definitely slowing now, as the last of the oxygen poured from the vents, and the reverse-propulsion engines continued to fire. The pod hit rough ground, shaking the craft so hard, Kade thought it would break apart. But now the terrain sloped gently uphill, and slowed the craft considerably.

With a final, horrible shudder, the craft settled to a stop. Kade gasped, unaware until now that he'd been holding his breath. The pod gave off a burst of steam and a series of mechanical groans. The cabin lights flickered then died. The only light—dull, grey and unrevealing—came from the small porthole set in the pod's hatch.

His equilibrium returning, Kade attempted a smile for Mariss' benefit. "That's that. This pod isn't taking us any further." He released the hatch and his own restraints. He scanned the external-environment readings. "Earthlike.

Breathable oxygen, uncontaminated, radiation readings normal—hell, even the weather is temperate at 60 degrees. We couldn't have asked for better. Thank the Maker." He exhaled and ran his hands through his hair.

"We're on Elysia now, aren't we?"

He glanced toward Mariss, who was unbuckling her restraints. "Yeah."

Equally shaken, Mariss attempted a smile. "Well, Quantum certainly knows how to show its passengers an exciting time."

Kade laughed. He was alive. *They* were alive. For a while, anyway. He rose and popped the hatch free. The hatch door dropped to ground level—and then beyond. Stunned, Kade stood in the hatchway and looked out and down.

And down, and down.

Mariss was right behind him. Anticipating his forward step, she bumped into him. Kade reacted by stepping back, hard.

"Ouch! What are you waiting for?"

"Mariss," he said, his voice low, serious. "Sit your fanny back down, right now. And don't move an inch."

"Why should I—"

"Mariss."

She must have heard the tension in his voice, for she complied without another word.

Very slowly, hardly daring to breathe, Kade got a firm grip on the hatchway and leaned out far enough to see how the pod was resting. The lifepod had stopped just a centimeter or two before the precipice. A few pebbles, kicked loose by the craft, tumbled into the ravine below. How stable the pod was, Kade had no idea. One thing was certain—he didn't want to stay here a moment longer than he had to.

"We're on the edge of a pretty sharp drop, Mariss," he said. "Stay put. I'm going out."

Kade backed up a few steps. Keeping a firm hold on the side of the hatchway, he took a running step and swung around the edge. He managed to plant one foot squarely on solid ground. He shifted his weight and was safe.

He glanced at the pod. It seemed secure enough in its precarious location. The track it had made screaming toward this drop was visible in the pre-dawn light as a shallow channel, littered with flattened plants and displaced dirt.

He heard a sound from the pod and spun to find Mariss leaning out of the hatch.

"Oh," she said softly, her eyes playing over the position of the pod. "Well, I think I can manage it. Hold on."

Just as Kade had done, she was backing up to take a run at it. "No!" Panic hit Kade hard in his gut. He stumbled over his feet racing toward her. If she couldn't make it—

Mariss swung toward him, her foot outstretched for the ground, reaching for it, the momentum of her swing sending her right toward him, but she was losing it, wasn't going to make it, not far enough—

Kade dove toward her. One hand gripping an extension on the pod, he stretched out the other and barely managed to grasp her wrist. Mariss fell forward onto him—she would have had enough power to make it, he realized belatedly—and into his arms. He yanked her hard up against himself.

He turned her away from the precipice and shoved her back against the side of the pod. Still holding her, he found himself staring into her eyes, a few inches away. Both were breathing heavily. Her face was flushed, a pulse visible at the base of her neck. An unwanted surge of desire swept through his body. *Just your body, Kade. It's been a long time between women.* She was soft, delicate, exquisite. And she infuriated him.

He shoved himself off her. "What did you think you were doing? You could have killed yourself!"

"I had to get out of there. I felt the pod shift."

"I was going to get a rope for you."

Her violet eyes flashed. "I didn't need a rope. And if you hadn't stood in my way, I would have had no trouble at all."

"Fine. I'll stay out of your way. But don't move from this spot, do you hear me?"

He stepped toward pod's hatch. Mariss grasped his sleeve. "What do you think you're doing?"

He threw her an irritated glance. "Getting supplies."

"Didn't you hear me? I said I felt the pod shift."

"All the more reason for me to get them right away, wouldn't you say?" He tore her hand off his sleeve and turned to swing back into the pod.

"Look at that," Mariss said, her voice hushed.

Kade followed her gaze across the valley below, to where a mountain range stretched to the sky. Dawn was breaking beyond the mountains, a streak of grey illumining their tips in stark silhouette. Above, where the night sky was losing its battle with the morning, streaked the largest comet Kade had ever seen. The fireball shed a tail of orange-gold in a magnificent arc.

"What is it?" Mariss asked, coming up beside him.

Kade kept his eyes on the fireball, mixed emotions surging through him. It signaled the end of a chapter of his life, of that there was no doubt.

And the death of a dream. A dream which had seen him through a lonely childhood and a torturous prison sentence. "The end of my piloting career. Can't say it isn't spectacular."

To his surprise, Mariss slipped her hand in his. Together, they watched the Quantum passenger ship incinerate in the atmosphere of Elysia.

SEVEN

Elysia: Jio Continent

Mariss glanced about, taking in the uninhabited valley below, the rocky range rising in the distance. "Where are we?"

"On Elysia," Kade muttered. He was on his knees, the gear from the pod spread before him. He had gone back into the pod several times for everything of value. He had been in there so long the last time, Mariss had almost gone in after him. When he finally emerged, he carried her cyber-unit. Right now, Mariss couldn't remember why she had risked her life on the ship to grab it. Maybe she was a little preoccupied with the sense of order it gave her life. Right now, she was as far from order as she had ever been. Yet she knew she would manage. She always managed.

"I meant where on Elysia? It's almost as big as Earth, Kade."

Kade shoved a pack of flares into one of two backpacks. "On the edge of a cliff."

Mariss sighed. The lifepod manufacturer generously supplied ropes, a compass, a medical kit with bio-scanner, a hand phase-gun, a bio-analyzer, a couple of standard-issue hygiene kits, an all-weather two-man portable tent with sleeping cocoons, and two packs to carry it all with. Also included was a transponder to signal passing ships or land transports. Kade kept it turned off. He also left behind the heavy atmosphere scanner, since they already knew Elysia had breathable air.

"We can't stay here," Kade said, lashing the folded tent to the base of the one of the packs. "They'll probably follow us."

Mariss was lost, physically and emotionally. In a flash, her concept of law and order had been destroyed. The police who had boarded the Quantum ship had been ruthless villains. And she...she had almost murdered one of them. She should be shocked by her actions, but couldn't manage to feel anything but exhaustion. But her logical mind still worked, and she knew she'd been right to do whatever it took to save Kade.

She had never bargained for this situation, but was forced to make the best of it. She felt reassured that Kade knew what to do. Mariss was certain he would do his best to see her to safety. His attempt to protect her from the cops proved that. She knelt beside him, began handing him things as he arranged the packs. "Why did they destroy your ship?"

His coal-dark eyes met hers, devoid of any illusions about life. "To cover up the mess they made trying to arrest us. If the ship were part of an investigation, the evidence of gunplay would be obvious. Questions would be asked. It's easier for them to pretend we resisted, and they had to blast us out of the sky."

"You're saying we're dead, then. Officially dead."

Kade shrugged. "Looks that way."

"Then why would they look for us?"

His eyes glittered in the pre-dawn light. "To finish the job."

Mariss looked away. "You should have let them arrest me."

His response was rough. "Like hell."

"You could have let them blame it all on me. If I went to court, I could have gotten off. I don't have a record. I could have proved my innocence, Kade. Somehow. But now you have nothing. I can still go to the Colony, but you have nothing, Kade. Nothing."

Kade rose and yanked her to her feet, his hands squeezing her upper arms painfully. Mariss stared in amazement at the fury on his face. "Do you have any idea what would have happened to you as their prisoner in the *weeks* it would take them to get you to a central court?"

Mariss felt tears welling up. Reluctantly, she nodded her

head. "Yes, I know." She could still feel the hands of the male cop groping her. She dropped her head. "I know."

Kade's expression softened. He slipped his fingers under her chin. "Don't look that way, Mariss. We have to be strong to get out of here alive. We can do it. You've got a spine stronger than Callodian alloy. You saved my worthless life, don't forget." His eyes held hers in a magnetic grip.

Mariss couldn't look away. Kade was strong in ways she had never experienced. Yet she had saved him. Her actions had been instinctive, surprising even herself. But now, she only felt scared. She wanted to lean on someone—no, not someone, *Kade.* Almost without her conscious awareness, she leaned toward him, yearning for reassurance, intimacy, more.

Surprisingly, it was Kade who resisted an embrace this time. He broke the gaze and looked toward the pod. "Before we leave, we have one more chore. Covering our tracks."

Mariss stifled the disappointment in her chest. She watched as he went behind the pod and studied the ground. He glanced toward her. "Don't just stand there. Give me a hand."

She joined him. Together, with their backs braced on the pod and their heels digging into the soft ground, they began shoving the pod toward the edge of the cliff.

At first, it only shifted slightly under their backs. Her muscles screaming, Mariss gasped, "This is so they won't pick up the pod on their scans?"

Kade grunted in response, his corded neck muscles straining with his effort. Mariss shoved as hard as she could, but her efforts were pitiful compared to Kade's. Worse, she was distracted watching his powerful biceps nearly rend the fabric of his jacket. The pod moved half a meter before Kade stopped to rest. He shed the jacket. Underneath he wore a form-fitting, short-sleeve blue shirt. The veins in his massive arms stood out.

"Again." Bracing his feet once more, Kade pressed his back to the pod. Mariss tried harder to concentrate this time, closing her eyes so she couldn't see the powerfully built man beside her.

The lifepod inched toward the point of no return. Kade

gave it one final shove. It tottered on the edge of the cliff for a suspended moment. "Get away!" Kade yanked Mariss to the ground.

With a horrendous screech, the pod slipped over the edge. Flat on her stomach, Mariss heard it smashing against the rocks lining the valley. If it hadn't stopped its forward motion before the drop, they would be dead now. So near death how many times in as many hours? It was scary to contemplate. Kade seemed to take it all in stride, though she knew he too felt the stress.

An explosion rent the air, a wave of heat pouring over her and receding, like opening and closing an oven door. "The pod?" she whispered.

Beside her, Kade nodded. "I rigged it to blow. With luck, they'll think we died in the crash." They rose and approached the cliff's edge.

Carefully, Mariss peered over it. Fifty meters below, the pod was an unrecognizable pile of molten metal, blackened and misshapen. Here and there, orange flames licked at the wreckage.

"I'll say one thing for you, Kade. You sure know how to show a girl an exciting time."

"You don't know the half of it, Sakari." Kade returned to their supplies. "Now, come on. Take this pack—" He thrust it out to her, and she grasped it automatically. "I'll take the heavy one. We have enough food and water for ten days. I only wish I knew which way to go."

"We can look in the databank."

"What databank?"

Mariss picked up her cyber-unit, which Kade hadn't remembered to put in her pack. "I have information on Elysia. Maps and survey information. We can narrow down where we are."

Kade smiled. "About time that thing proved useful."

Mariss propped it open on a boulder and keyed up a satellite map of Elysia. Kade pointed out Jio Continent, which he recognized as the one they had landed on. He found the plain and the mountain ranges he'd seen from space. With the help of the gradually brightening day, they were able to identify the canyon. From there, they estimated their location.

"There, that's the Colony," Mariss said, unable to keep the excitement from her voice. On the satellite image, it appeared as a glowing collection of smaller lights. If only they had landed closer.

"On the other side of Jio Continent," Kade said dryly. "So that means we go west." He looked away from the precipice and into the forest. "Easier than heading down that cliff, in any case."

Mariss tapped the keys and studied the screen. "It's 485.76 kilometers distant. The terrain changes several times. It will take us days." She lifted her eyes from the screen. "Kade," she hesitated. "I can go it alone. I know how to survive in the wilderness. I've been on a lot of scientific field surveys, sometimes by myself."

He cocked a skeptical eyebrow. "That anxious to get rid of me? Must not be enjoying this date."

"I'm not trying to get rid of you. But the Colony is *my* destination. What about you?"

Kade's eyes were unreadable as he gazed back at her. "Don't think I'm escorting you there because I'm a gentleman, Mariss. Hell, no. And I'm not the least interested in visiting that over-advertised excuse for a settlement you're so enthralled by."

"You mean the Colony?" Mariss tensed at his jibes. No man on Earth—on *any* planet—could make her so angry so fast. "There's nothing wrong with the Colony. It's a fine place to live! How can you—"

Kade cut her off. "I'm not wasting a second debating it with you. Unfortunately, that Colony of yours happens to be the closest civilization around." He sighed as he settled the pack on his shoulders. "From there, I'm catching the first transport available, so I can get off this Maker-forsaken rock and on with my life."

***

Despite calling Elysia Maker-forsaken, it was Kade who slowed their pace when they passed particularly striking vistas.

And Elysia was a remarkably beautiful planet.

The sunrise seemed to last for hours, orange and tangerine hues brushing the sky. During the morning, they traveled through a temperate forest. Every now and then, the trees broke before them to reveal cool, green valleys framed by snow-capped mountains. They entered a plain and followed a meandering stream toward a break in the mountains—their best hope for a pass beyond.

Mariss also found herself stopping, to analyze the plants. The trees had fernlike foliage, but at this altitude, were probably hardier than tropical plants. Some bore clusters of yellow berries which provided food for small, bluebird-reptile-like creatures they had noticed perching in the trees. The foot-long creatures were timid, running at the sight of them, so she doubted they were a threat.

The trunks of the trees were burgundy-toned and smooth, almost blemish free. Their slender elegance gave the forest an open, airy feel. Mariss plucked off a leaf. It curled in a spiral as she watched. She used the bio-scanner from the medical kit to determine its basic make-up. She stored the leaf in her pack to analyze in more detail later.

Her attention fell to the sprawl of undergrowth, and she knelt to collect samples of these plants and flowers as well. Before she was through, Kade's shadow fell over her. He was waiting with hands on hips, obviously ready to continue their journey.

The tangerine sunrise finally gave way to cerulean blue when the sun—so like Earth's—was well up. Kade slowed to look over the valley they were entering. Before they descended, Mariss stopped him. She lifted her fingers and gently touched the side of his head. Kade flinched. "There's blood, Kade. From where the cop struck you. I don't understand this. Why were the cops so...so—"

"Brutal? Hell, this isn't Earth. You think the good cops want to serve out here? It's death to a cop's career."

"Like piloting the outback run is death to a pilot's career."

He chuckled. "Something like that." He pulled a rag out of his pocket and dabbed at the wound.

"Didn't you pack a med-kit?" Mariss said. "I thought I saw one."

Kade readjusted his pack. "We don't have time for you to play nurse. Let's go." He started off.

Annoyed, Mariss followed. Kade was more hard-headed than a Keruvian mor-cow, and their skulls were denser than stone.

***

They ate lunch during a brief rest, then continued on. Mariss' legs were already aching. She knew she should have exercised during her time on the ship. While she went on frequent field excursions to study plants, they didn't involve endless hiking over rough ground.

She stared at Kade ahead of her, his steps never flagging. He wasn't in the least bothered by their journey. And why would he be? He was made for this, hardened inside and out.

She was determined not to slow him down, so whenever he asked if she wanted to take a rest, she declined. Unfortunately, the days were several hours longer than on Earth.

Nightfall was heralded by a sunset as long and beautiful as the sunrise. Twin crescent moons rose over the horizon. By then, Mariss could barely hide her discomfort. She almost kissed the ground when Kade called a halt and decided to set up camp in a clearing by the edge of the stream they had been following all day. Her legs gave out, and she sat on the ground.

***

Kade knew Mariss had been playing tough. He shouldn't have made that remark about how strong her spine was, even if it was true. He'd been referring to her spirit. But she was trying to prove it through her stamina.

Mariss deserved comfort. She was a delicate, elusive beauty who deserved to be pampered, cosseted, spend her days in a posh resort like the Colony, not traipsing through the wilderness with him.

He crouched beside her. He hated himself for failing her, for having gotten her into such a hopeless situation. He laid his land on her shoulder. "Mariss. I'm sorry about all this. It has nothing to do with you."

Her violet eyes looked black in the night. "What has it to do with?"

"You wouldn't believe me if I told you."

"Try me."

He sighed and sat down beside her. Both of them looked toward a distant mountain range, above which hung the two crescent moons. "You know Lorena?"

"Of course. She's rather unforgettable."

"Well, you were right about her. After you mentioned the vagon, I started noticing things about her behavior—the number of times she went to the lavatory, the length of time she spent there. Then there was the weight of your luggage. I think she smuggled the vagon on board in your case. Greasing the right palms probably made it easy. If the drugs were found, she would look clean—at your expense."

Mariss' eyes widened as they met his. She brushed a lock of hair off her face. Kade fought the urge to stroke it aside for her. "I remember now, when we first met. She seemed concerned I wasn't stopping at Fredon Outpost with the rest of the passengers. That must be why the vagon wasn't there when we checked my case. She snuck it out after we were under way."

Kade looked away toward the crescent moons, now rising above the trees. "I questioned her about it. I tried to be discreet, so I asked her to come to the cockpit at night, when the rest of you were sleeping."

Mariss murmured softly, "Yes, I saw her leaving your cabin that night."

Kade wondered what she had been doing up so late herself. Following Lorena? Keeping an eye on him? "After an intense conversation, she broke down and admitted it to me. I told her I would have to turn her in at Fredon. She offered me—compensation if I would hold off. I refused it. She was none too happy about it. Later, she told me she'd incinerated the stuff, was real sorry and would never do it again. And I believed her."

"But you never—" she faltered.

Kade cocked an eyebrow at her. "Slept with her?"

Mariss cleared her throat, clearly embarrassed. "I mean, why didn't they arrest her at Fredon?"

"As far as I know, they did. As soon as we broke interspace, I transmitted a message. That's why the cops were there when we arrived."

"Yet she managed to convince them it was *you* who had the vagon."

He shrugged. "Wasn't hard to do, Mariss. She had *me* convinced she'd gotten rid of the stuff. I imagine when the cops discovered my criminal record, they decided they had better catch up with me and take a look. Even better, Lorena left behind a present—for both of us," he added wryly.

"What a slank," she said, muttering a relatively mild term for a loose woman.

"Slank?" Kade cocked an amused eyebrow. "Goodness, Mariss. A little adventure brings out your salty side."

Mariss smiled warmly at him. "Oh, I can think of a few more choice words to describe Lorena. I just wasn't going to say them. But I'm partly to blame, Kade. I knew what she was up to. I was certain of it. It was my responsibility to make you aware of it. But I—I didn't try hard enough."

Kade didn't respond right away. He thought of their confrontation in the lavatory, how he had assumed she was flirting with him. Now he knew her better. Mariss was too serious to flirt—especially with him. She was not a woman to give her affection lightly. But she respected honesty. He spoke low, carefully. "I pushed you away."

"I let you," she said softly.

Kade watched her through the moonlight. She averted her gaze. "Next time, I won't," he promised.

"That isn't for you to decide," she said tersely.

Kade stood up, irritated at her cool rebuff. She was like a natural rose bush, he thought. Beautiful, but full of thorns for the unwary, for those who came too close to her lushness. Not that he had ever seen a natural rosebush, only the highly hybridized thornless ones. But he imagined visiting Earth, seeing all her wonders. Elysia was the closest he had gotten to

Earth he thought as he erected the two-man tent. Its beauty astounded him. He had grown up dreaming of being a pilot as a way to escape a dreary asteroid world. But he had always imagined piloting would take him to beautiful places, exotic places. Instead, until Elysia, he had only seen the seedy parts of the galaxy.

He glanced toward Mariss, where she sat nursing her blisters in the cool stream. Mariss had been lucky enough to grow up on Earth. When he felt like talking to her again, he would ask her how much Elysia was like her home planet. He watched as she emptied her backpack onto the ground next to her—which *he* had packed for her—and began repacking it to suit herself. Then again, maybe that day would never come.

Once the tent was erected, Kade took one of the two thermal cocoons and laid it outside. He crawled into it and fell asleep instantly.

***

The next few days brought them well into the mountain pass. Mariss was growing used to the walking, thanks to a shot of muscle relaxant Kade had given her at breakfast. He insisted it was safe.

She watched as he slipped the pill-sized capsule into the med-gun and shot it into her arm.

"On Rebus Five, a shot of this was worth more than a month's worth of liquor or an X-vid," he said off-handedly.

The remark caught Mariss up short. He was referring to his life as a convict, laboring day after day in the uranium mines. She had almost forgotten his past. Now it came rushing back to her, flooding her emotions.

How could she ever have feared him? She was mortified at how little she had trusted him, this man who had risked his life to preserve her honor, like some knight of old. Every night he gave her the tent without question, and slept outside like a personal guard.

Worse, she couldn't look at him without recalling other, more disturbing emotions which threatened her equilibrium and her sense of purpose.

He grinned at her over the med-gun, as if reading her mind.

Mariss forced herself not to reveal how much he was starting to bother her. The last thing she could afford was another confrontation, now that she was relying so much on him. There was nowhere for her to keep her distance on this journey. So she merely lifted her chin and looked the other way.

***

Kade called a halt for a mid-day meal when they reached an overlook. Mariss chewed on her carbo-protein jerky, washed down by the cleanest, clearest water she had ever tasted, from the nearby stream.

Kade was sprawled on the ground across from her. It had grown warmer as the day progressed, so he had removed his jacket. He was badly in need of a shave. Her eyes played over his rough-hewn face, its scruffy beard making him look even more the rogue. And she—she must look a sight. She kept her hair in a tight braid wound and fastened in back of her head. She hoped it didn't look as dirty as it felt.

Mariss had found some bio-soap in her pack, but used it only to wash her hands and face. She wasn't desperate enough yet to take a full bath in the frigid mountain stream. Kade hadn't either.

She also missed hot food. While adequate for her nutritional needs, the carbo-pro food source tasted blander with every meal.

"When we run out of food, we'll have to forage for edible plants," Mariss commented.

"Can you tell which are edible?"

"Well, those little blue lizard-birds are eating those yellow berries. My scanner, however, shows some questionable characteristics. I don't know how human physiology would react to them. The lizard-birds may have some mechanism to cleanse their system of the poisons, where we wouldn't."

A lizard-bird hopped across the ground within two meters of where they rested. Kade pulled some yellow berries from a low-hanging branch and began tossing them toward the creature. The creature inched closer. "How about eating the lizard?"

"Uh, I'd rather not," Mariss said. "Besides, you'd have to

catch one."

Kade tossed another berry at the creature, and it hopped within a meter of him. Swift as lighting, his hand shot out and wrapped around the animal. He scooped it up. He met Mariss' amazed expression and winked. "Record-fast reflexes, remember?" He gently unwrapped his hand from around the creature and held it out to her. "So what do you think? A tasty snack?"

"Be careful, Kade. We know nothing about the flora and fauna here. It could be dangerous. It may bite you."

The creature emitted a soft mewing sound, not unlike an Earth kitten. Kade held it aloft on his palm. The creature didn't run away while he turned it this way and that, examining it. "Cute, but not too appetizing."

The lizard leapt from his palm to his knee. Kade held out a few berries, and it pecked them off his palm. Then it sat back on its thick tail and unfurled its wings to their full half-meter length.

"It's beautiful," Mariss said. The webbing on the wings was as delicate as gossamer. "It seems to like you. I hope it's as tame as it looks."

"Sure you're tame, aren't you?" Kade addressed the animal, stroking it under its neck. The animal fluttered its wings. Mariss smiled at the sight of the hardened space jockey petting the animal. It warmed her. "You know what this little guy reminds me of?" he asked Mariss. "A dragon."

Mariss cocked her head. "You're right. It *is* a dragon. What an amazing coincidence."

"It may be more than that," Kade mused. "Perhaps Earthers are connected to this planet in some way. Parallel but asynchronous evolutionary tracks, or, to get unscientific about it, the same creative hand at work?"

Mariss shrugged. "I doubt anything mystical is at work. And we're lightyears away—too far for an exchange of species. It must be coincidence. But the plants do look similar to Earth's paleozoic specimens," Mariss said. "And this *is* a younger planet than Earth."

"Sort of like the Garden of Eden, then? A man, a woman,

a serpent..."

Mariss chose not to answer that observation. "If only I had my lab supplies from my case on the ship. I'd be able to do a more in-depth analysis."

The dragon leapt onto Kade's shoulder. Kade continued feeding it berries. "If I had my ship, we wouldn't be here."

She smiled at his logic.

Kade turned his attention from the dragon to her. "So, why *are* you here, Mariss?"

Mariss shot him a sharp look. "What do you mean?"

"This thing you have for mapping out your love life. You said something on the ship about trying it the other way, the natural way, and it not working. Some guy, some university geek, break your heart, or what?"

This line of questioning was *not* one she wanted to pursue with Kadin Land. "I really don't see that it's any of your business, Land."

Kade grinned like a cat which had cornered a mouse. It made him look entirely disreputable. "What'd he do? Cheat on you?" His eyes grew bright. "I know. Vagon. You said something about being familiar with it. I know you couldn't possibly be a user, so—"

Kade had no idea how right he was, and Mariss wasn't going to enlighten him. It stirred up far too many painful memories. She spoke firmly, as if talking to an unruly child. "If this is going to work, you and me on this journey, I suggest you keep your nose out of my business."

Kade laughed, a deep, throaty sound which made Mariss' nerves tingle. "I'm right. It was some guy who got whacked out on vagon and jumped every co-ed in sight. So now you're playing it safe with this silly mating service idea."

Mariss could no longer contain herself. She jumped to her feet and stared down at him. "Shut up! You're an insolent, ill-bred excuse for an interplanetary officer, and I'm not spending a moment more in your company." She snatched up her backpack and strode away, shouldering it as she went.

Kade made no move to follow her. Several minutes later, Mariss entered a deeper part of the forest, alone. Her steps slowed. She listened closely, but could hear nothing but the bright chirping of the dragons.

Branches crackled ahead of her and Kade burst from the trees. He stopped in front of her and closed the distance between them in one stride. "Don't you *ever* run off like that again, do you hear me?"

The fury on his countenance startled Mariss. His eyes glittered in the shadowy forest light.

"Get out of my way." She tried to move around him.

He easily blocked her path, not touching her, letting his brawny physique do the work. And he was quick. Whichever way she tried to go around him, he was there, in her way. She gave up.

"Are you through playing?" he said in exasperation. "Then listen up. I'm your damned captain, and you'll do as I say, do you hear me?"

"My captain? That relationship ended when your ship was blasted out of the sky."

"Like hell it did. This is a survival mission with me, the crew, seeing to the safety of a passenger from a Quantum ship. It's my duty to protect you. And that's damned hard to do when you disappear on me just because you get your feelings a nanomite out-of-whack."

"You're insufferable, Kadin Land."

His grin was cocky. "Yeah, I know."

"You know perfectly well Quantum doesn't want you anymore. So all this about being a captain—you're just fooling yourself."

"And what in the hell do you know about it?"

"It said so, right in your—" Mariss burst out before she thought. She had done it again, revealed information she should by rights have no knowledge of.

"Right in my personnel file, huh? What'd you do, memorize it? And you accuse me of being nosy. So, what did it say?"

Somehow, they had started walking again. Mariss told him about the entry which stated his chances for promotion were nonexistent. She sighed. "You would think they'd be a little more honest with you."

"Are you kidding? And lose their chance to use me up on the most unpopular run in the galaxy? But now—" Kade snorted. "Quantum can go shove itself into the nearest turbo-pressurizer unit and turn it on full, for all I care."

Mariss smiled at the image of the entire Quantum management staff shoved into a tiny depressurization chamber and imploded.

She felt his eyes on her. "But I'm still your captain, Mariss. Don't forget it. And don't ever disappear on me again."

His words rang with intensity. Mariss glanced at him, tried to read his expression. But he had turned his full attention ahead.

***

The following afternoon, as the sky began to turn orange, they reached the end of the mountain pass. They came to an overlook. An uneven plain dotted with forest and grasslands stretched below. There was no sign of the Colony on the horizon. But there was something else of interest.

Mariss pointed. "Look. Artificial structures."

Kade had already seen them. He was peering through a pair of field glasses. "A settlement of some kind. I can't make out any of the details. Looks deserted. Pretty small. It wasn't on your survey map, or if it was, we missed it. But it may have something we can use, even a transport."

"Or at least a shower and a hot meal."

Kade lowered the field glasses. "I'll go for that. We won't reach it until sometime tomorrow. We'll keep on today and camp on the lower slopes. That is—if you can manage. How are you doing? Need more muscle relaxant?"

"I feel fine," she said. It was true. The only complaint she had was a general tiredness, but that was to be expected. "I can push on until we make camp."

Kade nodded and turned away from the overlook. Mariss followed him as he hiked down the mountain.

EIGHT

The twin moons were rising as they walked along a high ridge, seeking a good place to pitch camp. The air was growing colder. Kade's jacket protected him well enough. But Mariss only had her flightsuit. It was an all-weather suit, but there were limits to its thermal abilities.

On top of that, Kade knew Mariss was growing tired. All afternoon, he had tried to keep her mind off their strenuous hike by drawing her into conversation.

He stuck to safe topics. She responded brightly to his observations on politics, the most recent planetary discoveries, news of settlements. Mariss seemed quite happy to share her views on these things. They were both residents of the galaxy, he thought ruefully. It was one thing they had in common.

Soon dusk fell, and with the magnificent sunset a sense of intimacy closed around them. They were crossing a ridge which gradually led downward toward the valley. The walking was easy, and the serene atmosphere—the beautiful light of the waxing twin moons bathing them—made Kade's thoughts turn personal. He couldn't keep his curiosity about Mariss to himself. "You've traveled a long distance from Earth, Mariss. I imagine someone's going to miss you," he commented as he walked beside her.

Mariss didn't look at him. "Why do you say that?"

"You look like the sort of lady with connections, with family and friends."

Mariss walked several steps before responding. "Adrian. Adrian Young will miss me if I don't arrive at the Colony soon."

He snorted. "I mean *real* family. Parents—"

"My parents are dead." She said it as a fact, without inflection.

"Yeah, join the crowd."

"I know you have no family," she said, her words gentle. "And that you were raised by your mother, with no brothers or sisters." Her voice became even softer. "It was in your file, Kade."

Kade sensed her pity, if that's what it was. He didn't want or need it. He warded her off with sarcasm. "I keep forgetting how fascinated you are with my personal life. Well, seeing as we have nothing better to do, tell me about *your* family. No parents living, so what about brothers and sisters?"

She shot a sharp glance toward him. "I'd rather not discuss it, Land."

Kade was determined to make it his business. "It's a simple question, Mariss." He chuckled. "Don't tell me. Your brother was convicted of murder, and you're ashamed of him."

"Not funny, Land." She readjusted her pack and lifted her chin. "My brother is a high-ranking official in the Diplomatic Corps. Perhaps you've heard of him."

Silence lasted the length of a heartbeat as understanding dawned. "Ambassador Jarik Sakari is your *brother*?"

"Yes."

Kade whistled low. His eyes played over Mariss' face, noted its resolute expression. It was obvious she was proud of being related to the high-ranking official, famous for negotiating peace treaties and helping to make the galaxy safe for expansion and settlement. Still... "He's older than you by a good fifteen years, at least. I'll bet you haven't seen him in eons."

"He's very busy, and extremely important." She furrowed her delicate eyebrows.

Kade could see her defensiveness rising like a shield. He was determined to slip under it before she shut him out completely. "Uh-huh. So what about sisters?"

Keeping her eyes straight ahead, she shrugged noncommittally. "One."

"Is she older, too?"

"No." Clipped, terse.

"Younger then."

"No."

"Then..."

She shot him a stormy look. "Figure it out for yourself, Land." She increased her pace, gaining several steps on him.

Kade stared at her back, amazed and delighted. "You have a twin!" She ignored him, her silence all the confirmation he needed. Kade strode forward, came even with her again. He looked her up and down appreciatively. "By the Maker, there are two of you. Is she an identical twin?"

Mariss didn't answer. Her chin merely clicked a notch higher, as if the topic under discussion was beneath her interest.

Kade's tone softened, his tone sweetly sensuous. "I just want to know if she's as beautiful as you, Mariss."

Incredibly, Mariss increased her pace once more. Kade stood there, stunned. He lifted his voice, his tone a sarcastic imitation of her own. "Why, Kade. What a nice thing to say. I'm flattered, thank you." He returned to his own voice. "You're welcome, Mariss."

If his needling had any effect on her at all, it was only to make her walk even faster. Kade jogged to catch up with her. He rounded on her, held up his hands. She stopped. He gave her a friendly smile. "Okay, Mariss. Let's talk honestly. Here's the deal. I see you safely to the Colony, so you can throw your life away on that blond blockhead Adrian Young. As a gesture of your eternal appreciation, you give me your sister's address." His smile grew broader, suggestive. "What do you think? I get a Mariss clone, you get—well, we won't mention what. And everybody's happy."

Mariss's violet eyes took on the cast of a summer storm. "That isn't funny, Land."

"What, is she already married?"

Her answer exploded from between tight lips. "Yes!"

She shoved past him and kept walking. Kade trailed behind, mystified and fascinated. He knew he was treading on thin ice, entering dangerous territory without a chart. But her barriers drew him. He wanted to see them shatter. He had an innate sense that something good would come from slipping past—or smashing through—the walls she had so carefully erected to keep prying people away. "Does she have any kids?" he prodded to her back. "Nieces, nephews who are going to miss Auntie Mariss?"

She shot back over her shoulder, "What would you care about children?"

Her words cut deep. He strode forward and grasped her arm, stopping her in her tracks. "Hell, I may be an out-of-work ex-convict space jockey, but I happen to think I may want to be a father some day. Got a problem with that?"

The question sounded harsh in his own ears. Her expression froze for a few precious seconds. Then she lost control, her chin quivering and her eyes filling with devastation. Her voice was like brittle steel. "If you *must* know, my sister is living on Earth, raising her own twins. She's living in *my* house, eating in *my* kitchen, and sleeping in *my* bed."

"And?" he prodded, as if he were digging at a splinter, feeling it was painful but necessary for her to speak.

Mariss backed up a step, her face a storm of emotion. "She stole my husband, okay? She stole him, and my life! She stole all of it!"

Kade's heart whapped against his ribcage. Whatever he had been expecting, it wasn't this. He felt ashamed to have teased her, yet was relieved she was finally opening up to him.

Mariss' voice rang painfully thin in the evening air. "I walked right in on them together, in my bed. I was blind and trusting and a stupid fool!"

She threw down her pack and approached Kade, her finger pointing at him accusingly, as if he were a stand-in for the man at fault. "And you know what he said to me? You want to know? He told me right there, in front of Ami, what a horrible disappointment I was as a wife, and as a woman. He called me cold, unresponsive to his needs." A wrenching gasp tore from her throat. "I had wanted so badly to make it work. I tried so hard to be a good wife, to make a good home for Roldo. I had already failed at marriage once. I really thought it was working! But he said I set impossible standards, that I expected too much from him. He said I—I *intimidated* him."

Kade listened to her in stunned silence. He let his pack slide off his shoulders and onto the ground. Any man who would be intimidated by Mariss had to be spineless. She was spirited, even a spitfire at times. But that was a great deal of her appeal.

Her voice turned from pain-filled to icy. "And Ami didn't even have the decency to cover herself when I walked in on them. She'd never succeeded in school, never had a boyfriend for more than a few months. But she stared at me, a victorious smile on her face, as though she'd done the cleverest thing in the galaxy. Even then she was already pregnant. I wanted to wait for children, but Roldo grew impatient. I guess I waited too long." She yanked her chin up. "So. Now you know."

Kade expelled his breath, amazed at her story, his heart aching for her. His words were low, intense, almost a whisper. "Damn. I'm sorry."

"What do *you* care?"

Her casual dismissal of his concern struck him like a physical blow. He grabbed her arm so tightly she gasped. "I care, Mariss." Their eyes clashed for a breathless moment. Before he could think it through, he yanked her to him, wrapped his arms tightly around her until the fight poured out of her and she grew soft and yielding in his arms. "I care," he murmured. He stroked the back of her head, settling her more firmly against him.

Mariss submitted to his attentions. She rested her head on his shoulder. He heard her sniffling quietly. "Shh. It's all a long way away, remember? You're here with me now."

When Mariss spoke, her voice was reflective rather than sad. "I had just gotten over Peck when I met Roldo. He was everything Peck wasn't—conservative, ambitious, serious. But at least Peck didn't cheat on me with other women. With—with my own sister. He didn't discard me for a better model, in the same package, no less."

"Here." Kade gently pulled her to sit beside him on the ground. "Mariss, look at me." She lifted her tear-streaked face to his. "I was teasing back there. I don't give a hill of Torindian krod about your sister. I don't want her address. She was worthless and cruel, and your ex- was even more contemptible. I'd like to stick the both of them in a spacepod and shoot it into interspace without a nav-scope. A one-way ticket. They could bounce around for an eternity, thinking about nothing but how vile they were to you."

Just as Kade hoped, his ridiculous description of a suitable punishment brought a flicker of a smile to her lips. "That's the best thing anyone's ever said to me," she said softly. "Thank you, Kade."

Kade felt the power of her gaze touch him deep in his heart. His arms ached to hold her. But he knew he must tread carefully. She was still healing from her betrayal, and her broken heart.

Mariss sniffled and wiped her hand under her nose. Kade poked his fingers into his jacket pocket, seeking something he could use as a handkerchief. His fingers brushed the softest cloth imaginable—the lingerie he'd stolen from her luggage. He'd forgotten about it. He shoved it aside and came up with the piece of rag he'd used to stanch the cut on his head. It was the best he could do. She accepted it gratefully.

She dabbed her eyes and began pulling herself back together. "Now you know my shameful secret. I never really told anyone before, but you forced it out of me."

Her eyes met his. He knew as well as she that he had done nothing of the sort. She had been looking for an excuse to talk about it for a long time. "I'm not done," Kade said. "Tell me about Peck."

She sighed. "It was the vagon, just as you thought. He was addicted even before we met at the university. But you know vagon. You can't tell when someone's using it. He claimed he took it so he could study better. We were both working on our degrees. I didn't like him using it, but I couldn't stop him. Then he began using it on weekends, and—in bed. To heighten the sensation, he said." She averted her face. "I guess what we had wasn't enough."

Kade waited patiently, trying not to think about showing her how good it could be, how good he was certain it would be, between them.

"Anyway, things grew worse, and I discovered he was not only using it, he was manufacturing it in the small botanical lab I had set up in our basement for my research projects. I was furious. Before I could do anything, the law caught him dealing. My own credibility was questioned, naturally. I had to defend myself against the university board, as well as fight off a police investigation. It was touch and go for a while. I thought my career would be over before it even began."

His voice rang with admiration. "But you did it. You held fast."

"Only because Peck insisted to the authorities that I had nothing to do with it. For that, I'm grateful to him. He never intended to hurt me, after all. It was the drug." She expelled a heavy sigh. "But he refused to let me help him. He served a short sentence, as a first offender. By the time he got out, he wanted out of the marriage. There was simply nothing left."

He gazed at her in awe. "You waited for him. How long?"

"Three years." She shrugged. "I would have waited longer. He was my husband." She shifted, her back straightening, as if casting off the past. "Now you know why I'm going to the Colony. To start a new life." She gazed at the first stars intensifying in the deepening twilight. "But we always carry the past with us, don't we? Half a galaxy isn't far enough away for me to forget."

Kade's voice turned husky. "That's where you're wrong." He slipped his fingers along her face, cupping her cheek in his hand. He urged her to turn her gaze to his, felt himself melting in her lambent eyes. Gently, slowly, so as not to frighten her, he guided her mouth toward his.

His blood surged as he watched her eyelids lower and her lips part in anticipation. At the last possible second, she yanked her face away. His lips grazed her cheek. "Kade. Kade, stop. I can't." She pulled away from him. "This feeling. I don't want it. That's how it always starts. I don't want romance, or even love." She grasped his hand and held it. Her amazing eyes met his, her voice almost a plea. "Just...be my friend."

Kade hid his disappointment behind a gentle smile. "You already have that."

NINE

Settlement A: Jio Continent

Kade and Mariss approached the collection of dilapidated structures carefully. Kade had put on the phase-gun holster, so the weapon would be close at hand—just in case.

Dun-colored pre-fab buildings were arranged in a circle with a courtyard in the center. Kade recognized the markings on the buildings. They belonged to the Explorer Corps, the elite Earth-based team which sent out expeditions and started colonies throughout the known galaxy. He stepped on a piece of debris—a portion of an electrical panel. He knelt beside it. "Part of a turbo-pump unit, looks like." He rose and scanned the settlement.

"Where are the inhabitants?" Mariss asked in the still air.

"Looks abandoned."

"But this land is so rich. Settling here would be easy—comparatively speaking."

Kade nodded, but didn't take his eyes from the buildings ahead. He advanced toward them.

***

Mariss watched Kade approach the silent buildings. She wished she also had a phase-gun, to protect his back. She knew her thoughts were illogical, but she had a bad feeling in her stomach. Something wasn't right.

"Drop the phase-gun and come here." A cultured English accent spoke the words. "Both of you."

Mariss looked around. Half a dozen men stepped from the shrubs, surrounding them, phase-guns ready to fire. She studied the nearest man. His clothing used to be a uniform of some kind. Now it was stained, dirty, ragged.

Kade had no choice but to comply. He tossed his phase-gun into the dust. Mariss moved closer to Kade, also raising her hands. "Take off the packs." Kade and Mariss did so.

The order had come from a tall, skinny man with stringy brown hair and a shaggy beard. Mariss noticed his shoulder patch, recognized the Explorer Corps insignia. She breathed out softly. They were Earthers, trained to settle, not to fight. Scientists. They couldn't mean to do them harm.

"We have no other weapons," Kade said. "We were stranded several days ago. We've been traveling by foot since then."

"This way." The leader nodded toward the courtyard. Surrounded by the men, Kade and Mariss passed into the settlement.

The courtyard was about 50 meters wide, with a dozen buildings fronting it in a ring. Mariss saw about fifteen people. Most were men. There were two women as well, older ladies with greying hair. No children were about, though part of the Explorer Corps' mission with their settlements was to build a society—which required children. A settlement such as this was designed to hold thirty people at first and expand to one hundred or more. But the base would open to additional settlers from Earth or other planets only after it was well-established and functional. For some reason, that had not happened here.

Mariss thought of the Colony, not far as a hovercar drove, just on the other side of the continent. She recalled its history, knew it had been built with private funds about forty years before. Perhaps that was the difference, and Elysia was more difficult to settle than it appeared. Perhaps the government-sponsored settlement was running out of resources. They certainly seemed interested in the contents of their packs.

Mariss glanced at Kade. He stared with a dark expression at the men scrounging through their supplies. She knew he would like to take on each one of them, but was treading carefully for her sake.

With a sudden revelation, Mariss realized she knew Kadin Land better than she knew most people. How and when she had come to understand him so well, she wasn't sure.

"Bring them in here, with their gear." Mariss and Kade were ushered into the largest of the shelters, which appeared to be a mess hall. The leader sat on a table in the center and directed Kade and Mariss to stand nearby. The armed men circled behind them.

"Nothing worthwhile here," said one of the men who was searching their packs. A moment later, he dropped the packs at their feet.

"Who are you?" the leader demanded in his cultured accent, so at odds with his mangy appearance.

Kade crossed his arms. "No answers until you call off your infantry," he said dryly. "Phase-guns make me nervous."

Despite his sarcasm, Mariss wondered if he wasn't speaking a partial truth. She still didn't know how he had murdered a man, and over what. But she knew he was more interested in piloting than in killing things.

The leader gestured with his hand, and the men lowered their weapons. "Very well. So who the bloody hell are you?"

"Kadin Land, Quantum Craftlines, pilot number 09264."

"We aren't arresting you, flyboy. Yet." The leader's hazel eyes flicked over Mariss and lingered too long for her comfort. "She yours?"

Kade shifted. "Yeah. Hands off."

"We'll see about that."

Mariss couldn't contain herself. "What are you talking about? I'm my own person. I don't belong to him—" she pointed at Kade, "—or to any man. Any man here," she quickly corrected, remembering Adrian Young. "We just need a transport, and we'll be gone."

"A transport!" The leader threw his head back and roared. The other men joined him. "A transport, she says. Wouldn't that be nice?"

Mariss said, "You don't have hovercars? I thought all Explorer settlements were fully equipped—"

The leader jumped to his feet and stared down at her. "Do we *look* fully equipped to you? We were raided." He swept his hands out. "This, darling, is all that's left. Impressed?"

"Raided by who?" Kade asked.

"Only the Maker knows. We were hit."

"Humans?"

"Yes, humans. People like you and me. Men. They took all our women, except Jessica and Helen. And our hovercars. We don't know where they came from, and we sure in bloody hell aren't in a position to follow them."

"How long ago?" Kade asked.

"A few years. And why am I telling *you* this?"

"What's your name? Sir," Mariss added hesitantly.

"Commander Tige Alexander, ma'am. At your service." He raised his hand in greeting and grinned at Mariss. His teeth were discolored, but Mariss could tell he had been a pleasing-looking man once. "And you are..."

Mariss returned his salute. "Mariss Sakari, botanist. Pharmacological botanics is my subspecialty."

"Pleased to make your acquaintance. Not often we see a new face. Never, in fact." Again, he roared with laughter. Mariss felt uncomfortable standing so close to him. She wondered if he was in complete possession of his faculties.

The commander began to pace. "I had thirty good men and women in my troop. Thirty of the brightest, smartest, most able Earthers. Why, this is the bloody New Frontier! We barely got our settlement up and running before we were hit. Took all our stores, took our transports, took almost everything of value, except Dwayne's data computers. He hid those." He gestured toward Dwayne, a small, bald man with a pinched face, who even now was working on an cyber-unit at one of the mess hall tables.

"Why haven't you contacted the Explorer Corps, gotten some assistance from them?" Mariss asked. Her question caused everyone to still. They glanced at each other, their eyes wide with fear.

The commander's lips curled up in a nasty smirk. "I was sent here to do a job. I'm going to do it, if it's the last thing I do."

"And your people feel the same," Kade stated, his voice like ice.

"Of course they do. Right, Harrison?" The commander didn't even look around to see if Harrison was paying attention. "Harrison, I can't hear you."

The skinny, pale man stuttered in response, "Y—yes, Tige. That's right. I'm with you. We all are."

"Helen?"

The woman spoke with more composure than Harrison. "We'll make it work, Tige. We all agreed." Mariss tried to catch the woman's glance, to read the truth there, but Helen avoided looking directly at her.

"We'd tell Earth about our plans, but our communications equipment isn't working anymore," Tige said, his smile doing little to hide his pent-up frustration.

"Listen," Mariss said. Kade threw her a warning glance. Mariss ignored him. "We're heading for the Colony. It's about three hundred kilometers from here. Have you heard of it? It's sponsored by the Iridion Corporation."

Tige scratched his chin. "Gee, let me see...the Colony...the Colony. I do believe I heard something about that Colony. Good luck getting any help from there."

"What do you mean?"

"We sent men there. They never came back."

"I doubt that's the fault of the Colony."

"Hell if I know. We sent a second expedition. They never came back, either. Now, either there's a black hole between here and the Colony, or the Colony is keeping them. Which do you think it is, darling?"

"Maybe they liked it so much, they didn't want to come back," Mariss said. The moment she said it, she wished she hadn't. The commander's face started turning an unappealing shade of purple.

He stepped toward her, enraged. "That is *not* what happened, little missy. Do you hear me? *Not* what happened."

Kade stepped between them, his fists clenched. "Get away from her," he growled.

Mariss held her breath as Kade and the commander faced off. They looked like two vicious Rebus Rats about to tangle over a scrap of food. Kade's eyes flashed, his leg muscles tensing as if he were about to spring.

To her relief, the commander finally broke the stand-off. He stepped back and shrugged, as if the confrontation had been meaningless to him. "Fine, go to the Colony. I'd like you to spend the night here, as my guests. Take advantage of our fine hospitality. It's a regular five-star resort! A bath, a hot meal...a good, firm bed. Then, tomorrow, you can be on your way."

"Thank you," Mariss said. Kade was staring meaningfully at her, as if trying to warn her. Mariss chose to ignore him. She glanced at Dwayne, who was tapping away at his cyber-unit. "Have you done much exploring here about? Do you have any information on the continent—the life forms, weather, terrain—"

"Babe, we know more than you'd ever want to know. Not that it does us any good. This is a damned stone-age existence we have here. You know something funny? We tried to plant crops last year. Our food processing unit was smashed in the attack. So me and my men—and our two women, of course—all highly trained, highly educated, had to clear land by *hand.* And try to cultivate it. Just like on Earth, thousands of years ago. Can you imagine that?"

A swell of contempt filled Mariss for this scientist, brought so ignominiously low. Her eyes strayed to Kade, who stood with crossed arms and an unsympathetic expression. He had been forced to work with his hands for years on Rebus Five, in the mine pits. She knew he thought as little of this commander as she did. If this man had any gumption, if any of them did, they would find a better way to live than sitting here decrying their fates.

"Must have been hard," she said. "But I was interested in sharing data. I have the latest satellite surveys of Elysia in my cyber-unit." She slipped it from the pack at her feet. She opened it and placed it beside Dwayne's, then studied his screen, craving the data she saw there. Species, subspecies, meteorological data—she and Kade may not make it to the Colony without it. "I see you have an extensive encyclopedia of Elysia. Maybe we can trade?"

Dwayne looked to where she stood behind him, his myopic eyes focusing on her for the first time. He started back, almost falling from the bench. "I...I..."

A hand slammed his cyber-unit closed. Tige towered over Dwayne, making the man shrink inside himself. His expression softened and he smiled at Mariss. "What Dwayne is trying to say is we'd be happy to give you whatever data we have—catalogued characteristics of forty-eight animal species and one hundred and fifty-three plant species, some of which are amazingly nasty. We'd love to do this for such a nice girl as you. But, there has got to be something in it for us."

"I said I have satellite surveys. Plus a little information on a few of the native flora, which I gathered on our journey from the crash site."

"Something more than that. We have twenty gigabytes of data, little lady. It took three years to compile. So it seems to me the least you can do is..."

"What?" Mariss asked. A prickle of fear roamed down her spine.

"Spend the night with me." His eyes scanned her from breasts to hips. "I want to rav you."

"No, she won't." Kade was hovering right behind her. "We don't need your data."

Mariss glanced from Kade's stony countenance to the commander. She looked at the man's grimy face with its yellowing teeth and half-crazed grin. "Yes, I'll spend the night with you, Commander Alexander."

TEN

Kade could see nothing but red.

It had taken only an hour to exchange the data. Now Mariss' cyber-unit was back in her pack, outside the door to the commander's private bungalow. Kade had immediately tried to dissuade Mariss from her course. But she had turned a deaf ear. The commander had hustled both Mariss and Dwayne across the courtyard and into his inner sanctum, followed by a pair of armed guards who stationed themselves outside the bungalow until Dwayne emerged, clutching his cyber-unit in sweaty palms.

After that, the men felt things were under control, and retired to the mess hall for dinner. Their commander could manage Mariss, of that they were certain. As for Kade, they ignored him.

Kade paced in the dust of the courtyard. The sun had long since set, and she was still inside, with *him*. Fighting for survival was one thing. But to think how she had jumped at the chance to spread her legs for that—that egotistical dictator!

Restless, Kade crossed to the mess hall. He didn't want to enter. Some of Alexander's men were inside, discussing their commander's good fortune in snaring such a young, willing beauty.

Kade slumped against the wall. He couldn't take this anymore. What was he doing to himself? What was he letting that violet-eyed vixen do to him?

Ever since Mariss had strolled onto his ship back at the Nexus Spaceport, he'd been responding like software she had programmed.

He was fed up with it. She had let him get closer to her,

but only as close as *she* decided was acceptable. When he pushed it, he'd been kicked and hit and whacked in the head.

He had gone out of his way to protect her and been rewarded with coolness and arguments—and this, the worst betrayal she could have perpetrated on him. After all he'd done for her, she didn't think twice before jumping into bed with that piece of krod. She loved bits and bytes and computers so much, so *damned* much, she would sell herself for them without a thought. It astounded Kade. Floored him. He couldn't comprehend it.

But he knew one thing. If she so much as looked at him with a flicker of interest, he'd be damned sure he followed through. He was through with being a gentleman. He'd been too gallant, that was his problem. By the Maker, he'd treated the little temptress like a *lady*.

Well, it was over, as of now. She wasn't going to turn a cold shoulder to Kadin Land after tonight. He would push past that cold wall she hid behind and *make* her see the truth, make her realize how she burned for him, too.

If he ever wanted to see her again, that is.

***

Mariss glanced over the sprawled body of Commander Jason Alexander. He was snoring deeply. One booted foot hung over the side of his cot.

The boots, she would have to remove them.

Mariss knelt and grasped a boot in both hands. She gave it a tug. It wouldn't budge. She yanked harder. It slipped off and threw her off balance. She fell hard on the floor, dropping the boot in the process. It clanged on the floor. She shot a glance at the commander, but he didn't stir.

She maneuvered the second boot off with greater alacrity. Next, she tackled his jacket, and his shirt. Both were filthy from sweat and dirt. Their laundry unit had apparently been smashed as well. Or maybe they had no source of power. As it was, she was working by the light of a solar-battery lantern resting on a table.

The man was undernourished, his ribs prominent, his skin pale. It wasn't too surprising that he backed off when Kade confronted him. There would have been no contest between the two of them.

Throughout her tugging and pulling of the fabric, Commander Alexander remained asleep. Mariss wondered if she had given him too high a dose of the somnolent plant's essence. She had picked up the plant on the first day, and analyzed it that evening after Kade had rolled into his cocoon. Its properties were classic sleep potion, and pure enough for her to use without reprocessing.

She had carried some of the plant with her since, in case it was needed. Never in her wildest imaginings had she expected to use it on a man who thought he was about to rav her.

True, she had harbored in the back of her mind the idea that if Kade had tried to force his way with her, she might use it on him. That thought shamed her now. The look on his face when she announced her intention to sleep with the commander—she had never seen such a shocked and devastated expression on any man. She told herself it stemmed from overprotectiveness and tried to ignore her heart's voice, which insisted there was much more to it.

She wasn't about to sleep with any of these men. Only with Adrian Young, after they were man and wife. And only him for the rest of their lives.

Leaning over the snoring man, she unfastened his pants. She hated this, but it would have to be done. She pulled his pants off, then his underwear. She prayed that the commander would think they had actually slept together.

As a final touch, she picked up a stylus and scrawled a note on the screen of the commander's cyber-unit, which rested beside the lantern.

"Thank you, commander, for a memorable evening.
— M"

Naked and oblivious, the commander never saw her leave.

***

Mariss shouldered her backpack and closed the door silently behind her. The courtyard was deserted. Night had fallen. The twin moons were riding high, now a quarter full.

Mariss had to find Kade as soon as she could, but had no idea where to look for him. She'd had no chance to explain her plan to him. Now they had to leave immediately, in case the commander wasn't convinced.

She traversed the courtyard and left the settlement by the same route they entered. There, on a rise a few meters distance, stood Kade, bathed in the moonlight. His pack rested at his feet. He also must have realized they needed to leave tonight. He was staring toward the settlement, and toward her.

She walked silently toward him. "Kade."

He said nothing. Nor was there a shift in his brooding expression. He had never looked so intimidating. She stopped in front of him. "I had to—"

As fast as lightning, Kade's strong hands were grasping her arms. He shook her, hard. "Don't you *ever* pull anything like that again!"

A bolt of fear combined with shock coursed through Mariss. She knew he had been angry, but he looked like he wanted to murder her. "Kade, let go of me."

Kade dropped her arms. He threw his hands wide and stepped back. "Gladly."

"Kade, I got the data! It's all been loaded into my cyber-unit. It has everything we need. There are several dangerous species we could easily have stumbled onto. Our supplies won't hold out forever. Now we know which plants we can eat. You know we wouldn't get very far without this information."

His teeth clenched, a muscle in his jaw worked furiously. He closed in on her. Mariss backed up a step. His voice was low, menacing. "I don't give a hang about the fragging data. Whatever made you think I cared about their data?"

"What *do* you care about, Kade?"

He ignored her question. He was only a few inches from her, his eyes boring into hers. "Whatever made you think you had to sell yourself for it? There are other ways!"

"Like murder?" she shot back.

Kade's expression froze, all the passion she had seen

vanishing as if it had never been. Mariss wished she could recall her flip remark. "Oh, no. I'm sorry, Kade. I didn't mean it." She touched his arm, but he yanked it away as if she were poison. Her voice dropped to a whisper. "I—I didn't let him rav me, I swear."

Kade's expression altered only slightly. His cool eyes were nailed to her. In a flash of insight, Mariss knew she had purposefully delayed telling Kade what had really transpired. She had wanted to see how he reacted to the idea of her sleeping so casually with the commander.

But her ploy had backfired horribly. Kade obviously cared more than he ever wanted her to see. It might already be too late to preserve his good opinion of her and save their fragile friendship. Desperately, she started to explain. "I didn't let him rav me," she repeated. "I never intended to. I put a sleeping potion into his drink. Juice from a plant I found a few days back. Before he could do more than kiss me, he started feeling its effects. He was out in just a few minutes."

Kade's voice was barely leashed fury. "You let him kiss you?"

"Yes." Mariss choked on the word.

Kade's hands slipped up her arms and under the straps of her pack. The pack—with its precious cyber-unit crammed with new data—landed on the ground. Mariss didn't notice. Kade pulled her closer, so close she felt her breasts press against his chest. "Did you like it?" he asked, his voice a rumble of barely contained emotion.

"No." Mariss felt herself drowning in his potent gaze.

Kade's hand drove into her tightly wound hair, loosening it enough for him to grip the back of her head in no uncertain terms. "You'll like this."

Mariss barely registered his meaning before Kade pressed his lips to hers. She felt the touch like an electric charge. His mouth covered hers completely, taking full possession. His lips moved over hers in sensual rhythm, hard and soft and unbelievably erotic. He was in control, demanding she respond.

And she did.

Mariss closed her eyes and reveled in the sensation. Her

lips parted, welcoming his tongue, returning his thrusts with equal fervor, tasting his potent, dark masculinity as if she had never tasted a man before.

Passion swept through her body, every nerve coming alive. She pressed Kade to her, slipped her arm around his muscular back, buried her hand in his thick, silky hair. Mariss craved his touch like she had never craved anything in her life. She was losing her sense in a swell of animal passion. She arched her back, pressed herself harder against him, stroked her breasts over his chest, entreating, inviting his touch.

Kade groaned deep in his throat. His hand slipped to her bottom, and he tugged her hard against himself, grinding his rock-hard erection into her pelvis.

A whizzing sound cut through her passion-fogged mind. Kade had already shoved her away. They were tumbling down the slope of the hill before she recognized what the sound was. A phase-gun blast.

"Halt!" a voice called out. "You must return to the settlement immediately!"

"Run. Now!" Kade commanded. He grabbed up both their packs as he shoved her forward. They sprinted toward the forest beyond. As they ran, Kade struggled to shoulder his own pack while managing not to drop hers. He got the pack over his shoulders just as a phase-gun blast singed the alloy frame. The blast would have hit him in the back if he'd been any slower.

Mariss chanced a glance back and saw two of the men from the settlement running after them. These men would know the terrain much better. And they weren't weighed down by packs. Maybe Kade alone could outdistance them, if he wasn't hauling all that equipment along. But he was never going to make it with her struggling to keep up.

She had no chance to consider why they were being pursued. An explosion crashed through the air, drawing the men's attention back toward the settlement. In one of the bungalows, flames shot into the night sky. A few seconds later, another explosion rent the air, this time from the opposite side of the settlement. To Mariss, it looked like the settlement was under attack.

The two men ceased their pursuit and started running back toward the flames. Mariss heard shouts of panic. Kade yanked on Mariss' arm, dragging her forward toward the trees.

It was at least half an hour of hard running—and stumbling—before Kade allowed her to stop and catch her breath. They were deep inside the forest canopy. No one seemed to be pursuing them. The forest was quiet, filled only by the sound of their heavy breathing.

Mariss collapsed against a tree trunk. "What happened back there? You did something, didn't you? The timing was too perfect."

"I rigged a couple of explosions."

"Of what?"

"Just some trash barrels."

"But why?"

"To get you out of there!" His eyes glittered fiercely in the shadows. "And to give us a chance to escape."

His dramatics infuriated Mariss. "They had agreed to let us go. What were you thinking? Or weren't you thinking at all?"

"They wouldn't have let us go. They were already making plans to keep you there, so all of them could—enjoy you."

Mariss shuddered. "I see."

"I hope so." He tossed her pack to her and she slipped it on. "Now let's get a move on. They might still be after us."

"Which way do we go?"

"North, further into the forest. We can swing around toward the east after we give the settlement a wide berth."

"That will add days to our journey."

"That's right." He stepped closer, his eyes locking with hers. Mariss could feel the heat emanating from his body. "Can't say as I mind."

Mariss averted her gaze. "Kade. I still intend to go to the Colony."

Kade slipped his hand in his jacket pocket and pulled out a silver orb the size of a baseball. "Mariss. Look."

She glanced up. "What is that?"

"While you were playing with the commander, I was looking around. I found this. Here." He tossed the orb to her. She caught it just before it fell to the earth. Its surface was shiny, even in the shadows, catching every bit of available light and casting it back. Inscribed on one side were the words, "Property of Iridion Colony, Elysia."

A frisson of trepidation roiled through her. "I...don't understand. What is it? Why did the settlement have it?"

"It's a battery. For the newest model hovercars."

Mariss stared at him as understanding washed over her. "You're saying people from the Colony visited the settlement. You think they're the ones who destroyed it."

"Got a better interpretation?"

"There could be other people on this planet, Kade. It's a big planet." Her eyes fell to the battery. "Someone from the Colony probably visited the settlement at some time."

"Visited? Is that all they did? Think about it. The Colony seems to be intentionally giving the settlement the cold shoulder. They're not that far. They could offer aid. Mariss, something is fishy here. I've felt it ever since I saw that hyped up hologram you showed us on the ship. I know you feel it, too. But you're ignoring your feelings." He ran his hand along her shoulder.

Mariss cleared her throat. She stiffened her spine and looked straight at him, so he would understand how serious she was. "Kade. What happened back there between us, before they began shooting at us...I've been under undue stress lately. I wasn't prepared for all this. The commander—I was terrified he would awaken at any moment. You can't—"

"Can't what?"

"Can't hold me to anything that may have happened. I mean—"

"Are you making excuses?"

"I'm trying to explain!"

His lips thinned. "I'll tell you what I think of your explanation, Mariss. I don't want to hear it. You want to ignore this thing between us, fine. You want to go to the Colony, fine. Just don't play games with me, woman. Do you hear me?" He pointed his finger in her face.

Mariss grabbed his hand and shoved the silver ball into it. "I never play games. That's what's eating you, Land. You got marooned in the wilderness with a lady. Well, I'm not sorry to disappoint you. You were never part of my plans."

She turned her back on him and strode through the trees, stumbling over the underbrush.

"Mariss," he called out to her. She ignored him. "Mariss, you're going the wrong way."

Mariss slowed to a stop. Chagrined, she returned to him. Without another word, he started off, leaving her to follow.

***

They hiked most of the night, striving to put distance between themselves and the settlement. Toward dawn Kade felt it was finally safe, and they made camp beneath the trees.

Kade shook Mariss awake far too soon, somewhere around mid-morning. He insisted they had to keep moving, in case the people of the settlement decided to pursue them.

Mariss was tired, sleepy and achy. She was filthy from days without a hot bath. She knew she stank. Kade didn't exactly smell like a bed of roses, either, though she hadn't minded the tang of his male scent the first few days.

Nor would she win any beauty contests. At least she wasn't trying to impress Kade. She would have failed miserably. He didn't seem to care whether she saw him at less than his best, either, though she had to admit the rugged, unwashed, unshaven look fit him better than it did her.

By the time the sun began to set, she was more than ready to call a halt. But Kade pushed on. They traversed the foothills of a second range of mountains, following them toward the east.

The weather grew almost too cold for her thermal flightsuit to keep her comfortable. She found herself stumbling on scattered rocks and small, scraggly plants. Kade plowed on, oblivious.

She looked up and slowed her steps. "What's that, smoke?"

Kade stopped and followed where she pointed. Puffs of white curled up from behind an outcropping to their left, in the direction of the mountain range. "Looks like steam," Kade said. "Let's take a look."

Without considering it further, he headed toward the outcropping.

An image popped into Mariss' head of a fire-breathing dragon ten times the size of the little blue ones in the forest. She opened her mouth to warn Kade to go carefully, but he was already heading around the outcropping.

"Mariss," he called out. "Mariss, come here."

Mariss joined him. In awe, she gazed upward at glistening limestone shelves, glowing in the orange sunset. The crystal terraces cascading down the mountain face reminded Mariss of a giant, multi-layered cake, lathered in icing.

But what drew her attention was something much more practical. Nestled at the base of the terraces were several hot pools. Mariss detected a mild hint of sulfur in the air.

She shrugged off her pack. "Tell me I'm not dreaming."

Kade was smiling with pleasure. "Nope."

"And it's so warm here. We're camping here tonight."

Kade deposited his own pack next to hers. "Yes, ma'am."

Together, they walked across the spongy grass to the edge of the nearest pool and gazed at it longingly. It was roughly oblong, about three meters across. The water was so clear, they could see the sandy bottom about four feet down. Steam wafted across its surface. A cushion of lichen coated the rocks along the edges.

Kade knelt and slipped a finger in the water. "Comfortable temperature."

"Do you think it'd be safe?" Mariss asked.

"Damned if I know. You're the scientist. You check. I'll set up camp."

Kade knelt on the grass and unpacked the bio-analyzer from his pack. He handed it to Mariss. "The fate of our personal hygiene is resting on your shoulders."

While Kade was erecting the automatic tent supports, Mariss scooped up a water sample from the pool and inserted the tube into the analyzer.

A few minutes later, the reading appeared. Mariss grinned.

"It's almost like bath water—with a little bit of sulfur added, but not at harmful levels. Temperature, 38.9 degrees Celsius. Looks like a bathtub to me!"

Kade was already sitting by the edge, yanking off his boots. He rose and tossed off his jacket. His shirt came flying after. Mariss glanced at his bare chest, and away again. "Um, Kade? Aren't we going to take turns?"

"I'm going in. If you want to wait, go right ahead. Could be a few hours, though."

Mariss shifted her feet. "At least turn your head."

"Turn yours." He shot her a cocky grin and began unfastening his belt. Irritated, Mariss turned her back. She stayed that way until she heard splashing, then peeked over her shoulder. Kade was swimming toward the far end of the small pool. He settled in place there, up to his chin in the steamy water. "Ah, Mariss, it's great! The best bath I've ever had. What are you waiting for?"

Mariss looked around and spotted a boulder a few meters away. She went behind it and stripped down to her underwear. Leaving her undershirt and panties on, she returned to the pool, a careful eye on Kade.

He wasn't even looking at her. He was dunking his head and scrubbing at his hair with the bio-soap from his pack. The soap was designed to break down immediately after use, making it perfect for use in a natural environment. Unaccountably disappointed, Mariss slipped into the pool.

The embrace of the hot water was incredibly relaxing. Immediately, every ache in her body began to dissolve. She slipped lower, lower still, until the water was up to her chin. Holding her breath, she took the plunge, completely immersing herself in the steamy water.

When she couldn't hold her breath any longer, she shot upward and threw her wet hair out of her face. She collapsed back against the pool edge, across from Kade. His eyes were on her now.

She watched him watching her. He was soaping his chest. It struck her then—they were taking a bath together.

"Can I have that soap when you're done?" she asked,

striving to sound composed, casual.

"Yeah. Here." He tossed it to her across the pool. She missed it.

Mariss sighed. "You should have handed it to me. Now I'll have to dive for it."

"I'll get it," Kade said in mock exasperation. He dived under and came up with the soap right in front of her. Mariss tried not to watch the drops of water roll down his chest. "There's a cave down there."

"Is there?" Mariss lifted a skeptical eyebrow. She didn't trust him not to be planning some move on her.

Kade shrugged. "Go see for yourself. On your side, at the bottom. About a foot high."

"I'll take your word for it." She held out her hand. "The soap, please."

Kade's lips curled in a smile. "Are you sure you don't want me to wash your back?"

Mariss fought down an answering smile. She knew what he was really after, and he wasn't going to get it. But she had to admit she liked him trying. "I can manage."

Kade shrugged, as if disinterested in her answer. "Suit yourself." He retreated to his end of the pool and sank down into the water. He laid back and closed his eyes.

Mariss breathed easier without him watching her every move. She fought down a surge of irritation at how easily she had dissuaded him from any amorous advances here in the intimacy of the pool. She didn't really want him to make a move on her. It was only her ego that expected it.

Her ego, and this amazingly romantic setting.

Conscious that her breasts were outlined by her wet shirt, she turned her back to wash her hair, since it involved lifting her arms in the air. She rubbed the soap between her hands, working up a thick lather, and massaged it through her hair. Washing had never felt so good. She had begun to think her hair would never be clean again.

Keeping her back to Kade, she arched her head back into the water and rinsed the soap out of her sprawling tresses. She closed her eyes, enjoying the feel of her hair separating as the grime washed out of it.

She sensed a shadow above her. She reopened her eyes. Her view of the evening sky was blocked by Kade's head. He was standing over her, gazing down at her face. "Let me," he murmured, slipping his strong fingers into her hair.

Mariss felt such a surprising surge of satisfaction at his interest she couldn't bring herself to protest. Kade cupped her head in his hand, allowing her body to float freely in the water. He ran his fingers along her scalp and through her hair, all the way to the roots, working the soap through it.

His touch felt so exquisite, Mariss didn't have the strength to tell him to stop. She merely relaxed and let him do his magic. He kept his hands solely on her hair and her scalp. There was nothing overtly sexual about his touch, nothing she ought to demand he stop doing. But she was aroused just the same. She felt his touch in every part of her body.

She gazed up at him. The fading light framed his rugged face, glinted off his slicked-back hair. High above, early evening stars were making their first appearance. The moment was magical, unreal, more vibrant than anything she had ever experienced.

Her eyes caught his and held. He wore an expression of deep concentration, almost devotion. Mariss forgot to breathe. When had this man she'd been traveling with become so irresistible? She closed her eyes, melting in sensation, half expecting to feel the touch of his lips on hers, half expecting to give in to him here, tonight.

It didn't happen.

"All clean." Kade helped her right herself. He squeezed her shoulders. Mariss felt the warmth of his palms, wanted him to slip his hands along her skin. But he removed them. She heard him splashing away, toward his end of the pool. "I'm going to get out now," he said casually. "Getting a bit overheated."

Mariss turned her back. But she couldn't resist a covert glance over her shoulder. Kade hoisted himself onto the edge of the pool. She watched him stand upright—wet, naked and fully aroused.

The sight sent a storm of heat through Mariss' body. She tried to will her desire away, but it only seemed to grow stronger. She argued with herself, clinging to logic. She had no business aching for Kadin Land. She simply wouldn't allow it.

Kade stooped to gather his clothing, his tight buttocks drawing her gaze. He crossed to the tent ten meters away. Their sleeping cocoons were equipped with thermal regulators, which would dry wet skin in a matter of seconds.

Mariss decided to wait in the pool for a few minutes, give him a chance to preserve his modesty. She slipped down into the water, resting her head against the rocks.

She fell into a delicious daydream. Knowing Kade had been desiring her as she desired him, with neither of them acting on it, was a tremendous aphrodisiac.

She couldn't help the fantasy that spun through her mind. He was out there, only a few meters away. She imagined him returning to the pool, naked and ready, slipping into the water, pressing her hard up against himself.

He would say nothing—nor would she. They would speak no promises, no words of commitment or of love. They would only seek to lose themselves in sensation, to satisfy their voracious physical needs.

And when they were sated, they would never refer to it again. They would continue their trek as before, and eventually go their separate ways.

But for those brief moments, they would be lost to everything but each other. He would take her here, in the water, her legs wrapped tight around his waist, his full length thrusting deep inside her, over and over, until ecstasy overwhelmed them both and she cried out —

A gouging, jabbing pain struck her calf. Mariss jerked away from the pain, opened her mouth to scream. But something powerful yanked her under the surface of the water. Sulfuric-tasting water filled her mouth and nose. She choked, thrashing about in a frenzy to break the hold of whatever unseen thing had grabbed her.

But her struggling was useless. She was being dragged

deeper, and held there. Her lungs started to ache. She couldn't hold her breath much longer.

Frenzied, terrified, she clawed at her leg, felt a slippery tentacle, an *alien* tentacle. She kicked, fought—all to no avail.

She hadn't managed to scream for help. Kade didn't know she needed him. He would never come until it was too late.

These thoughts flashed past her conscious mind in a matter of seconds. She only had a few moments left. She stopped tugging at the tentacle and struck the surface of the water, hoping Kade might notice the splashing, realize it was more than the usual sounds of bathing.

The creature yanked her leg again, whipping her body against the side of the pool, smashing the last of the oxygen from her lungs.

She was going to drown.

ELEVEN

Kade was trying hard to avoid looking toward the hot pool. He didn't want Mariss to have any excuse to accuse him of impropriety.

Not that he didn't think of it—more often than he would ever admit to anyone. But he knew she had no intention of allowing him closer. He wasn't her type; he wasn't what she needed, and she already had found her "perfect mate," as irritatingly ridiculous as that idea was. For her, it was real. And as far as Kade knew, she was right.

He heard the sound of furious splashing, and looked up from buckling his belt. Mariss was gone. The surface of the water roiled wildly.

Still wearing his pants, Kade sprinted toward the pool and leaped in. He couldn't see for a moment, so much sand had been tossed up.

There—Mariss was almost at the bottom, being pulled feet-first toward the small cave he'd seen earlier. Kade grabbed her under the arms and yanked her upward. Her head broke the surface, and she sucked in a precious breath.

"My leg," she gasped out, before being pulled back under.

Kade dove to the bottom. A yellowish, slimy tentacle was wrapped around her leg from her ankle to her thigh. Kade stomped on it, tore at it, yanked at it—to no avail. Mariss had been under too long. He again pulled her toward the surface, giving her a chance to catch another breath.

"Take a deep breath, I need to get the gun," he ordered.

He avoided the panic in her eyes as he swam to the edge, leaving her behind. He had no choice. Mariss was immediately pulled back under the surface.

Kade was back in a matter of seconds. The phase-gun didn't work well under water, but it did work. He sliced through the tentacle, and it began to slip from Mariss' leg.

Kade pulled her to the surface. She gasped for breath. He lifted her to the pool's edge and pulled himself out.

"My leg," Mariss cried softly.

"I know. I shouldn't have left you alone." He scooped her up and carried her toward the tent.

She gasped, "On Earth, almost nothing thrives in sulfur hot springs because the environment is too hostile."

Always the scientist. Kade smiled softly. "Mariss, don't try to talk."

In the tent, he laid her soaking-wet body on her sleeping cocoon and bent to examine the leg. It was raw, red, bleeding in places.

"Kade, it stung me. I can feel the poison moving into my system."

"Just try to relax. I'm taking a look."

"It—it stung me," she insisted. "It feels like a neuro-paralysis chemical. I—I can't feel my hands or my feet."

Kade yanked his head up, faced her. He wasn't trained in anything but basic first-aid. "Tell me, what can I do?"

"I'm trying to think. I have to think."

He pressed her hands together, tried rubbing them.

"I can't feel that, Kade. My arms are growing numb. I—I won't be able to breathe soon."

Kade's stomach clenched in fear. He felt impotent. "Tell me what to do!"

"Try...tavol. In the med kit. It's a neuro-stimulant. Give me a shot."

Kade struggled to open the kit. Then panic crept up on him as he eyed the fifty-plus miniature capsules of chemicals. He scanned for tavol, located it, yanked out the injector gun, almost had the capsule in the chamber—then dropped the pill-sized capsule.

He was all thumbs, a new experience for him. This tension, this need to hurry, yet think perfectly clearly, shouldn't be any different than piloting a ship through an asteroid storm.

He was an expert at maintaining a single-minded focus. His ability to push aside every consideration but the one at hand was legendary among his fellow pilots.

But not this time.

He couldn't keep from feeling overwhelmed. The panic slipped inside and gripped his bowels. With every beat of her heart, Mariss's body was pumping the poison through her system. With every wasted second, her chances of survival diminished.

And he couldn't hold onto the damned capsule long enough to insert it into the gun.

"I got it." A flush of satisfaction flowing through him, he lifted the gun to her arm.

"No, Kade. My bottom. It's faster. Roll me over."

Without hesitation, Kade turned her. He yanked her panties down and shot the chemical inside her body.

More gently this time, he rolled her onto her back. "Is it working?" he asked. He continued massaging her hands, though he feared it wouldn't help.

"I don't know. You did what you could." Mariss gazed up at him, her face composed, brave and sweet. Kade wished more than anything he could take her place. "Please, Kade, hold me."

Kade lay beside her and slipped his arms around her. She was small-boned, delicate, yet with a will of iron. She would survive this. She would. "How do you feel?"

"My—legs. I can't feel my legs anymore."

The medicine he'd fought so hard to give her was proving useless. The worst part was that he could do nothing to help her. Nothing. He stroked the wet strands of hair from her face. "You're freezing. Here." He tucked her into her cocoon and turned on the thermal heater. In a few minutes, she was dry.

"Kade. Don't let me go."

Kade lifted the edge of her cocoon and slipped in beside her. He pulled her close. Soon, he was as dry as she was. He was almost afraid to ask. "Are your legs still numb?"

"It's moved to my midriff," she said softly. "At least it's painless. My leg doesn't hurt anymore."

"Christ!" He swallowed hard, blinked back the sting of tears.

"Kade," Mariss said, her voice almost a whisper. "Will you tell Adrian what happened? I know he'll be disappointed when I don't arrive."

In that second, Kade wanted to kill Adrian Young. The mention of another man's name at this moment...And the man had never even *met* Mariss. Young would simply find another wife, another "perfect" profile. Mariss—the real Mariss—meant nothing to him.

But Kade—he knew he would never get over the pain of having Mariss Sakari die in his arms. His throat was tight with unshed tears. He choked out, "I was supposed to protect you, Mariss. I should have stayed with you."

"You haven't done anything wrong, Kade. You've done everything you could for me, despite how irritating I can be."

"You? Never."

"You know it's true. I'm just afraid, Kade."

"Shh. I know."

"I'm afraid. Over how you make me feel."

"You're going to make it, Mariss, so don't say anything you'll regret later." He tried to speak the words lightly, with gentle teasing. But he could hardly speak past the lump in his throat.

"I—I can't see very well." Her eyelids drifted closed. She managed to open them once more, revealing terror in their violet depths. She gasped, her entire body shaking violently. "Kade, I'm blind. I can't see anything. I can't see your face!"

That's when it became real. She was going to die right here, and he would be alone again. Mariss seemed to accept it, too. He spoke to her soothingly, saying nothing substantial, only caring. After awhile, his comforting words calmed her, and she stopped shivering.

She spoke softly into his ear. "Are you holding me?"

"Yes."

"I can't feel you." Her voice quavered with fear.

"I'm here, Mariss. I won't leave you."

"I know. You're such a good man, whatever you did before,

it doesn't matter, Kade. Don't let anyone tell you it does."

"No, no I won't."

"Promise me."

"I promise." He would have promised to bring her the twin moons of Elysia, if she had asked for them.

Her next words were so soft, he had to press his ear to her lips to hear them. "I wish...I'd met you..." Her words faded as her breath grew more shallow. Her lips formed the final word on a single exhalation. "First."

Mariss stopped breathing.

TWELVE

Kade breathed into her mouth for the hundredth time. He checked for her pulse. It fluttered under her skin, weak and thready, but it was there. Mariss could no longer breathe on her own, but her heart continued to pump oxygen through her system—as long as he continued to breathe for her.

A half-hour passed, and her condition remained the same. Kade's back ached from bending over her. His lungs ached from breathing for the both of them. But he refused to quit. Not while she still had a ghost of a chance.

He settled his mouth over hers again.

***

An hour crawled by. Kade sat back on his heels and felt for her pulse. He checked twice. Couldn't find it.

He swore and checked a third time. It was there. Remarkably, now it seemed stronger than before.

Was it only wishful thinking? Kade had wasted enough precious time wondering about it. He lowered his mouth to hers once more. Before he could breathe for her again, she moved—her chest rose on its own as she sucked in a deep, choking breath.

A surge of joy overwhelmed Kade as he watched her gasp and sputter. She was coming back to him.

***

Mariss moaned. She sensed light through her eyelids, but even this sensation hurt.

But no agony compared to the shooting, burning sensation in every cell of her body. The pain was everywhere. When she could suck in enough air, she cried out in anguish.

A voice answered her. "Thank the Maker, you're back.

You're back."

A man's voice, vibrant, emotion-filled, just above her. Mariss began to remember, though even thinking hurt. She cracked her eyes open to find Kade gazing down at her.

Tentatively, she licked her lips. Her tongue throbbed with the effort. "The drug must've worked. Interesting." She closed her eyes against the light.

Suddenly, bolts of agony coursed up her arms from her hands. Mariss screamed. Kade had picked them up and begun rubbing them. He stopped immediately. "I'm sorry. What is it, Mariss? What?"

"Side effects, I would guess," she murmured. Her vocal chords protested the effort to speak. "Everything hurts. Horrible pain."

Kade swept a tear from her cheek with his thumb. "I thought I'd lost you."

"Me too. Guess you're s—stuck with me."

"Looks like it. How about pain killer? We must have some capsules of aragon in the med-kit." He disappeared from above her.

Mariss tried to shake her head. It sent a bolt of agony up her spine. "No. No, Kade." He turned back to her.

"It may depress my systems again. Let's not mess with success."

"Antibiotics should be safe." Kade examined the wound. "I see the puncture mark. A lot of scrapes, but those are minor. The puncture worries me, though." Kade opened the med-kit and removed a small vial and the gun. He daubed the wound with a topical antibiotic, which burned like hellfire, layering pain on top of pain. He then applied a snug bandage to her calf. Then he held up the med-gun. "Can you roll to your side?"

"If you help me."

He did, again shooting the medicine into her hip. He put the gun away. "That's all I can do, Mariss. I'm sure no doctor." He stroked her forehead.

"There is one more thing you could do," she said softly.

"What?"

"Hold me and talk to me, to distract me from the pain."

She was shivering. She couldn't control it. Every nerve-ending screamed in agony as her body shook, but she couldn't manage to harden her muscles enough to stop.

Kade slipped into the cocoon beside her once again and enfolded her in his strong, warm embrace. Mariss couldn't help noticing how neatly she fit in his arms, her head tucking under his chin.

"So, you want me to talk?" he asked softly.

Mariss nodded. She hadn't yet decided which was worse—moving her head or speaking.

"That I can do. How about a story?" He thought a second. "Once upon a time there was a beautiful princess with long black hair, a sharp tongue and a cyber-unit she loved very much."

"Very funny." Mariss couldn't help thinking that she had almost died, without really knowing Kade—where he'd come from, what he had been through. Once they reached the Colony—if they made it that far—it would be too late. She prompted, "Tell me about you."

She could feel Kade's sigh through her entire body. But he began, finally, to reveal his story.

"You already know where I grew up. Tass Mining Colony. I know it doesn't look pretty in the holos, not like Earth. But my mom was the best. When I was about ten age-years, my dad was killed in an accident deep in the asteroid's interior. After that, my mom worked for one of the mining companies. She made a decent home for us. Still, I knew there were better places out there, in the wide sweep of the stars. I grew up dreaming of leaving Tass, of becoming a pilot. It seemed the best way off that rock. Only problem was I couldn't afford the training. So it looked like I was going to live on Tass all my life, work in the mines like my dad did.

"But a teacher of mine found out about a scholarship program sponsored by Quantum Craftlines, through Spanos Academy. He recommended I apply. So I did."

"You were a good student, then."

"Good enough."

Mariss knew he was being modest. He had to have been

the best to receive a full scholarship to the prestigious academy. She hadn't pictured him as a scholar.

"Nothing on Tass prepared me for the academy. It was sophisticated, exotic, exciting, everything I had ever dreamed. Not that it was easy. Oh, the flight training itself wasn't difficult, and I loved it. I was up there with the best of them. Problem was, the other students generally came from well-off families who had paid their way. They didn't think much of the upstart charity case from Tass taking one of the coveted spots in the elite ranks. I earned the respect of most of them by bettering them. When they came to see I wasn't going to be intimidated, most of them started to accept me. But there were a few..."

He fell silent.

"What about the women?" she asked, to get him talking again. The pain had receded slightly. Kade's story had done much to get her mind off the agony.

"The female pilots were more understanding."

"I meant girls."

"Yeah, well." He hesitated. "It isn't hard to get a date when you're in the elite corps." Mariss knew he was downplaying his appeal. She could just imagine him as a top-ranked academy student. He must have been incredibly popular.

"Anybody special?"

He sighed. "There was one girl...from Earth. A wealthy trader's daughter. Pampered girl. Pretty. Popular."

"What about her?"

He hesitated. "We were going to get married after I graduated."

Mariss wondered if she were forcing him to open old wounds which were better left closed. But she thought of how Kade had made her talk about what had driven her from Earth, her husband and her sister's betrayal. Sometimes it was healthy to share.

"What happened?" she asked quietly. She knew full well Kade never graduated from the academy. He was at the point in his story on which everything turned, all his actions since—his life since—hung on this one slim section of time.

"I found out my roommate Alan was selling exam answers to underclassmen. He didn't need the extra cash. His family was one of the wealthy ones." Kade sighed. "Before I could convince him to stop, the officials found out. There was an investigation. They discovered that the computer in our room held a databank of exam data. I hadn't noticed it. I'm not that swift with computers, not enough to hack around in them when someone wants something hidden.

"After a while, the suspicion turned to me. I was the poor kid from the backwater planet. It seemed more likely I was the one in need of extra cash. My mom had died the year before, so I had nothing beyond what came with the scholarship.

"I was, however, at the top of my class at the time."

"You were going to graduate First?" Mariss was astounded. She knew his flight scores were high. But his academics must also have been top-rate. Any pilot who graduated First would have had his pick of jobs with the best firms in the galaxy. She had seen profiles of the First graduates on the newscasts every year for her entire life.

Kade shrugged, as if it were unremarkable. "Yeah. Anyway, pilots—particularly young ones—are notorious for their competitiveness. I was a tempting target. A few words in the right ears, and the officials felt they had enough evidence to convict me. They leapt on the circumstantial evidence like it was proof. Alan's reputation—and that of his family—would be preserved."

"You were the designated fall guy."

"That's right."

Kade grew silent, lost in thought. Carefully, Mariss tried lifting her hand. It tingled, but not unbearably. Slowly, she brought it higher and laid it on his bare chest. His chest hair felt soft under her fingers, his skin warm, solid and alive. "Tell me the rest."

Kade slipped his hand over hers. "You're moving your arms. That's great."

Her eyes shone with humor. "Don't change the subject."

He smiled. "Yes, ma'am. With my future on the line, I did

what any red-blooded guy would do. I confronted Alan McChord—"

"Alan McChord? The son of the McChord Alloy magnate? I remember hearing about..." Mariss' voice faded. She had heard how he was brutally murdered while attending the academy. "I'm sorry, Kade. Please tell me the rest."

"I confronted Alan and demanded he confess to the authorities. With the backing of his family, he would get off with a slap on the hand. But that was my mistake, thinking I could convince him to do the right thing.

"He argued with me, started to panic. He thought our conversation was being recorded to use against him later. The next thing I knew, he had drawn a phase-gun and was holding it on me. Phase-guns were forbidden in the Academy. He must have bought it on the black market. Or traded test answers for it. Somehow I—I ended up trying to get it from him. We struggled, and—it went off."

"He was killed."

Kade didn't answer. Mariss didn't try to make him. She relaxed in his arms, felt the pain of her body fading as an even worse pain grew in her heart. She had actually been afraid of Kadin Land. How much it must have hurt him to see her terrified of him as if he were a cold-blooded monster. But she could do nothing for him now, except listen, and care.

"His finger was on the phase-gun's trigger button, about to depress it when I jumped him. I tried to stop him from shooting me, and forced the barrel up and away from my own chest." His voice dropped so low she almost missed his words. "I pushed it too far."

"Kade. It was an accident. You would have been killed if you'd done nothing."

"I shouldn't have been so fast. I scared him, pushed him over the edge."

Mariss thought of Kade's gifts, his amazingly quick reactions. In this case, they had brought him only grief.

"The Academy was desperate to avoid a scandal," Kade finally said, his voice growing bitter. "They wanted it over, and over quick. All they could think of was how it would look to have their name and top-flight image displayed all over the newscasts for months on end. That's what a trial would mean. Worse, the McChord family would do anything to cover up the truth about their son's dealings."

"That's why you accepted the plea bargain?"

"Hell, no. I didn't do it for them. I did it for me. They charged me with murdering Alan to cover up my crime of selling exam answers. A nice, simple motive, and a good resolution for them. And a life sentence for me. I had a public-defender for a lawyer, appointed by the Earth Tribunal. He told me straight—if I didn't accept the plea bargain and go quietly, the Academy had enough circumstantial evidence to crucify me. I believed him. So I pled guilty to third-degree murder and first-degree fraud. I had no resources to pay for better advice. No one on my side, so to speak. And I knew there *was* no other side, not for a boy from Tass."

Mariss hesitated, but she had to ask. "Your fiancée—wasn't she from a wealthy family?"

"She said, and these are her words, 'I have no intention of exhausting my youth waiting for a man with no future.'"

"She just gave up on you? How cruel. She deserves to be ejected into deep space without a suit."

He smiled ruefully. "Thanks for the sentiment. That's how I felt, too. She was all the family I had, then I lost her. But she had a point. I was sentenced to seven years hard labor on Rebus Five, working in the uranium mines. I slaved in the mines for only three years of my sentence. That makes me a lucky guy, in case you didn't realize it."

"Lucky," Mariss said dryly.

"It's exhausting, dirty work, you and the robots deep in the interior of Rebus's moon. Wearing a full environmental suit, yet doing hard physical work. Exactly the kind of work I had left Tass to get away from. Unhealthy, too. The rad suits weren't that safe. Exposure accidents happened every day. I seem to have made it through fine, but I'm probably infertile."

"Kade, no." Mariss blinked back a surge of tears. He had said he wanted children, but it was only wishful thinking.

"They put me on explosives duty—because of my quick

reflexes, they said. I had to rig rock walls to blow. Set the charges and get out fast. When things didn't go off as planned, I had to go back in and re-arm the charges."

"That's so dangerous! Why didn't they send robots in?"

He snorted. "Are you kidding? Robots are expensive."

"Kade," Mariss whispered, her heart aching for him.

"Anyway, a few years into my sentence, the mines were hurting for good pilots. A clerk in the office stumbled on the fact I was a pilot, so they put me on cargo-hauling duty. It wasn't glamorous, but it was a reprieve. They paroled me after I served five years of my sentence, with the understanding that I would continue to work for them for the remainder."

"Did you have to keep living on Rebus Five?"

"No. I lived on my ship. The rent was cheap, and it wasn't the Rebus Five Prison barracks, at any rate."

"Then you were hired by Quantum?"

"That's right. Even they had to scrape the bottom of the barrel to staff the outback runs."

"Kade," she chided. She then returned to the subject, a suspicion growing in her mind. "So now you live at the Nexus, where Quantum is headquartered?"

"Yeah."

"And you've only piloted outback runs."

"Yeah."

"So, you've never been to Earth, have you?"

He opened his mouth to reply, then snapped it shut. He shook his head.

"Those posters on your cabin wall, in the ship—you've never been to any of those beautiful places."

"No. But I've seen the holograms, Mariss."

She could tell he did not want her to feel sorry for him. "But it's not the same, not the same at all. A hologram can give you a general idea, but could never match up to being there and experiencing it for yourself."

Kade's eyebrows rose, and he smiled. "Is that a fact?"

"Yes!" Mariss insisted.

"Funny. That's just what I've been trying to tell you—about Adrian Young and the Colony."

Mariss had walked right into that one. She bit her lip, discovered it didn't hurt so much anymore. "Well, let's not talk about that. Maybe instead you can tell me what happened on Barron Outpost."

He arched a brow. "How do you know about that?"

"I have ways." She smiled softly. "I overheard the other officer mention it before we boarded. And, of course, I read your personnel file." Their argument about her prying now seemed so long ago.

Gently, he stroked her hair. "You're much sneakier than you appear."

"I know. So tell me."

He exhaled, then began. "That was my latest screw up. I met a young girl in the Outpost bar—a runaway who'd gotten in over her head. After she flirted with me and got nowhere, she began chatting up Grogarian soldiers, massively built men a foot taller than me. When three of them took her outside, I thought I should follow, just in case. Sure enough, they planned to… You know. Anyway, I wasn't about to take on three drunk and armed soldiers bare-handed. Instead, I rigged a small explosion as a distraction. It worked. The girl ran off. She disappeared into the outpost and I never saw her again."

"But you didn't get away." He didn't answer, but Mariss already knew he'd been arrested for drunk and disorderly conduct. He'd saved the girl, but had been punished for his good deed. Mariss' heart ached for this man who seemed to have been born under the wrong star.

His face looked drawn, and she knew she should let him rest. "I should probably sleep now, if you don't mind."

Kade started to pull away. Mariss tugged at his bare shoulder "Please don't leave. Not until I'm asleep. To be honest, after almost dying, I feel just a bit vulnerable right now."

Kade didn't protest as she snuggled against his chest and closed her eyes.

***

Mariss awoke. She felt she hadn't slept at all, but morning light was creeping through the flap of their tent. She was weak, hungry, and still in pain. The agony had faded to a dull ache. She rolled to her stomach, seeking a more comfortable position.

Kade lay beside her, his eyes closed, breathing evenly. She gazed at him, astounded at how close she felt to him. In the past few days, going through what she had with Kade, she felt closer to him than she had ever felt to anyone, except perhaps her twin sister Ami, when they were children.

Kade cracked his eyes open. He smiled and laid his hand on her back, his touch tentative.

"How do you feel?"

"Wretched."

He propped his head on his hand. "Understandable," he murmured, the word thick with sleep.

He ran his hand along her back.

"Mmm, that feels good," Mariss said. If she'd been a cat, she would have purred her pleasure.

A corner of his mouth tipped up. "No pain when I touch you?"

"No. I'm achy all over, and my leg is throbbing. But this feels wonderful."

"I'll check your leg in a minute." Neither of them made a move to get up and face the day. Kade seemed content to look at her, lie beside her, stroke her back from her shoulders to just above her bottom.

Mariss relaxed under his touch, anticipated his hand sliding lower, caressing and warm. Her eyes met his, and she knew he wanted to touch her in much more intimate ways.

His touch spread through her, engulfing her in an intoxicating mist. It felt wonderfully right. Yet she had never woken up beside a man who wasn't her husband.

Instantly, like recalling a bad dream, the image of Roldo flashed into her mind. Roldo holding her in their bed, in the early months of their marriage. Before the dissatisfaction, the anger, the betrayal.

What she was feeling toward Kade right now was very close to what she had felt for Roldo. She had thought Roldo her perfect mate, had drowned in his charms, had been lulled into thinking what they had was real, and he would always love her.

"The Colony."

Kade's hand froze on her back. "What about it?"

Mariss rolled to her side, away from Kade. "We have to get going. Adrian must be worried sick that I haven't arrived. I'm weeks overdue."

Kade sat up, his expression closed, all sense of intimacy extinguished like a candle snuffed by a cold wind. "You're going nowhere, Mariss, for at least a week. Have you forgotten you almost died yesterday?"

"No, but—"

"And your leg—you wouldn't last an hour on a hike." He yanked back the cover of her cocoon and bent to examine the dressing.

"But a week! I don't need a week to recover. I—"

Her voice faltered as Kade's expression grew stormy. "Do you think I like holing up here in the middle of nowhere playing nurse? This isn't my idea of a great time, Mariss."

Hurt flowed through her. Tears stung her eyes, and she blinked them back. "I realize that," she said softly. "I'm sorry. I know you didn't ask for this."

"Damn straight. Your leg looks better, but it has a long way to go. Today, you rest. Now, where the hell did I leave my shirt?" He ducked out of the tent.

Mariss heard his footsteps fade. Her heart heavy, she collapsed back into the cocoon.

***

The orange-yellow sun was straight overhead when Mariss managed to stand up and hobble out of the tent. Mist caressed the foot of the terraced slope, hovered in clouds over the hot springs. Kade was nowhere to be seen. Her leg throbbed so badly, it brought tears to her eyes.

Kade had done a credible job bandaging her leg. He had done so much for her, cared so much. And she would continue to rely on him. She had no choice. But what he'd said was true—he hadn't bargained for any of this. She was the worst kind of inconvenience to him. A nuisance and a trial.

Biting down the pain, she half crawled, half hobbled toward a stand of bushes behind the tent.

When she was through, she hobbled toward the tent again—and right into a furious, bare-chested Kade.

He supported her and she leaned into him, letting him take her weight. "Where in the hell do you think you're going? To the Colony?"

"Very funny. I had to *go*."

His anger faded. "Oh. Well, next time, tell me and I'll help you."

"Don't be silly. I can manage. Besides, it's private."

"Mariss, in case you haven't noticed, there's very little of you I haven't seen or touched." As if to prove his point, he scooped her into his arms. She felt weightless in his strong embrace. He returned her to the tent and her cocoon bed.

He helped her get comfortable. He folded his own cocoon into a makeshift pillow and placed it behind her back, so she could sit up and "play" with her cyber-unit, which he set beside her. "Now, stay put. I'm within shouting distance, just outside."

Mariss nodded. She wasn't interested in her cyber-unit just now. She couldn't take her eyes off Kade. She watched him through the tent opening as he approached the killer hot pool. He knelt beside it. Mariss wondered what he was up to. He lowered something into the water.

"Kade," she yelled, panic gripping her. "Kade, don't go *near* there! Kade!"

He looked toward her, but completed his task before he straightened and left the poolside. He held up his blue shirt so she could see it. It was soaking wet. He crossed to a flat boulder and spread it out to dry.

"I'm doing laundry, Mariss," he called to her. "I'll do yours next." He turned away and headed for the pool again. Mariss saw her flightsuit in his hand.

She almost leaped up despite her leg injury. "Not in *that* pool you don't."

Kade called back at her. "There are caves like that one in *all* the pools, Mariss. Some of the larger pools have two or three. It's back to sponge baths."

He knelt by the pool again and thrust her flightsuit into the water. Mariss bit her lip. She couldn't stand seeing him so close to that *monster*. "Kade, please!"

He ignored her.

"Kade, damn you! I don't need a clean flightsuit. Get your butt away from there!"

Taking his sweet time, Kade rose and squeezed the water from her suit. He laid it out on the boulder next to his shirt.

Mariss collapsed back against her makeshift pillow, cursing his bullheadedness.

He sauntered toward her, wiping his wet hands on his pants. "I'm being careful, Mariss. You shouldn't get yourself overexcited," he said mildly. "Now, take off your underwear."

A flash of heat swept through Mariss despite her aches and pains. "My underwear?"

"Yeah, your panties and undershirt. And your bra."

Mariss wasn't at all sure she wanted him *saying* the words, much less seeing the items themselves. "They don't need to be cleaned," she said.

He shook his head. "I've *seen* them, remember? Hand 'em over." He stretched out his hand, his face rock-hard with determination.

Mariss knew she wouldn't win this argument. She could hardly fight the man off. She crawled deep into the cocoon and stripped to the buff.

She tossed her underwear out. Kade caught all three pieces. "At least now you won't wander off someplace," he said.

He retreated toward the pool of horrors once more. Mariss held her breath until he was through playing with her underthings and had laid them out to dry.

He returned to the area in front of the tent, this time with a full expanda-bottle.

"What are you going to do now?" she asked, unable to keep the concern from her voice.

"An ancient ritual, performed only by men, done best with warm water." Kade ran his hand over his beard-stubbled face. "It's called...shaving." He knelt on his heels within sight of the tent entrance and opened the kit of personal items from his pack. He extracted the razor and proceeded to divest himself of his beard.

Mariss watched him perform his manly ritual. She couldn't help it. He was right in her line of sight. The morning mist had lifted. Sunlight glazed his brawny torso. Watching his muscular physique made Mariss all too conscious of her complete nudity in the warm cocoon.

Kade glanced toward her and caught her staring. Flushing with guilt, Mariss looked away. She feigned indifference and grabbed her cyber-unit. Being careful to remain fully covered in the cocoon, she propped it on her lap and turned it on.

Yesterday, she and Kade had been so excited about finding a ready-made bath, neither had thought to check the data she'd gotten from the settlement at such risk. Now she searched through it. Sure enough, there was an entry for the pool creature which had attacked and nearly killed her. One of the earliest expeditions from the settlement had stumbled on the pools and gone bathing, exactly as she and Kade had done. The expedition had lost two of their party in two different pools at almost the same time.

Mariss pondered that fact. It seemed an odd coincidence, unless these creatures all ate at the same time every day. "Kade..."

"Hmm?" He glanced toward her, his face half-shaven.

"This may sound silly. But maybe there's only one creature."

"What?"

"Only one. Living in the hot water under all the pools, with lots of tentacles. You never actually saw the entire creature, did you?"

"No. Just a tentacle."

"Then it *could* be one creature."

Kade shrugged. The sunlight rippled along his muscles. Mariss swallowed. "What good would knowing if it was one or several creatures do us, Mariss?" he asked.

"None, I suppose. But it's interesting."

His answer was blunt, bordering on cold. "I'm only interested if it means we get out of this wilderness faster, without any more threat to life and limb."

Mariss stopped trying to discuss it with him. Her eyes flicked from the screen to Kade, now combing his thick, dark hair. He'd been aloof ever since she had mentioned the Colony, and how Adrian would miss her. Which meant one thing—he had feelings for her.

As I do for him.

A dizzying heat flowed out from Mariss' chest through her body. Her heart expanded, and she felt she was about to fly. But she could not.

She recognized the signs, and it terrified her. This heady, intoxicating feeling, this hunger coupled with satisfaction, this exhilaration and contentment —

I don't want this, she thought frantically. *I refuse. I will NOT fall in love with Kadin Land.*

Adrian. She repeated the name to herself like a mantra. Adrian. But to her dismay, she couldn't recall the details of his face. Nor could she recall all the little facts about him, things which made him so special, so *right* for her. She had clung to thoughts of Adrian Young throughout the two months it took to arrange her move to this planet—and escape the betrayal of the people closest to her. It shocked her to realize she had put Adrian Young so far out of her mind in the past weeks.

Because of Kade.

You're just lonely, she told herself. *Kade's here, and Adrian's not.*

Liar, a small inner voice said. *You could have been stranded with any other man in the galaxy, and you wouldn't be feeling this way.*

All right, she admitted, Kade *was* attractive. Any healthy woman would notice that. And he was brave. And compassionate. And he had other qualities she was reluctant to define.

To her chagrin, she could not forget the way he had kissed her. Every nerve in her body responded to the memory, and yearned for more.

It's been a long time since you ravved a man, she reminded herself. That had to explain the intense cravings which had crept up on her in the past few days. Mariss determined to relegate these unruly emotions to a corner of her mind and simply not pay them any heed. She was *that* disciplined, at least.

Besides, Adrian had fine qualities, too, she reminded herself. She tore her eyes from Kade and pinned them to the screen of her cyber-unit, where she keyed up Adrian's profile.

He was twenty-nine. His parents had both served prominent positions in Earth Coalition government before moving to the newly founded Colony to raise their family.

Adrian had received an off-world education, at Earth's finest universities, graduating with top honors in two advanced degrees. His specialty was landscape engineering, transforming the mundane into paradise.

As a twenty-year-old wunderkind, he had recreated the landscapes of several prominent Earth parks in the name of the Iridion Corporation. Then, he had returned to Elysia and was performing his landscaping magic there. Having accomplished many of his professional goals, his fondest desire was to marry and raise a family.

He was dedicated to family life, valued personal and professional discipline, always strove to better himself. His sense of humor rating was 55, which was on the low side.

Mariss had known this before, but in her excitement at finding Adrian, at knowing such an accomplished man wanted her, she hadn't given it much weight. Probably because she had still been hurting at her husband's betrayal, and in no mood for laughter.

She looked toward Kade, but he had disappeared from view. She wondered what he would rate on the humor scale. He seemed to find things humorous no matter what their situation. It was probably a coping mechanism he had developed from living in the dismal environments of Tass and Rebus Five. This was what her logical mind told her. But her heart recognized a kindred spirit, someone who looked for the humorous in life to deal with harsher truths. So how would Adrian deal with them?

A chill drifted down her spine. She had no idea.

Exhaustion overwhelmed her. She could no longer think clearly about anything. Her leg had begun to throb fiercely once more, so she dosed herself with a mild painkiller. Now that she was out of the woods, she felt it would be safe. A few minutes later, her lids grew heavy with the effort to stay awake. She set her cyber-unit down and rolled into the cocoon, then fell blissfully asleep.

***

Kade let Mariss sleep. Toward evening, she woke up, and he brought her food, such as it was. More carbo-pro jerky. He was sick of it. Mariss didn't have much of an appetite. He couldn't blame her. He checked her dressing and tucked her in once more. She was asleep in minutes.

A glow in the dark caught his eye. Adrian Young's face stared out from Mariss' cyber-unit. Kade swept it up and looked at the man who was shortly going to have Mariss all to himself. When she was sick or hurt, it would be Adrian who would care for her.

He hit the power button, dissolving Adrian's face, and closed the cover, trying not to think about it. He had no right to think about it.

He gently slipped his own sleeping cocoon from under Mariss and stepped into the cool evening air outside the tent.

A sweet, feminine voice followed him. "Kade. You don't have to sleep outside."

Kade dropped the cocoon and ducked into the tent. Mariss was awake, gazing up at him. The sight of her, sleepy-eyed and vulnerable, her ebony hair tumbled in a riotous, uncombed mass about her shoulders, caused an unwanted surge of tenderness to spin through him. "Mariss, what do you want from me?" he asked softly.

Her large violet eyes were ingenuous. "Nothing. I thought you'd be more comfortable in the tent."

He couldn't stand it anymore. She was oblivious to the effect she had on him because she *chose* to be. Mariss wanted nothing from him but friendship. Oh, he knew she desired him. But only because he was here. What she valued was a man like Adrian—solid, respectable and clean. "You want me to lie beside you?" he asked harshly. "How about putting my arms around you. Is that what you want?"

"Kade—"

"You want me to stroke you? Run my hands over your body?"

She sat up, pulling up the edge of her cocoon to hide her naked breasts. "Stop it."

Kade crouched beside her. He locked gazes with her, wouldn't let her look away. "Let's cut to the chase. Do you want me to rav you?"

Mariss opened her mouth in shock. "I—I only asked if you wanted to stay in here, like you did last night."

"Last night you were sick and injured. Tonight I just may rav you, good and hard. You've lusted after me ever since we met. I told you before not to tease me, woman."

Mariss was silent for several long heartbeats. Her words were low. "Kade, if we did...What would it mean to you?"

Fury uncoiled in him. She wanted Adrian Young, but obviously she'd use Kade to pass the time until they arrived at the Colony. Then she'd go her own way. He rose slowly and towered over her. "The same thing it would mean to you. A good, hard, mindless rav. But right now, I sure as hell am not in the mood."

He tore his eyes from her pain-filled expression and left the tent.

THIRTEEN

Neither of them referred to the incident over the next few days as Mariss healed.

She grew stronger and told Kade the fierce throbbing in her leg had faded to a dull ache. She began walking around the campsite, once again modestly dressed in her blue flightsuit.

Kade watched her come toward him as he shaved by the pool. "I think I'm ready to start out again, Kade," she said. "And I really wish you'd stop playing so near the water."

"Gee, Mom, I know how to swim," he replied dryly. His gaze swept over her. She looked good. Her color was back. She almost sparkled in the brisk morning light, the sun shining off her newly cropped hair.

Following his gaze, Mariss touched her bare neck, and the ends of her shorn locks. "Does it look too terrible?"

"You look like you just dropped a heavy weight off your shoulders."

Biting her lip, she smiled shyly. "I feel that way. Roldo always wanted it long, so I thought I did, too."

"Well, if Adrian wants it long, it'll grow," Kade offered. It was hard to think about, but he had to face facts.

Some of the glow went out of Mariss' face.

Her hair had turned into a rat's nest by the time she managed to rise from the bed the day before. Kade had helped her wash it—bringing the water to her this time—and tried to comb it out. "Just cut it off," Mariss had cried out when the comb snagged for the hundredth time.

"Are you sure?"

"I want it off. I'm sick of taking care of it," Mariss said. "I don't have any way to do it out here."

"We won't be out here forever."

She had flung back the tangled damp mass and looked straight at him. "Do you want me to keep it long?"

Kade wasn't in a position to demand she wear it one way or another. But he had thought back to when he had met her. She had worn her hair pulled back, in a tight braid wound high on her head. It had looked like the expression of a woman afraid to let go. "I'll get the knife."

It was done in a matter of seconds, the full one-meter length on the ground.

Now her hair fluffed about her face, highlighting her large eyes, softening her exotic features. His heart swelled with tenderness as he gazed at her. She was more beautiful than she had ever been.

His eyes dropped to her leg. She was still favoring the injured leg. "Let's give you another day at least, Mariss," he said. "It'd be foolish to push our luck. I know you're anxious to get to the Colony, but—"

"No, that's fine. I can wait, if you think it's best." He stared at her, waiting for her to elaborate. "I mean, we'll get there eventually."

Kade sighed. He replaced his razor in his hygiene case. She was a hard woman to figure out sometimes. Just when he was certain she was dedicated to Adrian Young, she would say something like this, or look at him a certain way, and he could think of nothing but making love to her.

***

Mariss watched Kade press the tent collapse button. The tent folded itself into a roll no larger than half a meter. He lashed it to the bottom of his pack.

Mariss was itching to get started again. Her leg only hurt a little, and Kade had finally accepted her word that she was ready.

She glanced about, thinking how close she had come to dying right here. She would have, if it hadn't been for Kade. Her eyes moved to him. He was standing perfectly still, his head cocked to the sky as if waiting for something to happen.

It was an odd, strained posture. “Kade?”

He didn’t answer her and seemed oblivious to her presence.

A moment later he ran toward her, dragging his pack. “Grab your pack and follow me.” He pounded past her. Mariss picked up her pack, slipped it on, and jogged after him.

He disappeared around a rocky outcropping. Before Mariss reached it, he reappeared, sans the backpack. He grabbed her arm and yanked her, forcing her to move uncomfortably fast. He pulled her into a cave entrance.

“What’s—” she started to say. Kade slapped his hand on her mouth to shut her up.

He whispered in her ear. “Police fly-by. Be calm, be quiet, and maybe they won’t notice anything.”

She nodded and he released her. “They can’t see us, can they?” she whispered.

“No, but if they see evidence we’ve been camping here, they may land and look around in person.”

“Then—”

“Then it’s all over, honey. I only have a third-level phase-gun. No match for their cannons.”

Mariss recalled the guns they had used, the gun she had used to shoot the cop and save Kade’s life. It was five times as large as Kade’s phase-gun. “They want us dead.”

“Can’t think of another reason for the fly-by. Listen.” Together, they sat on the floor of the cave and listened to the ships passing overhead, back and forth in a search pattern. Mariss huddled next to Kade, and he slipped his arm around her. She pressed her cheek against his, but kept her gaze riveted to the cave ceiling as the ships passed above.

All around them, it was dark. As her eyes adjusted, she could see the highlights of Kade’s face growing sharper. Beyond, the cave stretched to unimaginable depths.

It seemed to take hours, but finally, the sound of the ships began to fade. They were moving on. Mariss relaxed only after she felt the tension leave Kade’s body. He sighed and wrapped his other arm about her, cradling her head, his fingers entwined in her hair.

A moment later, his mouth slipped over hers, gentle yet

insistent. Mariss kissed him back, his attentions washing away her fear, and Kade intensified the kiss. All her defenses began to collapse as she allowed him full access to her mouth. She couldn't help herself. This was what she had wanted, ever since he had kissed her at the settlement, and even before. Kade's arms around her. Kade holding her. Kade's lips wreaking havoc with her senses.

His teeth tugged at her lower lip, sensuous and playful. He outlined her lips with his tongue, then covered her mouth completely with his. Mariss melted in his arms. She was losing her battle to dedicate herself to Adrian Young.

Kade brought his lips lower, traced the contours of her neck. Mariss could hardly breathe. His touch was like fire on her skin. His teeth teased her earlobe, and a shock of sensation poured through Mariss. "This isn't happening," she said breathlessly.

"My body thinks it is," he countered, equally breathless.

"I'm engaged to be married."

He pulled back, cupped her face in his hand, traced her swollen lips with his thumb. He smiled crookedly. "Mariss, I'm not looking for a lifetime commitment, here."

His words stung, despite her better sense. "You're not?"

"How could I be? I don't know what I'm going to be doing three months from now, much less for the rest of my life. Hell, I don't even have a job, Mariss. Or a home. I have nothing to offer."

That didn't matter to Mariss. She had a career, after all. She pictured herself back on Earth, coming home to Kade after a hard day's work, how he would pull her into his arms, kiss her, make love to her anytime she wanted. She rather liked the image of Kade as her "kept man." But she knew if such a thing came to pass, he would grow as intimidated by her as Roldo had. Or would he? Kade seemed pretty certain of who he was. No. He would never be intimidated by her. *Bored*, perhaps...

Kade continued, his words soft, seductive. "I learned long ago not to live for the future. It's the moment you're living now that counts. Nothing else."

She swallowed hard. "What about Adrian?"

He glanced past her, toward the sunlit entrance and smiled indulgently. "Do you see him here? I don't."

Mariss' voice trembled. "Kade, I don't engage in casual sex. "

His eyes met hers, held. "What we have isn't casual."

"Kade, I can't—" Movement caught her eye, over Kade's shoulder, coming from the deepest, darkest part of the cave. It moved quickly, slithering toward them. A pungent, sulfuric smell burned her nose.

Mariss screamed and jumped to her feet. A slimy yellow tentacle slapped about the chamber, moving toward them. It was as thick as her waist, tapering off to a pointed end. Its root was somewhere deep beyond, in the darkness. Mariss knew what it was—she was painfully familiar with the creature.

Before she had a chance to run, the tentacle shot toward them, lightning fast. Kade jumped over it, then ducked when it swung back around. He was quick, but not quick enough to avoid a second tentacle which had joined the first. The second tentacle slapped him to the ground and hovered over him. A sharp stinger protruded from its end, dripping with poison. It moved toward Kade, ready to strike.

Mariss jumped under the tentacle and yanked Kade's phase-gun from his holster. She fired it upward toward the wildly moving tentacle, missing widely. The blast ricocheted off the cave walls, deafening her. Smoke filled the cavern. She tried again, not certain where she was shooting. A bolt hit one of the tentacles. It writhed as smoke poured off it. A few seconds later, the creature withdrew.

Kade was pulling himself to his knees. Mariss dragged him to his feet, then ran with him out of the cave.

Out in the sunlight, Mariss caught her breath. "It was the same creature, just as I thought," she panted.

"Probably," Kade said, his hands on his knees. He righted himself and looked at Mariss.

Mariss glanced away, unable to face him after their intimate encounter in the cave. The brilliant sunlight had shocked her back to her senses. She wasn't going to make love with Kade. Of course she wasn't. She'd been afraid and feeling vulnerable. And Kade had been scared, too. It meant nothing else.

Kade was gazing at her, his muscular arms crossed and his expression speculative. He had returned for their packs, but wasn't donning his. Mariss had the feeling he was reading her thought processes. All business, she turned her back to him and slipped on her own pack. "Let's push on. We have a long day of hiking ahead of us."

"Somehow, I knew that's what you'd say," he said.

***

Mariss kept her distance from Kade for the next few days. She read and re-read her profile of Adrian Young. She cited facts about him over and over in her mind as she walked behind Kade. She reflected on why the computer had matched them up, thought about the scientific studies which showed that people with such compatible scores as theirs would make perfect life mates.

But her unruly heart continued to plague her with images of Kade's body, of his face. The memories played havoc with her senses. She plodded along, placing one tired foot in front of the other. But her thoughts were far away...Kade washing her hair in the pool. Kade waking up beside her. Kade caring for her, kissing her, saving her life.

"Would you look at that."

Mariss pulled herself from her reverie. She joined him at the top of a rise. They were leaving the mountains and forest behind. Below stretched grasslands and shrubs.

But Kade's eyes were fastened on a notch in the hill they were passing, ten meters away. Floating in the air, weightless and beautiful, were hundreds of disks no bigger than her hand. They reminded Mariss of jellyfish from Earth's seas. But these were airborne. They clustered together, hovering in a group about two meters off the ground. The sunlight reflected off them as they swirled gently in the breeze.

"Are they alive?" Kade asked.

"I'm sure they are," Mariss said. "But I'm not sure if they're plants or animals, or something else." She shrugged off her pack and knelt on the ground, then she opened her pack and slipped out her cyber-unit. As she powered it up, Kade approached the disks. One disk broke away from the others and floated toward him.

"Kade, don't go any closer. Wait until I see what these things are." Mariss tapped at her keys, bringing up the databank from the settlement. She began scanning the entries on the various life forms.

She glanced up. Kade hadn't listened to her. The disk had settled on his shoulder. He didn't seem to mind, just gazed at it in fascination. Concern grew in Mariss as she watched Kade move toward the main mass of disks, away from her. They began to land on his body with delicate grace. He stretched out his arms, allowing them access.

"Kade, stop that!" Mariss leapt to her feet. An image of a disk had appeared on her screen along with the words:

LEVEL FIVE DANGER: FATAL

Kade didn't seem to hear her, nor did he seem to be in pain. Then his knees crumpled, and he collapsed on his back.

FOURTEEN

Euphoria flowed through Kade—endless, a river of joy, love and goodness. The moment the first disk had touched his shoulder, Kade had felt the euphoria flowing outward from the disk, into him, enfolding him.

Vaguely, he heard Mariss calling his name. Then, he no longer knew his name. Nothing mattered but this sensation of exquisite pleasure. Everything before had been turmoil. Now he had a new awareness.

As other disks landed on him, the sensation increased to unbearable heights. Somewhere beyond the light of pure sensation, someone cried out to him to get away, that he was in danger. But he knew it wasn't so. He would never be in danger or in pain again.

He was on his back, his body covered in the warm comfort of the disks. He gazed upward. The cerulean sky shone with more vibrance than ever before. A young woman appeared above him, her terrified face screaming down at him.

Then she was beside him, trying to knock the disks off him. One by one, the disks lifted from Kade and floated toward her, landing on her.

Unconcerned, Kade watched as she was transformed by the disks, a beatific expression covering her angelic features. As more disks landed on her, she crumpled to the ground beside him.

A thought slipped into Kade's consciousness. One idle thought. *She's going to die, just like I am.*

The thought found its way past his euphoria. It disturbed his calm. Kade began to struggle with the drug-like spell. He forced himself through it as if it were mud. He strove to recall anything painful, anything which might distract him from the euphoria caused by the disks.

That woman beside him was going to die.

He didn't know who she was, or why he cared. But it was enough. With his last bit of strength, he lifted his hand and knocked one of the disks aside. It hovered uncertainly above him, and tentatively started floating back to land on him.

Kade did not like to be thwarted in anything. He sat up and swatted at more of the disks, sending them spinning away from his body.

He couldn't remember where he was, or why...had even begun to forget *who* he was. He reacted like an animal, clinging to self-preservation by sheer force of will.

He knocked the last disk away, and his head began to clear. He knelt by Mariss and knocked the things off her, at the same time fending them off as they tried to resettle on him. He grasped her under her arms and dragged her away from the area.

The disks hesitated, as if uncertain what to do. They didn't seem to be able to follow them from the immediate area. In a few minutes, the disks had coalesced back into one colony.

Kade pulled the awakening Mariss to her feet. Together, they stumbled a safe distance away and collapsed on the grass. Kade leaned back against a boulder, breathing heavily. Mariss panted, too. He fought to recapture his equilibrium. "Mariss. Are you all right?"

She nodded, at first unable to speak. "I saw on my cyber-unit that they were deadly, just as you were being attacked. So I went after you. How did we get away? They were all over you."

Kade shrugged. "I guess euphoria doesn't agree with me."

***

"Those things are the reason the people from the settlement never made it to the Colony," Mariss pronounced. She sat beside Kade, her cyber-unit beside her. She had read the complete entry on the disks, and was still amazed they had gotten away.

Kade shot her a skeptical look. "The settlers knew about

the danger? It was in their databank?"

"Oh, yeah." Mariss was still shivering from their close brush with blissful death. Kade removed his jacket and settled it over her shoulders. She slipped her arms into the sleeves and nestled in it. The jacket was stiff and tailored on the outside, yet soft inside. It carried Kade's scent. She inhaled deeply and began to relax.

Kade raked his hand through his hair. "By krod, those things—that feeling—it was almost as good as sex."

"It was better than sex," Mariss said, her words firm.

Kade looked at her askance. "Your husbands weren't worth ravving, I take it."

Mariss stood up suddenly, a little off-balance from her brush with pleasant death. She steadied herself and stared down at Kade. "My husbands were fine. At least at first. But I just don't think it's that important."

Kade's lips wore a teasing smile. "It's important if you care about who you're with."

"Hah, and how long does that last? Until the morning after?"

"Sometimes longer."

Mariss paced in front of him. "Sex is a tool men use. Like that commander back at the settlement. Oh, don't get me wrong. Women use it, too. Like Lorena."

"You're talking from your past, Mariss. You let your experiences decide how you feel."

She faced him. "Of course I do! I'm not stupid. I can learn from experience. Doesn't everyone? No, Kade, it would be more foolish to repeat my mistakes."

His voice wasn't loud, but it rang with intensity. "Because of Roldo, you'll never trust another man, is that it?"

"Is that so hard to understand? He told me he loved me, Kade. That's why I married him."

"The sex wasn't good even then, was it."

Mariss looked away. "It was good with Peck in the beginning. We were both young and randy. It was pleasant, and fun. But he grew bored with it. He wanted to experiment all the time. I felt like we were involved in a science project. I didn't like what it had come to mean to us."

"What about Roldo?"

She shrugged. "He said I had enchanted him, and he had to have me. And he did want me, for awhile. Until he grew bored and turned to Ami. She was always less inhibited than me." Her voice dropped, but she tried to maintain a casual tone. "Some women are good at it. Apparently, I'm not. But I'm intelligent. Some women aren't. So I guess it all evens out in the end."

"Come here," Kade commanded. He extended his hand to her. Tentatively, Mariss allowed him to grasp her hand. He urged her closer, then pulled her onto his lap. He started running his hands over her slender frame, under the jacket. "You're crazy to think you aren't desirable, and crazy to think you aren't good at sex."

Unlike Lorena, Mariss wore her flightsuit closed to the neck. Kade's fingers slid along the fastening, urging it open. Before Mariss could put up much of a fight, he had slipped a hand inside and cupped one of her breasts. "You fill my palm."

"Kade, you're embarrassing me," she said. She shoved ineffectually at his shoulders. But she didn't put up a proper effort, not with him caressing her like this. Her body felt liquid, insubstantial, wonderful.

"Embarrassed?" he murmured. "Why?"

"They're so small."

"They feel just right to me." His fingers were sliding over her nipple in a sensuous, undeniable rhythm. It tightened under his touch.

Breathless, Mariss tried to speak calmly. "Peck suggested I have them enlarged."

Kade snorted. "Mariss, you're perfect as you are. Compact and sleek, like a panther." Kade's palm ran down her side and up again, his thumb teasing her aching peak as he nuzzled her neck.

Mariss knew she was about to give in to him, open herself to the incredible sensations he was causing in her. It reminded her of the euphoria disks, but it was so much better, because Kade was the cause.

In a panic, she thought of Adrian—patient, true Adrian—who even now was awaiting the arrival of his future wife. Her spine stiffened. "At least I know *one* man finds my type appealing. Adrian."

It worked. Kade slipped his hands from her. His voice was leaden. "Adrian."

She nodded, sliding off his lap to sit beside him. "Adrian specified his preference for type in his ideal mate, so he must like skinny, dark women with flat chests." As she spoke she refastened her flightsuit, avoiding Kade's gaze.

Kade's muscles tensed. "That means you did, too." His voice had an odd, distant quality.

"Did what?"

"Specified what you find physically appealing in a man."

She nodded, more concerned with stilling her shaky nerves than discussing the Computer Mating Service of Iridion. The application process seemed so long ago.

Kade wouldn't let it go. "This thing was pretty detailed, I suppose."

"Well, yes. There were two hundred questions on appearance alone. And other, more important elements to consider, had even more questions. Then there were psychological profiles, questionnaires for my friends to fill out—"

Kade was still on appearance. "Two hundred. Covering... what? Skin coloring, hair coloring—"

Mariss nodded, unsure where the conversation was leading, but knowing in her heart it wasn't good to discuss it with him.

But Kade pursued it, relentless. "Facial features?"

"Kade, it doesn't matter. I don't remember exactly. Why are you so interested?" She cocked her head at him, her words light, flip. "Are you planning to apply for a mate?"

"You must be joking. I *know* how to choose women. And I don't select them off a menu."

"Neither did I. I merely ranked preferences—"

"And they gave you Adrian Young. How close did they come? Were they in the neighborhood?"

She slowly nodded, her stomach tensing.

A stark, angry expression crossed Kade's face, intensifying his sharp features. "Like hell. They were right on target, weren't they? You envisioned a blond, Adonis-type with perfectly sculpted features, and that's what you got. That's why that program's so damned expensive. Every customer is satisfied. Tall, blond, aristocratic Adrian Young really *is* your ideal mate."

Understanding hit Mariss so hard it physically hurt. She had been blind not to see sooner what was eating at Kade. "You're good-looking, too, Kade. Different from Adrian, but certainly handsome."

He wouldn't look at her. "What did your husbands look like?"

"Peck was a slight man, slender, blond hair. Average, really. But he had a wonderful sense of humor, in the early years. Roldo is—more hefty. Scholarly. Distinguished. He has light-brown hair."

Kade's hand fastened around her wrist like a vice. "Then why are you so hot for me? The short guy with the big nose and the dark coloring?"

She yanked her arm free and stood up. "Kade, stop it. You're not short to me. And you don't have a big nose. It's more—aquiline."

Kade followed her up. "Forget my nose. I got used to it a long time ago. I mean it, Mariss. Why? You're so damned certain you know what you want, so why have you been lusting after me from the moment we met?"

Mariss recoiled from his fierce demeanor. "How dare you say that!"

"I dare because it's true. You know it and I know it. Hell, you're afraid of ravving me. You know how good it would be, and you're terrified Adrian will never measure up. And you're right. Well, I hope your Nordic giant satisfies you, Mariss, if anything ever will."

She turned away and snatched up her cyber-unit, jamming it into her pack. She didn't want him to see how deeply his remarks cut. It was true. She *had* pictured her ideal mate as someone who looked just like Adrian. She had never imagined being with a dark, intense man like Kade. But now, her preferences seemed like a childish fantasy. Kade pushed every button in her, from physical to emotional.

Like right now. He knew exactly what to say to infuriate her.

She allowed her fury to bubble to the surface. She spun on him. He was standing right behind her. Their eyes clashed so strongly, Mariss could feel his intensity washing over her in waves. "You can have your jacket back. I don't want anything from you, Kadin Land." She stripped it off and hurled it at him.

The jacket flew through the air and Kade caught it. But something else fluttered to the ground. Mariss gazed at the shiny fabric. She recognized it, but couldn't immediately place it.

Kade stooped to snatch it up. But he wasn't quick enough. She'd seen it first.

Mariss planted her foot on it, then squatted beside him. "Get your hands off," she growled. Kade dropped his hands and rose.

Mariss lifted the crumpled item of clothing from the ground and held it up. It was soiled from being mashed in the dirt, but it was still elusively sensual. Her lingerie—a wedding gift from one of her friends. She had thought it lost on the ship along with the rest of her belongings.

She lowered the garment and stared at Kade, rage filling her. "You—you—" The words clogged in her throat.

Kade took a step back, crossing his arms defensively. "It fell out of your case on the ship. I forgot I had it."

"Like hell you did. I distinctly remember putting it back in my case! You thief!" She shuddered. "What have you been *doing* with it all this time?"

"Hey, now. That isn't fair." Kade advanced on her, his jaw muscles tightening. "You make me sound like a pervert or something."

"It seems nothing is sacred to you. Not even a bride's honeymoon clothing."

He shot her a look of pure scorn. "You don't even *like* sex, remember? So what are you so mad about?"

"You animal!" Mariss raised her hand to strike him.

Blindingly fast, he grasped her wrist and pinned it behind her back. His lips came down on hers, hard, unyielding, demanding. Before Mariss could protest his brutal embrace, it was over. He shoved her away so hard she stumbled and almost fell.

"Take that with you to your wedding night. It's all you'll ever get from me."

Mariss wiped her mouth off with the back of her hand. She gazed at Kade, seeing him with new eyes. He was reacting out of anger. And pain. He was just as vulnerable as she was—perhaps more so. "You're the one who's hot for me! You accuse me of lusting after you, but *you're* the one!"

Kade stood there like a rock. Mariss knew she was right. "All this time you've made me feel guilty for wanting you, but you're the one who's suffering. You're just too stubborn to admit it."

"What's the fragging point?" he growled. "I wasn't invited to this party, Mariss."

Mariss stared at him, her anger dissolving like mist in the rising sun. Kade turned away from her and shouldered his pack. He walked off, leaving her standing there alone.

Mariss watched him go. She looked down at the lingerie balled in her fist. Her fingers relaxed. Kade had carried this flimsy garment in his jacket pocket, right beside his heart, ever since that night on the ship. She admitted she was flattered. All this time...Had he kept it to remind himself of her? Or to keep her from wearing it for Adrian? Either way, Mariss knew what it meant.

Kadin Land was falling in love with her, as wild and surprising as that thought might be. More importantly, what should she do about it?

FIFTEEN

Mariss woke to a whirring sound. The artificial noise was unexpected in the early morning quiet. She pulled herself to her elbows and looked toward the mouth of the tent.

Kadin wasn't in his sleeping cocoon. Worry tugged at her. He'd been silent and pensive the day before, ever since she confronted him about her lingerie—and his feelings.

She slipped into her flightsuit and stepped outside. A shiny red land car hovered above the ground beside their tent. It bore the markings of the interstellar police. No one was inside.

Mariss stepped back toward the tent entrance, her eyes darting about for any sign of the police, or Kade.

"Right here," Kade said, as if reading her mind. He walked toward her from a nearby outcropping, last night's washing in his hands. "Get packed. We're going for a ride."

He ducked into the tent to start packing.

Mariss followed him as far as the tent entrance. "Kade, you can't just walk off without telling me what's going on. Where did this car come from?"

His voice, coming from the tent, was muffled. "The cops."

She stuck her head in the entrance. "You stole it?"

"They sure as hell weren't giving it away." He imploded her cocoon and slipped the softball-sized bundle into his pack. He tossed Mariss her boots, then stepped outside and began dismantling the tent. "Get a move on. We don't have all day."

Mariss couldn't begin to fathom what Kade had been thinking. "Kade, you have to tell me what you've done."

He spoke casually. "I saw them yesterday, from a distance, patrolling the countryside."

Mariss had seen nothing. But she recalled Kade stopping

on a knoll and staring with his field glasses for quite some time toward the wide plain. She had thought he might be looking at the large, slow dinosaur-like creatures which grazed there. "You never said anything."

"We weren't in danger. They were heading the other way." He carried the folded tent to the car and tossed it in the back.

"Then how did—"

"We caught up to them last night. After you went to sleep, I heard their car and their voices as they drove by. So I hiked over to their camping spot on the other side of that hill." He gestured. "There were only two of them. Don't worry, they won't follow us."

She ran her hands along the side of the sleek car. "How can you know that? You didn't kill them, did you?"

Kade shot her a sharp look.

Mariss instantly regretted her remark. "I'm sorry, but—"

"I shot them, all right. With tranquilizer. They'll sleep well until mid-day, maybe even evening." Kade rose and tossed his pack in the back seat. "Now, if we push hard, we'll probably get to the Colony some time in the middle of the night, well ahead of them. If the place is as wonderful as you say, they'll take us in and protect us. It's privately owned, right?"

"Yes, but—Kade, you've taken an incredible risk. These are the interstellar cops! You yourself said they want us dead. They'll come after you, after *us.* You should have let well enough alone!"

"You'll be safe in the Colony."

"Kade—"

He faced her, his dark eyes cold and impersonal. "I want this trip over as badly as you, Sakari. Now, get in."

He retracted the passenger-side door, and Mariss slipped into the cool interior.

***

Mariss sat beside Kade in the cop's hovercar, speeding at more than 200 kilometers per hour due east, toward the Colony. They clipped along at such a fast pace, Mariss began to wonder if they wouldn't arrive by early evening. It was amazing the difference having transportation made.

She didn't like it.

She didn't like it at all. Kade had risked his life—*was* risking his life—stealing this car. When the cops found out, they could be pursued by airships. But Kade seemed perfectly satisfied to write his own rules in life, like when he had set the explosions back at the settlement. He knew she wanted to get to the Colony, so he had found a way to make it happen, regardless of the consequences.

Mariss realized that a selfish man who only wanted to rav her would have sought to prolong their trip, not bring it to a speedy end. But obviously Kade had another agenda.

She watched the chronometer flip to 1300 hours. It was already afternoon. The upholstered seat was sinfully comfortable, enfolding her body and contouring to it.

In a few short hours, she would be at the Colony, and her time alone with Kade would come to an end. He sat beside her, a foot away, but his eyes were pinned to the plain they crossed, and the horizon rushing toward them.

For the most part, Kade followed the winding river that they had hiked beside their entire trip. The elevation was falling, and they were heading for the sea. When a hill or escarpment rose up before them, Kade shot the car up to a high altitude. Otherwise, they skimmed the surface at a dizzying pace.

Mariss watched him handle the car like an expert, his lean, strong fingers sure at the controls. He was extremely gifted, she knew. The power of his hands—she recalled their touch on her body like the bearers of pure magic.

She bit her lip to fight back the betraying emotions. At the Colony, he would catch a transport, and be out of her life forever. She would be married—to a man she didn't even know—promising to live with him at the Colony for the rest of her life. She knew in her heart Kade would never want to return to Elysia.

She would never see him again.

As the kilometers rolled past, an idea formed in her mind. At first it seemed impossible—something a woman of restraint could scarcely imagine. But as the seconds passed, her conviction grew, and with it, a new sense of freedom. She couldn't allow Kadin Land to simply walk out of her life. Not if he wanted the same thing she did.

"Kade."

"Hmm?" He kept his eyes forward, toward the onrushing plain.

"Can I ask you a question?"

"What?"

"You said you like to live for the moment, for today."

"What of it?"

"Well, if you had the chance to get something you badly wanted—but you knew you could only have it once and you would have to give it up after enjoying it for a day—would you still want it?"

Kade shook his head and eyed her out of the corner of his eye. "Getting philosophical on me, Sakari?"

He had started calling her by her last name. Mariss knew it was his way of putting distance between them. "Just answer me."

"You mean like this police car, don't you?" He caressed the control panel. "Not bad, is it? I could handle owning one of these babies."

"Well, sort of like the police car, yes."

"Then you know the answer. There's no reason not to take what you can, when you can. Especially if you know you'll never have a chance at it again."

Her heart hitched. The die was cast. She gazed at Kade's profile, carefully imprinted it on her memory. She would never forget this day as long as she lived. "Yes, Kadin Land, I know the answer."

***

To Kade's surprise, Mariss insisted they not try to reach the Colony that night. Toward evening, she told him to pull up in a tropical oasis nestled between high cliff faces. A small stream fed the main river.

Kade stopped the car and tapped out an impatient tattoo on the control deck. "Don't you want this trip over with?"

"Tomorrow is soon enough." Mariss retracted the door

and stepped out. She gave him a warm smile. "You pitch the tent. I'm going to...take a bath."

Not an unreasonable idea, Kade thought. By following the plain from the mountains, they had entered a more tropical region of the continent. The air was balmy, and exotic scents spiced the air. He recognized the flora from Mariss' holo of the Colony. There were several kinds of flowers growing wild, as well as ferny plants and ones with huge leaves.

He expected to see Mariss pull out her bio-kit and start sampling the flora as he set up camp, which she usually did. But she seemed preoccupied, pacing near the stream.

Because of Adrian, he thought ruefully as he unpacked the car and set up the tent. She was about to meet him, and she was nervous. It was to be expected. That was why she wanted to stop tonight instead of pushing on. She probably wanted to clean up and look presentable.

Kade studied her. She had tanned considerably since their trip began, and her shorter hair gave her a more carefree appearance. The serious scientist was hard to detect. To him, Mariss was a sight better than presentable. If Adrian Young couldn't see it, he was a fool. Unfortunately, the man wouldn't be able to miss it.

The idea frustrated and angered Kade, but he rebelled at such strong emotions. He had already given up all hope of meaning anything to Mariss Sakari. It hadn't happened after all they had been through together. Now, he knew it never would. He had spent all day trying to accept that fact.

Kade moved the car into a thicket of shrubs, so it would be invisible from the air. The clearing itself was surrounded by cliffs on three sides. It was sheltered, and most likely safe.

Mariss disappeared downstream, probably to take a private bath. The water here was much warmer than the streams in the mountains, Kade thought, chewing a piece of jerky. He may have to bathe himself, later.

"Kade."

"Yeah?" He didn't look at her. He was sitting in the evening shade of tall trees trying not to think about her. The last thing he needed was for her to strike up one of those "let's be friends" conversations.

"Kade." More insistent this time. She probably needed help with something, and he, designated servant of Mariss Sakari, was going to have to help her.

"What?"

A long pause. Finally, Kade glanced over his shoulder.

His eyes absorbed what he was seeing long before his brain did. His blood surged and his pulse began to beat erratically.

"Mariss." He whispered her name on the evening breeze. She was standing not three meters away, dressed in nothing but that skimpy piece of lingerie which had caused him so much trouble.

It was causing him trouble of a different sort now.

Shyly, Mariss took a step closer. Kade found himself on his feet, but couldn't remember standing up. He could see right through the fabric. As he knew it would, it revealed everything about her, yet tantalized and teased him with the promise of greater pleasure.

Her body was slender, yet with an underlying layer of muscle, no doubt strengthened by the rigors of their overland trek. Her sculpted legs were long for her height. Her hips curved gently to the tiniest of waists. And her breasts—her dusky nipples were already erect, visibly pronounced through the thin fabric. He swallowed hard. His eyes slipped lower, to the apex of her thighs.

As if knowing where he was looking, Mariss ran her hands up her thighs slowly, inviting him to gaze at her feminine essence nestled in its bed of black curls.

Kade tore his gaze from her body and met her eyes. She was smiling at him, her expression a mixture of shyness and pleasure. Kade licked his lips. She was giving herself to him, after all this time. After agonizing, sleepless nights dreaming of ravving her, of loving her, of making her his own. She took another step toward him. "Stop. Don't come any closer," he rasped out.

She hesitated, a flash of uncertainty crossing her face. *She thinks I'm going to reject her,* he thought. The idea was almost laughable. He could barely keep from leaping on her as it was. But he wanted to do this right, he wanted to go slowly, to show her everything that existed between them, yet remained unspoken.

"Turn around."

Another slight hesitation, then compliance. Kade ached with desire for her. He was fully aroused just looking at her. Her sweetly curved bottom was completely exposed in the costume, the thinnest thong sliding up behind to fasten at the small of her back.

And it was all for him.

***

Mariss waited, hardly daring to breathe. She felt sinfully erotic, standing there essentially naked, advertising herself for his pleasure. She knew he was gazing at her—all of her, and taking his time at it.

The next thing she knew, Kade had crossed the distance between them, pressed his rock-hard physique against her back. She could feel his heat through the thin cloth.

His palms slipped to her behind, cupping her bottom, sliding across her skin with fire and promise. He swept his hands along her hips, over her flat stomach and down along her thighs, pressing her hard against himself. She could feel his erection in the small of her back.

His breath was hot in her ear. "Feel how much I want you, Mariss."

"Yes," she said, already weak. This was what she wanted. She could think of nothing but this. Nothing else. Tonight, she would be his, and past and future would no longer exist. They would enter a vortex of their own making, blocking out everything that had gone before, and all that was to come. Only this moment existed.

Kade's palms, rough yet sensuous, slid upward along her sides, slowly, as if determined to imprint the feel of her on his memory. Mariss had never felt anything so delicious as his hands moving against her body, the slippery fabric sliding with his caresses. She ached for him to slide his hands higher, touch her breasts. But he held off satisfying her craving, teasing her by stroking her shoulders and ribcage, making it all the more sweet when he finally cupped her breasts.

Kade was right, Mariss thought in a daze. Her breasts fit perfectly into his palms. He burnished her erect nipples with gentle rotations, sending shocks of pleasure through her.

She bit her lip and arched her head back onto his shoulder. She lifted her arms and cradled his neck, giving him full access to explore her entire body with his seeking hands. He took full advantage of the invitation.

His sleeves were rough against her skin as he enfolded her. She had a wild, burning need to feel his bare skin under her own hands. Mariss turned in his arms and tugged his jacket off. It fell to the ground. She ran her hands up his chest, slipped her hands under his shirt and helped him remove it.

Now his magnificent chest was hers for the pleasure. She ran her lips over his skin, kissed his small male nipples, flicked her tongue down his chest.

She felt his muscles tense and release under her seeking hands. He was warm and hard and wonderfully strong.

Kade urged her upward, into his embrace. But Mariss slipped away. "No. Strip off your pants, Kade. I want to see you."

This time she enjoyed watching him hesitate—just a second, before he complied. A moment later, he was naked before her.

"Turn around." Kade gave her a look that seemed to question whether she was serious. "Just do it."

He did. Mariss approached him again, cupping his small, tight buttocks in her hands, squeezing and massaging. She had never felt a man with a body like this, so full of power. It filled her with awe. To think this man—*this* man—was going to rav her, here, tonight.

She slipped to her knees, and guided Kade so he faced her. She pulled him into her mouth. He gasped, shivering with pleasure, his fingers knotting in her hair. "Blessed Maker," he cried. "Oh, Mariss."

Mariss had done the same for Peck—he had demanded it. And she had done it for Roldo—he had expected it. But Kade's simple, surprised reaction was the most gratifying thing she had ever felt with a man. The act of pleasuring him in this way was delight itself.

"Mariss," Kade said, his voice heavy with strain. "Slow down. I want to do this right."

She slipped her mouth off him and raised her eyes to his. "This is right."

She took him again, teased him with her teeth and tongue. He groaned, thrusting his hips forward. She sensed he was about to burst. She pulled back and stood. He reached for her, but she stepped away again. She gave him a teasing smile. Dusk had settled among the trees by the stream. She spun and darted away, toward the stream, her laughter crystalline in the evening air.

Kade was right on her heels. Mariss had barely splashed into the stream before he caught up with her. He yanked her around and slammed his mouth onto hers. Her laughter was extinguished in the flood of sensation he unleashed as they embraced in the stream.

He broke the kiss. "You've had me dancing after you so long, woman, I won't let you get away again."

She moaned as he kissed her, his mouth devouring hers. She had also thought to take this slowly, but all the passion, the denial of the past weeks, had built into an inferno. Mariss pulled him hard against her, clawing at his back. She was wild for him, could never get close enough. She found herself climbing up, encircling his waist with her leg. She knew she would die if she didn't have him inside her, *now.*

Kade growled, a primal, animalistic sound that set Mariss afire. Vaguely, she heard cloth tearing. Her lingerie spun up into the evening air and drifted onto the surface of the stream, then swirled away.

Kade scooped up her bottom and impaled her. Mariss gasped as he thrust into her as deeply as he could. His presence was hot and hard inside her, stroking her in places she had long forgotten could feel—and she had never felt anything so intensely.

"Oh, Mariss, I've wanted this so long," Kade cried. Mariss

tightened her legs around him, locking her ankles, cradling his head against her breast. Keeping himself buried inside her, he carried her to the bank and pressed her against a mossy slope. Half in, half-out of the water, he rode her hard and furiously. He was wild and uncontrollable, pounding into her, taking her with him to the brink of oblivion.

Mariss arched her hips, dug her fingers into his back, did whatever she could to bring him even closer. "Kade," she cried. "I must—I can't—"

An explosion of sensation obliterated her senses, stronger than anything she had ever felt. Mariss sank her teeth into Kade's shoulder. Dimly, she heard him cry, "Scream it out, Mariss, don't hold back."

When the next wave of pleasure hit her, Mariss cried out so loudly, a flock of dragon-lizards were startled from their tree nests and batted away into the night.

She heard the echo of her cry in Kade's voice, felt his heated juices inside her as he joined her in ecstasy, spiraled with her into the vast reaches of the cosmos where nothing mattered but this.

***

Mariss had not even begun to recover from his loving when Kade picked her up and carried her to the grass above the stream.

The light of the full twin moons bathed well-defined muscles on a body she was finally free to explore. Her hands drifted along his chest and arms as she lay in Kade's embrace. She gazed up into his rugged face, now softened with tenderness.

She recalled her experiences with Peck and Roldo. With Peck, it was never good enough. He had made lovemaking a chore. Roldo placed her on a pedestal before marriage, and afterward had expected perfection from her. She had tried to meet his high standards, but failed. Only now, in this brief interlude with Kade, did she feel completely free to express her desires as *she* wished. It was a revelation. "You were right," she said softly. "I *am* good at sex."

Kade chuckled, his teeth glinting in the starlight. "Maybe

you'll listen to me next time we disagree."

"Kade," she said softly, uncomfortable that he should suggest a future time. But no, not now, it wasn't right. She would not let reality intrude. She was still in the vortex, she and Kade. She stroked his cheek. "I didn't mean for it to be so quick."

"Me neither. But we can spend all night at it until we get it right." He winked at her. Despite her devastating orgasm of a few moments before, Mariss felt her body coming alive again—all because of his teasing. That's when she realized the truth. She had completely lost her heart to this man, on the eve of meeting her new husband.

No, her logical mind insisted. *Don't think of it. Think of tonight, and tonight alone.* "Did I surprise you?"

Kade gave her a look of disbelief. "You've got to be joking. I must have looked like an idiot staring at you with my mouth hanging open. But I've never had a finer surprise, I can tell you that." He kissed her gently, his lips drifting over hers. "Or a more perfect lover."

Mariss' gaze fell to his shoulder, where the moonlight revealed the deep indentations of her teeth. Tentatively, she touched the wound. "I actually bit you," she said in awe. "I never did such a thing before."

Kade smiled down at her. "Do you realize what this means?"

Mariss hesitated. "What?"

"I'll have to bite you back."

Before she could protest, Kade was nipping her lips, then her neck, drawing a line of little bites downward across her breast. She stopped thinking of protesting as tingles of pleasure danced through her.

Kade's teeth settled on her nipple. He tugged it, rolled it with his tongue. Mariss closed her eyes and lay peacefully, melting into the sensations he caused.

While his mouth teased her nipple, Kade stroked her body, slow, sensuous caresses up her thighs, along her stomach. He slipped his hand over her other breast so it wouldn't feel neglected, his fingers toying with her nipple.

Mariss felt anything but neglected. She basked in his tender, skillful attentions, a sinfully languorous feeling sweeping through her. Every muscle in her body was relaxed. She had never felt so comfortable with a man.

Then, imperceptibly, her feelings changed. *She* changed, opened up to strong inner drives surging to the surface. Mariss allowed herself to obey the urges as desire pulsed through her. Feeling wanton and wild, she spread her thighs indecently wide. At the blatant invitation, Kade caressed the insides of her thighs, coming near but not touching her womanhood.

Mariss grew even more bold. She rocked her pelvis, inviting his touch at the center of her pleasure.

Kade's fingers drifted across her mound, swept lower, teasing her mercilessly. His forefingers slipped along her folds, driving her wild. Kade played her like an instrument, his fingers moving in gentle rhythm, then tugging at her hard, demanding.

Mariss arched toward him, seeking more. Soft throbs of pleasure crashed into uncontrollable, driving desire, which receded in decreasing waves, only to return with greater force. Mariss moaned and wrapped her arms around his, tugging him toward her, entrapping his hips with her thighs. She was more than ready.

"No. Not yet," he commanded, slipping from between her aching thighs. His mouth grazed her stomach and dropped lower, taking the place of his fingers at the apex of her thighs. Tenderly, then with more demanding force, his lips and tongue began to wreak havoc on her senses.

Mariss almost sobbed, she craved him so badly. He was working her desire to a fever pitch. "Rav me, Kade. I can't stand it any longer." She knew she was begging him. She had never begged a man before. The only rational part of her mind left decided she felt so uninhibited only because she would never see Kade again.

Kade trailed worshipful kisses along her welcoming thighs. "Not yet. Not until I'm good and ready." He slipped his fingers inside her. Mariss sobbed and bucked beneath him as he stroked her. He planted his free hand by her head and locked eyes with her. His voice revealed his strain. "I love to see you like this—wild, uncontrollable. This is who you are."

"Kade, please," Mariss cried. "I need you in me. Take me, now."

Kade nodded assent. "Now." He slipped between her thighs and entered her with deliberate slowness, causing a long, torturous pleasure so exquisite Mariss could hardly stand it. She grasped his face in her hands. "I want to look in your eyes, Kade. Watch you." She wanted to imprint his face on her memory.

"Yes," he whispered, his voice harsh. Mariss knew then he was as moved as she. "You're so beautiful," he groaned.

Never taking his eyes off hers, Kade entwined their fingers, lifting their hands above their heads. He locked them there on the soft grass while he moved in and out of her, perfectly in control this time, knowing exactly what he was doing to her.

This time when she crested the peak, Mariss felt tears on her cheeks.

SIXTEEN

Mariss was stretched out fully on Kade, resting peacefully, her body touching his from her toes to her head. Their contact was complete.

When the deep night had brought cooler temperatures, he had carried her to the tent, thinking they would sleep. They hadn't.

He ran his hands up her back in languorous strokes. She had just ridden astride him, commanding his body to obey until passion obliterated everything but the feel of her sweet possession. Both of them were thoroughly sated now. Kade wondered if he would ever be able to move again. "Sweet, beautiful woman," he said softly. "You are the most surprising thing ever to happen to me."

Mariss tensed slightly under his hands, so slightly he wasn't even sure he'd felt it. But she laughed softly, lifting her face to his, her violet eyes lambent. "You must have had dozens of lovers, Kade. Don't fool me."

"I've had a few," he said. "Mostly port-side stuff. One-night ravs."

"Like this?" She laid her head back on his chest.

"Mariss, a one-night rav doesn't begin to describe what we've shared tonight, and you know it. This is like nothing else."

"I know." Her voice was so soft, Kade barely heard it. He was suddenly filled with a desire to tell her everything he felt for her. But he restrained himself. He had nothing to offer a woman like Mariss Sakari, sister of a renowned diplomat, accomplished scientist, beautiful woman. She deserved so much, but he hadn't a clue how he could provide it for her.

Not yet.

"Mariss. Look at me," he gently commanded.

Almost reluctantly, she obeyed.

"Mariss, sweetheart. You aren't a one-night anything to me. I want you to know—"

She laid her fingers on his lips. "Kade, you don't have to say it. It doesn't change anything."

Kade sighed in relief. She understood his quandary, and accepted it. He outlined her lips with his thumb. He would never grow tired of gazing at her, of holding her. An unexpectedly strong swell of romanticism filled him. "Sweet Mariss, I want to give you the stars."

"This was free, Kade," she said, all innocence. "You aren't required to pay for it—like you did those port-side women."

Kade playfully slapped her bottom, and she squealed. "I never *have* to pay for it, or have you forgotten the likes of Lorena? They haunt spaceports, too. I have to beat 'em off."

"Must be the uniform," she said dryly, her fingers swirling in his chest hair. Kade swatted her rump again. One thing led to another, and he discovered he *could* move after all.

Only later, after Mariss was sleeping peacefully beside him, did Kade realize she had effectively channeled their conversation away from intimate declarations to playful humor. He reveled in her moods, whatever she might choose to surprise him with. He would never grow tired of her.

***

Kade stirred awake. He stretched, feeling a delicious satisfaction in every part of his body.

Last night... Images played through his mind, images of Mariss. He smiled to himself, recalling how she had seduced him, how they had spent all night making love until, exhausted, they had fallen asleep in each other's arms.

She had brought to life his every fantasy. But she was exquisitely real. He had never felt so close to another human being. For the first time in his adult life, he was no longer going to be alone. There had been other women, women who wanted to form liaisons with him. But he had always preferred the freedom of being on his own—until now.

Mariss filled a hollowness inside him he could only now acknowledge had been there for years. He was not accustomed to sharing his deepest feelings. And last night hadn't been the time for words. But Kade had demonstrated to Mariss in no uncertain terms how he felt about her. And there was no doubt she felt the same.

He turned his head toward her cocoon, now linked with his. She wasn't in it. He wiped his hand over his face and sat up. "Mariss?" he said softly.

No response. He ducked out of the tent and looked around. She was sitting by the stream, using a comb and a small hand mirror to fix her hair. She was already dressed in her flightsuit.

Still naked, Kade came up to her. His heart swelled at the sight of her. He crouched behind her. Slipping his hands along her shoulders, he tilted her head back and kissed her. "Good morning."

Mariss leapt to her feet. "Kade. You should get dressed. It's getting late."

"According to who?"

"It's probably after 1100 hours. The Colony is—what—maybe four or five hours away? Going directly east, I mean. But if we have to travel up or down the coast, well, it could take all day to get there."

A deep foreboding grew in Kade's chest, tightened in his gut. He rose slowly to his feet and peered at her closely. "What's the hurry?"

"Adrian is waiting for me."

"Adrian!" He clung to a single thread of hope. "You mean you want to tell him. About us. Get it over with."

Mariss returned her comb and mirror to her hygiene case and snapped it closed. "Tell him? I don't plan on doing that, Kade. It would cause trouble in my marriage." She strode past him toward the tent.

Kade stood there in stunned disbelief. After their glorious night together, she still planned to go through with it? Anger slammed through him like a punch in the gut. He strode after her, rounded on her. "You're still planning to marry Adrian Young? After last night?"

Mariss walked around him and crawled into the tent, where she imploded both their cocoons. She tossed them out. His clothing followed, landing at Kade's feet. Her voice came from deep in the tent, terse and emotionless. "I suggest you get dressed, Kade. Unless you want to show up at the Colony as you are."

Fury surged through him. He snatched up his clothing and retreated, pulling it on as fast as he could. He sat on the ground and yanked his boots on. Fully dressed, he was now on equal footing with the traitorous Mariss Sakari.

***

Mariss crawled out of the tent. Kade was waiting for her. She almost ran into him. "Why don't you get the transport while I implode the tent?"

He ignored her request. His hands grasped her shoulders. She tried hard to avoid his stormy expression. "What in the hell is going on here, Mariss? How can you give yourself to me like that, and plan on marrying someone else?"

"Let go of me. I gave you what you wanted."

He shoved her away in disgust.

She spoke harshly. "You said you wanted to live for the moment. You told me if you had a choice, you would choose to experience something you wanted at least once, even if you could never have it again. You said so. And I knew you wanted me."

"I thought you were talking about the police car!" He raged at her.

It always starts like this, Mariss thought. *With misunderstandings, arguments.* She didn't need the baggage which passion carried with it. "I'm sorry. But you know I have to do this."

Kade moved closer, his hands up, his voice more reasonable. "Why? Sure, you made a commitment, but things have changed. They won't hold you to it. If there's a contract or something—"

"It has nothing to do with that!" Mariss flung back. "Don't you see, how can I possibly trust myself? I have a terrible track record, Kade. I *can't* trust my own feelings. Besides, what kind of future do you have planned for us?"

Kade expelled a breath. "I don't know. I haven't thought that far." His words grew intense. "But I know I want you."

Mariss stepped away from his yearning expression. "Well, I *have* thought ahead," she said coolly. "Something would happen. I know it would. You'd grow tired of me, of us. I won't go through that again, Kade, so just let me be."

She knelt down and began retracting the tent supports. She could feel his eyes boring into her back. After a long moment, he left her. Mariss blinked hard to keep the tears at bay. She hadn't expected spending a single night with Kade would affect her so. He had taken complete possession of her in every way, and she had reveled in it. But she had to force down all the emotion she felt and think with her logical mind. It was the only real choice she had.

She heard the sound of the car starting, coming toward her, idling. Her expression composed, she glanced up. Kade got out and began tossing their things into the back. She sighed heavily. He seemed to have accepted her decision, which was good. But the knowledge did not make her happy.

She slipped in beside him and he engaged the drive. Soon, they were speeding once more toward the Colony.

***

They traveled in silence for most of the morning. Kade's expression was unreadable. He hardly acknowledged her presence. Mariss knew he was furious with her. But what else could she do?

He never said he loved you, an inner voice reminded her. But that wasn't the reason she was going to Adrian. Of course not. She had vowed never to trust love long before meeting Kadin Land.

They lifted over a rise, and Kade slowed the transport to a standstill. It hovered in the air a meter above the ground. The first thing Mariss saw was the sea. Blue-green and magnificent, it stretched to the horizon far distant.

"There's your Colony," Kade said flatly.

Mariss followed his gaze. North of their position, by the sea, was the loveliest settlement Mariss had ever seen. A blue globe rose from the center of a neatly laid-out collection of structures which sparkled in the sun. From what she could see, the buildings were nestled among tropical plantings and connected by a sophisticated tram system.

The Colony was larger than she thought it would be. More than a settlement—a true city. And she had never seen a more organized, a more beautiful city. It beckoned her like all the promises of happiness she had ever held dear. There at the Colony was where her heart lay. She knew it. It had to be so.

Mariss glanced toward Kade and her chest tightened painfully. He was gazing at her, his expression impassive. She would have preferred some emotion, even anger or pain. But this...blankness. She hated it. She pulled her gaze from him and fastened it on the Colony.

Kade lowered the car to the ground. "Get out, Mariss."

Shocked at his command, she nevertheless obeyed. If he wanted her gone, she would go. She retracted the door and stepped out.

He gunned the engine and the hovercraft shot forward, arcing toward a stand of trees on the right. Mariss watched it disappear into the tropical forest there. She stared hard, unable to believe it. Just like that, Kade was leaving her? Without another word?

She glanced about. The Colony was only a couple of kilometers away. It would take her less than half an hour to walk. But is this really what Kade intended, that she go the rest of the way alone?

She sighed and started to walk, feeling more lonely than she ever had in her life. She had no right to feel this way, as well she knew. But she couldn't help it. Kade had been more than her lover. He had been her friend.

Disconsolate, she cast a final glance toward the trees where he had vanished.

She stopped short, relief flooding her. Kade was walking toward her. He had merely been disposing of the hovercar, out of sight of any passing airships. Of course. Kade still needed to visit the Colony to gain transport off Elysia. She was reading too much into his actions. She wasn't the center of his life, never had been. He had other concerns than her and their brief, confusing relationship.

Kade strolled up to her. "I—I didn't think you were coming back," Mariss said.

"Hey. I don't like this planet enough to *stay* here," he said, his lips cocked wryly. "Besides, the least I can do is make sure this Adrian character is everything he's advertised to be before I dump you on him."

"Gee, thanks." Her heart warmed. Somehow, in the past moments of separation, the man who was her friend had returned to her.

***

When they were half a mile from the Colony, a sleek blue hovercar drove up to them and stopped. On its side was emblazoned a stylized blue and gold crest depicting the Colony rising white and beautiful beside the sea.

The hovercar carried a couple, both dressed in silky, clean tunics with silver belts. "Greetings!" called the woman as she stepped briskly out. "You're Mariss Sakari, aren't you? We've been expecting you. When you didn't show up, your stats were transmitted to all of us at the Colony. We take care of our own."

Mariss gazed at her. She had freshly styled cornrows ornamented with jewels. Her ebony skin glowed, and her makeup was perfect. She was glamorous and sophisticated and civilized. And she had an open, inviting expression filled with welcome. Mariss had finally arrived at the Colony. "Yes, I'm Mariss," she breathed, filled with relief that their journey was over. She did her best to quash the niggling sense of disappointment at having ended a dramatic and emotion-filled episode in her life.

"I'm so glad you're safe," the woman said. She clasped Mariss' hands warmly in her own. "We were all so worried about you." She smiled toward Kade and raised her palm. "I'm Kip."

Kade nodded. "Kade."

"Kip and Kade! Sounds like a comedy act at the Solon. That's our favorite lounge at the Colony." She laughed lightly, her smile revealing neat, straight teeth. "Now get in, both of you. You look like you could use some pampering."

She retracted the back door for them, and Mariss stepped aboard. Kade followed, more reluctant than she. "This is Jord, my husband," Kip said. She gestured to the driver, who tossed them a polite wave.

"Nice to meet you," he said pleasantly. He was a tall man with long, fair hair.

Jord spoke into a com-unit, alerting the Colony that they would be bringing in guests—one of whom was very special.

"Mariss, you look different from your holo," Kip said. She was sitting sideways, her arm over the seat in order to talk with her passengers. "Less...delicate?"

"All that walking," Mariss said wryly.

"How far have you come?" Kip asked. "We expected you weeks ago. Then the interstellar police told us you had probably been killed in a spaceship accident." She gestured gracefully with her perfectly manicured hand. "Adrian will be so thrilled when he learns you're alive, you have no idea. He refused to accept even the possibility you had died."

Her words warmed Mariss. Even long distance, even having never actually met her, Adrian cared. He believed in her, in *them.*

"We crash-landed in a lifepod beside a huge ravine," Mariss said. "I believe it's called Loner Canyon, according to my satellite survey map."

"Why, that's the other side of the continent!" Kip exclaimed. "Can you imagine that, Jord? They hiked from the other side of the continent all the way here."

Mariss nodded. She didn't mention the stolen police hovercar which had taken them half the distance. She hoped no one figured out they couldn't have traveled on foot all this way in such a short time. Yet she *had* been injured, and they had rested for more than a week by the hot pools. So maybe it evened out. She hoped so. The last thing she wanted was to cause trouble for Kade.

The vivacious Kip kept up a flow of conversation the short distance to the Colony entrance. Fascinated, Mariss absorbed the view as they passed into the city. Kade was slouched in the seat beside her, impassively staring ahead.

On either side of the entrance, massive ornately carved pillars rose thirty feet in the air. They entered a broad boulevard paved with glossy tiles which glinted in the sun. Since the cars rode on anti-grav cushions above the ground, the roads were designed to be beautiful as well as delineate transportation corridors.

Jord swung the car toward the first building they came to, fronted by a tree-filled park with an intricately sculpted fountain. The building's architecture was low, curved, sprawling, yet gave the appearance of perfect harmony with its surroundings. Tropical trees and plants softened visible edges. A profusion of flowers burst from shrubs and vined trellises, their perfume sweetly scenting the air.

Mariss knew they hadn't entered the Colony proper yet, but these first sights thrilled her. "It's even more beautiful than the holos," she said in amazement. "Everything—every detail, is so *perfect.*"

"Isn't it, though?" Kip said. "No matter how long I live here, I can't get over it. It's...paradise. But that's not the best part of living at the Colony." She glanced toward Jord, who squeezed her hand.

Mariss looked from one to the other. They seemed deeply connected, with a perfect bond between husband and wife. A sense of hunger gnawed in her, to have what these two had. Despite herself, her gaze slipped toward Kade, who seemed bored. She knew better. He was absorbing everything about this place. She wondered what his verdict would be. She knew she shouldn't worry so much what he thought. They would soon go their separate ways, and she would be meeting her own life mate. She asked Kip, "How long have you been here?"

"Five years—is that right, Jord?"

"Five, and three months," he said with a nod.

"I came to be with Jord," she said. "And he came to be with me. We were from different star sectors. But we came together because of the Colony and Iridion's special program. If it wasn't for that, we would never have met." Her voice filled with emotion as she gazed at Jord's strong profile. "He was selected especially for me, just as Adrian has been for you."

Despite Kade's passive expression, Mariss knew in her heart the conversation made Kade uncomfortable. She tried to change its direction. "What are your fields?"

"Medicine. I'm a physician, Jord's a bio-researcher."

Mariss nodded. A good match. Mariss recalled the CMSI's philosophy in matching professions. A husband and wife should have professions similar enough to speak the same technical language, yet different enough to preclude undue competition between partners.

Jord stopped the hovercar in front of the entrance to the large building.

"This is our administration building," Kip supplied. "Administrator Locke will see that you're both settled, and then—" she winked at Mariss. "Adrian."

Kip bounced out of the car. Mariss joined her on the festively tiled pavement before the grand sweep of stairs leading to two gold doors.

While Jord came around the car, Kade stepped behind Mariss. His front just brushed her back. Heat burst through Mariss, a potent reminder of their night together. *It's only sex,* she thought fiercely. *And he's doing it on purpose.*

He lowered his lips to her ear. "It's showtime, Sakari. Time to meet your perfect mate."

To her relief, his sarcastic drawl went unheeded by the happy couple, who were leading the way up the steps, hand-in-hand.

The four of them were met by a man in his fifties, Mariss guessed, with thick white hair and youthful skin. He was dressed in a white, full-length tunic covered by an overtunic of the purest blue. He introduced himself as Locke, the Colony administrator, and welcomed them warmly—especially Mariss. "My lost lamb," he said with a fatherly smile, as if he'd known her for years.

After Kip and Jord helped with the introductions, they disappeared in the hovercar.

The administrator ushered Mariss and Kade into a glass elevator. One floor up, it opened onto a pleasant sitting room which provided a sweeping view of the Colony through tall, open-air portals.

"Come. Sit, and we'll talk," Locke said, gesturing toward a conversation area decorated with potted palms and wall holos of the sea.

Locke sat across from them, his curious eyes glancing from one to the other. Mariss and Kade had taken up positions on the same sofa, side by side, despite the availability of seats. She asked herself why, but abruptly dismissed the question as irrelevant.

Kade immediately asked about transports.

"An off-world transport arrives approximately every six weeks," Locke said, his smile cool. "From Quantum Craftlines. Their schedule has been rather unpredictable lately."

Kade's eyes narrowed. If the administrator was trying to insult him, he was doing a good job, thought Mariss. "I'll wait for the next one," he said, equally cool. "If I may be allowed to impose on your generous hospitality, that is."

Locke must have sensed the veiled sarcasm of Kade's words. "Of course. You are welcome to enjoy our hospitality as long as necessary," he said. "The Colony welcomes any and all visitors. You may take meals in the dining halls, or in your room. And enjoy our many amenities, from massages to tennis courts to bric-ball tournaments. Then there's the library—" He stopped himself and chuckled. "I do go on. I'm quite proud of the comforts of the Colony, as you can well imagine."

Mariss nodded, thinking the Colony sounded like a resort more than a working settlement. The promotional holos had mentioned living and working here. But then, Kade wouldn't be interested in those aspects, so Locke wasn't mentioning them.

"Both of you will stay here in our guest wing." Locke gave Mariss a gentle smile. "Until your wedding, of course. I think Adrian has prepared quite a nice surprise for you."

Mariss felt her initial tension fading as a thrill of

anticipation surged through her. She wasn't being interviewed, for heaven's sake. She had already been admitted. And Kade could care less what these people thought of him. She knew that with certainty.

"Kip mentioned your difficulties when we were introduced, but I'd like to know the details," Locke said, his deep voice cultured and assured as he regarded both of them. "Your ship was struck?"

"We were boarded by the interstellar police, but they didn't act like police should," Mariss said. Beside her, Kade stiffened. She glanced at him. He was sending her a warning glance. But it was too late.

Locke's white eyebrows arched. "The interstellar force? We try not to get involved in affairs outside the Colony. We police our own, though it's hardly ever necessary."

"Yes, that's the agency. They tried to...molest me, and hurt Kade," Mariss explained. "Things got out of hand. They forced us to flee the ship. That's how we ended up stranded on the surface."

Locke shook his head. "That's terrible." He was leaning forward, his hands clasped between his knees. His face was creased with concern. "Very distressing. I just don't understand it. While we keep our distance, we at the Colony have a solid understanding and relationship with the police who patrol this sector. They've never been anything but respectful toward our citizens."

Mariss hesitated. "I didn't tell them I was coming to the Colony."

"Perhaps you should have. It would probably have made all the difference."

Kade snorted. "So they abuse only non-Colony citizens?"

"Of course not," Locke said. "But I can't see them behaving in such a way without provocation." His blue eyes sparked as he eyed Kade.

A tingle of dread welled up in Mariss. It was already starting. Kade was already showing his antagonism toward the Colony—in front of the leader, no less. But he was right. "We did nothing but submit to being boarded and searched," she said firmly. "Without probable cause."

"Hmm. Very distressing." Locke sighed. As if closing the topic, he added, "I'll speak with them and see what I can do. I'm sure it's all a misunderstanding."

"No, it's more. I—" Mariss began.

Locke's attention was drawn by the approach of a thin woman in a white jumpsuit. He stood and joined her. She held out a clipbook for him to consult.

Kade leaned close and murmured in Mariss' ear. "Smart move, Mariss. You trying to get rid of me permanently, or what?"

"You didn't do anything," Mariss said tersely. Then she remembered his theft of the cop car. "Much."

"With these Colony stiffs, a little goes a long way. Trust me. As far as they're concerned, I'm as welcome as a Poro attack."

Mariss rolled her eyes at his comparison with the nasty flying-slug insects from Divinion. Locke had made them both wonderfully welcome. Before she could protest his assessment, Locke returned. He gestured for them to rise. "Please come. I have something to show you." He strode off, confident they would follow. And they did.

They stepped onto a balcony and down curving steps which cast a pearlescent sheen in the sunlight. They looked as if they were made of polished marble, but weren't at all slippery to walk on.

The steps led down to a broad terrace fronting a rectangular garden. Beyond clusters of trees, Mariss caught glimpses of the blue- and green-tiled roofs of other structures. Homes, perhaps, or offices. And beyond those gleamed the massive blue dome.

And, she saw more citizens. They strolled by, men and women, alone and together, some holding hands, others chatting in groups. Most wore tunics, every color of the rainbow. Others wore white jumpsuits. Mariss wondered if the jumpsuits meant some sort of rank, or job description. Those who wore them seemed to have business in and around the administration complex. More than a few of the women she saw were visibly pregnant.

"There he is."

Mariss and Kade both followed Locke's gesture. Mariss knew him instantly, the man she had come to marry. "Adrian," she said softly. He was standing by the edge of the terrace, showing a young man the proper way to control a pruning 'bot which floated about a topiary shrub, nipping off branches here and there.

Adrian's back was partly turned to them. He was dressed in a white jumpsuit. His hair was brilliant in the sunlight, more gold than blond. His features were straight, perfectly proportioned. He was tall, well-built—an Adonis, Mariss admitted to herself. He was exactly as he appeared in the holo, yet he was real.

Mariss didn't feel so real. She felt as if she were in a play of some kind, acting out a predetermined role, that of future wife. She shook her head, trying to regain a sense of equilibrium. This was a moment she had waited months for—*years* for—meeting the man she would finally spend the rest of her life with. But her wayward thoughts were darting around, capturing nonsense, noticing things like the wrinkles in his jumpsuit pockets.

As if sensing her presence, Adrian turned and gazed toward the approaching threesome. His eyes fell on Mariss, and he froze as if entranced. Without giving his assistant a glance, he passed the 'bot controller to him.

When they were five meters away, Locke held back. Even Kade respected the importance of this meeting, allowing her to step forward alone. Adrian closed the distance between them and clasped her hands warmly in his. He smiled broadly, his eyes sliding up and down her frame. Mariss gazed at his face, studied it, compared it to her memories. She almost felt she knew this man. Almost. He, at any rate, was obviously pleased with what he saw.

"Mariss. We've been together so long in spirit, and now, finally we meet in person." His voice was deep, melodic. He leaned down and kissed her cheek. Mariss got a full sense of his height. He was so much taller than she, she had to crane her head back to look into his face.

"Yes," Mariss said, her words fleeing. What was the right way to address a stranger who would soon be her husband? *He's not a stranger. He's your perfect mate, remember?*

Adrian was speaking, and she concentrated on his words. "Tell me what happened. Your pilot wrecked his ship?" His eyes flicked toward Kade.

Her hands still clasped in Adrian's, Mariss reluctantly looked over at her lover of the previous night. He had obviously heard Adrian's remark. His eyes were as dark as gathering storm clouds. Mariss pulled Adrian over. "Adrian, this is Captain Kadin Land. He saved my life."

Kade's eyes clashed with hers, and Mariss forgot to breathe. *He saved my life,* her mind repeated the litany. But even that powerful statement couldn't begin to sum up everything he'd been to her.

Kade tore his gaze from hers and faced Adrian, his expression becoming closed, cool. "Adrian Young. I've heard a lot about you," he said. His voice sounded perfectly polite, but Mariss knew it was all for show.

Adrian smiled, his lips widening over clean, white teeth. "Good of you to care for Mariss. Thank you for seeing her safely to me."

He seemed to expect some sort of acknowledgement, a "you're welcome," perhaps. But Kade said nothing. Adrian shifted his weight from foot to foot.

In contrast, Kade stood as still as a rock. Mariss couldn't help comparing the two. They were as different looking as she could imagine two men being. Adrian was garbed in pure white. He was perfectly clean and neat, not a hair on his golden head out of place.

Kade hadn't bothered to shave this morning, so stubble darkened his chin. His stance was bold, his feet spread and arms crossed, as if Adrian was the visitor to *his* territory and not the other way around. Deep, penetrating eyes looked out from a rugged face which had seen more than its share of trouble. Adrian's eyes were sapphire blue, calm, non-threatening. He looked like he had faced nothing more terrifying than a final exam.

He makes Adrian look like an android. Where did that thought come from? Angry with herself, Mariss forced her mind away from such disloyal comparisons. She had just met Adrian. He was *her mate.*

"Mariss," Adrian said, drawing her attention. "You look different from your holo. I had specified long hair in my preferences, I recall."

Mariss touched her shorn locks. "It was difficult to maintain long hair in the wilderness."

"Hmm. Well, it will grow, won't it? Though it will take years to reach its former length." He tapped his chin. "You know, the lab is experimenting with some growth enhancers. Perhaps..."

"I plan to keep it short," Mariss said. "I like it this way."

"We'll have to discuss that. But later." Adrian laid his large, manicured hands on her shoulders. Such an innocent touch, but Mariss knew another man who had touched her in such a way and caused havoc with her senses. She waited for a similar reaction from Adrian's touch, some sign she was sexually attracted to him. It didn't happen.

I'm tired from the trip—and last night. If Adrian had been naked, I wouldn't feel anything sexual. Kade wore me out. Besides, she was stressed over this meeting. She knew these factors played a large part in her lack of reaction. After all, she had wanted Adrian before, fantasized about him before. She had to be patient. They would have years together to find their feelings. Years. Besides, she hadn't expected romance. Nor did she have use for it.

"I've built us a house," Adrian said. "I can't wait to show it to you."

"Gee, I bet you already picked out the curtains and pictures for the walls, too." Kade's sarcastic words cut into their intimate moment.

Adrian frowned, knowing Kade was insulting him. But he clearly couldn't understand why. "Of course. Mariss' tastes are well known to me. And we agree almost 100 percent." He shifted his body to cut Kade out of the conversation. "Which reminds me, Mariss. We can be married two weeks from today. That should be sufficient to make the final arrangements. All the pre-planning has already been done."

Locke stepped beside Kade. "How nice, you'll be able to attend the nuptials. We do weddings up big here in the Colony. Weddings are quite meaningful and unforgettable occasions to us."

Kade slid his hand along his unshaven cheek, resting his jaw in his palm. Mariss wondered what expression he was hiding behind his hand.

Locke laid his hand on Kade's shoulder. Kade ignored him, his eyes fastened on Mariss. Mariss found it hard to look away. She was feeling guilty, and she hated it. She had never promised Kade anything. He had known about Adrian from the first.

"Why not visit your guest room?" Locke prodded. "Perhaps rest before dinner? Or, you could look around, enjoy the amenities."

Kade continued to ignore him. He shifted his gaze away from Mariss, staring toward a fountain several meters away.

"And you're coming with me, so I can show you your new home." Adrian tapped a control on his belt and summoned a transport. A tram zipped up to an established stop a few feet away. Adrian slipped his arm around Mariss' shoulders, steering her toward the tram, away from Kade.

Mariss looked back. Kade was staring at them, his hand still shielding his expression, and his thoughts.

SEVENTEEN

Kade tasted blood. The administrator had finally given up and left him alone. He pulled his hand away and gazed at it.

He had bitten his palm. He had wanted to bash Adrian Young's head in, and the only way he could contain his burst of violent emotion was to do violence to himself. But to hear the way he talked about her hair, the way he implied Mariss shouldn't have cut it, as if he *owned* her. It infuriated Kade.

Then, seeing the man's hands on her shoulders, the way he pulled her toward him as he discussed their *wedding...*

Kade had known all along it would come to this, but until now, he hadn't actually believed it. Adrian Young hadn't really existed. But today the man had become real, and he was even better looking than his hologram. Perfect features. A smooth tan. The man *was* good-looking, Kade grudgingly admitted to himself. Like one of those statues in a museum, or one of those models selling hydronic toothpaste. Mariss couldn't help falling for him. Hell, she had specially selected him!

A warning chime rang from above his head. Kade glanced about, but didn't see the source of the sound. A female voice rang from the same hidden speaker. "Injury, Sector J, East Terrace. Injury, Sector J, East Terrace."

Before Kade could figure out what the voice meant, a tram pulled up at the same station Mariss and Adrian had left from. A petite blond woman garbed in a white tunic leaped out and rushed over to him, clutching a med-kit.

But Kade forgot about his bleeding hand as he stared at her. He could hardly believe his eyes. She didn't belong here, in this time, in this place. Not her.

When she was halfway to him, her own steps slowed. For a long moment, they merely stared at each other, memories returning, not all of them pleasant.

"Kade?" she said softly.

Kade finally managed to speak. "Yeah, Farra, it's me." His voice was rougher than he intended. "Believe it or not, they let me out of prison. Despite you."

***

"Finally, we're alone." Adrian slipped Mariss' hand into the crook of his elbow as they sat side-by-side in the tram. The automatic transport increased speed as it moved along grav-rails toward the city center, and the huge blue dome rising above surrounding structures.

"We only met a few moments ago," Mariss pointed out.

His sculpted lips twisted in a smile. "But I got you away from that pilot."

Already, Kade was coming between them. She had never intended for this to happen, but it was her own fault for allowing herself the weakness of falling for him. She tried to sound casual. "Why would you be concerned about Kade?"

"He had a look about him—feral, almost. I didn't care for the way he was staring at me."

Kade had *intimidated* Adrian. Mariss stared at the man she was going to marry. He grumbled, "That pilot better understand all our women are taken."

"You think he's going to try to rav them in the few days he's here?" She couldn't contain a sarcastic edge.

Adrian frowned. "Not all women have standards as high as you do, sweet."

Sweet? Mariss found herself irritated by his use of the surprisingly intimate term on such short acquaintance.

He continued, "Some women actually find a rough, uncultured demeanor appealing, though it's hard to fathom."

Mariss hesitated, but she couldn't let his remark go unchallenged. "How do you know what standards I have?"

"I know everything about you, sweet, as you know about me. I have your bio memorized." He patted her hand. "You needn't fear you will surprise me."

Mariss nodded slowly. Of course. To him, she had no mysteries yet to reveal. She fidgeted in the seat, trying to get used to the idea.

"Look. There's one of our elementary schools. This is the one closest to our home, where our children will go." Adrian touched a control on his belt, and the tram slowed to a stop. The car was open-air, and Mariss had a good view of the school grounds. Children were playing on bright, freshly painted equipment.

"They're on a break. Physical fitness is valued as an important component of a well-rounded academic program. We have a student-teacher ratio of five to one. You couldn't find a better education anywhere." His voice rang with pride. "Every student is rigorously schooled to the highest academic standards here at the Colony. No matter what walk of life the student may someday choose, he or she will be a success. It's virtually guaranteed."

Mariss watched the children at play. She guessed their ages at around eight or nine. All of them were good-looking, active, apparently happy. Any parent would be proud to call such children theirs. Yet the scene nagged at her, left her unsettled. *You're starting to think like Kade. Stop it.*

As Adrian started the tram again, Mariss finally realized what was bothering her. None of the children seemed too loud or too rambunctious or engaged in disagreements of any kind. "Why are they so well-behaved?" she asked Adrian. "I've never seen such a well-ordered bunch of kids."

Adrian shrugged dismissively. "They have quality parenting, Mariss. Parents like us. Think about it. No one who might cause social problems is even allowed in the Colony—except to visit," he added dryly.

"You're thinking of Kade," Mariss said.

He shrugged. "Anyone can tell he's trouble. It doesn't take much more than a passing glance to see that."

Mariss withdrew her hand from his arm. "Kade didn't have it so good as a child, Adrian. He turned out remarkably well considering what he's been through. I really don't want to hear you say anything against him. He happens to be my friend."

Adrian seemed to consider her remarks. Then he chuckled. "I believe we've had our first disagreement, Mariss." His blue eyes sparkled. "Thank goodness it was over something so unimportant."

Mariss opened her mouth to retort, but forced herself not to. Adrian wanted to end their discussion, and she was willing as well. After all, in a matter of weeks, or even days, she would never see Kadin Land again.

Mariss sighed, trying to shake off a heavy weight forming in her chest. She kept her eyes on the street below, where a Hispanic mother was operating a hoverstroller with a plump baby inside.

Adrian followed her gaze. "Did you notice the quality of the children at the school?" he asked softly.

"Quality?"

"Because of our policy of post-conception quality checks, we have achieved zero birth defects."

"Post-conception quality checks?" Mariss frowned. Then she understood and nodded. Adrian tended to pepper his conversation with institutional doublespeak. She would have to become accustomed to it. He was obviously referring to the standard DNA and blood tests pregnant women were given to rule out birth defects.

They were passing through a residential area. Each street they passed was paved with tiles in colors which harmonized with the gaily painted houses. No hovercrafts clogged the streets. "The Colony is strictly mass transit," Adrian said, as if reading her thoughts. "Except for maintenance and exploratory functions. It cuts down on the congestion and the potential for accidents considerably. And we have a very high proportion of parkland. One for every neighborhood, as well as public parks near the shopping and working areas. And the seashore."

Finally, to her relief, Mariss felt a surge of excitement begin to thrum through her. This was why she had pulled up roots and come so far. The lifestyle here seemed wonderful. She had seen no sign of vandalism, of grime, of disrepair, of anyone unhappy with life. It was truly remarkable. The Colony was a paradise, just as it had been advertised. She pointed toward a street lined with mauve tile and fronted by beige homes with neat lawns and gardens. "Does our house look like one of those?"

Adrian smiled, his blue eyes twinkling. He really was remarkably handsome, Mariss thought as she gazed up at him.

Really. He was.

"You'll see."

Mariss watched a young couple leaving a house with two school-aged children in tow. The father supported a baby against his chest. The house was single-story, not much different from its neighbors.

The young family met another family on the street, with a teenaged boy and a girl of about ten. As a group, they headed for a park at the end of the block. All were wearing unisex tunics of various solid colors.

"Where are the old people?" Mariss asked as the tram moved to the left of the dome and headed north. Everyone she had seen so far was relatively young.

"Most of our older citizens are serving throughout the galaxy, lending their vast experience to better society for all of us."

"And the rest?"

"If they're too old to serve, they return here to retire. Most prefer to live in a separate Colony," Adrian said. "They have different concerns, different lifestyles, from our family residents."

"Where is this separate Colony? I thought there was only one."

He hesitated. "It's not far."

"Oh. Close enough for family visits then."

Adrian shrugged. "If a family wishes it."

"Is today a day off? I see both parents with the children. But then, some of the children were in school, weren't they?"

"The children are schooled in shifts, so that they may have more individualized attention. Family life is highly valued here, Mariss. You know that. Work hours are extremely flexible. Many people work out of their homes."

Mariss understood that. She planned to set up a botanical laboratory in her new home—if Adrian hadn't already done that for her. "My research—who's paying for it? I mean, who will my employer be?"

"Why, the Iridion Corporation, of course. Look. There's our house."

Mariss looked where he pointed. She gasped. The house was on a rise, with a sweeping view of the ocean. It was fronted by columns and its own open-air terrace. The home she had owned with Roldo would fit inside it three times over. Mariss was sure of it.

Other houses nearby were equally impressive. This neighborhood was much fancier than the homes they had passed earlier. "Adrian, it's so—elegant," she said, smiling at him. "I don't understand. Why?"

"I'm a member of the Council, Mariss. I was appointed last year. But I didn't include this information in my bio, for I didn't wish to attract a woman who was a social climber."

"So it's a very prestigious honor?"

"Yes. There are only fifty members of the Council out of a ten-thousand-member population."

The transport slowed to a stop at a station below their new home. Adrian stepped out, helping Mariss onto a golden tiled street. "And you were raised here at the Colony, weren't you?"

"Yes, as it said in my bio. I'm of the second generation. Truly, Mariss, my membership in the Council was the only fact I did not disclose. There are no secrets between us." Again he tucked her hand in his arm and escorted her up the curving walkway to their front door.

Mariss had imagined the Colony holos showed only the best of the settlement. She had never in her wildest fantasies imagined herself living in anything as ornate as this small palace. "And I thought I was coming to help settle a frontier," she said softly, as Adrian pressed a control on his belt and the gold front door retracted.

The house was immaculate, an architect and designer's

dream. Adrian allowed her to absorb the amenities: a thick carpet, exquisite artwork. Most amazing of all, a waterfall tumbled from somewhere beyond the living room wall and over rocks into a wide pool on the outdoor terrace beyond. "I selected the plants for their beauty and aromatic characteristics," he said of the plants lining its sides.

"You designed this? I've never seen anything like it."

"Watch." Adrian clicked a button on the wall, and a shower of color lit up the waterfall and pool. After a moment, it transformed from gold to red, then to greens and blues. "You can set it to any color band and frequency you prefer. There's a steam bath, too, in the bedroom suite."

In a daze, Mariss followed his broad frame toward the other end of the sprawling house. There, she saw the hot tub, just as Adrian said. It looked remarkably like the limestone pool she and Kade had bathed in. She bit her lip, fighting off memories of Kade and her at the hot pools where she had nearly died in his arms.

She had to put it behind her. She knew it would be difficult, but her time with Kade had been only a moment of her life. A fleeting, memorable thing, but not substantial enough to carry into the future. How could it be? Even now, Kade had let her go—with Adrian. He hadn't even tried to convince her to stay with him. *As you wanted him to,* her logical half insisted.

"Mariss? Is something amiss?"

Adrian was staring at her, concerned. Mariss shook her head.

"I asked what you thought of the bedroom."

Mariss looked toward the massive bed resting in a seashell that glowed iridescently. "It's an actual Kiopin shell, taken from a creature that lives a fathom deep." He took a step toward her, his voice solicitous. "It sheds the shell naturally, in case you're concerned we hunted it."

"It's—phenomenal," Mariss said, her voice catching. This was her marriage bed. *Her marriage bed.* And she would share it with this man, this stranger, who kept staring at her as if she were failing at something. She blinked hard to regather her thoughts and smiled at Adrian. "I'm extremely impressed,

Adrian. I had no idea all of this awaited me."

To her relief, he grinned, obviously pleased at her response. "I had several special features built in just for you," he explained. "I know what being organized means to you, as it does to me." He showed her the highly organized closet system, with sections and compartments specially designed for every possible personal item. The bathroom was the same way. In both, half the space was occupied by his things, all neatly in their places, and half was empty, reserved for her things.

And there was a personal exercise room off the bedroom, with exer-units for both of them. "I work out every day at 0900 hours. You are welcome to join me at that time, or pick a time suitable for yourself."

Another unwanted memory flashed into her mind of when she had walked in on Kade exercising on the ship. She valiantly tried to shut it down, but his image continued to haunt her. She realized with a start that she had been constantly in Kade's company for weeks on end. This was the first time in days they had spent time apart. Now, she found she missed him keenly. She wished she was sharing her discoveries of this city, and this incredible house, with him.

What are you thinking? Show him where you plan to live with your new husband? Point out the bed, perhaps? She may be nothing to Kade but an entertaining rav, but even a hardened guy like him would find that hurtful.

Adrian led her back down the hall, passing two empty rooms for "their children" on the way. They entered the kitchen. In awe, Mariss watched him demonstrate the computer-organized storage units and the ergonomically laid out appliances. "No wasted motion. Everything in its place. Exactly as you prefer it. As do I."

Numb, Mariss nodded. It was so much to absorb at once. But Adrian expected some kind of response. "It's—very nice," she said finally.

He nodded. "Why not look around? I'll make us a refreshing drink."

Mariss wandered back into the living area. The pool that started inside led beyond the terrace, where a second waterfall tumbled and disappeared somewhere beyond her view. The design gave the impression that the water traveled all the way to the sea beyond. Perhaps it did.

When Mariss turned her gaze from the magnificent view, she began to notice details of the decor. The walls were done in subtle, unobtrusive earth shades and textures. Jewel-toned glass vases stood on occasional tables along the walls and in the hallway. Comfortable, ergonomically designed chairs and sofas were clustered about tables and a computer programmable fireplace. A corner nearby was set aside as a study, with text-disks on shelves from floor to ceiling.

The decor was the epitome of good taste. It was also the epitome of *her* taste. Mariss ran her fingers along the wall. She recognized the colorant. It was the same as a sample which she had been shown as part of the application process, when she had been asked to select her preferences among several samples. She hadn't known her choices would be used to decorate her home. She supposed it made sense. But it made her feel odd, to be predicted so well.

There was something else familiar about the place, even beyond the recognizable colors and patterns. It finally struck her. *It's like the home I made for Roldo.* A home she had tried hard to forget in the intervening months since finding her sister there, invading her territory. Her life with Roldo had haunted her while she went through the Iridion Corporation's selection process. She must have chosen these preferences because she could think of little except what she had given up—and keeping her life in perfect order so it could never happen again.

Adrian entered, followed by a servo-hoverbot holding a tray with two tall, icy drinks.

Mariss turned to him. "Adrian. It's very nice. But I may want to change a few things."

"Change things? But why?"

She sighed. "I know you've put a lot of effort into it."

He shrugged. "Some. But we have people who do much of the labor for us. What would you like changed?"

"I don't know. Perhaps the wall texture. Just some of it, not all. Maybe something bolder would work better."

"I suppose it might, but you selected subtle earth tones as your first preference, with jewel tones as an accent. I agree with your original selection."

"That was before I knew how the information would be used."

"I see." He considered a moment, then smiled. "Well, the walls then. Anything else?"

She stepped over to a picture, an abstract in bold blues and reds, which hung over the fireplace. "This picture. Maybe on a different wall. I don't know. I think I'd like to see something with a little life in it. I know—do you have any paintings of the blue dragons?"

"Blue dragons? You mean the ornithotiles?"

"The dragons from the forests. They're so beautiful, some artist must be painting them."

"I suppose so, yes." He stared at her, mystified. "I thought you preferred abstracts."

"Just one different picture. Something...inspiring." *A rugged space jockey holding a dragon on his palm, its outstretched wings fluttering in the breeze...*

Adrian's brow furrowed. "I don't understand. How could your tastes have changed so drastically in just a matter of weeks?"

Mariss shrugged, also at a loss. All she knew was this house wasn't *her* house. It bore the shadow of a place where she had once lived, once thought herself happy, when she had tried too hard and lost so much.

But she wasn't that person anymore. Everything in this house was precisely in its place. But now the organization disturbed her, felt confining. She had the urge to mess it up, to throw a few pieces of clothing around.

Her eyes fell on the sofa, each pillow in its place. "You've been living here, Adrian? How long?"

"Since it was finished, about four months."

She ran her hand along the sofa. "But it's so neat. You didn't know I was arriving today, so you didn't clean it for me."

"The servobots take care of the clutter. I have programmed

them to do so. And, like you, I prefer everything be in its proper place, so I can easily locate what I need, when I need it. That's one of the things we share, Mariss, a sense of order. The way some people live, it's appalling. Clothes strewn about, empty glasses, papers piled everywhere. It's enough to give one the shivers."

An image popped into Mariss' mind, of Kade sprawled on the sofa. His shirt was open, his bare feet on the coffee table. He probably left rings on the end table because he didn't use a coaster. His shoes were tossed on the floor. He would probably kick them off the second he came in. Yes, she knew how it would be, living with him. No, there wasn't anything orderly about Kade. He was too vibrant, unexpected—*alive. That's what you want,* an inner voice insisted. Mariss shook it away.

Why did Adrian's organization disturb her now, when she had striven for years to keep her life perfectly organized? With sudden insight, Mariss understood herself better than she had in years.

After Peck and his drug habit had disrupted her life so completely, she had taken to organizing things because she couldn't control her *life*. And during the bleakest days of her dismal marriage to Roldo, even before discovering Ami and him together, she had made an effort to force organization, causing an even deeper rift in their relationship.

She had always assumed she was right about the importance of order. But strangely, now, when Adrian expected her to have such a need, it was gone. She no longer felt she was about to lose control of her life if she lost control of the little things.

Oh, she would always be an organized person. But she would never again be obsessive about it. She kicked off her shoes and settled on the couch, curling her legs under her. She watched Adrian reach for her shoes, set them side-by-side next to the couch. She would have done the same thing, before.

Before—what?

She reclined on the sofa, trying to absorb the ambiance of her new home. Adrian passed her a drink and sat across from her. He leaned back, but his posture remained neat, orderly, contained. Mariss wondered if Adrian ever sprawled. She gave him the benefit of the doubt. He was probably so stiff because he felt a little nervous, as she did, as if he were being interviewed for a job.

Silence fell. Mariss thought rapidly, selecting a topic she knew they could discuss easily as professional colleagues. "Don't you find exotic botanicals the best class to study for insubstantial toxins?"

Adrian nodded thoughtfully. "Yes, I do. I believe that was in my profile. Such shared opinions is why we were matched."

"Oh. Of course." Mariss considered a moment. "Well, then, how about the study of poisonous plant species. Do you agree with Herendon's theory of their use as medicinal boosters?"

Adrian nodded again. "Yes. As do you. You seem to have forgotten how complete the selection process was."

Mariss sighed, a sense of restlessness growing within her. "Well, what *would* you like to discuss?"

"Perhaps...my position on the council? I have not completely filled you in about that."

"All right."

He began to talk, and Mariss tried to listen as he described each of the council members and their roles, and his role as a socio-guidance expert. She blinked twice and yawned, her train of thought derailing into more images of her past, and her attempt to understand what had changed within herself.

"Mariss? Mariss." Adrian's voice was growing insistent. Mariss focused on him. "Obviously, you're tired. We've stayed here long enough. I shall return you to your guest room at the administration center, where you may rest and freshen up before dinner."

"Can't I just crash here?"

His sculpted lips tightened. "Absolutely not. You mustn't sleep here until we're properly wed. I know you do not rav men who aren't your husband. You said so in your profile."

Mariss gritted her teeth. She was starting to hate the damned profile. *I ravved Kade—and I'm glad.* The words popped into her mind, but she replied, "I only meant to take a nap, Adrian."

"Of course you did. But the principle is the same, Mariss. We shouldn't try to stretch the rules to suit our whims, or order will be lost. Come." He extended his hand, and Mariss grasped it, allowing him to pull her to her feet.

EIGHTEEN

Farra seemed to recover from her shock first. Numbly, Kade watched as she became all business. "You injured yourself." She gestured toward his hand, which hung at his side, the blood dripping onto the terrace.

Farra set the med kit in the air. It hovered there on antigravs. She popped it open and removed an absorbent material. Lifting Kade's hand, she pressed it into his palm. "Hold this until we get to the med station. It's a short ride away."

She led the way. He followed, still amazed to be seeing her again. He wasn't sure how he felt about it. He had never completely forgiven her, that was certain. But now, he couldn't even begin to imagine himself married to her.

Farra stepped into the tram, and Kade sat across from her.

Her cornflower blue eyes settled on him, intent, questioning. "Kade, what are you doing here? You haven't been recruited, have you? No, you were a pilot, of course." She smiled softly. "The best. Are you on a commercial run?"

"You could say that," he said dryly, not keen on sharing much with her. "I'm here until another transport arrives, at any rate."

She nodded. He examined her more closely. She was still petite, her soft-blond hair as baby fine as ever. Her beltless blue tunic hung loosely over her frame. Now that she was seated, Kade saw that her belly swelled underneath the fabric. "You're pregnant."

She smiled and nodded. "With my second."

"So, you applied for that computerized mating program, then?" Kade envisioned Mariss in Farra's place, sitting across from him, pregnant with Adrian's child. Pregnant, as she could never be by him. He blinked hard, feeling like an idiot for caring so much about something so completely beyond his control. Mariss was lost to him, as he always knew she would be.

"Kade? You're a thousand miles away. I know what you think of me, and—Oh. Here's our stop." True to her character, Farra had assumed he was thinking of her.

She rose and stepped off the tram, Kade trailing behind. She led him into the med station, which was sparsely occupied with a few people in blue medical uniforms like Farra's.

She took him past the reception desk and a row of seats where a few Colony citizens waited their turns, and into a private room with a patient bed and a wall of medical equipment. She directed him to sit on the bed.

Kade complied, feeling oddly displaced. Mariss was who-knew-where doing who-knew-what with that stranger, and he was here with his ex-fiancée, a woman he had hoped never to see again. But his former animosity was almost entirely gone, blunted by time, distance, and passions which had become directed elsewhere.

Farra was staring at him again. She tugged at his hand, extracting the bloody cloth, and examined the wound. "These look like teeth marks. Kade, did you bite yourself?"

Kade yanked his hand away. "It's not even deep. Leave it alone."

"Don't be so stubborn. I can mend it in a few seconds." She pulled over a waist-high device and set his hand in a tray, strapping it down tight. Kade recognized the unit. He had been healed of injuries several times on Rebus Five, so he could be returned to the mines to work again. But he'd never heard of the expensive procedure being done for something so minor as a skin tear.

Farra had settled herself at the controls behind the machine. "Hold perfectly still." A moment later, orange lasers arced down from the top of the unit and sealed his skin. "There. All better."

Farra had always enjoyed talking like a little girl, Kade

recalled now. She always made the most of her innocent, childlike appearance. He had found it endearing back at the Academy.

She rose and disconnected him from the unit. Kade flexed his fingers. His palm was as good as new. "Now, why did you bite your hand?" she asked, gazing at him intently.

"I was hungry."

"Very funny, Kade. I always did like that dry sense of humor of yours. If you're really hungry, the main dinner is in a few hours. I imagine you're staying in guest accommodations?"

He shrugged. "Yeah, I suppose."

"Then my husband and I will join you. I'll get a sitter for Elaine. She's my baby."

Kade nodded. He wasn't in the mood for polite conversation, but at least it would distract him from thinking too hard about Mariss being with that Adonis of hers.

"I'm glad you're here, Kade," Farra finally said. "You look good."

His mouth quirked wryly. "Thanks. So do you. You're all grown up."

She actually blushed. Kade found himself responding to her warmly. She hadn't been a mean girl all those years ago. Just weak, forced by convention to obey her parents and their plans for her. "Kade, you do look good, all tanned and...And, well, I don't recall you being so toned." The admission seemed to take a lot out of her, as if she was embarrassed to be talking about his body. "You look wonderful, really. But you don't look happy."

Kade's brow creased. "Farra, what are you trying to do? Psychoanalyze me?"

"No, I'm just a medic. But Kade, happy people don't bite their hands."

Kade snorted. He shoved off the bed. "I think I'll go wander around this place, see what it's about."

"Wait." She laid her hand on his arm. "Stay here. Talk with me. I—I've thought about you a lot over the years, about what I did. Or rather, didn't do."

He turned slowly to face her. "Yeah? Well, Farra, I did, too. I spent a hell of a long time on Rebus Five thinking about it. I'm all thunk out. So—" He walked toward the door.

"Kade, I'm trying to apologize." A tear rolled down her cheek. Kade sighed. He came to her side. She brushed the tear away and swallowed hard, looking at the floor rather than at him. "I was wrong, Kade, to listen to my family. I know that now. I knew it then. I wanted to help you, but they wouldn't let me!" She turned her tear-stained face to him. "They were so insistent that I...that I let you go."

Kade wasn't in the mood for this. It had happened so long ago, it was as if it happened to someone else. But he didn't like to think of Farra—married mother and wife—suffering because of him. He gave her shoulder a reassuring squeeze. "Farra, I know. It's okay. I never expected you to wait all those years for me. No woman would do that." Except Mariss. She was loyal. She had waited for her first husband while he was in prison, and the man hadn't even appreciated it. Even now, Mariss was remaining loyal to Adrian. He admired that about her, but cursed what it meant to him, to *them*.

"Kade, that's why I came to Elysia," Farra continued. "To escape my family. They wanted me to marry someone else. But I refused. I—I still loved you."

Kade sighed. "Farra. I don't know what to say." He didn't love her. He didn't know if he ever had. He had wanted her, of course. She had been pretty, popular, rich, and out of all the available pilots in training, she had chosen him.

"So I joined the Explorer Corps."

Kade's attention riveted to her words. "The Explorer Corps? You mean the settlement a hundred kilometers from here, on the plain? You came here with them? I thought you went through the Iridion Company's mating service, like my—"

"Like your what?"

"My—my friend."

"You have a friend here? Who? I know everyone here."

"I doubt you know her," he said. "She's new. I brought her here."

Farra shrugged. "Oh. Well, we can meet at dinner, if she's new. All the new ones stay in the administration building. Is she maybe why you—no, of course not. You said you were leaving. Whose is she?"

Kade opened his mouth to reply, but couldn't say the name. The idea of Mariss *belonging* to another man was more than he could stomach. With supreme effort, he forced his thoughts from Mariss. He had to concentrate on something else. He had a hunch it could prove important. "How did you end up here, if you came to Elysia as an Explorer?"

She hesitated. "It's kind of a strange story."

"So try me."

"I was kind of...well...forcibly recruited."

Kade stepped back, amazed. "Damn it, I knew it. They kidnapped you, didn't they?"

"Yes." The word was a whisper. "Me and about seven other women. They needed more women for the men here. I didn't want to—" Suddenly, Farra grimaced. She grasped her temple, her lips twisting in what could only be described as pain.

In an instant, Kade was holding her, supporting her. He helped her sit on the bed. "Headache?"

She nodded. "They come on suddenly, without notice." Her color began to return. "I'll be okay. Just give me a moment."

Her pain filled him with concern. "Is the baby okay? Should I send for a doctor?"

She shook her head. "I'm fine. It's already passing." She breathed deeply. Then she looked at him, her eyes unnaturally bright. "Now, where were we? Oh, yes. How I came here. I met a man, and he and I—I discovered he was my perfect mate. Now, I'm quite happy. More than I can say." She smiled at him, her eyes misty, faraway.

Kade stared at her in disbelief. Before her headache, she had been about to discuss the details of her kidnapping from the settlement. Now, she was rambling on about her perfect mate.

The hair on the back of his neck prickled. Things were definitely not quite right in paradise. And damned if he wasn't going to learn why.

***

"Kade."

Mariss stared into his face, feeling more awkward than she ever thought possible. He returned her gaze, his expression stony. But his eyes held a banked fire.

Mariss and Adrian had come across him just inside the entrance to the dining room. She had wondered all day what he was up to, but hadn't expected to see him tonight. Her surge of gladness was dampened considerably when she felt Adrian tugging at her elbow in an effort to draw her away.

But their path was blocked by a petite blond who, Mariss now realized, was with Kade.

"Is this your friend, Kade?" the blond asked, looking from Mariss to him. She glanced at Adrian's hand on her elbow and smiled. "Oh, you're Adrian's mate. We thought you'd never arrive, and that our poor Adrian had been stood up." She giggled.

Mariss forced her gaze from Kade to the woman and back again. "I see you've been busy making friends," she said to him, knowing her words sounded far too tense for casual conversation.

"Not surprising, considering his type." The words were Adrian's, spoken in her ear. She knew they were just loud enough for Kade to hear. "But I didn't expect Farra to fall for his brand of charm."

"I confess. Farra and I are...old friends," Kade said, his gaze glued to Mariss.

Mariss was filled with jealousy which her logical mind couldn't dismiss. She knew she was letting her vulnerability to Kade show. She couldn't help it. This whole scene was growing more twisted by the moment. Kade and a woman from his past—

She's pregnant. And she was also rattling off something about a husband waiting for them. Mariss was obviously overreacting. Besides, she herself had no claims on Kade. So where had all that primitive emotion come from?

Farra was speaking. "Come, Adrian. You two have to join

us for dinner. Haram and I insist. And I know Kade won't mind seeing his friend again."

"Certainly," Adrian said. He didn't look especially pleased at having run into Kade again, or at sharing a meal with him. But obviously he was too polite to object. Farra led the way to the table where a man of Arabic extraction—presumably Farra's husband—waited.

Introductions soon were dispensed with, and Mariss found herself sitting across from Kade and Farra. Naturally, Adrian sat beside her. Farra's husband, Haram, was on her other side, at one end of the table.

The servo-bot arrived and they placed their orders. Kade asked for a Klinian ale, which confused the 'bot. "We do not indulge in spirit-weakening beverages here at the Colony," Adrian said, his lip curling as he looked at Kade.

Kade sat up straighter. "You mean to tell me this is a dry city? I should have guessed."

"I'm not at all surprised this disappoints you, Mr. Land," Adrian said.

Farra did a credible job of keeping the conversation on safe topics, such as the weather and the fun she and her family had at the beach. Mariss soon learned that Farra had known Kade while he attended the Academy. While she talked, Mariss tore her eyes from Kade and looked about the room. It was on the second level of the administration center in the south wing, and gave out on a view of the Colony. In the distance, the massive dome lit up the night skyline.

It was a lovely sight, a romantic sight. Or could be. But Mariss felt about as romantic as a prickly shrub on Jiva Five, the volcano world. Her eyes kept flicking to Kade. He was slumped in the chair, his penetrating gaze on her, his arms crossed over his brawny chest. He was still wearing his short-sleeve uniform shirt, but it had been laundered. Mariss had showered and changed in her assigned guest room, and Adrian had brought her a tunic of lemon yellow to wear. It was comfortable. And, it branded her as a Colony resident.

Kade caught her gaze with his own, stealing her breath away. His eyes held a knowing glint. He knew perfectly well she had been staring at him. Mariss was afraid if he so much as crooked his finger, she'd follow him somewhere, anywhere, and spend the rest of the evening in his company, and in his arms, completely forgetting why she had come to the Colony in the first place...

"Mariss?" Adrian was speaking to her. "Farra asked us a question about our life together. I hesitate to answer without consulting you first."

"What?" Mariss turned her attention to her future mate.

With a giggle, Farra waved her hand dismissively. "Don't worry about it. I know the Colony can be overwhelming at first. Meeting so many new people, *and* your future husband, all in the same day." She gave Mariss a friendly smile. "I was asking if you're planning to start a family soon."

"We—we have to marry first," Mariss said.

"That's just a formality, though," Farra said.

"I don't think of it that way."

"Gee, Mariss, tell us how you view it, then. This...mating thing." Kade's snide words intruded on the conversation and grabbed their attention. Adrian stiffened beside her. And Farra—she seemed very curious about Kade's reaction, her pretty blue gaze jumping between the two of them.

Mariss faced him squarely, her chin up, trying to hide all evidence of her nervousness. "Kade, I believe I've shared my opinion on the subject with you more than once."

His eyes glinted in the light of the fire-orb decorating their table. "You certainly did. *More* than once. How could I ever forget it?"

His tone infuriated her. He had no right to speak to her like this in front of all these people—her new friends, her future husband. She knew with certainty that they would soon figure out what he was talking about, if they didn't already know. She had to change the subject, now. "I want to start a family right away, I think," she said, her eyes only on Farra. "Are you having your first?"

"Second. You can start very soon. They like it that way, here at the Colony. Lots of babies. But you have to be screened first. And then there's the in vitro processing. It can be time-consuming. Something to do with quality control, they say."

"In vitro. What do you mean?"

"Farra." Haram, so far a quiet man, spoke commandingly, and Farra seemed to fold into herself.

She didn't answer Mariss' question, so Mariss repeated it. "What do you mean by in vitro processing?"

"It's simple, Mariss," Adrian said. "Nothing to lose sleep over. We do it every day here.

"I don't understand, Adrian. Please explain it to me."

"Of course, dear." Adrian placed his hand over hers possessively. "The conceptions are done outside the uterus. The children certainly are beautiful. Haven't you noticed? That's the reason."

"You mean to prevent birth defects? It sounds so unnatural."

"You're a scientist, Mariss. You especially should understand. We have developed methods to screen for desirable characteristics. This way, no conceptions continue past the elementary zygote stage that aren't children who are completely wanted, in every way."

"You mean screened for birth defects?" Mariss said again, still waiting for confirmation.

But Adrian didn't answer her directly. "Only the quality zygotes are used—reinserted into the mother for gestation, yes. A perfectly harmless procedure."

Kade leaned forward, his arms on the table, his broad shoulders hunched. "So tell me, Adrian. What characteristics *do* you screen out? Hereditary diseases?"

"Of course. Otherwise, why bother?"

"What about near-sightedness?"

"Well, yes, I believe that's one."

"Children who would need corrective lenses or eye surgery aren't allowed to be born? How about kids prone to allergies?"

"I'm not certain, but I believe so. I know of no second-generation child who has allergies."

"So, are there intelligence requirements? All the dumb kids are weeded out? And the ugly ones, too? How about height requirements? Or do all the children have to grow up to look like you?"

Abruptly, Adrian rose. "You are insulting, sir, and a poor excuse for a Colony guest. It's no wonder a person of your... caliber cannot understand. Mariss, I do not know how you managed to spend time in this person's company as long as you did. I insist we leave this minute."

"Adrian! This isn't a proper way to behave, is it?" Farra prodded. She leaned across the table to Mariss. "He's an easy one to irritate sometimes. Very gung-ho on the Colony."

Mariss refused to move. Kade was asking tough questions, but she also wanted the answers. "You don't allow pregnancy to proceed naturally? I've never been told this. Why—"

"Mariss, come with me." Adrian tried tugging on her hand.

She snatched it back. "I don't think so, Adrian. I would like a few answers. Besides, I haven't eaten yet."

Adrian finally had to admit defeat. He retook his seat. Mariss couldn't help finding that fact more irritating than his show of walking out. For goodness' sake, if he said he was leaving, he should have followed through on it. Her eyes met Kade's. He wasn't even trying to hide a smirk.

Mariss looked away, filled with embarrassment over Adrian's behavior. She should be angry with Kade for attacking her future husband, but that wasn't how she felt at all. Nothing was working out like she thought it would.

"I'll tell you more about the Colony, Mariss, when we are alone," Adrian said, his tone reassuring. "You will understand everything perfectly once you complete your orientation training. I believe it is set for tomorrow. And none too soon."

"Orientation? What's that?" Kade asked. "She has to learn how to be a proper wife and mother, or just a good little Colony citizen?"

"Kade," Mariss said firmly. "I'll deal with this. Please don't get in the way again."

"Excuse me, Mariss." Kade's reply was ice cold. "I'll do my damnedest to keep your desires in mind."

"Thank you."

They stared at each other. Mariss knew everyone at the table felt the tension between them. She couldn't do anything to prevent it. She realized now there was still too much left unsaid between her and Kade. If they never saw each other after today, if they never spoke about what had occurred between them, she would never be able to put what they had shared in its proper context.

The waiter-bot delivered their meals, the best food Mariss had eaten on this planet. For the moment, she shelved all her concerns in her enjoyment of the meal.

The rest of dinner was restrained. Mariss watched Kade's face from the corner of her eye, while trying to appear to ignore him. His attention switched from wry disgust as he looked at Adrian, to irritation when he caught Mariss' eye. And Farra—he stared at her as if trying to decipher a puzzle.

Toward the end of the meal, Farra invited Mariss to accompany her to "freshen up." Mariss did, glad to get away from the festering undercurrents at the table.

In the women's room, Farra looked at Mariss in the wall-sized mirror. "I thought you should know about Kade and me."

"Know what?"

"He and I were...engaged once."

Mariss stared at her in disbelief. "You're the one? The one who *left* him?"

"Don't look at me that way. I don't see you planning to stay with him."

"Me?" Flustered, Mariss almost dropped the brush she was using to tidy her hair, the hairstyle Kade had given her. "Of course not. I'm here for Adrian."

"Uh-huh." Farra eyed her closely. "Listen. Kade's hurting something fierce. It's been years since I knew him, but people don't change that much. It's all over him. In case you can't see it. I don't think you're really looking."

"What are you talking about?" Mariss said, trying to sound casual. She didn't want her one-night fling with Kade to haunt her new life here in the Colony after all the effort she had put into coming here.

"If you care for Kade, if you have a chance with him, why are you even here?"

"What makes you think Kade and I—"

Farra ignored her protest. She clasped Mariss' arm, her grip surprisingly strong for such a petite woman. "Don't stay," she said, her words fierce. "If you have any other options—"

Farra suddenly fell silent, as if hit by a stunning force. She stepped back from Mariss, her entire demeanor growing relaxed. "Wasn't that a nice meal? Haram and I enjoy eating out here. It's so pleasant in the evenings." A smile drifted across her face, beatific, serene.

Mariss didn't understand what was going on. Farra's behavior was completely bizarre. Adrian spoke of strange childbearing customs, and Kade—Kade she understood. He wanted the truth. So did she. Didn't she?

Her thoughts in turmoil, Mariss followed Farra back to the table.

***

Mariss was dreaming of a palace with blue dragons guarding it. She was standing on the terrace with Adrian, looking out to sea. But after a while, the scene shifted, and he was kissing her.

No, it wasn't Adrian. His image faded, as insubstantial as smoke, and Kade took his place, unbearably real. Heat flowed throughout her body as his lips and tongue worked magic on her pliable mouth. She heard herself moan, felt her body stir.

A second later, she was fully awake. And she wasn't dreaming. She *was* being kissed. Her moan turned into a shriek as her eyes shot open. Kade sat on the edge of her bed, smiling like a cat.

Mariss pressed herself against the headboard, yanking her blankets about her. "Kadin Land. What are you doing in my room?"

She tried to sound imperious, but her voice came out breathy, weak.

"I had to wake you up. It seemed like a good way, if you hadn't screamed. But I don't think anybody heard."

"Get off my bed, Kade."

He shook his head. "Nope. You're going to listen to me, and listen good. I've spent all night prowling around this place—"

"What time is it?" Mariss looked toward the wall clock. It was 0324. "Don't you ever sleep?"

"Not when I'm in a place as screwed up as this one, lady."

Mariss sighed. She should have expected Kade wouldn't give up. "I've seen a lot of the Colony today, Kade, and screwed up is hardly what I'd call it. It's beautiful. It's more than I ever dreamed it would be. And the holos didn't lie at all, you have to admit that."

"Yeah, well, you were given the official tour." Her bare foot was outside her blanket. To her surprise, he scooped it up and settled it in his lap, his strong fingers beginning a deep, relaxing massage. He continued to talk, all the while stroking her foot and ankle. At first, Mariss tried to pull her foot away, but he wouldn't give it up. He ran his knuckles along her instep, rubbing gently, and Mariss stopped wanting to try. Kade would never cease to surprise her.

"You can't tell me that stuff about pre-selecting babies didn't get to you," he said. "I could see it all over your face."

"Well, I admit it sounds odd," she agreed grudgingly. "But Adrian says there's a good reason, and it's nothing to be concerned about."

"And you trust that android?" Kade sneered.

Mariss jerked her foot away. "He's not an android. He's just not like you."

"Yeah, I know. He's your idea of Mr. Dreamboat." Kade reclaimed her foot, his fingers working along her Achilles tendon. "Well, I snuck into the lab where they weed out the babies. It's in that dome at the center of the complex, by the way. I'm no scientist, but it looked damned suspicious to me. The little dishes—"

"Petri dishes?"

"Yeah, they were labeled with codes. I wrote a couple down." He set her foot in his lap and pulled a slip of paper from his jacket pocket. "I thought if you could hack into the computer with your own unit, you might be able to find out what they stand for."

Reluctantly, Mariss accepted the paper from him. She glanced at it and set it on the nightstand. "Probably just the mother and father's names, Kade. And control numbers. Batch...numbers." As soon as she said the last words, she regretted it. Her eyes met Kade's. The idea was horrific. Processing babies like they were a product. It couldn't be that bad. Kade was making it up. Making it up to scare her, to get her to leave here with him.

"I overheard the lab techs talking. I heard them discussing which ones were 'viable,' and which ones weren't. They were laughing about it. It made the hair stand up on the back of my neck."

Mariss sighed. "That just means which ones would be likely to survive, once implanted in the mother, Kade. Really. I know. I talk that way about plant specimens I grow in the lab." Mariss grimaced. Again, the image wasn't a good one.

Kade set her foot down. It was tingling with relaxation. He retrieved her other foot from under the blanket and settled it in his lap. "Then there's Farra. She was one of the women kidnapped from the Explorers settlement, Mariss. She told me about it. Or, she started to. Until she got a tremendous headache. Then she seemed to forget all about what she was going to say. It was bizarre."

Mariss stared at him. For the first time, trepidation took hold. "I—I noticed something like that. When Farra was telling me to..." *Leave here, with Kade.*

"To what?"

"I don't exactly recall. But one minute she was saying one thing, the next she seemed completely calm and changed the topic."

Kade shook his head. "I knew this place wasn't normal. You can't stay here, Mariss. We have to leave."

"And I knew that's what you were building up to. But you're taking little things and blowing them up into huge ones. You were always against this place, Kade. You're just looking for problems. But I don't happen to feel that way. This is my home now. I belong here, with Adrian."

His eyebrow arched. "You still set on that guy? He's a worm."

Mariss ignored his comment. "You're jumping to

conclusions. Farra is just one person. She probably has migraine headaches. They can be so fierce, it makes you forget what you were saying."

"This wasn't a migraine, Mariss. And she *was* kidnapped. She told me that much."

Mariss crossed her arms. "So what are you suggesting? Mind control? I'd say that's a little farfetched, Kade. Haven't you noticed how happy everyone is?"

"Exactly." His expression was serious as his eyes clashed with hers, intense, seeking. "You're a curious woman, Mariss. Remember on the ship how you found out about my past? And how you made me investigate your luggage? You wouldn't give it up. And the vagon. You discovered it first. You *knew* something wasn't right." She could tell he admired this quality in her. The thought elated her. "That's who you are. Don't let them make you forget it."

"I don't really think the situation is the same," she said softly.

He grimaced. "No, it's worse. Did you notice how many of the women around here are pregnant? I swear, Mariss, it's a regular breeding farm."

"Now, why would they do that, Kade? Think about it. They have a near perfect society here. Surely they wouldn't let the population get out of control." Mariss closed her eyes, feeling waves of pleasure ascend from her foot throughout her body as he massaged it.

"Oh, there's room to expand yet. Entire sections under development."

"Adrian didn't show me that."

Kade's hands stopped moving on her foot. "So what did he show you? Your little love cottage?"

"Yes. But it isn't little. It is—huge."

"Yeah?" His fingers slowed, aggravation plain in his words. "I get it. None of what I'm telling you matters. Adrian is rich. He's one of the top colonists, so of course he's rich. That's his appeal, isn't it? That and his plastic looks. And babies."

Mariss gazed at him, her heart tumbling in her chest. Is

this what she had wanted all along, for Kade to fall in love with her and commit himself to her? Despite the pain romance had always caused her? Carefully, seeking some kind of admission, she said, "Kade, you sound jealous."

He sat back, smirking. "Jealous? Hell, why? We just shared a rav, Mariss. I'm not a possessive guy."

Mariss' surge of excitement faded just as quickly. She was right to stay here with Adrian. He offered her commitment, companionship, a secure life. And none—*none*—of the dangerous trappings of romance.

"I understand," she said softly. She would never have romance with Adrian. She had imagined she would, despite telling herself it didn't matter. She had fantasized they would fall in love once they met. That sparks would fly. But now she knew theirs would remain a relationship of mutual respect, nothing deeper. For she already had given her heart away.

Kade's finger tilted her chin, forcing her eyes to meet his. "But I don't like to see my friends hurt."

And to Kade, she was only a friend, despite what she felt toward him. "I promise I won't be hurt, Kade."

He leaned forward, his hands on either side of her hips. "Then be honest with me. Is this place everything you dreamed of? Is Adrian really perfect for you?"

She couldn't tear her eyes from his. *Perfect...* What had she ever thought it meant, a man being perfect for her? "Is Adrian as god-like as you imagined him to be? As all-powerful?" Kade continued, his words growing increasingly sarcastic.

His words struck a raw nerve. Mariss didn't recall giving strength of character a low ranking in her original survey. Yet Adrian seemed to lack backbone.

But the last person she wanted pointing out Adrian's flaws was Kade. She flung off the covers and slipped out of bed. Kade followed her up. "Get out, Kade. You don't know what you're talking about. You're trying to cause trouble, for me and for him. Things would be so much easier if you stayed out of it."

"Yeah, I bet they would." He walked toward her. She

backed up. A moment later, she felt the wall of the room against her back. She was wearing a white tunic, a bedgown they had provided for her. Kade looked her over from her head to her toes. "Nice. I kinda like you in a tunic. You've got great legs. It's too bad it means you're turning into one of *them.*"

Mariss had been staring at him as well, at his powerful chest and arms, at his narrow hips. And remembering the feel of his naked skin against hers, of her legs wrapped around him as he moved inside her...She had to get him out of her room, and fast. She edged toward the door. "You have to leave, Kade. This isn't right. I'm engaged to someone else."

He planted his hand by her head, preventing her escape and looked down at her. Mariss stood frozen, trying hard not to show her reaction to him. "Don't sweat, Mariss. I'm not back for seconds. I had my fill last night."

So why was he inching even closer? And why couldn't she tear her eyes from his? "Is that so?"

"Yeah," he drawled. "Damn, I like this little outfit." His finger slipped along the curved neckline. His touch sent a surge of desire through Mariss, so strong she felt her knees folding. She forced herself to lock them.

"Does Adrian's touch make you feel like mine does?" Kade asked, clearly aware of her reaction. "Like you want to wrap yourself around him and not let go? Or does he leave you cold, like a dead fish?"

"Of course not. He and I fit well together—perfectly. Adrian and I have many things, important things, in common." She batted his hand away.

Kade lowered his mouth toward hers, his breath dancing over her face. "You think that's really enough? You'll be bored stiff in a week, Mariss."

His words alarmed her, because subconsciously, she had started to wonder if it weren't true. "Please remove yourself from my quarters, Kade," she said stiffly. "I prefer not to be insulted in my own room."

Kade straightened. "Damn, I hate it when you get that prissy tone in your voice. You sound just like that blond lunkhead you think you want to marry."

"How dare you—"

"It also makes me want to kiss it away."

She had been too distracted to notice, but Kade had slipped his hand behind her head. Now he clasped it strongly and pressed his mouth to hers. At the intimate touch, a powerful surge of desire swept through her, sweeping logic away. With her last coherent thought, she realized she had to stop this before it went any farther, or she would be flat on her back in the bed, and he would be on top of her. Making love before they arrived here was one thing. But she had met Adrian now. How could she start a new relationship with him after such betrayal?

She tore her mouth from Kade's. "Back off, flyboy."

Her insulting tone struck him hard; she could see that. She regretted her words the moment she said them. But they worked. He stood back and crossed his arms.

"Excuse me, M. Sakari. I forgot. You had a nice, uncomplicated one-night rav and now you're done with it." He sneered at her. "Hell, so am I, for that matter. I just got a little bored hanging out in this place. It seems like it'll be forever before I can get off this rock."

He crossed toward the door.

"Kade."

He responded to the softness of her voice and looked back at her. "Yeah, what?"

"What will you do? Once you leave here?"

"Why in the hell do you care?"

"That isn't fair."

He shrugged, but he didn't answer her question. "Just follow your gut, Mariss. It's the only thing you can trust. Dig around. If you find nothing, great. Live a long and happy life here. Raise a dozen babies. But if you *do* find something, you'd better know it now, before you become another Farra. Before it's too late."

Once the door closed behind him, Mariss slumped against the wall. He had come in here without an invitation and stirred everything up. She no longer knew what to believe—about the Colony, about Adrian—about her feelings for Kade, and his feelings for her. One minute he was telling her he had taken his fill of her, the next he was all over her, as if he couldn't get enough. *Sex isn't love,* she reminded herself sternly. And she had the battle scars to prove it. Kade acted jealous. He sounded jealous. Any woman would believe he was jealous. But for what? Jealous for her body, or her time, or just on general, possessively male principles?

Or was he jealous for her love?

Mariss couldn't think about it. Her mind was dead tired, her heart in turmoil. She only wanted to sleep. But Kade had also stirred up questions about the Colony. And he was right. He knew her too well. She *was* a naturally curious person.

A moment later, her cyber-unit was humming softly atop the small desk in the room, the scrap of paper Kade had scrawled on lying beside it. She had plugged her cyber-unit into the wall socket which led to the main Colony computer and had already read the public-access material—information on amenities, features, history. Now she began to probe deeper...

NINETEEN

Mariss walked through the entry doors onto the front steps of the administration building. Adrian had said he would meet her here and take her to her orientation.

She smiled to herself. It was a beautiful day. Crisp, clear, golden. The colors seemed extraordinarily bright, the scents of nearby flowers richer than she'd ever smelled. The Colony was an exquisite place to live.

She vaguely recalled being disturbed in the night, by Kade of all people. He'd said some things to her, unpleasant things.

She frowned, recalling bits and pieces of their talk. They seemed to float up from her memory as if through a fog. She felt pleasant now, happy. Did she really want to remember?

But Kade was involved. She couldn't help wanting to think about him. A tingle shot through her right temple. Mariss rubbed it.

She had awakened surprisingly late, but refreshed, feeling more confident and sure of her future than she had in weeks. She and Adrian would build a beautiful future together. Now, her serenity was disturbed, like pebbles tossed on a clear pond. She shook her head.

Her cyber-unit. She had used it to hack into the Colony databanks. Of course. But what had she learned? She couldn't remember.

"Mariss! Good morning." Adrian strolled up the steps toward her from a waiting hovercar. "You look exceptionally well-rested. I knew a good night's sleep would work wonders for you." He kissed her temple.

"Adrian." Mariss gazed up at him, liking the feel of his lips on her skin. He was more handsome than ever, stronger, more assured than he had seemed yesterday. Yesterday had been confusing in myriad ways. But today, she knew she belonged here with him. How could she have ever doubted it? It was so clear to her now.

He smiled brightly, and Mariss noticed again how attractive he was—his golden hair gleaming in the sunlight, his eyes a brilliant azure. "Come. I think you'll enjoy what we have in store." He led her to the hovercar, and she slipped in beside him.

He steered the car through the grounds of the administration complex, arriving at a small building set away from the main area. He got out and helped her down, just like a perfect gentleman. "Mariss. Before you go in, I want to speak to you, seriously, about something."

"What?"

He pulled her from the walkway to a stretch of verdant grass and clasped her hands in his. "It has been brought to my attention that you spent part of the night using your cyber-unit to move into areas you don't have proper clearance for."

Embarrassment flushed through her. How had he known?

He patted her hands. "No damage was done, sweetheart, but it's important for you to understand that it's best if you limit your computer use to your own programs."

The soft wash of warmth she had felt for him began to dissolve in the harsh reality of his words. "Adrian, how did you know about this?"

He chuckled. "We know almost everything that happens here at the Colony. For our own protection. What if you hadn't been my future wife? What if some otherworlder had been trying to gain access? We must protect ourselves, our way of life. That's how we manage to maintain such a paradise here on Elysia."

"But how did you *know?"* Mariss was starting to realize Adrian frequently side-stepped her queries.

"You triggered a security alarm when you passed the first level, Mariss. I don't know much about computers myself, but I know you must have been doing something you shouldn't. Locke asked me to speak with you about it, explain the situation. Now, don't look so upset," he said, lifting her chin with his lean, tanned finger. "No harm was done. Just don't do it anymore, all right? We have plenty of other entertaining—and safe—diversions."

Clasping her hand, Adrian led the way toward the front doors. But Mariss remembered now, with crystal clarity, something she *had* stumbled onto. The listing of citizens who had been "dismissed from service." Her steps froze, and she slipped her hand from his. "Adrian, I want to visit the old people."

Adrian turned slowly and stared at her, a mystified expression on his face. "Old people? What do you mean?"

"Where are the old people?"

"I told you before, Mariss. Most of them are serving the Corporation off-world, in high-level posts."

"I mean the elderly ones, Adrian."

"They're in a neighboring colony."

"Then take me there."

He chuckled, the sound ringing unnaturally in the still tropical air. "They prefer not to be disturbed. There really aren't that many, Mariss. The Colony is a young settlement."

"Then your parents. I want to be introduced to them."

He frowned. "My parents died, Mariss."

"I'm sorry."

"It's all right, Mariss. There's nothing to worry about." He laid a reassuring hand on her arm. His blue eyes grew intense. "Trust me." He slipped his arms around her and tugged her close. Lowering his head, he kissed her. Really kissed her. Mariss met his kiss, worked with it, leaned into him. He was too tall. Mariss felt she had to stretch to meet him halfway. And it was pleasant—merely pleasant. With a stab of longing, she missed Kade more than she ever had.

Adrian lifted his head and sighed with satisfaction. "That's better. You and I will be a happy couple, I guarantee it. Now, come." His hand on her back, he began to maneuver her toward the doors.

Mariss dug in her heels. “Then why can’t we conceive our children the natural way? I’m willing to take the risk, Adrian.”

He studied her, so Mariss continued. “What if we made love outside somewhere, on a picnic or something, and—it just happened? I got pregnant? It would be our child, regardless of its characteristics.”

He nodded, “Yes, that’s true.” Then he smiled, his long fingers playing along her bare arm. “You’re that anxious to consummate our marriage, that you would mate in the open? Isn’t that rather...uncivilized?”

“I know you want to wait,” she said firmly. “But you haven’t answered my question. What if I get pregnant without this in vitro business?”

“It won’t happen, Mariss. These things are controlled, for our own benefit and the benefit of the Colony at large.”

“Controlled, how?”

He sighed, running his hand over his handsome face. She knew she was a trial to him, and not exactly what he had been expecting. If she hadn’t met Kade, would she be asking all these questions?

“Tell me about the in vitro fertilization. Kade was asking some good questions last night at dinner. I want the answers.”

“I told you all I know. There are no birth defects. Surely you don’t want one of our children born retarded, or...damaged in some way?”

“Maybe it’s not my first choice, but if that’s what the Maker of the Universe gives me, I would still love my baby.”

“Why, when it can so easily be prevented? It’s not a horrific procedure, Mariss. Merely sensible. At the 32-cell stage, the zygotes are screened for fifty-two thousand birth defects. The defective ones are discarded.”

“Are birth defects all you screen for? Then why is every man around here almost two meters tall? And Kade is right. Why is everyone so perfectly beautiful?”

He grimaced. “Mariss, you’re beginning to try my patience. Obviously, tall people have tall children. As for beauty, Land is merely jealous of us.” In a nervous gesture,

Adrian laced his thumb in his belt, his long fingers tapping out a tattoo rhythm on the belt's surface.

Mariss smiled wryly. "Now that, I seriously doubt. Besides, what you say is nonsense. Offspring often take on characteristics of the mother. I'm not particularly tall."

"We have a method to screen for height passed on through the father," he said carefully, his fingers tapping away. "Spermatozoa which carry a recessive, defective gene for height are not allowed to fertilize the eggs."

"*Defective?* Since when is shortness a defect?"

"Mariss..." he said in exasperation. "It's just an expression."

"What's the cut-off?"

"What? The cut-off?"

"How short can a man be?"

"1.82 meters."

It was several centimeters taller than Kade. "I see. So a man like Kade—he'd be considered too short?"

He threw his hands up in exasperation. "Who cares? You indicated in your preferences that you preferred taller men." Mariss bit her lip. She *had* indicated that, out of a girlish notion that taller men were somehow stronger, sexier. Her ex's had been average. This time, she had been shooting for perfection.

Adrian continued, "Studies show that tall men are perceived as having greater leadership potential, greater charisma. And good looks also count. You know that's true. Handsome people are rewarded. They're looked up to. Doors open for them. Our sons and daughters will be given every advantage, Mariss. Every chance to be leaders in the civilized galaxy. It's our way." He traced her cheek, turned her face up to his. "Besides, just look at you. You're a product of genetic manipulation yourself. I see it in your eyes."

Mariss blinked her genetically enhanced violet eyes. She didn't know if Adrian was trying to be intentionally funny with his pun, but she doubted it. "That was my parents' decision, not mine."

"But you indicated on your application that you willingly accept such a concept. Am I not right?"

"I *may* have..." Probably because she'd been thinking of her own situation. She would hate for people to consider her different because of the color of her eyes. "But prenatal eye-color selection was a fad. You know that. I would have been perfectly happy with brown eyes. I certainly don't think it's necessary."

Adrian shrugged. "Of course not. That's why this is even better. We *don't* manipulate the genes. We make the best of our existing gene pool. It's much *cleaner* that way, don't you think?"

"No, I—" Adrian was confusing her. But one question burned in her mind. She cocked her head, her eyes narrowed. "Tell me, Adrian. If Kade wanted to join the Colony, would you allow him in?"

Adrian didn't even hesitate. He crossed his arms, his handsome mouth pinched with distaste. "No. He is completely unacceptable in many ways, least of which is his inadequate height."

"Kade is hardly inadequate. And if it's not his height, then what? What would keep him out?"

Adrian threw out a hand in exasperation. "He's undisciplined. Problematic. Anyone who looks at him knows that." He exhaled, his expression becoming more gentle. He settled his hands on her shoulders. "I know you fancy he's your friend, sweetheart. But you don't know about him. *I* do. I've looked into it. It turns out your so-called friend Kadin Land is a felon. He's an *ex-convict,* Mariss. He's not Colony material at all."

Mariss smiled wryly, a sinking feeling in the pit of her stomach. "If you're trying to shock me, Adrian, you're failing miserably. I know all about Kade's record, and his past. I don't appreciate you digging into his personal files. It's none of your business. How *did* you learn about it, anyway?"

"We have a special understanding with the Interstellar Police in this sector, Mariss. I simply had to ask, and they allowed me access to his record."

Mariss cursed herself for mentioning the difficulties she and Kade had had with the cops. It boded no good. She prayed

Kade would be able to leave with little difficulty. Certainly Adrian didn't want him around. She lifted her eyes to him. "Adrian, Kade's record doesn't tell the whole story. It wasn't his fault."

"Of course he would tell you that. *All* convicts say that. None of them are ever guilty. Your Kadin Land is known to be a consummate and practiced liar."

"No." Kade hadn't been lying to her. She knew it in her heart. But somehow, Adrian was managing to stir up doubts where none had existed before.

Adrian squeezed her shoulders. "Mariss. You should have nothing more to do with him. He's unstable. You know in your heart that what I'm saying is right."

Mariss *knew* what he said wasn't true. But for some reason, she *wanted* to believe him. She shook off the feeling, knowing how hurt Kade would be if she even thought such a thing of him. "His record isn't *him,*" she insisted. "The incident at the Academy was years ago."

"Incident! He murdered a fellow student, in cold blood! Besides, it's not just his past that has me concerned. He's been arrested numerous times over the years. He was arrested only months ago, Mariss. On Barron Outpost. He was inciting a riot. He's a drunk, and he flaunts authority."

"No," Mariss said firmly. "He told me about what happened on Barron Outpost. He was helping a runaway girl who'd gotten in over her head. She was about to be raped by these—*men,* more than Kade could take on alone. So he set a small explosion as a distraction. It worked. The girl got away, disappeared into the maze of the outpost. But unfortunately, Kade didn't. He was arrested."

Adrian looked at her in disbelief. "And you truly believe this tale he told you? *Mariss,"* he chided. "You're too unsophisticated, too easy to exploit. Your mind doesn't work like *his* does, so you can't conceive of someone lying to you like he does. Frankly, Mariss, I cannot understand a woman of your high calibre even giving the man a second glance, much less proclaiming him your friend." His voice intensified. "It's *me* who deserves your kind regard. *Me.* Remember me?

You traveled lightyears to be with me. I've waited all my life for you."

He cupped her face in his hands, his eyes pinning her in place. His voice dropped, becoming deep, husky with emotion. "I saw you, Mariss, and I knew you were the one I was destined to share my life with. Don't throw away our future over this. Kadin Land is no good. He will always *be* no good. I know his kind. He could never commit to anything important. But I *can*. I can commit to you, to us. I swear it, on my life."

After such a pronouncement, Mariss could only nod weakly.

"Good. Now come. You have important business, and so do I." He escorted her inside and left her in the care of an administration staff member, then departed with the promise to pick her up once her session was over.

***

The orientation had been thorough and surprisingly enjoyable. Through a combination of holos, vids, and interactive virtual reality, Mariss had gained a much fuller understanding of the philosophy behind the Colony.

A man in an administration-style jumpsuit had led her to an enclosed room, where she had been seated on a comfortable mauve couch. Once the holo began, Mariss watched with polite interest as it took her through the history of the Colony's founding and discussion of safety and security features. After several hours, she had actually dozed off. But when she woke, she was already on the review, and since she knew the correct answers, she was certain she must have been listening even while asleep.

She was beginning to regret her earlier discussion with Adrian. Now she understood not only the philosophy behind the Colony, but its many benefits. She couldn't remember the details of her discussion with Adrian, or what she learned during the orientation, but her fears were greatly diminished.

She glanced at Adrian as he walked beside her in the tropical garden. Exotic plant specimens, many of them from off-world, lined the walls and decorated sculpted hillsides. Adrian explained that entrance to this particular garden was restricted to a select few, but he had certain privileges and was able to obtain access whenever he wanted. Mariss would be included in this privilege in her own right, after a time.

Adrian must have sensed her eyes on him, because he turned and gazed at her with love in his eyes. Why had she fought him? Mariss wondered. She couldn't think of single reason. He led her to sit on a plasticene bench. She was wearing a full-length tunic in preparation for a formal dinner he had invited her to. A private dinner.

"Mariss." Adrian slipped to his knee before her. "Give me your hand."

Mariss extended her hand, and he clasped it. He slipped a box from his robe. Snapping it open, Mariss saw the jewel catch the light even before he removed the ring. He slipped it on her finger. "An ancient Earther rite, but fitting for my bride," he said, his blue eyes intent on her face. "We are now officially engaged." He rose and sat beside her. "I have moved up our wedding to the day after tomorrow."

"So soon?" Mariss stared at the red, translucent stone. It was shot through the center by a gold star. It was gorgeous. But a niggle of worry swirled in her chest. It wouldn't go away, even though Mariss was certain she had nothing to worry about.

"Certainly you have no objections?" Adrian smoothed her hair off her face. "You did so well at the orientation that I have been given permission to wed you even sooner than I had hoped. And, I confess, I am anxious to consummate our union." He leaned close to her, running his hand up her side, his palm warm on her tunic-clad body. He ran his lips along her neck, spoke huskily into her ear. "My sweet, I will enjoy you. As you will enjoy me." He tugged her closer. Despite the sense of euphoria his touch now seemed to engender in her, Mariss could feel her body resisting him. Her mind seemed to crave his touch, but she knew in her heart she really didn't want him. Even to herself, she made no sense.

An instant later, she was on her feet, backing away from Adrian. A primitive impulse had awakened in her, telling her to maintain distance between them.

Adrian rose as well, confusion and puzzlement mingled on his sculpted features. Again his fingers began tapping out a nervous tattoo on his belt. "Mariss? You run from me?"

She shook her head. "No. Not at all. I'm just—not ready yet. Please. You said it would be two weeks before we were wed."

"I will not reschedule our wedding date. It took too much effort to change it."

A piercing headache was starting to throb behind her temples. Mariss pressed her fingers to the spot and massaged, but it did little good. "You should have consulted me, Adrian. A woman has a right to have a say in her own wedding."

He stared at her for a full minute. "Very well, I agree. Next time, I will consult you. But for now, our wedding is the day after tomorrow, after you complete your orientation."

The headache had already begun to recede. Mariss lowered her hands. "I thought I completed that today."

"The first part is completed, that's true. Tomorrow, you will have a physical. Nothing complicated, but it is important we establish your health and ensure your body is prepared to have our children."

"I already had a physical, when I applied for this program, remember?" she said dryly. Usually it was Adrian reminding *her* what she had done to apply for the Computer Mating Service of Iridion.

He nodded. "Of course. But things change. People change. And that was months ago. Don't forget you had a traumatic time in the wilderness, Mariss. We're just going to check you over, make certain you're perfect in every way." He clasped her hands. "I have faith everything will turn out wonderfully well." He leaned forward and kissed her forehead. "The Maker knows, I am a patient man. I have waited years for such a perfect mate. I can wait a few more hours."

Mariss nodded, feeling she had been granted a reprieve, but not certain from what.

***

Mariss stepped from her bathroom and stared. She shouldn't be surprised, not after last night. Kade was sprawled on her bed, his head resting on his arms, watching her. She hadn't seen him all day. Just the sight of him filled her with joy. She had the wild urge to run to him and throw herself on him.

With supreme effort, she restrained herself. But she couldn't help meeting his broad smile with one of her own. "You never do knock, do you?"

"I had to see how you liked your little orientation today."

"Why do you care so much?" she prodded, hoping, wishing for some indication of his inner feelings.

But true to form, he shrugged dismissively. "Wondered if you realized yet what a mistake you made in deciding to come here."

She walked toward him, stared down at him. He may be feigning a relaxed pose, but she knew he was coiled as tight as a spring. She had come to read Kade's moods remarkably well. The thought pleased her immensely.

But then a wall seemed to drop across her thoughts. She shouldn't think about Kade. Not now. Now, her energies belonged to the Colony. "I—I don't feel I made a mistake."

"What?" Kade dropped his feet to the floor. "Why in hell not? Didn't you ask any questions, tap into their computer, anything?"

"Yes, I did. I used my computer last night, I think. And I talked to Adrian..." Mariss began. *That's right, she talked to Adrian. Before the orientation. They had argued, about Kade, about pre-selecting babies. Why had she forgotten that?* Mariss sat beside Kade. "Kade," she said carefully. "I'm not sure of anything anymore. I think things aren't quite right, but I'm not sure how."

Her words triggered an immediate response in Kade. He wrapped his arms around her, his strong hand stroking her back. Mariss curled into him. It felt like coming home. She sighed with contentment. The wall in her mind began to dissolve, and she experienced all her feelings for Kade in full. At that moment, nothing else mattered—not her future, not whether he returned her feelings—nothing but Kade. Her emotions stirred her so deeply, she found her eyes moist. She blinked hard.

Kade spoke softly to her, his voice tender. "Mariss, you don't have to stay. I can take you from here. I'll find a way. There are some freighters in the docking bay. I've seen them. We can steal one."

Mariss pulled back. "Kade, that's dangerous. Especially for you. If the cops catch you again—"

"Dammit, Mariss, you think I care?"

Mariss felt herself falling into the depths of his eyes. She laid her hand on his chest, felt his strong heartbeat. "Maybe *you* don't, but *I* care."

Kade saw her ring sparkle. "What's this?" He lifted her hand and examined the engagement ring. He whistled low. "Mariss, this thing is worth a fortune."

"I suppose it is."

"Trust me, it is. It's a Jovian fire stone, for God's sake. You could buy a starship with this." He looked in her eyes. "*He* give you this?"

Mariss nodded. She opened her mouth to speak, but couldn't think of anything to say.

Kade slipped off the bed and paced across the room. He kept his broad back to her. "I can help you get off the planet, Mariss, if you decide you want out. Damn straight, I'll do that." He raked his hand through his thick hair. "But I need to know where you want me to take you."

"What do you mean?"

He turned to her, his hands on his hips. "Just that. Where will you go? Back to Earth?"

"I—I haven't thought that far. No, not to Earth. I was thinking..." *With you,* she thought to herself, afraid to give her words voice. "I don't know."

Kade's shoulders sagged. "Maybe we'd better find out a little more about this place before rushing you out of here," he said, his voice hollow. "I don't want to ruin your future for nothing."

"Kade, you wouldn't be—"

"Come on. Let's find out what makes this place tick. Then you'll know what you're getting into, one way or the other."

He thrust his hand out, and she took it. He squeezed it reassuringly before they slipped into the hall.

They traveled together down the corridor only a few feet from her door. Kade stopped at a door labeled "Staff only." He tapped the button, and it retracted to reveal a stairway. "I rigged the button last night, so I could get in and out. Usually, it's locked."

Mariss nodded. His talents never ceased to amaze her. The door closed behind them, leaving them in darkness. But Kade was prepared for this, too. He slipped a handlight from his jacket pocket and flicked it on. "This way." He led the way down a flight of stairs, then another flight. From there, he entered a second door.

They traveled through what was obviously a service corridor, with exposed pipes and vents in the ceiling. Dim wall sconces provided yellowish light. Mariss hadn't thought about what was *under* the complex. But it was so immense, it was like another city down here. Corridors ran in every direction, stretching into the dark beyond, intersecting other corridors.

As if reading her thoughts, Kade whispered, "These corridors lead everywhere. I've been all through this city, Mariss."

"But—why?"

He glanced back at her, his eyes catching the dim light. "Why do you think?"

Mariss felt herself blushing in the dark. She held his hand tighter.

They walked for what seemed miles, and probably was. Here she was again, on a long hike with Kade. She rather liked the idea. No, she loved the idea, she finally admitted. For the most part, they didn't speak, for fear of being overheard. Now and then, Kade named the part of the Colony which was above them, or where a service door went. They passed a wider area where service hovercars were parked, each stamped with the Colony's blue-and-gold crest.

"The dome is just ahead," Kade said. A second later, he froze. He yanked Mariss down behind a hovercar.

Mariss barely breathed. Then she heard it. A hovercar, coming their way. She remained as still as she could, until the sound of it filled the tunnel before them. Then it vanished down the corridor in the direction they had come.

"Colony security," Kade whispered. They waited several moments in silence in the dark.

"Kade." He glanced at Mariss. "I don't think you should be doing this. It's too dangerous."

"Mariss, we've already decided. Don't argue with me now. Come on." He stood and stepped tentatively into the corridor, then waved her forward.

Finally, Kade stopped at a service door and opened it. They moved up several flights of stairs, coming out into a finished hallway with what looked like a series of laboratories exiting off it.

"There are computers in all of them, Mariss. Take your pick."

Mariss nodded. She read the names on the doors. One immediately piqued her interest. It read "Screening criteria."

"This one." She nodded toward the door. Kade slipped a device she hadn't seen before from his jacket. He tapped in a code and the door retracted.

"Where did you get that?"

"From an unobservant security guard," he replied nonchalantly.

Mariss stared at him, speechless. She had been spending her time being pampered and courted by Adrian, and Kade had been risking himself getting into all sorts of trouble on her behalf.

While unoccupied, the lab was obviously in use. Besides panels of computer controls, there were tables and desks, printouts, bulletin boards, schedules, papers and disks everywhere.

Mariss parked herself in front of a control panel. "I think I can access this one. It's similar to ones I used at the Institute where I worked."

Kade stayed by the door, guarding it, while she went to work. She moved into the main databank. Where she expected to find a list of the criteria used to select suitable offspring, instead she found a listing of criteria used to choose applicants to the program.

Fascinated, Mariss scanned the requirements. She knew most of them from when she applied to the program. But there were others which hadn't been shared with her. For women, their fertility quotient was weighted heavily. As was overall health. None of this was too surprising. The Colony prided itself on being a place for people to raise families. Mariss hadn't realized infertile people were completely excluded, however. Her eyes flicked to Kade. Another reason he would be found unacceptable. She found the idea appalling. Even if a person couldn't have his or her own biological children, he or she could still make a good parent, and a wonderful mate.

Also given strong weight were the ability and desire to conform to the dictates of a higher authority. Mariss grimaced. Naturally this was important, she reflected. Just look at Adrian's reaction to Kade, a maverick if ever there was one. As for why she had rated high in this, Mariss thought she understood. When she first applied, she had just exited a terrible relationship. All she had wanted was a safe haven. Of course she had wanted to conform. She had wanted to be *loved.*

An offshoot of this was the desire to avoid conflict. Mariss sighed. Yes, she had certainly exhibited that characteristic throughout her second marriage. She hadn't wanted to confront Roldo for fear of losing him. And look what happened. She had lost him anyway.

But since then...She glanced toward Kade and smiled. She had been anything but docile toward the man who was even now standing guard to protect her. Kade brought out the worst in her—or, more accurately, her spirited best.

Her eyes drifted down the screen. Another factor was given an even higher rating than the rest put together. In fact, if the candidate scored below the 75 percentile ranking in this particular characteristic, their application was rejected. No exceptions.

"Kade," Mariss said, her voice weak.

He joined her at the terminal.

"I know why they wanted me. I know now."

He laid his hand on her shoulder. "Mariss, what? What is it?"

She turned her gaze to his. Of its own accord, her body began to shake. "I'm highly susceptible to brainwashing."

TWENTY

"That's it. We're out of here."

The words were barely out of Kade's mouth before the wind was knocked from him. He gasped in pain and sagged to the floor, barely catching a glimpse of a pair of Colony security guards standing over him.

The next instant, a terrific pain sliced through his brain, and everything went black.

The last thing he heard was Mariss screaming.

***

"I knew he was trouble. Didn't I say so?" Adrian was livid. He stood in front of Mariss, his tall frame filling her vision.

"If you hurt Kade, I swear, I'll—"

"You'll what?" Adrian strode back and forth in front of her, his pace choppy, quick. "My God, Mariss, I can't believe you were with him, late at night, getting into areas you have no business entering. It was like a childish prank!"

As soon as Kade had been knocked out, she had been escorted from the lab and returned to the administration center in a security hovercar. Adrian and Locke had been waiting. Adrian convinced Locke he could manage Mariss if she were left with him.

So it turned out that they were now together in her guest room. Mariss had nagged him mercilessly about Kade until she received the concession that he wouldn't be harmed, his movements merely "contained" until an off-world ship arrived.

"I want to see Kade."

"You can. Tomorrow," Adrian said. "He's been taken to the clinic for the injury to his cranium. I wish you wouldn't become so worked up over this, Mariss. He's not worth your concern. Look at the trouble he's already gotten you into!"

"*You're* the one who's worked up. And it was because of *me,* Adrian, that we went to the lab. He knew I was worried that you haven't been straight with me."

Adrian propped his hands on his hips. "In what way, Mariss? Tell me. I have done *everything* for you. Built you a house, paid for your transit here, given you a beautiful ring. *Everything.*"

Her voice grew chilly. "I saw the criteria, Adrian. The criteria for selection. I know why I was chosen to come here."

Adrian looked at her blankly. "Yes, so? Of course you know. You're my match. Though, frankly, I'm beginning to wonder if there wasn't some mistake."

"Because I'm not as weak-willed as you would prefer?"

"Mariss, that isn't fair."

"Isn't it? Isn't that important to living here, being willing to conform? But the winner, the one that *really* puts it over the top, is suggestibility! I couldn't believe it when I read it, but it's true, isn't it? You're brainwashing people!"

Adrian stared at her several seconds, his fingers idly tapping at his belt in that nervous habit he had. Then he started to chuckle. His chuckle grew into a full-blown belly laugh.

"What's so funny? I don't find it funny!" Mariss cried, frustrated beyond belief.

"Mariss, the computer you were so ungraciously hacking into contained records on a student's lab project. A student's, not the files for the Computer Mating Service. This poor student's project has nothing to *do* with you, or with any Colony resident. The fellow is working with white rats."

She felt her anger begin to drain. "Rats?"

Still chuckling, Adrian nodded. "Yes, Mariss. Rats. How much of the file did you read?"

"I thought I read enough." She lifted her chin a notch. But a sense of embarrassment was starting to overwhelm her. In a detached part of her mind, she noticed Adrian's long fingers slide away from his belt.

He closed the distance between them, his laughter fading. "Do you really trust me so little?" he asked softly. "I would never do anything to hurt you, Mariss. Never. I—I can honestly say, I love you."

"Adrian." She let him hold her, resting her head on his chest. Her emotions surged and roiled, drowning her in confusion. Adrian said he loved her. She had learned never to trust those words. But still, he had said them. He may even mean them. And what had she done but return his honest emotion with distrust, with fear? She was an appalling excuse for a future wife.

Mariss sniffled. Gradually, a sense of calm enveloped her. She honestly wasn't certain what she had become so worked up about.

Adrian pulled back and cupped her face in his hands. "There now. Don't cry." He brushed tears from her cheeks and kissed her nose. "Everything will be fine, sweetheart. Just trust me, okay?"

Mariss nodded, feeling weak beyond belief. "I'm sorry, Adrian. I just wasn't prepared for the—the post-conception screening idea. It scares me. Can't we bypass it?"

Adrian sighed. "Perhaps we can. I have more than a little pull around here. Besides, just look at us." He turned her to face the mirror over the bureau. Mariss saw them standing side-by-side, he, tall and glorious; she, only reaching his shoulder, her face ravaged by emotion. "We are a perfect couple, aren't we? Our children will be especially blessed."

Mariss nodded. Soon, Adrian allowed her to slip into the bed, to sleep, while he remained close by her side.

***

Kade opened his eyes and squinted at the bright light. His skull throbbed. The pain was centered behind his left ear.

"Just relax, Kade. The effects of the anesthetic will wear off in a moment."

It was Farra's voice. Kade blinked a few times, until he was able to focus on her. Her blond hair encircled her delicate face like a halo as she looked down at him.

"Mariss." His throat was tight, his tongue stiff. He swallowed and tried again. "Mariss."

Farra smiled. "She's here, Kade. Waiting to see you. That's

why I woke you up. My husband resealed the fracture in your cranium. But you need to rest."

"Out. How long?"

"You've been here since the night before last. And don't worry about your friend. Adrian's been seeing to her. She's just fine. In fact, here she is."

Kade twisted his head toward the door. A fuzzy Mariss stepped into his field of vision. He stretched his hand toward her, but she came no closer than a meter from the bed.

"Kade, I'm sorry you got hurt, especially since it was on account of worrying about me," she said, her voice soft, melodic.

Kade's chest suddenly ached with the need to touch her, but she wasn't taking the hint. He tried to wave her over, his hand moving weakly. "Mariss, come here."

"No, Kade. I...I don't want to upset you further. I'm only here for a few minutes. Adrian said I could see you, but the doctor recommends I not stay long."

"Adrian?" The name struck him like a blow. Kade could focus better now. He saw her face. She seemed to be hiding her softness under a firm mask. "He's around?"

"He's waiting for me in the reception area. I know you're wondering why I'm with him. But believe me. We were wrong in what we thought. I understand everything better now, and—" she laughed lightly. "I was really jumping to some bad conclusions. We both were."

Kade stared hard at her. Mariss didn't seem her old self. Or maybe it was just the blow to his head that had him confused. If she would only come closer, let him look into her eyes... "Mariss, please. Come *here.*"

Tentatively, as if afraid to get too close to him, she moved toward the bed.

He dropped his voice to a whisper. "What about what you learned? The brainwashing? You read the file, remember? About why you were chosen to come here?"

An embarrassed smile wreathed her face as she dropped her eyes. "We made a very stupid mistake, Kade. No one's being brainwashed here. We stumbled onto a student's project.

Everything's fine, really. You have to trust me on this."

Kade's intuition nagged at him fiercely as he looked at her. Something wasn't right, but he was too sore and drugged to put his finger on it. And his heart wasn't helping. All he could think about was losing her forever to Adrian Young and the Colony.

Mariss seemed to read his expression. "I'm much happier than I've been in a long time," she reassured him. "Everything's finally working out for me. Please, Kade. Be happy for me."

Happy? That was a laugh. Of course he wanted her to be happy. That's all he ever wanted. But he wanted her to be happy with *him.*

She took a half-step back, reclaiming her distance. Her voice brightened as she changed the subject. "I hope you're going to feel better soon. I was in a clinic yesterday, too, one at the dome. For my physical. And guess what? I get to go back today."

He glanced at her trim, healthy body. "What in the hell for?"

"It's sort of a pre-wedding thing." Her voice ended awkwardly. "My—my uterus isn't quite ready for babies after all. Something about unneeded tissue which has formed."

Her medical talk swept past him. All Kade could hear was one word. "Wedding?"

"It's tomorrow, Kade. I wish you could attend. But a transport is arriving later this morning, and Locke has gotten you passage on it." Her voice dropped, grew poignant. "Perhaps this is for the best. It might be kind of awkward, considering."

Kade was more awake now. "Yeah, considering," he said dryly. Considering he had been locked in a passionate embrace with this woman just days ago. Considering he couldn't stand to see her with another man. Considering he was in love with her. But now, finally, it seemed their paths were going to separate.

"Well, I have to go. They'll let you know about the transport. I don't think I'll be seeing you again. I—I want to thank you. For everything."

Her eyes finally met Kade's, clear and honest. The impact sent a shock through Kade's heart. She meant every word she said. Mariss Sakari was leaving him for good.

"Mariss, don't go," he said on a breath. But she had already turned and left the room.

***

"Kade. Kadin Land, wake up."

Kade's cracked his eyes open. It was Farra again. This time, she spoke to him with a sense of urgency. "They're coming for you, Kade. You have to wake up now."

Kade wasn't in the least groggy this time. He remembered his visit from Mariss and a flurry of questions plagued his mind. "What time is it?"

"It's just 1015, Kade. But the transport is set to leave at noon."

Kade swung his legs over the side of the bed. "Farra, Mariss said something about going to the hospital. What was that about?"

Farra shrugged. "Probably the usual cleansing procedure. We all go through it."

"Yeah? Well, I don't like the sound of it." He planted his feet on the floor. "Can you look up her medical record?"

Instantly, Farra's fingers traveled to her temple. But she gazed at Kade a moment before nodding, almost reluctantly. She turned to a wall unit and tapped a few keys. "Here's her record. Results of yesterday's physical, a few other notes. She's fit." She glanced toward Kade. "Is that what you're worried about, whether Mariss is healthy?"

Kade smirked. "Not exactly. Let me see it." He leaned over her shoulder. The language was in medic's code, and Kade could decipher very little. Just dates and readings and levels. He wasn't certain what he was looking for. Something about brainwashing maybe. It was just a last-ditch attempt to change things, he knew that. But still..."What's this? Post-mitosis intra-cleansing?"

Farra didn't answer, just stared at where he pointed.

"Farra? What is it? Is it something important?"

"I suppose that depends on your point of view."

"What in the hell does that mean?"

She turned her large blue eyes to him. "It means she's scheduled to have an abortion."

TWENTY-ONE

Kade stared at Farra, numb, confused. Her words didn't register at first. They didn't make sense. Suddenly, feeling returned with a vengeance. Kade felt as if he'd been slammed in the stomach. All the oxygen drained out of his lungs. He couldn't catch his breath. He stumbled back. Farra's image swam in front of his eyes. "That's not possible. You read it wrong."

Farra looked at the read-out again. "No. That's what it says." Her eyes were huge as she looked toward Kade, who had slumped against the bed. "Kade," she said softly, "is it yours?"

Kade was fighting with what he was hearing, trying to fit the news into what he knew about his own health—*they said I'd almost certainly never be able to have children.* It wasn't his, that's all there was to it. Couldn't be. She was pregnant before their flight from the Nexus Spaceport. Still...she had shown no signs of pregnancy in all the time they had spent together, even when she had nearly died. "How old is it? I mean, how far along is she?"

Farra's eyes returned to the readout. "Only a few days. Conception is pinpointed at 2499.6/06. That's four days ago, Kade. Only four days. The day before you and she came here."

Kade sucked in a breath, his lungs aching. Moisture welled up in his eyes. *My baby.* Damn it all, it was his baby. *Our* baby.

Then the full truth of the revelation settled in. Kade's stomach twisted as if it was being turned inside out. "She's getting rid of it?" He shoved away from the bed, every muscle in his body tense, ready for battle.

"This afternoon, yes."

Kade repeated, "She's getting *rid* of it? Like hell she is. Where in the hell is she?"

"At the central clinic, in the west sector."

Without another look at Farra, Kade stormed to the door—and found it locked. "Open this up, damn it!" He pounded on it.

Farra rushed to his side. "I can leave, but you can't. Not until the guards come." Her voice fell. "I'm sorry."

Kade turned on her, his hands gripping her slender shoulders. "For the love of the Maker, get me out of here."

"I—" Farra pressed her fingers to her temple. "I—I can't."

"You have to! They're going to kill my baby!"

Farra pressed her eyelids closed. A moment later, she opened them, a new resolve in her eyes. She turned to a cabinet and opened it. She removed a vial and pressed it into Kade's palm. "That's all I can—"

She moaned and collapsed in a chair. Kade moved toward her, but at that moment, the door opened and a pair of Colony security guards entered. Kade managed to slip the vial into his pocket unseen, still not knowing what it was. "Kadin Land, you're coming with us," said the first guard, a slender brunette. She gestured, and her subordinate—a hulking redhead—spun Kade around and snapped a pair of manacles on his wrists.

"What in the—" Kade shoved the woman aside, but she apparently expected resistance. She delivered a swift sidekick into his stomach.

The hulking fellow supplied a chop to his back, bringing Kade to his knees. "No more funny stuff, buddy. Get up."

The hulk yanked him to his feet, and Kade found himself being marched out the clinic door and into a security vehicle. The passenger section was encased in solid plexiform. He was sealed in.

The car slipped into a tunnel and descended for a few feet before leveling out. Kade fumed. Time was draining away, running through his fingers like sand while he was led around by these idiots. "You have no right to detain me," he said.

The guards ignored him.

When he wasn't thinking up fruitless ways to escape, his mind was filled with thoughts of Mariss, and their baby. A miracle, that's what it was. And she was going to let them kill it.

Rage coursed through him. She wasn't even going to tell him! If she were only here now, he thought, flexing his fingers despite the manacles, he'd wring her neck! She had become so like these people—these sterile-minded, rigid, heartless people—that she would dispose of his child—*his child!*—in order to carry out their breeding program.

But his child wasn't good enough for them. For *her*. Not good enough to live.

The hovercar swept into a huge docking bay. Kade saw what awaited him and shuddered. The craft was black, with the blood-red insignia of the interstellar police. They had come for him. *No doubt the Colony turned me over, gladly.* Kade wondered if Mariss knew. Bitterness welled up. He wondered if she even cared.

He was placed in the ship's brig. Only one guard had been left to watch over him, and a young one at that. The rest were probably off enjoying the Colony's amenities.

The guard was reading a magazine. Or a comic book, more like, Kade thought ruefully. Since the guard's eyes were turned, Kade felt it was safe to find out what Farra had shoved into his hand before he was taken from the clinic. She had seemed in such pain when she did it. For all their medical advances, even the Colony couldn't seem to fix a simple migraine.

He slipped the narrow cylinder from his pocket. Xygathene. 65 percent solution. Kade smiled. It would do the trick. He eyed the youthful guard, who looked almost too young to shave.

Without warning, Kade cried out in agony, slamming his body into the side of the cell.

The guard was instantly on his feet. "What? What is it?"

Kade gripped his stomach, writhing in agony on the cell floor. He cried out again, a wordless, hideous sound which echoed painfully loud in the chamber. The young guard responded as most inexperienced people would—he flicked off the shield on the door and hurried to Kade's side.

Kade hit him in the face full force with a blast from the xygathene spray. He stuffed it back into his pocket. The guard collapsed in a heap. Kade rose and gave the cylinder a grateful toss. Painless, instant, and effective. As a prisoner, he'd been on the receiving end of the drug more times than he cared to recall. It felt good to dish it out to one of *them.*

He stepped toward the cell exit, then paused and looked back at the prone body. He had to think smart. Shove his feelings away for awhile, if he was to get through these next few hours. For starters, this kid was going to loan him a little something special.

***

Mariss stared ahead as the hovercar sped down the main streets of the Colony. A medic was beside her at the controls. Adrian had work to do and said he'd meet her after the purification.

Purification. What an odd term for a simple laser procedure. But the Colony had its way of referring to things. Part of its culture. She knew, in time, she would become used to it.

The hovercar moved toward the west sector of the Colony. Where the largest clinic was, Adrian had told her. Since they were following the tram line's route, Mariss wondered why Adrian had insisted a hovercar take her personally to the clinic. But, he had been extremely solicitous in the past day. Ever since she had followed Kade into the dome late at night and made a perfect fool of herself. It was a wonder Adrian still wanted her.

The hovercar slowed. Mariss looked up. A red-uniformed star cop was standing right in the center of the roadway, holding out his hands for them to stop. Sunlight glinted off his blood-red helmet, its smoked visor covering his face.

The medic downshifted, jerking Mariss forward. The car slowed, but continued to hurtle toward the cop. The cop stayed planted in the street, not giving one centimeter.

"He's insane!" the medic said, slamming on the reverse thrusters. Hovercar engines were so fine-tuned, brakes usually weren't necessary except in an emergency. The car stopped instantly, a meter from the cop, who hadn't even flinched. The medic looked around for the accident or problem, but there was no hint of trouble. "Officer, what is it? What's going on? Where are the security guards?"

The cop approached him. "Step out. We're conducting a search."

The medic complied, leaving Mariss sitting in the car. As soon as he was away from the car, the cop vaulted into the driver's seat beside Mariss. "I'm commandeering your transport. Security reasons," he told the shocked medic.

Mariss stared at the cop, apprehension giving way to something else...That mouth—that chin! Her jaw dropped. A thrill shot through her. Kade was going to steal her away, take her from her wedding, keep her for himself. After everything they had been through.

But she didn't want him to. She wanted to marry Adrian. *Didn't she?*

Kade shoved the car's engine on full. He didn't head toward the Colony entrance, as Mariss thought he would. Instead, he angled the hovercar straight for the dome, which rose from the center of the Colony. No, this didn't make any sense. "Kade?"

He tore off the helmet and tossed it in back. When she saw the expression on his face, Mariss wished he'd kept it on. His jaw was set in a grim line, his eyes were like chips of granite.

"Kade, what are you doing? You can't do this."

Then he turned on her, truly turned on her. The fury in his eyes was so intense, she hunched away from him against the hovercar door.

"How could you do it?" he demanded, his words like shards of ice. "It may mean nothing to you, but I happen to want it!"

Mariss stared at him, confused and afraid. "I don't know what you mean! You knew I was marrying Adrian, when we came here."

"That's no excuse!"

"Kade, you can't kidnap me like this! This is crazy!"

"*I'm* crazy? Is that why you don't want it, because I'm *crazy?* Afraid it's genetic? Well, I've just found out a little something that'll make you think twice about who's crazy, woman."

He had lost it. Truly lost it. There was no other explanation. Adrian's dire warnings about Kade's instability came back to her. "Kade, this isn't the answer. Let me go."

"Like hell I will!"

Anger coursed through Mariss. "How dare you take me! You have no right!"

"I have every fragging, bloody right, woman." The engine screamed as he pushed the hovercar to the max. A moment later, they were passing under the arched entrance to the dome. Mariss gazed upward. On both sides rose floor upon floor, more than thirty from the ground level to the top. Hovercar ramps criss-crossed the interior, allowing access to all floors.

But Kade ignored the neat rampways. He pulled back, and the car's nose pointed almost straight up. Mariss hung on as it shot upward past level after level. Finally, he pulled the car out of its arc and leveled off, cutting the engine at one of the hovercar parking spots three quarters of the way to the top. A surge of nausea swept through Mariss. Gamely, she swallowed it down.

Slipping the cop's helmet back on, Kade leapt out and came around to her side. "Get out."

Mariss discovered her fingers frozen on the hovercar door, she was gripping it so tightly.

Kade pried her fingers off and lifted her out. "Walk." He shoved her forward, none too gently, into a hallway.

"Where are we going? There will be security guards all over this place," she said.

His smile looked wicked under the cop's helmet. Mariss saw him palming a phase-gun in a holster at his side. She shivered. This was insane, all of it. She had a dreadful feeling Kade was going to get killed, and for what?

The scientists and lab techs they passed stepped aside and did nothing to interfere. Kade's cop uniform was enough to deter them from asking any questions. He must have been counting on that. The security guards also let him pass.

He stopped in front of a lab door and entered a security code. The door opened to admit them. Shoving Mariss in front of him, he entered.

Mariss glanced around. They were in some kind of lab, that was certain. But what kind of lab? And why?

"Kade, please, if I ever meant anything to you, tell me what this is about."

Kade laughed hollowly. "That's rich. Really rich." He shoved past her. "It's supposed to be right through here. Damn, that kid gives good directions."

He pushed through a swinging door. A couple of brown-garbed techs looked up and stared.

"Everybody out!" Kade barked. The techs complied instantly. Mariss wondered at the effect of the cop's uniform on the lab techs. No one even asked any questions.

She faced him, grasping his arms. "Kade, tell me what this is about. *Now.*"

His lips were thin. "You tell me. Let's take a look around, shall we?"

"Let's not, and say we did."

The voice was Adrian's. Mariss looked over Kade's shoulder and saw him standing there, pointing a phase-gun right at Kade's back. "Mariss, move aside. I'll protect you from this deviant sociopath."

Kade's phase-gun was in his hand before Mariss saw him move. Adrian cried out as his own phase-gun spun away. It took Mariss a moment to realize Kade had blasted it out of Adrian's hand.

"If you want to play with guns, learn how," Kade said dryly. "Now, how about you take off your belt?

"What?" Massaging his hand, Adrian made a weak attempt to paste a smile on his ashen face. "That's a silly request."

"Oh, is it? You've got some kind of controls on it. I'm giving you one warning. Take it off, or I shoot it off."

Adrian slowly unbuckled it and dropped it to the floor. "That's a nice boy," Kade said. "Keep your hands in the air, and I won't have to use this again."

"Kade, give the gun to me," Mariss said. "Please."

Kade stared at her. At least Mariss thought he was staring at her. She couldn't tell through that smoked visor. A muscle in his jaw tensed and flexed. "So, you don't trust me, Mariss? Why am I not surprised?"

His remark stung her so badly, Mariss felt tears forming behind her eyes. She blinked hard. This was the man who had saved her life, seen her to safety. What was she thinking?

"I—I don't know. I can't think." Mariss rubbed her head. Thoughts were forming and reforming in her mind faster than she could grasp hold of them. "What's going on?"

"Let me tell you a little story. Wonder why I'm dressed like this? Because lover boy was having me arrested."

"You deserve it!" Adrian cried. "You're a criminal."

Kade ignored Adrian's outburst, directing his comments at Mariss. "Guess where I spent the last hour? On board a cop's ship. And guess what I found when I managed to slip past the guard?"

"No one cares, Land. Just crawl back into the hole you slithered out of and leave decent people alone!"

Kade turned to him. "You're starting to get on my nerves, buddy."

"You're psychotic!"

"And you're plain evil. Mariss, do you have a headache right now?"

"Yes." She glanced at him in surprise. "I do. How did you know?"

"It's a side effect. Think of your first husband, what was his name?"

"Peck? Why—" Mariss stared at Kade in amazement. Peck had gotten headaches from abusing vagon. But only after years, and only when he was suffering from overdoses.

"Think about it, Mariss. Think!"

Kade seemed desperate for her to understand. She fought to collect her thoughts.

"Haven't you been feeling strange lately? I'll bet you have. Sharper sometimes, yet vague other times. As if you're ready to believe what people tell you, do exactly what they say without question. If what I found in that cop ship is any indication."

"Don't tell me you found vagon."

"Kilos and kilos. Enough to drug this entire place several times over."

"And so what?" Adrian said. "Cops are *supposed* to confiscate illegal drugs, am I right? Really, Land, you're building up some sort of case based on thin air. He's really quite sick, Mariss. Delusional."

Mariss' thoughts were coalescing now. She was beginning to feel like her old self. She turned on Adrian. "Kade is about the most centered person I have ever met." Was it her imagination, or was Adrian beginning to perspire?

He threw out his hands, beseeching her. "Don't give him a moment's consideration, Mariss. He's always been a liar and a troublemaker. It's in his genes."

Mariss gazed at Kade, wanting suddenly to see his eyes. As if sensing her need, he slipped his helmet off and dropped it. His eyes locked on hers, held. "He has never lied to me," Mariss said softly.

"Don't look at him that way!" Adrian said. "You can't trust your heart, Mariss. You never could."

His words, his sharp tone, brought Mariss up short. Trembling, she faced her fiancé.

"You know I speak the truth," Adrian said, his words honeyed, soft. "That's why you came here, isn't it? Because you always fall in love with the wrong kind of guy?" There was a snideness to Adrian's words which Mariss had never heard before. It frightened and angered her.

"Mariss, just go see for yourself." Kade gestured with the gun toward a swinging door leading into the heart of the lab. "The kid said it happened in the inner lab. Try through that door. Go on. Take a look."

"Mariss, stay here," Adrian said.

Mariss ignored his command. She found herself walking toward the door, pushing it open. A second later, she was inside.

"What do you see?" Kade's voice came to her from the

main room.

The first thing she noticed was the immense vat in the center of the room. It was at least ten meters high and five around. It gave off a purple glow. Inside, jellyfish-like disks hovered in the air, clustering together. "Kade, there are euphoria disks in here," she called back. "A vat full of them. Like the ones that nearly killed us."

"You're kidding!" Kade sounded as surprised as she was.

Mariss glanced around, suspicions growing, cementing. "And I smell vagon. Very strongly." She looked toward the benches and equipment on the tables. Some she recognized, some she did not. But this was obviously a processing lab.

Something shiny caught her eye. She stepped toward a countertop. A euphoria disk lay on its back on the counter, in a dish. It was obviously dead.

Mariss stepped away from the counter, understanding flowing through her, filling her with trepidation, fear, and a sense of betrayal so deep she wanted to scream.

"They're mixing the two," she called to Kade. "Vagon and some substance from the disks. Probably the chemical which makes people feel so good."

People like her, who had found herself feeling happy when by all other measures of logic, she should have felt furious or upset or emotionally torn. They had tried to convince her she didn't love Kade. They had tried to convince her she belonged here. That she was someone she wasn't.

Mariss turned her back on the lab, anger coursing through her. Suddenly, she felt more alive, more aware, than she had in days. She slammed back through the door to confront Adrian. She stepped up to him, stared up at his handsome face. "All right, start talking. How much of that stuff did you give me?"

He laughed weakly. "Mariss, you're being unreasonable, jumping to conclusions. We use the drug that we make here to *help* people. It's a medicine."

"He's such an honest guy," Kade said wryly. "The thing I can't figure is how you're delivering it. I haven't gotten any, I'm sure of it. So it can't be in the food or the water, unless it's only in certain people's meals. Maybe it's in the air? Maybe you gas people at night, while they're sleeping."

Adrian kept his back to Kade, his eyes on Mariss. "Don't listen to him, sweet," he said, his voice soothing. "Don't let him get you worked up over nothing. This is merely a research lab. Don't forget, tomorrow's our wedding day. Don't let this—this *criminal*—cast a shadow over us."

He laid his hands on her arms. Mariss shook him off and backed away.

Adrian didn't give up. He closed the distance between them until Mariss backed into a counter.

"There are better, happier things to think about, sweetheart," he said. "Now, just come with me. We'll take care of your purification, and everything will be fine."

"Purification!" Kade's fury echoed off the walls.

Mariss and Adrian both jumped.

Adrian tried to appear casual as he turned to face Kade. "Removing toxins from her body," he said casually. "Nothing more."

Kade's jaw muscles worked furiously. His words, when he spoke, hit Mariss with the force of a sledgehammer. "My child is not a toxin!"

Mariss stared in shock. "Child?" Suddenly, things began to fit. The "excess intra-uterine tissue" she had been told needed to be removed. "My God. You mean I'm *pregnant?"*

Kade's gaze met hers, clung. His voice was raspy. "You didn't know?"

Relief, joy, emotions too new to be named poured through Mariss. She and Kade had started a life together. No wonder Kade was so angry with her. He thought she *knew*, that she wanted to rid herself of it. Her words were soft yet firm. "Kade, I didn't know. I didn't know." She blinked back tears. "I'm pregnant with your baby," she said, filled with awe. "Kade, I didn't think you could be a father. I didn't even think about taking precautions."

Kade smiled ruefully. "Me neither. Not once." Their eyes met as memory of their wild, passionate night returned.

"Baby! It's hardly that." Adrian's harsh voice cut rudely

into their conversation. “Just a collection of cells, errant cells, taking up a position in a host organism where they don’t belong.” He slipped his arm around Mariss. “Mariss, let us cleanse you of them, so we can start our lives together in the right way. We’ll have children—plenty of them—but they will be screened, genetically cleansed of all imperfections.”

Mariss backed away from him, toward Kade. “No—I would never allow you to take my child. You were going to steal it—kill it—without even telling me! You *bastard.”* She turned away from his outstretched arms and found herself enfolded in Kade’s strong embrace. Mariss pressed her face into his chest, felt the slick, unfamiliar cop’s uniform under her cheek.

Kade held her tight, pressed his face against her hair. Mariss never wanted to leave him. But she knew they were far from safe. Reluctantly, she looked toward Adrian.

He was staring at them, his blue eyes unnaturally bright. Mariss expected him to be furious, to be hurt. But he maintained an unnatural calm. “We could never allow the offspring of such a lower-class creature to live here at the Colony,” he said, his eyes sweeping over them. “So you *must* allow us to abort it. Soon, Mariss, after *he* is gone—you will see I’m right.” He advanced on them, reaching for Mariss.

Kade lifted his booted foot and planted it in Adrian’s stomach, shoving him back so hard, he sprawled on the floor. “If you come near her again, you’re a dead man,” he said, lifting his phase-gun.

Mariss didn’t doubt Kade meant every word. She could see in his eyes his desire to squeeze the trigger. But he restrained himself.

Adrian scrambled to his feet and backed away. He began moving toward the door, until Kade’s voice stopped him. “Not another inch. Go into the corner and stand there.”

Adrian complied, moving to the corner away from the door. But a smile curled his sculpted lips. “This is a farce, Land. You’ll never get out of here alive. I alerted security before I entered this room.”

“Get us off-world transport, or *you* won’t get out of this

lab alive."

Adrian shook his head. "I'm sorry, Land. It's already too late. They're coming for you now. In fact, they're already here. This time, you'll be terminated. And you—" he looked to Mariss. "You will be re-educated, your thoughts cleansed, and that—that *thing* you're carrying removed."

As if on cue, the door flew open and three security guards entered, phase-guns readied. Kade fired at the first guard, stunning him. He tumbled to the floor. But the second guard fired off a volley toward the both of them.

"Not the girl!" Adrian screamed as Kade shoved Mariss to the floor, out of the line of fire.

Mariss rolled to her back and kicked her feet toward the guard, tripping him. Caught by surprise, he stumbled, letting off a stream of phase bolts, which sparked through the air in streaks of red before he hit the floor.

Kade kicked the phase-gun away from the man who had lost his balance, but by the time he looked up, the third guard had seen the lay of the land and was making use of it. He was holding the muzzle of his gun to Mariss' head.

"Drop it or she dies," he said flatly to Kade.

Kade froze. A moment later, his phase-gun clattered to the floor. He lifted his hands.

Mariss looked up at him, devastated. She had caused this, all of it. If she hadn't been so blind—

Adrian approached Kade, now that his hands were manacled and three men surrounded him. His handsome face was transformed by a wicked smirk. In the next instant, he rammed his fist into Kade's stomach. Kade grunted and doubled up. Mariss cried out, feeling Kade's agony as if it were her own.

"Adrian, no!" Mariss cried, knowing as the words left her mouth they would do absolutely no good.

Adrian ignored her. He grabbed a fistful of Kade's hair and yanked his head back. "That's for laying your filthy hands on my woman. And this—" He slammed his fist into Kade's jaw and Kade's head snapped back, "—is for contaminating her with your dirty seed."

Blind with fury, Mariss threw herself at Adrian, pounding on his back. Adrian shoved her to the floor. When she managed to look up, she saw that three more security guards had joined the first set. All but one formed a tight knot around Kade and escorted him out the door. The last guard waited to assist Adrian with her.

Mariss lost sight of Kade as Adrian wrenched her to her feet. Before he led her from the lab, Mariss did the only thing she could. It was futile, but it felt good. She tore off the expensive ring he'd given her and threw it in his face.

"That's the last straw, Mariss," Adrian said, his voice like ice. "You'll regret that little gesture. And you'll learn never to do anything like it again."

He shoved her ahead of him out the door, the guard following to ensure her compliance.

TWENTY-TWO

Mariss was in hell. She was strapped to a table, waiting for the appearance of a doctor who was going to steal Kade's baby from her. She writhed, trying to loosen her restraints, but it was useless. Steel mesh bands no human could tear through held her down.

Frightening images of her trip in the hovercar to this "clinic" stormed through her consciousness. She had passed through high gates to find herself in a land of lost souls. The old people she had asked Adrian about came here to "retire"—but from what she had seen, their stay was unnaturally short.

Others came here, too, ones her age—the intractable few, the terminally ill, the disfigured, those who had lost touch with reality from too much euphoria-vagon doping. The imperfect ones.

Mariss shuddered, recalling the incident when their hovercar stopped. A man had launched himself toward the car, breaking free of his two keepers, crying out meaningless gibberish into her face. The two "medics" yanked him away, wrestled him to the ground, stunned him and dragged him away. She had overheard one of them say that the patient was "serving" the Colony as a test subject in the discipline chamber.

The three medics Adrian had given her over to would not answer her questions. But Mariss already knew what lay in store for her. She knew, now that she had time to think of it, she had been branded a troublemaker. And troublemakers were brainwashed into being proper Colony residents, or, failing that, terminated.

Terminated—

A tear leaked out from under her eyelid. Kade might

already be dead.

A medic entered the treatment room, this one a middle-aged woman. "What's going to happen to me?" Mariss asked.

The woman ignored her. Mariss tried again, but for all intents and purposes, she was treated as a non-person. The medic lifted a device toward her. She struggled away from it, but it was too late. The device contacted her skin, and the medic hit the release button.

Mariss began to lose consciousness. Her last terrifying thought was that when she awoke, she would be a different person.

***

"You're supposed to be an example, so they're waiting to kill you." Farra spoke to Kade from the top of the pit. She was on her knees, her hands grasping the edges, above where a forcefield pulsed.

"Farra?" Kade peered up through the dimness to see her blond head looking down at him. He had been thrown in this five-meter deep hole in the sub-basement of the dome after being dragged from the lab. "How did you find me?"

"Everyone knows about the execution, Kade. I mean, the disposal action. They're pretty rare." Farra massaged her temple.

Kade rose to his feet. "Farra, can you get me out? I beg you. They're going to hurt Mariss. I have to help her. Do you have any idea where they've taken her?"

"You *have* got it bad, haven't you?" She smiled softly. "I'm not supposed to, Kade. I bribed a guard to let me in here, and—" She cried out and clutched her head, this time with both hands.

Kade watched her, understanding dawning. "Your head. What's wrong, Farra? What did they do to your head?"

It was a moment before Farra replied. "I can't tell you. I can't. I want to help you, if I can. To make it up to you."

"Farra," Kade said softly. She should know by now he had forgiven her. "Be careful."

"I'm not really supposed to be here—in the Colony, I mean. It doesn't work very well with me, but they needed women." She grasped her head again, huddling there above the steel rim of the hole.

Kade waited, anxious for her, for Mariss, for himself. After what seemed an eternity, Farra recovered enough to look down at him again. "I'm going to leave this here." She set a phase-gun next to the rim of the pit. "It's for you. I have to trigger the shield release, then you can climb out."

Kade nodded.

"Mariss is in the subcolony on the east side. That's where they take the difficult ones for re-education."

Kade nodded again, and she disappeared. A second later, he heard the barely detectable whine as the shield cut out and a ladder descended from a platform above. He wasted no time in scrambling up.

He pulled himself out, snatching up the phase-gun. There was no sign of guards in this inner chamber. But Farra was lying in a heap on the deck, just under the control pad. Kade knelt beside her. He took her pulse. There was none. He pressed his head to her chest. Silence.

Farra was dead.

Kade gazed at her still, doll-like face in shock. No one was about. She hadn't died from a phase-gun blast, that was certain. There wasn't a mark on her.

He knew the cause of her death. Because of her disobedience, Farra had paid for his freedom with her life.

***

Kade only had to stun three guards before making his way into the sunlight. Once he had knocked out the guard at the prison entrance below ground, he avoided the sub-level corridors. He took to a service passageway, crawling along it until he pushed through a manhole cover.

He found himself in a park. The idle Colony residents were entertaining themselves with tennis and bric-ball. He tucked his phase-gun under his jacket and sauntered over to a hovercycle parked by the curb. He casually glanced around before getting on and juicing the engine. In a flash, he was tearing down the street.

His heart pulled him toward the subcolony on the east

side, but he resisted. He had seen the entrance from a distance, but having no idea what lay beyond, he hadn't explored further. He had no idea how many guards there were, what type of security checks existed. And he knew he was probably already being pursued, his escape discovered.

No, there was no time. There was only one way to get in and get Mariss out quickly, and that wasn't on a hovercycle.

The docking bay lay to the south of the administration center. He pushed the cycle as fast as it would go, flying it higher than its design limits so he could avoid the traffic on the streets below. The docking bay was a place he'd checked over very carefully. All along, he'd had a hunch he would need to get away quickly.

He had just been there this morning on the interstellar police ship. But he'd seen a couple of other promising craft. Nothing fancy. Cargo haulers only. But they would suffice.

He dropped altitude and—before the docking crew knew what hit them—flew into the hangar bay at top speed. He cut the engine and coasted right for the open hatch of a freighter being off-loaded. Deck hands cried out and leapt for cover. Kade's hovercycle didn't come to a stop until it impacted the bulkhead inside the craft.

The crash threw him off, and he banged his shoulder painfully on the deck.

He heard voices outside coming closer and had his phase-gun out before he scrambled to his feet. A deck hand stood behind him near the cargo section, his hands in the air, his face white.

"Get off," Kade said. The young man didn't hesitate, nearly falling in his effort to get away from the half-crazed man in the black prison jumpsuit.

He slammed his hand on the hatch control and it began to ascend. He ran to the cockpit and started the pre-flight procedure, bypassing all the usual safety checks. He only had moments to spare.

He heard more shouts, and what sounded like phase-gun fire on the hull of the ship, just as the engines slipped into the readiness range. With the controls set to manual, he engaged all six of the ship's engines.

They responded more readily than he would have expected, considering he didn't wait the full cycle for them to warm up. The ship burst from the docking bay.

He angled it up, above the Colony, knowing he was only flying by luck now. He didn't even know if the ship was fully fueled. He glanced toward the indicators. Half filled. Good enough.

He flew the angular ship to the Colony's east side, and the subcolony. There, he switched the engines to hover and began scanning the buildings laid out below. Grey-toned, sad and ugly compared to the Colony proper. The dozen or so people near the entrance on the broad sweep of greensward stopped and stared at the ship hovering above them.

"It's showtime," he said to himself as he lowered the ship toward the stretch of lawn inside the subcolony entrance. He flicked the communication switch, giving him external access, and started talking.

"Attention. This is a fully-armed Class IV starship. My phase-turrets are locked on the big building just ahead of me. If you don't bring out a woman by the name of Mariss Sakari, I'm going to blast the building apart. In case you don't believe me, watch this." Kade leapt from the pilot's seat to a side-seat where a gunner would sit—if he had one. He centered the gun's crosshairs on a large tree and let lose a short burst. The tree went up in flames.

Kade saw the people below him running about like frightened rabbits.

He clicked on the intercom. "Bring Mariss Sakari out, or I'll find something else to blast. How about a building this time?" He felt a vicious satisfaction at having power over this place after what they were trying to do to Mariss. "See that little shed? The blue one in the corner of the lot? It's next. I hope no one's inside."

One person ran out, his hands out. Kade gave it five more seconds. No one else appeared.

"I don't see Mariss yet," he chided. "Okay, here goes."

He blasted the shed apart. Pieces flew everywhere. The

people below were in a full-fledged panic now. He kept his eyes on his scopes, knowing it wasn't beyond the realm of possibility that another ship could be sent after him. So far, the skies were clear of competition.

Just when he thought he'd have to seriously destroy something, he spotted a trio emerging from the main building, their hands in the air. More precisely, the men on each end were waving. In the middle was a dark-haired woman whom they seemed to be supporting.

They hurried as best they could to the center of the lawn. Then, the two men dropped the woman on the ground and rushed back full speed to the main building.

Kade gingerly set the craft down near the woman's prone body. He couldn't see her very well. They had damn well not be pulling a fast one, substituting some other female. When the ship settled down, he rushed back to the hatch and slammed his hand on the button. He crawled out before it was half-way down, knowing this was when he was at his most vulnerable.

But no one shot at him. He ran to the woman's side and scooped her up. It *was* Mariss. She was groggy, drugged, only half-awake. So, what else was new?

Kade sprinted up the hatch ramp with her.

Back in the cockpit, he settled her in the co-pilot's seat. A moment later, he lifted the ship away from the Colony, then the continent, then the planet. He couldn't get away fast enough. He pushed the engines to their max. He knew he wouldn't feel safe until he was deep in intersystem space, lightyears from this sector.

Beside him, Mariss stirred and moaned. Kade tore his eyes away from his scopes and looked over at her. She was pale, but she was alive. His eyes flicked to the hem of the knee-length hospital gown she wore. Her legs were bare. No sign of blood, of anything having been done to her. But he knew the chances were slim that he'd gotten her out before they stole her baby. Too much time had passed. He was certain of it.

Their baby. He sighed. It had been a short-lived miracle indeed.

***

The effect of the anesthetic lingered, but Mariss shook it off. She felt very cold. She shivered, and rubbed at the goosebumps on her arms.

She looked at Kade beside her, recalled the incredible scene of a few moments earlier when, half-drugged, she had been dragged from the clinic and tossed on the ground, only to see a gigantic ship fall from the sky and land beside her. "Will I ever stop being surprised by you, Kadin Land?"

His wry smile, so close to her, filled her with pleasure. "I hope not."

"You have no idea what you looked like, but that was one incredible scene back there."

This time he broke into a full-fledged grin. The ship was pulling out of the atmosphere into the blackest reaches of space. Kade's eyes and hands seemed to be everywhere at once—on the controls, on the cockpit viewport, tapping commands into the nav-computer. "How do you feel?"

"All right. Better. They forced me awake with a shot of stimulant. I was completely under, so they could—oh, God." She pressed her hands to her abdomen. Had they stolen her baby? She couldn't tell. She hadn't even known she was pregnant until just before she had been taken—and Kade had been arrested.

"Kade—you were to be killed! How did you get away?"

He began to tell her the story. Mariss listened in fascination. "Poor Farra. Why did she die?"

Kade's lips tightened in a grim line. "Something they did to her killed her, but I don't know what."

"That's horrible."

"Yeah, and it could have been you."

"Krod, I feel so stupid." Mariss sank down in the seat, burying her head in her hands. "I don't know how I could have been so blind."

"Don't be so hard on yourself. Even *I,* skeptic that I am, didn't imagine anything like this."

"I just wish I understood it. I mean, why? Why go to so much expense, so much trouble? None of it makes a bit of sense."

"Yeah, I know. I've been too busy to think much about it, but you're right. It doesn't really make a lot of sense."

Mariss sighed. "What now?" she asked tentatively. "Where are we headed?"

"Well, it looks like—damn!"

The ship shuddered as a blast from a ship's gun hit them. "It's a Class V Draconian cruiser." Kade slammed his palm on the panel before him, and the shields engaged.

"From the Colony?"

"You could say that. It's the cop ship that was docked there. I had a feeling they were letting us get away a little too easy. They just didn't want a mess on their front lawn." As he spoke, his hands flew over the controls. "Hold on!" The ship arced at a precipitous angle back toward the surface of the planet. Mariss grabbed the arm rests as her stomach lurched sickeningly. Kade took the clunky freighter into a steep roll, slipping right under the police fighter, out of its line of fire.

At the same time, he was entering information into the navigational controls, attempting to set an interstellar space-jump that would take them away from the planet. "Just a few seconds is all I need, and we're out of here."

Mariss tore her eyes from him as an immense cruise ship filled the view out the cockpit window. "Kade," she said softly.

He glanced up. The freighter received another buffeting blow from the police fighter, which had turned back toward them and resumed firing. But now, in their path of escape, hovered an immense cruiser, its sleek silver hull glinting in the light of the Elysian sun. On its side was emblazoned the falcon logo of the Earth Coalition Diplomatic Corps.

"We're almost in range of their tractor beam. I'm going to—"

Mariss laid her hand on his. "No. Don't. Let them take us aboard. It's all right."

"Mariss, what in the—"

Mariss met his eyes. "Let them intercept us."

"What?"

"It's better than the cops! Kade, we can't run away and

hide. We have to tell them about the Colony, about what's going on there. Think of all those people! People like Farra."

She could see Kade consider her words in the precious seconds before the nav-beacon rang, announcing the coordinates were locked in for the interspace jump. His hand hovered over the controls. He looked at her once more. She saw Kade's internal battle, his willingness to trust her fighting with his common sense. Finally, he threw up his hands. "Okay, you win."

A scant second later, she felt the tug of the tractor beam from the cruiser.

A voice came over their communication link. "By authority of the Earth Coalition, we are taking your ship aboard to be searched."

The message repeated. Kade pressed the intercom button and acknowledged the message. He shot her a skeptical look as they were pulled aboard.

TWENTY-THREE

Mariss followed Kade out the hatch into the cruiser's massive docking bay. She came up short, right behind him, watched in amazement as he lifted his hands. Tentatively, never having gone through this before, she raised her hands as well.

Surrounding them at the base of the freighter were half a dozen security guards, their weapons pointed straight at them. "Keep your hands up and advance slowly, one at a time."

Kade walked down the hatch ramp, and was immediately surrounded and searched. Mariss followed, hesitant and afraid. She hadn't expected this kind of reception. A few questions, definitely. But this was an army!

It was her turn. After a female security guard finished patting her down, her hands were cuffed behind her. Mariss glanced at Kade. She had to admit he looked the part of a criminal in that worn prison jumpsuit from the Colony. He needed a shave, and his face was turning black and blue where Adrian had slugged him.

But Mariss looked deeper. His mouth was set in a grim line, his eyes like stone. She knew being treated like a criminal was the last thing he wanted to experience. He had already traveled this route more than once and had hoped never to go through such humiliation again.

For Mariss, it was a new, unsettling experience. She wanted to scream, "I'm innocent, believe me," yet even now, felt guilty simply because she was being treated as if she *were* guilty. And she hadn't done anything but protect herself from people who wanted to harm her.

They were escorted from the docking bay into a holding room, where their photos were taken, their bodies scanned for disease, and their retinal patterns recorded. Finally, someone seemed interested in talking with her. A woman with a hand-unit asked her name.

"Mariss Sakari," she said softly.

"Mariss Sapati? Spell it, please."

"Mariss S-A-K-A-R-I."

The woman's gaze whipped up from her clipboard. She scanned Mariss' face thoroughly. "Lieutenant Tarin," she called out. "I believe we have a situation here."

The next thing she knew, Mariss was separated from Kade and taken to a nicer section of the ship, a reception room. The manacles were removed. Mariss massaged her wrists and yanked on the hem of the bedgown, wishing she was wearing something that covered her better.

As if hearing her thoughts, the female guard who had accompanied her settled a robe on her shoulders. "This will keep you warm. He's on his way. I recognized your name, Ms. Sakari. Why didn't you speak up sooner?"

Mariss narrowed her eyes as she stared at the stately blond in the tailored blue-grey uniform. "Do I know you?"

Before the guard could respond, a voice called out, "Mariss? Mariss! My God, it is you!" Its owner was a small-boned man of medium height in his late forties. He wore a rich, turquoise robe, a sign of his status.

Jarik Sakari swept his sister into his strong embrace. A sob tore from Mariss' throat as she returned his hug. It was only now that she realized how terrified she had been over being arrested. Now, everything would turn out all right.

She gazed at her brother's narrow face, noted a few new lines. His black hair was combed straight back from his high forehead, his temples touched with white. "Jarik, I had no idea this was your ship. But we needed a safe haven. I hoped the Coalition Diplomatic Corps would provide one."

The joy in Jarik's dark-brown eyes dimmed. "You must tell me exactly how you ended up in the company of a convict, Mariss."

"A convict? You mean Kade?"

"Kadin Land, the man who piloted the ship. We were

alerted to be on the look-out for him by the interstellar police. They said two fugitives were entering space from Elysia, trying to escape." He lowered his voice. "Please, Mariss. You can confide in me. Was it a kidnapping?"

"Of course not! Kade *rescued* me."

Jarik seemed confused by her news. He glanced toward the female guard, who was watching the exchange with interest. "Come, let's go to my private office."

Soon, Mariss was seated in one of Jarik's thick, comfortable chairs in what could only be described as a suite. This was his working office as an Earth Coalition Ambassador. At one end, on a dais, was his desk and a massive, high-backed chair. At the other end was a round conference table and banks of computers. Mariss was seated in the conversation area in the center of the room.

Jarik had insisted she take a moment to bathe and change. She did so as quickly as she could, slipping on the full-length gown of lavender without noticing its silkiness. Her mind was on Kade. Jarik had been deflecting her questions about Kade and his whereabouts, and Mariss found she couldn't wait any longer. "Where's Kade? He should be here, too. We can both tell you what happened. The Colony isn't what it pretends to be, Jarik."

"So you keep saying. Perhaps you should start at the beginning."

"Gladly. But first, tell me where Kade is. Please."

Jarik nodded. "Fair enough. He is being held in the brig. Even now, arrangements are being made to transfer him to the custody of the Interstellar Police."

Mariss bolted to her feet. "You can't do that! He hasn't done anything!"

Jarik seemed prepared for her outburst. His cool, dark eyes calmly studied her as he retrieved the hand-unit from his desk. He flicked it on. "These are only a few of the twenty-three outstanding charges against him, Mariss. Felony theft of a police hovercar. Breaking and entering. Illegal use of explosives. Tampering with security systems. Assault. Theft of a hovercycle. Hijacking a hovercar. Theft of a freighter.

And, finally—" his eyes met Mariss'. "Murder."

"Murder! Kade didn't—"

"A young lady was found dead outside his prison cell at the Colony, Mariss. Land has been implicated in the murder."

Frustration surged through Mariss. "But he didn't kill her!"

"Were you there?"

Mariss hesitated. "No."

"Then how do you know he didn't?"

"I thought people were innocent until proven guilty."

Jarik sighed. "Yes, Mariss, that is so. But Kadin Land has a criminal record, and—"

"I am sick to death of hearing about Kade's record!" Mariss cried, startling even the placid Jarik. "What about everything he's done for me? Doesn't that count for anything? He took care of me, protected me, saved my life! He's rescued me so many times I'm starting to lose count. I would not be standing here talking to you today if Kadin Land hadn't risked his life for me."

Jarik held up his hands. "Mariss, slow down. Please. Sit. Let's discuss this."

"I'm *trying* to discuss this."

Jarik nodded. Finally, his implacable expression broke, and he smiled. "I must say, Mariss, I have never seen you so passionate about anything."

"Then you must know I'm serious. Kade is a wonderful person. He just never got the kind of breaks you and I have gotten, Jarik. He didn't come from a wealthy family like we did. He's—he's a survivor. And he's helped *me* survive. I can promise you, if you give him to the cops, you'll regret it."

Jarik stared at her, his dark eyes intent. A voice interrupted from the viewer behind his desk. "Your Honor, we have a communication coming in from the police cruiser. Commander Pluto Orin."

"Put him on."

The police chief's face filled the man-high screen. Mariss gasped. It was the same man whose leg she had blasted when Kade's ship had been boarded above Elysia, all those weeks ago. "Ambassador Sakari. I have it on good authority you have taken the fugitives into custody. We are ready to receive them at the first opportunity."

Jarik sighed. "Excuse me, Chief, but I'm afraid I cannot comply with your request until I have conducted a thorough investigation of the situation."

The chief's jaw tightened, and he frowned. "Nonsense. You have no business with them. This is *our* sector to patrol. If you don't hand them over immediately, I'll file a complaint. It could start an incident."

Jarik didn't take the bait. He replied smoothly, "I understand the need to maintain proper relations with your branch of the government. Nevertheless, I have a situation with the woman which must be resolved. So for now, I cannot release them. Authority rests with me, as the highest-ranking representative of Earth's government in this sector, to decide on release of prisoners in my custody."

The chief's face spasmed with anger. But then he seemed to force a smile to his face. "Very well, I can bargain. You keep the woman. Just give us Land."

"I will consider your request. You will be hearing from me."

Jarik ended the transmission. Instantly, Mariss ran to her brother and clutched his arms. "You can't give Kade to them. You can't. They'll *kill* him. The Colony was going to terminate him! Jarik, I beg you, don't let them win."

Jarik stepped away from Mariss. His brow creased in thought, he turned his back to her. Mariss waited tensely in the silence. Jarik was not a man of many words. But when he spoke, people listened. Finally, he was ready to speak. "I came to this sector a few days ago, Mariss, because the Coalition hasn't sent representation to this part of the galaxy in years. This may be a factor in a growing problem with vagon smuggling which has come to light."

"I know. I know all about it."

"Do you? You must tell me." He lifted his hand. "But first, let me tell you the other reason I elected to come here. I knew you had run away to join the Colony. It seemed like such a drastic step to take. I know why you did it, and I can't say I blame you. Except running away seldom solved anything. I looked forward to the opportunity to check on you, see if you were happy. Ami has been worried sick—"

The response was automatic. "Ami? Worried about me? Fine time to think of that."

"Mariss, your bitterness is showing."

Mariss thought about his words. Then she smiled. "Actually, Jarik, I don't feel bitter anymore. In a way, I'm grateful to Ami. I realize now I was dreadfully unhappy with Roldo. I didn't want to admit it. Well, I admit it now. But I don't *care* anymore. I really don't. I *care* about Kade! You have to let him go, Jarik. You're the fairest man I know. I can't believe you wouldn't see past his record to the fine man beneath. Please give him a chance! You don't know him like I do. If it wasn't for him, I'd be—another person."

Finally, the entire story burst from Mariss, from when she met Kade and he escorted her to the Colony to their experience there. Then forward, to their horrible last day and their frantic escape. She left out the personal aspect of her relationship with Kade, not knowing herself where they stood anymore. There had been so little time to talk, to sort out her feelings.

Despite her terrible experiences with men who professed to love her, she could no longer deny her feelings for Kade. He was unlike any man she had ever met. He brought out sides of her she hadn't known existed, made her feel more alive than she ever had. No, he wasn't perfect. No man was. Certainly not Adrian. But—just maybe—he was perfect for her.

"Mariss?"

She had fallen silent, thinking of Kade, of the baby they had almost made together. She hadn't told Jarik about it—there was no reason, yet. The Colony's attempt to brainwash her was damning enough without that personal tidbit of information.

She gazed at Jarik, pleading with her eyes, her voice, her heart. "Let him have free access to the ship, while you investigate the Colony's doings. I swear he won't get into trouble. I'll stick to him like glue. I promise."

Jarik's eyebrows lifted just slightly, which for him was a huge show of emotion. Mariss suspected she had shocked her brother. "I have never in my life seen you fight so hard for anything as you're fighting for this man's freedom," he said. "I scarcely know you, Mariss. You were always so quiet and well-behaved, the sensible one. Ami is the sort to get into trouble, not you."

"Well, maybe we're more alike than I ever cared to admit."

Jarik gazed at her thoughtfully, then finally nodded. His voice took on the tone of a pronouncement. "I have already dispatched a preliminary investigative team to the Colony to look into the vagon smuggling situation. But after what you have told me, I will increase our effort by ten-fold, and explore every aspect of the Colony's administration. It may be run by a private company, but even the Iridion Corporation must answer to Earth's human rights directives."

"And Kade?"

"I will personally interview him. Then I will give you a decision."

Mariss' shoulders slumped. It was a small concession, but at least Jarik would have a chance to see what she saw in Kade. "Very well. I'd like to stay while you bring him in."

"First, I want you checked over carefully by our physicians. I want to know if there are any lingering effects from your ordeal. I also want to collect any trace evidence of drugs in your system, for use in future prosecution."

Mariss nodded, irritated that she couldn't see Kade yet. But she was confident he was safe—for the moment.

***

Kade was growing fatigued. He'd been taken from the freighter to the brig, then to the medic station for a series of scans and tests. They hadn't answered his questions about Mariss' whereabouts, but they *had* mended the bruise on his face so only traces of it were still visible. No one treated him poorly, but neither did they acknowledge his presence as a person.

Then a pair of armed guards escorted him from the security section of the one-thousand-person star cruiser into a much nicer section, away from the throbbing engines toward the fore of the sleek, long ship.

The guards brought him to an anteroom, where a young man in a tailored suit waited behind a desk. He spoke into an intercom, and a few moments later, a pair of double doors adorned with the falcon logo of the Diplomatic Corps slid open.

The guards pushed Kade forward and followed him as he entered. Kade's steps slowed as he took in the opulent surroundings. Not so much opulent as elegant, he decided on closer inspection. Nothing was overstated. Merely the finest possible desk, finest possible chairs, and—

"So. You are Kadin Land, the one who brought my sister from Elysia."

Kade stared at the man before him, at his fine, flowing robe and the familiar features. Kade had forgotten Mariss had a relative of such rank. He had forgotten just how far above him her family was. He had indeed forgotten. But now that she was back in the warm embrace of her family, the truth hit home, hard. What could he possibly offer her? Nothing. He had nothing.

"Yeah. And you're Jarik Sakari—the ambassador. Mariss' brother."

Jarik's smile of greeting was frozen as he looked at Kade. It was no wonder. Kade was staring at him stonily. He knew exactly what Jarik saw when he looked at him. A convict about to serve more time, a danger to good people, quality people.

But Jarik surprised him. Smiling warmly, he gestured with his fine-boned hand toward the round conference table at the end of the room. "Please. Sit down. We have much to discuss."

Kade hesitated a moment, but hell, he had nowhere better to go. He stepped to the table. Since he was unable to pull out his own chair with his hands manacled behind his back, Jarik did it for him. The guards hovered behind him, ready for any move on Kade's part, any threat to their leader.

Kade watched Jarik closely as the ambassador took the seat across from him. Was this a civilized form of interrogation? he wondered. Or was Jarik really interested in the truth? "Where's Mariss?" he asked, knowing his voice sounded overly harsh.

"She's at the medic station, being thoroughly examined. As she tells it, she has been through quite an ordeal."

A corner of Kade's mouth twitched. "You could say that."

"Mariss has told me what happened. Now I want to hear what you have to say."

"So you can compare notes? See if I'm lying?"

"Not at all. I'm trying to fill in the gaps. Mariss wasn't with you much of the time. So, please. Start at the beginning."

Kade sighed and began his story. Afterward, Jarik was silent for several minutes. Kade rolled his shoulders, trying to relax them despite the manacles. Jarik gestured to the guard standing behind Kade. "Remove the manacles, please."

The guard hesitated, then obeyed.

"Thanks," Kade said, rubbing his wrists.

"Your comfort was only part of the reason I had them removed," Jarik said. He laid a sketch screen before Kade. "I need you to show me where in the Colony these labs are. My investigative team needs to be able to find them."

Kade took up the stylus and began to draw on the touch-sensitive screen. He described the locations of each of the places he'd visited, how he'd made use of the underground passageways and gotten past the security systems. To his surprise, Jarik seemed to listen as if he believed him. This was a new experience for Kade. The last time he'd been branded a criminal, no one would hear what he had to say. Except Farra, and she'd been too frightened to do anything.

But Jarik seemed to accept him as an equal. Time slipped by, and Kade began to open up, explaining more and more of the Colony's inner workings, and what had happened there.

After sketching the layout of the vagon-processing lab, he looked up and found Jarik's dark eyes watching him intensely. "Why did you do it?"

"What?"

"Go to all this trouble? Why didn't you simply enjoy the massages and spas and relax while you waited for transport off the planet?"

Kade's fingers tightened around the stylus. There was no way this side of the universe he'd tell Jarik Sakari the truth about that. So he gave him another truth instead. "I'm a curious guy. And I learned years ago that things which seem too good to be true usually are. There's always a catch."

Jarik seemed to accept his statement. He nodded and asked him another question about the lab.

Behind Kade, the door opened. Instinctively, since his back was turned, Kade spun in the chair toward the sound. Mariss breezed in. Kade's heart jumped in his chest, then squeezed painfully. She crossed the room, the full-length lavender gown she was wearing clinging to her lithe figure. Its color brought out the violet in her eyes, which appeared bright, excited like a child's. A chiffon cape attached at her shoulders fluttered as she neared the table. She looked like a princess.

Kade swallowed as he gazed at her face. She was looking right at him, a mysterious smile on her lips. She was positively glowing. Naturally. She was back with her family, out of danger. Kade, on the other hand, was going back to prison.

Nevertheless, when she stretched out her arms to him, he felt his body responding. Without conscious intent, he rose to his feet and took a half-step toward her.

The guards reacted instantly, stepping in front of him, keeping them apart. Their phase-guns were pressed to his chest. Mariss stopped a few feet from the table, her arms dropping to her sides.

One of the guards slapped the manacles back on Kade's wrists while the other kept his phase-gun on him.

"Kade," Mariss said.

"Yeah, it's me," he said hollowly. "Back where I belong." He shook his manacled wrists.

"It shouldn't be like this," she said.

Her words were pointless, Kade thought. Now what? Was she going to throw a princess-like fit and get Jarik to dismiss all twenty-three charges against him? Not likely. Women like her knew better than to go out of their way for men like him.

But her voice was surprisingly firm. "Jarik, let him go. This is an insult. He should be our honored guest."

"Mariss, this doesn't concern you," Jarik replied. "However, I don't believe he poses an immediate threat. Mr. Land, please resume your seat. No one except the guards are allowed to have physical contact with the prisoner."

Kade slumped into the chair.

Jarik spoke to the guards. "Please remove the manacles, so we may continue."

Mariss took a step closer. "Kade, I came to tell you..." Kade looked toward her, though it hurt to do so. Thinking he'd never hold her again, never be with her again, was almost more than he could stand. The time they had spent together, exploring the beauty and danger of an alien world, would live only as a dream in his memory. No more would they laugh together, tread the forests side-by-side, rely solely on each other for support, solace, love.

So instead, he kept his emotions carefully hidden. He needed to remain tough. That's how he would survive. Nothing would crack through his shell into his heart again. He refused to let it. Or he wouldn't be able to go on living.

He could see Mariss seeking answers in his expression, looking for a vulnerability he refused to show her. He had come so close—too damned close—to revealing the wealth of love he had for her.

It had been so easy when they had traveled together in the wilderness to forget the great gulf that lay between them. But she was a child of privilege. She was at home in these magnificent surroundings, like a jewel in its proper setting.

Kade could no longer deny the truth. Mariss Sakari deserved a hell of a lot more than a broken heart caused by a doomed man.

Mariss continued to gaze at him, her heart in her eyes. Her words were low, carefully spoken. "The doctor examined me, Kade. I'm the same as I was before they took me to that clinic. Exactly the same."

Exactly the same. Kade sucked in a breath. She was still carrying his baby. It was incredible. He must have rescued her in time.

His spirits immediately sagged. For what? The last thing

Mariss needed was to have the child of a convict, the burden of raising it falling on her shoulders alone. "It's not too late to remedy that," he said, forcing his words through a tight throat. "Maybe you'll get lucky and you'll lose it. It's still pretty early, after all."

His words had an instant effect on her. She began blinking rapidly, attempting to keep back her tears. But Mariss was no actress. Kade knew he had hurt her deeply. She turned away from him.

Kade waited a moment to rein in his emotions before turning back to his sketch. He glanced at Jarik.

The ambassador wore a slightly pained look. "Please, continue your sketch," he said, rising. "I will return shortly."

Kade bent over the sketch screen and continued his work. At least it offered a minor distraction.

TWENTY-FOUR

"She is pregnant, then?" Jarik asked Dr. Uru. The tall, black woman nodded.

Mariss sat with them in the conversation area of the suite. She kept touching her abdomen, thinking of the new life nestled deep within.

Dr. Uru had come to give Jarik a full report on her condition. Mariss glanced toward Kade, but he kept his back to them, more interested in his sketches. The guards stood at attention on either side of him like bookends. Apparently, Kade had lost interest in his child. It didn't make sense. Just this morning he'd been furious at the idea she wanted to rid herself of it. But now, away from the Colony, away from Adrian —

He's come to his senses. Now that there was the possibility of a commitment between them, he had realized the mistake he would make loving her.

"Yes, she is most definitely pregnant," Dr. Uru said. "And Kadin Land is the father."

"You screened its DNA—and his?" Jarik asked, his voice low as he glanced toward Kade.

"Yes. No question."

"Of course there's no question," Mariss said. "I could have told you that, Jarik. I'm not exactly...free with my body."

"Free enough," Jarik shot back, his emotional reaction showing just how distraught he was.

"That isn't fair." The joy Mariss felt upon learning she was still pregnant had been dampened first by Kade, who had turned cold on the idea, and now by Jarik.

Before Jarik could reply, the doctor spoke up. "Of much greater concern is the implant in her temple."

Mariss gasped. "The *what?"*

"What are you saying?" Jarik asked.

The doctor glanced at the screen of her hand-unit and tapped a few keys. "During our physical, we scanned her entire body. Not only did we detect the pregnancy, but we discovered a small device had been implanted in her temple. I don't know its purpose, but it should not remain in her body. Unfortunately, removal could prove dangerous."

"How?" Jarik asked.

"It's nestled near the part of the brain which controls free will. It is now in a stasis mode. But I detect an energy frequency within which could disrupt the flow of Mariss' thoughts, or her will. I'm not certain how it's triggered, but to be safe, it must be removed."

Mariss touched her temple, recalled the painful headaches she had suffered at the Colony. When had the implant been placed in her skull? She didn't know. She knew it was before she began having headaches, which had come on her during her arguments with Adrian. Probably her first night there, after she had tried to hack into the main computer. She hadn't been as docile as Adrian expected—because of the doubts Kade had raised. And Adrian had implanted this—device—to control her.

The realization made her sick. What if she had arrived there without Kade? By now, she would be addicted to vagon and Adrian's slave. A perfect little breeding machine.

Thinking back now, she recalled how the headaches had come on her, how her thoughts had become muddy, her perceptions skewed. After a while, she had willingly believed whatever Adrian told her. An image popped into her mind of Adrian's fingers tapping on his belt, his voice trying to convince her of something. "He was controlling me with the belt he wore. Some kind of wave frequency, I would guess. And that vagon-euphoria—I probably received it at night, in the air, since I always woke up feeling...happy."

"This is criminal," Jarik said. "An outrageous breach of galactic human rights."

He said more, but Mariss missed it. She was thinking again of her headaches...Farra had also suffered from headaches. "Farra. That's it, that's how she died." Mariss rose and began to pace before the couch. "Don't you see? Kade didn't kill her. This proves it!"

Jarik considered her remark. "It certainly could indicate that, according to her behavior as Land described it, leading up to her death. But did he have prior knowledge of these...brain implants?"

"No, I don't think so. Why should it matter? He didn't kill her!"

"If that could be proven somehow..."

"Ambassador, I highly recommend removal of this implant, particularly if it caused another woman's death," the doctor said. "But I'm not certain how. It appears to be attached to the brain tissue itself. If I could see one of the implants up close—or see how the procedure was done. But as it is, I would only be guessing."

"My sister's body is not something to deal with lightly," Jarik said. His brow furrowed. Mariss waited, expecting a solution. Jarik was famous for his creative solutions.

"You want an implant to study? I can get you one."

All eyes turned to Kade. He began to rise. Obviously curious, Jarik waved the hovering guards off.

Kade stood before them on the dais, his hands on his hips, giving the impression that *he* was leading the meeting. Mariss recognized that cocky stance of his. Despite the humiliation of his arrest, he maintained that arrogant attitude which had so rubbed her the wrong way when they first met. Now, her heart ached with love—foolish, unrequited love of an intensity she had never felt before.

"What are you proposing, Land?" Jarik asked.

"I can go back in, bring you what you need. One of the implants. Or, maybe better—Farra's body."

Jarik seemed to be considering the outrageous proposal. And Dr. Uru was becoming excited. "A body with an implant? That would be ideal. I could autopsy—"

Panic struck Mariss full in the chest. "He can't! They'll kill him on sight!"

"Undoubtedly," Jarik said. "If you fall into police hands, I will be unable to get you back in time."

Mariss spun on Kade. "It's too dangerous. I won't let you."

"And what if I don't go in?" Kade strode closer. The guards followed, phase-guns at the ready. Kade concentrated his argument on Jarik, ignoring Mariss. "What if the good doctor here cuts into her head and can't get the thing out? Or what if there's a fail-safe mechanism? Trying to take it out could trigger it and kill her."

He turned his gaze to Mariss. His dark eyes burned with intensity. Mariss knew then that he still cared. Kade tore his gaze from her and addressed Jarik. "Who can do it better than me? I know the place. Your people don't. Besides, they're working above board, aren't they, Jarik?" No one seemed to notice the familiar way Kade spoke the ambassador's name, without the formal title. "I'll bet Locke, that administrator, has agreed to cooperate fully with the investigation. But even now he's working out ways to thwart you, covering his tracks, covering the Iridion Corporation's conspiracy. And you can't do anything about it."

"This is true," Jarik said. "We must follow the proper search and audit procedures."

"And where does that leave Mariss?" Kade asked. "Your investigation will take weeks. When they see they have no choice, they'll destroy all the implants. And it may be too late."

Mariss strode over to Kade, faced him squarely, forcing him to look at her. Only a foot separated their bodies. The alert guards moved closer. Mariss wished they'd go away. She wanted to talk to Kade alone. So she spoke to him as if they *were* alone, her voice low, impassioned, filled with memories of everything they had shared—the challenges, the intimacy, the arguing, and the love. "Why would you do this? You don't have to. The investigators will learn the truth about the Colony, Kade. They *will.*" She raised her hand to lay it on his arm, but stopped herself before the guards intervened. "You don't have to do this," she repeated, fighting the overwhelming desperation that swept through her.

When Kade responded, she knew she had lost. His gaze grew intense, his darkly rugged looks set with harsh determination. Despite the guards, he lifted his hand and stroked her cheek with his fingers. Mariss sighed at the tender touch. It was a simple gesture, but it conveyed worlds of meaning. "Yeah, Mariss Sakari. I damn well do. For both of us."

***

While evening fell over the Colony below, in the docking bay members of Jarik's crew worked against a tight deadline to prepare a small cruise ship for its mission. In all, it would carry six members of Jarik's investigative team, plus one "stowaway"—Kadin Land.

Kade had allowed the ship's doctor to implant a tracking device at the base of his neck. Ostensibly, it would allow them to assist him if he were cornered. But Mariss knew its real purpose was to make it impossible for the arrested man to attempt escape. She hadn't asked, but she suspected it also contained enough toxin to kill Kade, should Jarik deem him a threat in any way.

Kade didn't protest the implant. She knew his mental energies were on the task before him. He was letting nothing distract him. She watched him standing patiently, arms crossed and feet spread, as the ship finished refueling. The two guards continued to stick to him like glue. Other crew members began boarding. Soon it would be his turn.

Mariss turned to Jarik, who was watching the proceedings from beside her, at the edge of the docking bay. "Let me speak to Kade in private. Just for a moment."

Jarik looked at her, his expression immutable. In response, he lifted his wrist communicator to his lips and gave an order to the head of security. "Allow Ms. Sakari to address the prisoner. Retreat to five meters."

"Thank you, Jarik." As the guards stepped back from Kade, Mariss strode over to him, forcing herself not to run. His gaze turned to her, watching as she closed the distance between them.

She stopped before him. His expression was implacable, but Mariss didn't let that deter her. "You'd better come back," she said softly. She set her hands on his shoulders and kissed him lightly on the mouth.

Kade reacted instantly. He pressed her against him, lifting her off her feet and holding her there as he kissed her thoroughly. Mariss wrapped her arms around his neck and held on tight, meeting his kiss with equal fervor. She never wanted to let him go. The exquisite pleasure Kade gave her was tinged with fear and sadness at the knowledge that he would soon be in grave danger.

Finally, both of them breathless, he released her mouth. But he kept hold of her body. Mariss whispered, "I love you so much."

Kade let her body slide against his until her feet touched the ground. He cupped her face in his hands. "Sweet, beautiful woman. You're forgetting your terrible track record. You shouldn't let yourself fall for a guy like me. I'm the worst you could do."

Mariss blinked back tears. "No, Kadin Land, you're wrong. You're the best."

Further words failed them both. Mariss studied his face, imprinting every feature on her memory. She knew Kade was doing the same. There was far too much to say, and time had run out. Kade finally spoke, his voice husky. "Tell him—or her—something good about me."

Mariss forced a smile to her lips, tried to sound nonchalant. "We'll both tell him." There. She'd said it. *I want a future with you.*

Before Kade could respond, another voice broke in. One of the guards, standing a few feet away. "Excuse me. It's time to board."

"I have to go." Kade stepped back. Reluctantly, Mariss allowed him to slip from her arms.

"If you don't come back, Kade, I swear I'll—I'll..." She couldn't think what. Her voice dropped almost to a whisper. "Just come back."

Kade's cocky grin returned, as if in defiance of danger. "You won't get rid of me that easily, woman." He turned from her and strolled up the hatch ramp. At the top, he lifted his hand in a wave before disappearing inside.

TWENTY-FIVE

Mariss lay on the sofa in Jarik's office, with a clear view of the screen. Throughout the night and into the following day, the leader of the investigative team provided reports and updates.

In the middle of the night, the viewscreen flickered to life. Anxious, Mariss sat up, but it was the team leader, not Kade.

"We've discovered that these implants become dangerously erratic after a resident leaves the Colony," the leader reported. "There's a transmitter in the blue dome which ensures it works properly, but when a person gets out of range..." He hesitated. "It's as if the recipients are programmed never to leave."

"My God," Jarik murmured, casting a sideways glance at Mariss.

"Only the intractable ones get the implants, when the standard protocol of drug-induced brainwashing doesn't work by itself. When a person thinks the wrong thoughts, it causes pain, reinforcing the nightly brainwashing. But it goes beyond that. Some person close to them—called a controller—can also transmit a signal, which punishes the person for not complying."

"You found records on this?" Jarik asked.

The leader gave a small smile. "Actually, that prisoner you sent down coerced it out of one of the Colony leaders, a man named...," he glanced at his slate, "Adrian Young." He chuckled. "It was something else to watch. Land didn't lay a hand on him. Just intimidated the hell out of him. The guy was practically in tears." He caught himself and stopped smiling. "Sir."

Mariss bit her lip, worrying over Kade's methods. Not

because of Adrian—that bastard deserved whatever Kade saw fit to dish out. But Kade had made his presence known to Adrian. Had Adrian managed to alert others? Just then, a piercing headache hit her, and she stopped trying to think.

All day she had been fighting headaches, which radiated from her right temple, surging in and out of her head like rivers of fire. The doctor had wanted her to rest in the medic station, but Mariss refused. She wanted to watch Kade's reports, see him, know he was safe. Reluctantly, Jarik had allowed her to stay at his side.

"Did you learn anything about their motivation?" Jarik asked.

The team leader shook his head. Soon, he signed off.

But as dawn came to the Colony, the team leader provided the final piece of the puzzle. They discovered records on men and women—decision-makers and leaders in government and business—who held allegiance to the Colony. Once Colony residents, they now wielded power throughout the civilized galaxy.

"All famous, all influential. All secretly working for the Iridion Corporation, which apparently has some kind of secret agenda to take over the Earth Coalition," the team leader told Jarik. "It's astounding. The organization of this effort—the timespan involved—it's mind-boggling. Every year, they send more secret delegates out, give them false backgrounds to cover their origin. But every one of them holds allegiance to Iridion. They're completely manipulated by the Corporation, yet poised to take over every facet of our society, from big business to politics to science and the arts."

"And this is documented?"

"Now it is," the team leader said with confidence.

"Keep me posted."

The team leader signed off. Jarik turned to Mariss, frowning slightly. For him, it was a huge show of displeasure. "If much more time had passed before we learned about this, the galaxy as we know it would no longer exist."

"And my children—if I had married Adrian—they would be raised to become *weapons,"* Mariss said. "I had no idea.

When I applied to come here, it all sounded—"

"Too good to be true," Jarik concluded. Both of them were thinking of Kade, who had single-handedly brought the conspiracy to light.

"I hope he's all right," Mariss said, her voice strained.

"Me, too. I misjudged him."

"It's his background. It trails him like a demon."

Jarik laid his hand on Mariss' shoulder. "It takes someone special to see past that to the man beneath."

Mariss gave him a gentle smile. "Thank you, Jarik, for doing just that."

Jarik's secretary alerted him that another transmission was coming in—this time from Kade. His face filled the screen. He had obviously been up all night. Beard stubble shadowed his face. His hair was mussed. Mariss' heart went out to him. She wanted him back, safe and sound.

"Farra's body is out of the question," he told Jarik. "They incinerated it, I'm sorry to say."

Jarik nodded. "I don't find that surprising, considering our investigation is well under way."

"Me neither," Kade said.

Mariss rubbed her temple as a new wave of pain hit her.

"Mariss has been experiencing headaches with increasing frequency," Jarik told Kade now. "Dr. Uru says the implant is beginning to fire erratically. She is concerned about possible...brain damage if it isn't removed quickly."

Kade's lips twisted in a humorless smile. "Nothing like a little pressure, is there, Jarik? All right, listen. I've located the lab where the implants are made. There should be samples there, and maybe information about them, too. But with this investigation going on, the place is sealed tight. Security is doubled, tripled in some cases. Your boys are working to get in through proper channels, but hell could freeze over before they succeed. I'm pretty sure any evidence will be gone by then—hidden or destroyed. So I'll either have to convince someone to let me in there, or come up with a more creative solution."

Mariss had a hunch that solution involved explosives.

Neither method would be easy. "Kade, don't," Mariss said, stepping into view so he could see her. "Confronting Adrian was risky enough. Don't let anyone else see you. It's too dangerous."

His eyes widened as they fell on her. "Mariss? Jarik, shouldn't she be resting?"

"You know my sister," he said dryly.

"Yeah. Yeah, I do. I think I know what I'm going to do. I'm on it." Kade cut the transmission, before he heard Mariss say, "Be careful."

***

Time passed in a confused jumble. Mariss struggled to remain conscious through the blinding pain, headaches so fierce she felt her brain was about to explode. Then the pain would fade as if it had never been, and she could focus on the progress reports Kade was making. Already, morning neared. Why wouldn't he return to her? What was he after? She could no longer remember.

"I'm going to blow the door." The words came to her on a misty wave. They sounded so close, almost as if Kade were in her head.

"How will you keep from getting caught?" That was Jarik. Mariss forced open her eyes, saw her brother's stern features as he faced a black screen. Where had Kade's image gone? He must not be able to transmit it.

How will you keep from getting caught? The import of Jarik's words spun around and around in Mariss' head, finally taking on meaning. She had missed Kade's answer. *Kade...*

She forced her lips to work, forced the words through her uncooperative throat. "Tell him to come back. The risk—it's too great."

Jarik ignored her, and Mariss realized she'd only spoken the words in her head. Her body was no longer obeying her commands.

A blast of agony cut through her, much worse than before. Her head felt like it was cleaving in two. Blackness descended, and she lost consciousness.

***

Kade's finger hovered over the switch. At the slightest pressure, the remote sensor would trigger a miniature bomb he'd tucked under the laboratory door. The sliding metal door was all that separated him from his goal, retrieving an implant device.

Unfortunately, even if he blasted through it, he would immediately be caught, the implant confiscated. So far, he'd seen at least a dozen Colony workers pass by the door in the last ten minutes. The explosion would draw even more people, and he'd be history. As it was, the longer he remained in hiding here, behind a large rectangular planter, the more he risked discovery. And time was running out for Mariss.

He had to figure out a plan, come up with something…

Glancing sideways, he noticed a man and woman talking. Both wore the traditional Colony tunics. The man seemed about his size—taller, perhaps, and maybe less broad in the shoulder, but he couldn't waste time waiting for a perfect match. Now, if Kade could only get him alone…

As if reading his thoughts, the man said goodbye to his companion and turned toward Kade. In a few seconds, he'd pass him by. No one else was in sight. Kade jumped to his feet and confronted the man.

"Yes? Who—" He didn't have time to complete his question. Kade laid him low with a blow to his jaw. The man fell like a ton of rocks.

"What a tough guy," Kade smirked. Colony men were far too soft. He dragged the man behind the planter just before two more people came around the corner. Working fast, he stripped the guy and changed into his clothes.

The man began to come round. Kade didn't have time to waste tying him up and gagging him, so he punched him again. The man fell back, his eyes closed. "Sorry, Charlie," Kade muttered.

Holding up the remote, he jammed the trigger. The explosive had been designed to make minimal noise and incinerate only the target. Still, there was enough of a blast to draw the attention of several passers-by, who congregated around the red-hot debris where the door had been, their voices rising in consternation.

Kade walked toward them. "Terrible, isn't it?" he said. "Such blatant vandalism. What's the galaxy coming to?" He continued walking, right by them into the lab.

This was definitely implant central, a manufacturing plant for the wicked devices. The things were everywhere—on workbenches, in neatly tagged rows in glass cabinets, in containers stacked along the walls. The voices outside grew more numerous, and Kade knew he didn't have a moment to waste before someone noticed him and wondered what he was up to. Grabbing a handful of implants from the nearest workbench, he jammed them into his pocket and walked quickly—but not too quickly—back out the door.

Ten minutes later, as he entered the last hall on his way to the ship, he began to feel victorious. He would make it. A few more paces brought him to the hangar bay. No one was in sight. He sprinted toward the ship. Once he secreted himself inside as a "stow away," he'd send a final, scrambled transmission to Jarik. Jarik would recall his men, and he'd be on his way back to Mariss.

"Halt!"

Kade debated ignoring the voice, but his running to the ship might jeopardize the men Jarik had sent. He didn't want that. He slowed his pace and turned around, preparing to deal with what was no doubt an over-eager guard, someone he could easily take out.

He turned around and found himself facing Locke, the Colony administrator. A man who would no doubt recognize him. Three armed guards accompanied him.

"Holy krod," Kade swore under his breath. He couldn't allow these goons to get their hands on him. He had to do something, or the implants would be lost.

Glancing sideways, he noticed a second ship about twenty meters away being fueled for take-off. Had enough fuel been put in the tank to make it off-planet? He was wearing a Colony outfit—would Locke's guards risk shooting one of their own without being certain who he was? There was only one way to find out. Expecting any moment to feel phaser fire in his back, he turned and walked toward the second ship, ignoring the calls to halt.

He'd made it halfway when a blast of phaser fire took a chunk out of the ship's side. He broke into a dead run, sprinting toward the gangway.

***

Mariss felt hands touching her body, gently, but full of business. Dr. Uru's voice came to her through a groggy haze. "Mariss, I'm going to move your head, so I can shave part of your scalp. Relax, now. It won't hurt."

Mariss heard the whir of the shaver, its touch cool on the skin by her temple. Her head felt like it was spinning off her shoulders, but the pain had receded somewhat.

After a while, the shaver stopped. Another voice came to her, as if from under water fathoms deep. "Let me see her. Just for a moment."

Murmuring voices. She couldn't make out the words.

Then a rough palm settled on her cheek. "Mariss? Mariss, look at me."

She cracked her eyes open. The light hurt her eyes, but she fought the pain. Kade was bending over her hover-stretcher, his eyes intent on hers. He gripped the stretcher-rails, blocking out her view of anything but his face. Not that she wanted to see anything else. Her heart swelled with relief. "Is this a drug dream, or are you really here?" Her voice sounded alarmingly weak to her own ears.

Kade gave her a smile. "I said you wouldn't get rid of me that easily."

A tear leaked from the corner of her eye. She wasn't even aware she was crying. She felt the moisture roll down her temple, along her newly shaved skin.

Kade brushed it away. She had never seen such a tender expression on his face. "I brought back samples of the implants. Dr. Uru already took a good look at them. It has to come out right away. Something about being away from the Colony. The lucky few who get one are never allowed to leave."

He means *leave alive,* Mariss thought. She tried to nod, but it hurt too much.

"I did my part, Mariss. Now you have to do yours. Fight. Use that iron will of yours." His voice intensified. "Come back to me."

Mariss nodded slightly, weakly.

His voice broke. "I love you, woman." His eyes flicked to her stomach. "Both of you."

She smiled at his reference to their baby and tried to smile, to let him know she understood. "About time you admitted it, too." She tried lifting her hand toward his face. Her hand felt like it was going to float away.

Kade caught it and pressed it to his lips. "Yeah. It damn well is."

* * *

"Please. Your pacing will drive me over the edge."

Kade turned from the starfield view in front of him and strode back toward where Jarik was sitting. "How can you be so calm? They're slicing into her brain in there!"

"Dr. Uru is excellent. And—I am concerned. I merely don't show it as flamboyantly as you, Mr. Land."

Kade turned away again, pacing toward the viewscreen. Three hours had gone by, and still Mariss was in surgery. He had asked himself a thousand questions in those hours—was the ship's medic station well enough equipped? Did Dr. Uru really study the implants enough to know what to do? And—worst of all—was it already too late?

He tried not to consider the possibility that Mariss would survive the surgery just fine, but come out a senseless vegetable. Or—someone else. The implant could have caused irreversible damage to her mind, changing her personality forever.

Then, there was the baby. Whether it would survive the surgery was also in question.

"You will have to learn to control your emotions if you hope to establish your presence as a leader, Kadin Land."

Jarik's words barely registered, until Kade passed his chair a second time. He pulled up short. "What are you talking about?"

"Stop that infernal pacing and take a seat. I'll explain."

TWENTY-SIX

Mariss was sitting up in bed. Her head throbbed—no surprise there—but the sharp pain of the headaches was gone.

She listened to the voices in the anteroom and waited, excitement filling her. Her ordeal was over. And she knew something special was about to begin.

She heard Dr. Uru's voice. "Physically, she's fine."

"The baby?" That was Kade.

"Also fine."

A heavy exhalation. "Thank the Maker."

"Can you tell yet if there is any damage?" Jarik speaking now. Mariss listened closely.

Dr. Uru's voice. "Time will tell."

Kade's voice. "*I* can tell." A few seconds later, he was there beside her. He sat on the edge of the bed and held her hand. "Mariss, darling." He grinned. "Damn, I like the sound of that. Mariss, darling."

She laughed. "I made it through, so I expect to be hearing it a lot."

"Damn good thing you did, too." He seemed to change gears, think of something interesting to share. "Hey, you know, when I went back to the Colony, I happened to run into Adrian Young. You know Adrian, your old boyfriend?"

"That isn't funny, Kade." Why in the galaxy was he discussing Adrian? She never wanted to hear that name again.

But Kade continued, his voice casual, "We shared a Klinian ale, got to talking. You know, he's really not such a bad guy. A little stiff, but you know how that can be."

This was too much. Mariss tore her hand from Kade's. "How can you say that? That bastard, idiot block of wood tried to brainwash me. He *was* brainwashing me. He—"

She stopped cold. Kade's deep laugh filled the room. Behind him, Jarik had entered, and he was laughing as well. Even the somber Dr. Uru was chuckling. "What? What's so funny?"

"We're just glad to see you haven't changed," Jarik said.

Understanding dawned. "Ah, I get it. You thought I might be passive and submissive and mindless, is that right? The way Adrian wanted me to be. And this was a test. Well, Kadin Land, I did *not* appreciate it." He was still chuckling. She knew he was merely relieved and could hardly be angry over that. And the fact he knew exactly how to determine her "state of mind" showed just how well he understood her.

"It wasn't funny, Kade. Not in the least." She bit her lip, trying not to smile. But she failed. "However, I may forgive you, *if...*"

"If what?"

She crooked a finger at him. Kade leaned closer, and she whispered in his ear. Her words recalled a particular tropical night, making love with wild abandon in the stream; in the grass; in a tent made for two.

Kade's smile changed character, becoming suggestive, intimate. "I can manage that. In fact, I could manage it right now." His hand swept slowly along her side, pausing beside her breast. His thumb stroked terribly close to its crest, despite the fact they weren't alone.

"Excuse me, but Mariss should not be over stimulated," Dr. Uru said stiffly. "Too much excitement isn't good for her recovery. Now, I have other patients to see." The doctor left them.

"I'd say it does the patient wonders," Mariss murmured, her eyes on Kade alone. Despite having dangerous surgery just hours before, her body responded immediately and fervently to his touch. It seemed like forever, though it had only been days since they had made love. She craved him like she craved light, water, food. So much had happened, and they had been forced apart by will and circumstances, both at the Colony and now on this ship. But now—

A sudden realization struck. "The guards? Where are those two bookends who've been trailing you all over the ship?"

Jarik seemed happy to answer her question. "There's no need for them. Land is a free man. All the charges have been dropped, by order of the Earth Coalition. The Interstellar Policemen involved in pressing charges have been suspended from their positions pending a thorough investigation into their involvement in the vagon smuggling ring."

"That's wonderful!" Mariss squeezed Kade's hand. "I knew they couldn't keep you down."

"There's more," Jarik said. "Kade has agreed to accept a proposition of mine. He's going to remain here, on Elysia, and manage the Colony as an extension of the Earth Coalition."

"Stay here?" The words stuck in her throat. Did that mean he was leaving her?

"He's going to make the Colony the first true city of Elysia," Jarik continued, oblivious to her distress. "It will be public, open to settlers. He'll be the governor of a new territory."

"But why Kade?"

Kade shrugged. "I'm no administrator, but Jarik thinks this frontier planet needs a hard-headed, no-nonsense type. Like me."

"Kade has a great ability to think on his feet," Jarik explained. "For instance, the way he retrieved the implants. He blew open the door by jerry-rigging an explosive device. Then, he impersonated a Colony resident and almost walked out without being noticed. Until—"

"Locke spotted me. I had to steal another ship."

"A remarkable escape," Jarik said casually, as if admiring an action-adventure vid.

The thought of how close Kade had come to being killed terrified Mariss. Except it was over now. Finally over.

Jarik continued to speak. "The Colony is devoid of leaders, now that those involved in the Iridion conspiracy have been arrested, like that Adrian fellow. The rest of the citizens have been drugged with vagon too long to take control of their lives without guidance. Land was wasted as a commercial pilot.

My own opinion of his abilities has been confirmed by a report I received, filed by a Mr. Chan of Quantum Craftlines on his conduct as a captain."

"Mr. Chan," Mariss said. "Oh, yes. That was his real name, but we knew him as Mr. Lee. The Oriental man who was going to report on you to your superiors." She grasped Kade's hand. "Was it too awful?"

Before Kade could reply, Jarik did it for him. "On the contrary, it said that while Kade's attitude left something to be desired, he was diligent, handled the ship remarkably well in dangerous situations, managed to keep the passengers calm and relieve tense situations. Also, as is proper for a Captain, he courteously yet firmly declined offers of sexual favors from the two single women on board."

"The *two* single women?" Lorena had been all over Kade—but her?

Kade was gloating. "Even he could see you were flirting with me, Mariss."

Mariss punched him in the arm.

Kade shrugged. "So, having no better offers, I said I'd take the job. On one condition."

"And that is?"

He hesitated. "If you don't want to go back there, well, I'd understand, considering everything you went through." His words grew enthusiastic. "We can change it, Mariss. There's so much to build on. But—"

"But—?"

"I thought I was making myself clear." Kade cleared his throat. He seemed almost nervous. Mariss didn't recall him ever being nervous. His vulnerability was a revelation, endearing him to her all the more. "I don't plan to live there without you. If you'll have me, that is."

"Are you asking me to marry you?"

"Well, of course! Isn't that what I just said?"

Mariss paused, knew she had to ask. "You want me because of the baby?"

He looked insulted. "Hell, no! Because I love you! And you love me."

Joy filled her. She launched herself at Kade and held his hard body tight against hers. "Yes! Yes, yes, *yes.*"

Kade's hands stroked her back as he whispered in her ear, "I'm not ever letting you get away, woman. Ever. Not like those other men. Just remember that. This is a lifetime thing."

Mariss was in heaven. She knew marriage to Kade wouldn't be perfect. Both of them were human and flawed. They would have wonderful times and hard times and stressful times. She wouldn't have her perfect marriage, her perfectly secure future, her perfect anything—but she knew, for her, Kade was her perfect mate.

"I'll be leaving you alone," Jarik said. Mariss glanced up at him, met his smile with her own. "It looks like you finally got it right, little sister." He quietly left the room.

Kade was tracing kisses along her neck and face, stopping now and then to speak. "Do you know...what Elysia means, darling?"

"What?" Mariss gasped as his teeth teased her earlobe.

He whispered, his voice silky, "It's an ancient Greek term for paradise."

Warmth flowing through her body, Mariss managed one word. "Paradise."

"Yes. I didn't want to mention it before, in case it convinced you to stay—with Adrian. But now..."

She smiled and pulled back to gaze into his eyes. "Now, Kadin Land, it will truly be paradise—*our* paradise."

ABOUT THE AUTHOR

I've always loved books. I first started writing books in second grade. My teacher discovered my first story, which was about a band of cute animals (hey, I was seven!) who follow a new road only to hit a dead-end. She suggested I read it to the class. Being the smallest, youngest, and shiest kid in class, that was like suggesting I go before a firing squad. So I let her read it.

I've since learned it's not so scary sharing my work with others. In fact, it's downright fun! After earning a journalism degree from the University of Oregon, I worked as a newspaper reporter, which gave me a solid foundation in grammar and writing on deadline. But putting people on the spot with tough, probing questions didn't mesh with my personality. Instead, I applied my writing skills in the crazy world of corporate/government public relations.

After more than a decade of writing for everyone but myself, I picked up Jude Deveraux's *Knight in Shining Armor* and fell in love with the romance genre. I devoured historical romances by the truck full (along with squeezing in a Dean Koontz or medical thriller here and there), then realized there were other wonderful types of romance, including contemporary, futuristic, and paranormal.

When I'm not writing, I'm gardening, making crafts, traveling, reading (of course!), and spending time with my husband and teenage son. I love to hear from readers. Please contact me via e-mail at TracyCozzens@aol.com, or visit my web page at http://members.aol.com/TCozzens to join my mailing list.

DON'T MISS
TRACY COZZENS'

ARABIAN KNIGHT

ISBN: 1-893896-15-3

For more than a thousand years, Kasim al-Jinni has suffered a string of masters who used his jinni powers for their own selfish desires. Kasim has resigned himself to his deserved fate, for he failed young Prince Hajji and allowed evil to enslave the land of Zharinda. But when his new master Lindsey McCullough releases him from his magic jar, he discovers she has a kind heart. He longs to give her the one gift her miraculous, modern world cannot do— restore the use of her legs.

After ten years in a wheelchair, the thought of being healed makes Lindsey nervous. Her overly critical parents have finally accepted that Lindsey will never achieve greatness like the rest of her family. She long ago abandoned dreams of love and family, taking solace in her own small, safe world.

When Kasim tricks Lindsey into wishing her injury healed, she meddles in his life—wishing him free of the curse that enslaves him. To her shock, her wish sweeps them both back to ancient Zharinda. Worse, Kasim has lost his jinni powers and can't return Lindsey to her own time unless he overthrows the malevolent power which holds the land in thrall.

Thrown into the heart of an Arabian adventure, Lindsey and Kasim are soon embroiled in magic, court intrigue, and a prophecy that promises Kasim to a lovely Sultana—despite the yearning he feels for Lindsey. He cannot change his fate, which has been written in the stars for more than a thousand years. He cannot abandon his homeland to the hand of evil. Yet Lindsey deserves a true Arabian Knight...

AVAILABLE NOW